Leaving Everything Most Loved

Leaving Everything Most Loved

A Novel

Jacqueline Winspear

An Imprint of HarperCollins*Publishers*

HarperCollins books may be purchased for educational, business, or sales promotional use. For information, please e-mail the Special Markets Department at SPsales@harpercollins.com.

FIRST HARPERLUXE EDITION

HarperLuxe™ is a trademark of HarperCollins Publishers

Library of Congress Cataloging-in-Publication Data is available upon request.

ISBN: 978-0-06-225344-6

13 14 ID/RRD 10 9 8 7 6 5 4 3 2 1

To my family—all of you,
wherever you are in the world or
wherever you may roam:
godspeed.

*The family, that dear octopus from whose tentacles
we never quite escape, nor in our innermost
hearts never quite wish to.*

—DODIE SMITH

You shall leave everything loved most dearly, and this is the shaft of which the bow of exile shoots first. You shall prove how salt is the taste of another man's bread and how hard is the way up and down another man's stairs.

—DANTE, *PARADISO*

All the people like us are We, and everyone else is They.

—RUDYARD KIPLING, "WE AND THEY"

I have learned that if you must leave a place that you have lived in and loved and where all your yesteryears are buried deep, leave it any way except a slow way, leave it the fastest way you can.

—BERYL MARKHAM, *WEST WITH THE NIGHT*

Prologue

London, July 1933

Edith Billings—Mrs. Edith Billings, that is, proprietor of Billings' Bakery—watched as the dark woman walked past the shop window, her black head with its oiled ebony hair appearing to bob up and down between the top shelf of cottage loaves and the middle shelf of fancy cakes as she made her way along with a confidence to her step. Mrs. Billings considered herself to be a woman of some integrity, one who lived by the maxim "Live and let live," but to be honest, she wondered what a woman like that might be doing on her street; after all, she should keep to her own patch. Billings' Fine Bakery—or "Billingses" as the locals called it—did a fair trade in morning coffee and afternoon teas, and Edith didn't want her regulars, her "ladies" as she referred to them, being upset by someone who had no business walking out of her own part of town. There were a lot of her kind, to be sure— you could thank the East India Company going back three hundred years for that—but all the same. On her street? That woman with her colored silk, her jangling bracelets, her little beaded shoes—and, for goodness' sake, just a cardigan to cover her arms. *What's she doing here?* wondered Edith Billings. What does she want around these parts, with that red dot on her forehead? And what on earth happened to "When in Rome," anyway? It'd be painted dots one minute, and curry with roast potatoes the next, if people weren't careful.

Elsie Digby, aged six, was outside Billingses when the lady with the dark skin clad in silks of peach and pink walked towards her. She'd been left to rock the baby carriage while her mother bought a loaf of bread, and now she pushed back and forth with a solid rhythm against the carriage handle, yet with barely a thought to minding her new brother. The lady smiled as she approached, and Elsie blushed, looking at her feet in sensible brown lace-up shoes. She'd been told never to talk to strangers, and she was afraid the woman might speak to her, say a few words—and the woman was, if nothing else, a stranger. But as she came alongside Billingses and passed Elsie, a corner of the woman's sari flapped against the girl's bare arm. Elsie Digby closed her eyes when the soft silk kissed her skin, and at once she wondered what it must be like to be clothed in fine silk every day, to walk along with the heat of late summer rising up and bearing down, and to feel the cool brush of fabric touching her as if it were a night-time breeze, or breath from a sleeping baby.

Usha Pramal, respectfully dressed in her best sari, could feel the stares of passersby. She smiled and said "Good morning" when proximity brought the person within comfortable distance. There was no reply. There was never a reply. But she would shed no tears and worry not, because, according to Mr. and Mrs. Paige, their God was watching over her, as He watched over all His children. She had said a quick prayer to Jesus this morning, just to keep on acceptable terms with the Paiges and their deity, but she also bowed to Vishnu and Ganesh for good measure. Her father would have been appalled, but he would also have said, "Never burn your bridges, Usha. Never burn those bridges." She would not be here for long anyway. Her pennies and shillings were mounting, along with the pounds, and soon she would be able to afford to make her dream a reality; she would book her passage and at last return home. *At last*, after all this time, after seven long years, she would sail away from this gray country.

When the pain of separation seemed to rend her heart in two, it was her habit to walk to a street where there were shops that sold spices, where the aroma of familiar dishes cooking would tease her senses and set her stomach churning. And she could at least see faces that looked like hers; though at the same time, the sense of belonging was out of kilter, for many of those people had not been born in India and spoke in an unfamiliar dialect, or their names were constructed in a different manner. And even the other women in the hostel were not of her kind, though the Paiges thought they were all the same, like oranges in a bowl. Perhaps that's what happened if you had only one God to watch over you. Yes, she was wise to honor the gods of her childhood.

Usha had left her customer's house with a silver coin in her hand, a coin she would place in a velvet drawstring bag kept well inside her mattress, along with other coins earned. Whenever she added a florin or half-crown—riches indeed—it seemed to Usha Pramal that as she looked into the money nestled in the rich red fabric, it began to glow, like coals in a fireplace. And how she had worked to build that fire, to keep it alive. Soon she would have her ticket. Soon she would feel the damp heat of her own country, thick against her skin.

It was a tight little gang of street urchins, rambling along the canal path, who discovered the body of Usha Pramal. At first they aimed stones at the globe of colored silk that ballooned from the green slime of city water, and then they thought they would use a broken tree branch to haul it in. It was only as they hooked the fabric that the body turned, the face rising in the misery of sudden death, the dead woman's eyes open as if not quite understanding why there was a raw place on her forehead where a bullet had entered her skull. That morning, as Usha Pramal had painted a vermilion bindi to signify the wisdom nestled behind the sacred third eye, she could not have known that she had given her killer a perfect target.

Chapter One

Maisie Dobbs maneuvered her MG 14/28 Tourer into a place outside the bell-shaped frontage of the grand country house. She turned off the engine but remained seated. She needed time to consider her reason for coming to this place before she relinquished the security of her motor car and made her way towards the heavy oak door.

The redbrick exterior of the building appeared outlined in charcoal, as the occasional shaft of sunlight reflected through graphite-gray clouds scudding across the sky. It was a trick of light that added mystery to the flat marshlands extending from Kent into Sussex. The Romney Marsh was a place of dark stories; of smugglers, and ghosts and ghouls seen both night and day. And for some years this desolate place had offered succor to the community of nuns at Camden Abbey. Local cottagers called it "the nunnery," or even "the convent," not realizing that Benedictines, whether male or female, live a monastic life—thus in a monastery— according to The Rule of Benedict.

It was the Abbess whom Maisie had come to see: Dame Constance Charteris.

Whether it was for advice that she had made the journey from London, or to have someone she respected bear witness to a confession of inner torment, she wasn't sure. Might she return to her motor car less encumbered, or with a greater burden? Maisie suspected she might find herself somewhere in the middle—the lighter of step for having shared her concerns, but with a task adding weight to the thoughts she carried. She took a deep breath, and sighed.

"Can't turn around now, can I?"

She stepped from the motor car, which today did not have the roof set back, as there was little sun to warm her during the journey from London. Her shoes crunched against the gravel as she walked towards the heavy wooden doors. She rang a bell at the side of the door, and a few moments later a hatch opened, and the face of a young novice was framed against the ancient grain.

"I'm here to see Dame Constance," said Maisie.

The nun nodded and closed the hatch. Maisie heard two bolts drawn back, and within a moment the door opened with a creaking sound, as if it were a sailing ship tethered to the dock, whining to be on the high seas once more.

The novice inclined her head, indicating that Maisie should follow her.

The small sitting room had not changed since her last visit. There was the rich burgundy carpet, threadbare in places, but still comforting. A moldering coal fire glowed in the grate, and a wing chair had been set alongside another hatch. Soon the small door would open to reveal a grille with bars to separate the Abbess from her visitor, and Dame Constance would offer a brief smile before bowing her head in a prayer. Maisie would in turn bow her head, listen to the prayer, and echo Dame Constance as she said, "Amen."

But first, before the Abbess could be heard in the room on the other side of the grille, when her long skirts swished against the bare floorboards with a sound that reminded Maisie of small waves drawing back against shingle at the beach, she would offer her own words to any deity that might be listening. She would sit in the chair, calm her breathing, temper her thoughts, and endeavor to channel her mind away from a customary busyness to a point of calm. It was as if she were emptying the vessel so that it could be filled with thoughts that might better serve her.

The wooden hatch snapped back, and when Maisie looked up she was staring directly at Dame Constance. The Abbess always seemed beyond age, as if she had transcended the years, yet Maisie remembered a time when her skin was smoother, her eyes wider, though they never lost an apparent ability to pierce the thoughts of one upon whom her attention was focused.

"Maisie. Welcome to our humble house. I wonder what brings a woman of such accomplishment to see an old nun."

Maisie smiled. There it was, that hint of sarcasm on the edge of her greeting; a putting in place, lest the visitor feel above her station in a place of silent worship.

"Beneath the accomplishment is the same woman who was once the naive girl you taught, Dame Constance."

The Abbess smiled. It was what might be called a wry smile, a lifting of the corner of the mouth as if to counter the possibility of a Cheshire cat grin.

"Shall we pray first?"

Dame Constance allowed no reply, but bowed her head and clasped her hands on the shelf before her, her knuckles almost touching the bars of the grille separating Maisie and herself. Maisie rested her hands on her side of the same shelf, feeling the proximity of fingers laced in prayer.

She recognized the words of Saint Benedict as Dame Constance began.

"And let them pray together, so that they may associate in peace."

When the prayer was finished, when Maisie had echoed Dame Constance's resolute "Amen," the Abbess allowed a moment of silence to envelop them as she folded her arms together within the copious sleeves of her black woolen habit.

"What brings you to me, Maisie Dobbs?"

Maisie tried not to sigh. She had anticipated that first question and had sampled her answer, aloud, a hundred times during the journey to Romney Marsh. Now it seemed trite, unworthy of the insight and intellect before her. Dame Constance waited, her head still bowed. She would not shuffle with impatience or sigh as a mark of her desire to be getting on with another task. She would bide her time.

"I am troubled . . . I feel . . . No. I have a desire to leave, to go abroad, but I am troubled by the needs of those to whom I feel responsibility." Maisie picked at a hangnail on her little finger. It was a childhood habit almost forgotten, but which seemed to claim her when she was most worried.

Dame Constance nodded. To one who had not known her, she may have seemed half asleep, but Maisie knew better, and waited for the first volley of response with some trepidation.

"Do you seek to leave on a quest to find? Or do you wish to run from some element of life that is uncomfortable?"

There it was. The bolt hit the target dead center, striking Maisie in the heart. Dame Constance raised her eyes and met Maisie's once more, reminding her of an archer bringing up the bow, ready to aim.

"Both."

Dame Constance nodded. "Explain."

"Last year . . ." Maisie stopped. Was it last year? Her mind reeled. So close in time, yet almost a lifetime ago. "Last year my dear friend Dr. Maurice Blanche died." She paused, feeling the prick of tears at the corner of her eyes. She glanced at Dame Constance, who nodded for her to continue. "He left me a most generous bequest, for which, I confess, I have struggled to . . . to . . . become a good and proficient steward." She paused, choosing words as if she were selecting matching colored pebbles from a tide pool at the beach. "I have made some errors, though I have found ways to put them right, I think; however . . . however, in going through Maurice's papers, in reading his journals and the notes he left for me, I have felt in my heart a desire to travel, to go abroad. I believe it was in the experience and understanding of other cultures that Dr. Blanche garnered the wisdom that stood him in good stead, both in his work and as a much-respected friend and mentor to those whose paths he crossed. Of course, he came from a family familiar with travel, used to expeditions overseas. But I now have the means to live up to his example, so I have this desire to leave."

"I see. And on the other hand?"

"My business. My employees. My father. And my . . . well, the man who loves me, who is himself making plans to travel to Canada. For an indefinite stay."

Dame Constance nodded and was silent. Maisie knew it would not be for long. *She's just lining up the ducks to shoot them down, like a marksman at the fair.*

"What are you seeking?"

"Knowledge. Understanding. To broaden my mind. I . . . I think I am somewhat narrow-minded, at times."

"Hmmm, I wouldn't doubt it, but we all suffer from tunnel vision on occasion, Maisie, even I." Dame Constance paused. Again there was the catch at the corner of her mouth. "And you think journeying abroad will give you this knowledge you crave?"

"I think it will contribute to my understanding of the world, of people."

"More so than, say, the old lady who has lived in the same house her entire life, who has borne children both alive and dead? Who tends her soil; who sees the sun shine and the rain fall over the land, winter, spring, summer, and autumn? What might you say to the idea that we all have a capacity for wisdom, just as a jug has room for a finite amount of water—pouring more water in the jug doesn't increase that capacity."

"I think there's room for improvement?"

"Improvement?"

Wrong word, thought Maisie. "I believe I have the capacity to develop a greater understanding of people, and therefore compassion."

"And you think people want your compassion? Your understanding?"

"I think it helps. I think society could do with more of both."

"Then why not take your journey, your Grand Tour, to the north of England, or to Wales, to places where there is want, where there is a need for compassion and—dare I say it—some nonpatronizing, constructive help from someone who knows what it is to be poor? You have much to offer here, Maisie."

"I take your point, truly I do—but I think going abroad is the right thing to do."

"Then why ask me?"

"To align my thoughts on the matter."

"I see." Dame Constance paused. "And what of those you say you cannot leave—your employees? Your father? The man who loves you? Maisie, I know you well enough to know that you could find new positions for your employees, if you wish. Your father, by your own account, is a fiercely independent man—though I could understand a certain reticence to leave, given his age. And your young man? Well, I suspect he's not so young, is he? I imagine he would want you to go with him, as his wife."

Maisie nodded. "Yes, he has made that known."

"And you don't want to?"

"I want to take my own journey first."

"Your pilgrimage."

"My pilgrimage?"

"Yes, Maisie. Your pilgrimage. Where do you intend to go?"

"In reading Maurice's journals, it seems he spent much time in the Indian subcontinent. I thought I might travel there."

"Do you know anyone there? Have you any associations?"

"I am sure there are people who knew Maurice, who would offer me advice."

" 'Pilgrimage to the place of the wise is to find escape from the flame of separateness.' "

"I beg your pardon," said Maisie.

"It's something written by the Persian poet Jalāl ad-Dīn Muḥammad Rūmī, from a more recent translation, though most of his work remains in his original language."

"But . . ."

"I believe the words you find most startling are 'the flame of separateness.' "

Maisie nodded.

"Then go. Go to find out who you are—*Know Thyself*, as written at the entrance to Delphi. Know thyself, Maisie Dobbs, for such knowledge is freedom. Extinguish the flame of doubt that has burned in you for so long, and which—I suspect—stands between you and a deeper connection to someone with whom you might spend the rest of your life."

"There are more recent reasons for that separateness, Dame Constance. Matters of a confidential nature."

"You would not have come had you not felt trust."

"James—the man with whom I have been, to all intents and purposes, walking out with for some months now . . ." Maisie paused. *A year.* In truth a year had passed without engagement, cause for some gossip within their social circle. "James is associated with certain men of influence and power, one of whom I have had cause to cross. I know the man orchestrated the death of another man—one I knew and had affection for—though it was not by his own hand, he has others to do his . . . dirty work. He is a powerful man who at the same time is serving our country in matters of international importance, and is therefore untouchable."

Dame Constance bowed her head, then looked up at Maisie again.

"So, I suspect you feel compromised. I know of your work, and it would seem that you were powerless against a man who is beyond the law, so you have become disillusioned with the law."

"Disillusioned with myself, I think. And though I grasp why James must follow this man, I find I admire him for wanting to be of service, yet sickened that it requires him to throw in his lot with such a person."

"So, perhaps the leaving is to set this episode behind you, to distance yourself from the grief associated with death, and also with a feeling that you have failed because you could not win against those who ensure that this man you speak of will be able to evade justice. But remember this, Maisie—according to The Rule of Benedict, the fourth rung of humility requires us to hold fast to patience with a silent mind, especially when facing difficulties, contradictions—and even any injustice. It asks us to endure. Thus I would suggest that you might well see justice done, in time. Patience, Maisie. *Patience.* Now go about your work. Seek the knowledge you crave, and remember this: you have expressed your desire, so be prepared for opportunity. It may come with greater haste than your preparations allow." She paused, and there was silence for what seemed like a quarter of an hour, though it might only have been a minute. "I am sure that, because you have voiced your desire to venture overseas, a direction will be revealed to you. Now, lest I be thought of as heathen, I should balance the esteemed Persian poet with our beloved Benedict."

The Abbess met Maisie's gaze; neither flinched.

"Listen and attend to the ear of your heart, Maisie. Before you leave, let us pray together."

And though it was not her practice to pray, Maisie bowed her head and clasped her hands, wondering how indeed she might best attend to the ear of her heart.

Chapter Two

London, September 4th, 1933

S andra Tapley, secretary to psychologist and investigator Maisie Dobbs, placed her hand over the cup of the black telephone receiver as Maisie entered the office.

"It's that Detective Inspector Caldwell for you." She rolled her eyes; Sandra bore a certain contempt for the policeman.

Maisie raised her eyebrows. "Well, there's a turn-up—wonder what he wants."

She took the receiver from her secretary's hand, noticing the telltale signs of bitten nails.

"Detective Inspector, to what do I owe this pleasure, first thing in the morning?" As she greeted her caller, Maisie watched the young woman return to her typing.

"Good morning to you, too, Miss Dobbs."

"I thought you liked to get down to business, so I dispensed with the formalities."

"Very good. Now then, I wonder if I could pay a visit, seeing as you're in."

"Oh dear, spying on me again, Inspector? Now that we're off to such a good start, I'll get Mrs. Tapley to put the kettle on in anticipation of your arrival."

"Fifteen minutes. Strong with—"

"Plenty of sugar. Yes, we know."

Maisie returned the receiver to its cradle.

"I can't stand that man," said Sandra, stepping out from behind her desk. "He needles me something rotten."

"He likes needling people, and I shouldn't really needle him back, but he seems to be so much more accommodating when he's had that sort of conversation—there are people who, for whatever reason, always seem to be on the defensive, and they're better for being a bit confrontational. If they were taps, they would be running brown water first thing in the morning. At least he's not as bombastic as he used to be—and he's coming to me about a case, which is the first time he's done that. It must be something out of the ordinary, to bring him over here. Or someone's breathing down his neck."

"I'll keep out of his way then."

"No, don't. I'd like you to be here—and what time did Billy say he'd be back?"

"Around ten. He went over to see one of those reporters he knows, about that missing boy."

"Finding out more about how the press covered the story, and what they might have known but didn't report, I would imagine." Maisie looked at the clock. "Looks like Billy will cross the threshold at about the same time as Caldwell and whichever poor put-upon sergeant he brings with him this time."

Detective Inspector Caldwell, of Scotland Yard's murder squad, did indeed arrive on the doorstep of the Fitzroy Square mansion at the same time as Billy Beale, assistant to Maisie Dobbs. And he was not alone, though the man accompanying Caldwell was not a police sergeant, but a distinguished gentleman who wore an array of service medals. Maisie watched from the window as Billy greeted Caldwell in his usual friendly hail-fellow-well-met manner. Caldwell shook his outstretched hand, and in turn introduced the gentleman. Billy must have recognized that the visitor had served in the war, because he at once stood to attention and saluted. The man returned the salute, then gave a short bow and extended his hand to take

Billy's. Billy shook the man's hand with some enthusiasm, and Maisie was at once touched to see the respect Billy accorded the visitor. Her assistant had served in the war, had been wounded, and still suffered the psychological pain inflicted by battle. The war might have been some fifteen years past, but there was a mutual regard between men who had seen death of a most terrible kind. Given the color of his skin, his shining oiled hair, and his bearing, the man who Billy was escorting up to the office along with Caldwell had likely served with one of the Indian regiments that had come to the aid of King and Country.

Maisie could hear Billy's distinctive footfall on the stairs and his voice as he welcomed the visitors, asking if the Indian gentleman had been in London long. Sandra was already setting out cups and saucers, and the tea was brewed in the pot, ready to pour.

"Miss Dobbs, may I have the pleasure in introducing Major Pramal—he served with the Engineers in the war. We didn't know each other, but Major Pramal said he'd met my commanding officer."

"I'm delighted to meet you, Major Pramal. And good morning, Detective Inspector Caldwell—you've been a stranger."

The Indian gentleman was about to return Maisie's greeting when Caldwell interrupted.

"I thought you were about to say just 'strange' then," said Caldwell, removing his hat and taking a seat before being invited to do so. "I've been busy, Miss Dobbs."

"Please, Major Pramal." Maisie held out her hand towards a chair.

"I am honored to make your acquaintance, Miss Dobbs, though please forgive me for correcting you—I was not a major in the war, as I am sure Mr. Beale already knows; it was not possible for an Indian man to be a commissioned officer until after the war—I was a sergeant major." He was seated, and then went on. "No, only British officers could command us until 1919. In any case, I would prefer to be known as simply 'Mr. Pramal,' though as I said, I appreciate Mr. Beale's respect for my contribution."

Maisie looked at Billy and suspected he had made the deliberate error to antagonize Caldwell—it seemed to be a sport among her employees.

Sandra handed cups of tea to the guests, and Billy pulled up a chair alongside Maisie's.

"Well, we'll get straight to the point, Miss Dobbs," said Caldwell. "Sergeant Major—I mean, *Mr.* Pramal— has come a long way, from India, on account of the fact that his sister was discovered dead."

"Oh, I am so sorry, Mr. Pramal. Please accept our deepest sympathies for your loss—and your sister was such a long way from home."

"Indeed, Miss Dobbs. We miss her from the deepest place in our hearts, but my family was very proud of Usha. She had been the governess with an important family—a governess, mind you. Very important person in the bringing up of children."

Caldwell rolled his eyes, and Maisie saw that Sandra had witnessed the look and was shaking her head.

"How can I help? Inspector?" asked Maisie

"Mr. Pramal here is—understandably, I'll grant you—not very happy with the police investigation, and—"

"My sister was murdered, Miss Dobbs. In cold blood, her life was taken. It was no accident. A bullet at short range is never an accident."

Maisie looked at Caldwell. "Inspector?"

"Mr. Pramal has a point. We've drawn a blank. I've had some of my best men on this case, and still not a hint as to who might have murdered Miss Pramal. When Mr. Pramal came to us, he pointed out that he had knowledge of your services, and that he intended to come to you directly if we didn't bring you into the fold. I felt it would be better if we kept ourselves apprised of what steps you might take towards a satisfying conclusion. So we're here together."

"I see. Right." Maisie looked at Billy, then glanced at Sandra before she stood up from her chair and walked to the window. Caldwell had told her only part of the story, so she could either challenge him—ask for more details—or she could take his account as truth, and accept the case. Or she could turn them both away, saying she had too much work at the moment. It would have been a lie, but she wondered if she really needed the annoyance of working with Caldwell of Scotland Yard.

But as she turned back into the room, having been with her thoughts for only half a minute, Maisie saw something in Pramal's eyes, a look of despair, of yearning. His eyes were those of a man who had been strong, but was now almost beaten by grief. It was as if the bones in his body, used to a certain correct posture, were all that stood between him and collapse. Now there was no choice. They were all looking at her: Billy, Sandra, Caldwell, and Pramal.

"Mr. Pramal . . . we should begin. Time is always of the essence in this sort of case—and so much time has been lost already." She glanced at Caldwell. "How long since Miss Pramal's body was discovered?"

Caldwell reddened. "About two months now, I'm sorry to say it, but we hit a dead end early on, and never picked up the lead. And of course, Mr. Pramal has had a very long journey from India—weeks."

"Where did it happen?"

"Camberwell. That's where the body . . . where Miss Pramal was found. In the canal."

"All right. Here's what I think we should do, if I may make a suggestion, Inspector Caldwell? Perhaps Mr. Pramal could remain here for a while, just to give us his viewpoint." Maisie turned from Caldwell to the Indian gentleman. "Would that be convenient?"

The man bowed his head, then looked at Maisie. "I have all the time needed, for my sister."

"Good. Inspector, perhaps I could visit you later, at the Yard, and we can discuss the case—I am sure there will be no problem in allowing me to view your investigation records, in the circumstances."

"In the circumstances—"

"Good," said Maisie, cutting off any dissent that Caldwell might have expressed. In that case, Inspector, I'll walk with you down to your motor car?"

As they stood on the downstairs threshold, Maisie folded her arms against a cool breeze that had blown up to chill a fine day in what promised to be one of the warmest Indian summers she could remember.

"What happened? It's not like you to lose the thread—assuming you found it," said Maisie.

Caldwell shrugged. "I've had a lot on my plate, Miss Dobbs. She was an Indian woman, knew hardly anyone, and she turns up dead. There was no one pressing me for a result, so it went to the bottom of the pile—mind you, we had a go at finding who did it, but it's not as if there was anyone to answer to, and the press weren't all over it—no grieving relatives, nothing your *Daily Mail*s and *Mirror*s could make hay with. Then he comes along—the brother. Of course, it takes, what—six weeks to come over on the boat? There had been a letter saying he was on his way, but I suppose it went into the file and the next thing you know—"

"She wasn't the right color, so no one bothered."

"Now, don't be like that, Miss Dobbs. You know me, straight as a die—I don't make any distinction whether the deceased is one of us or not."

Maisie sighed. "You know my usual fee?"

"Only too well. So does the Commissioner, and the bookkeeper."

"Tell him to keep that checkbook at the ready."

"Tell *her*. The bookkeeper who deals with my department is a she."

"Good. I'll be paid on time then." Maisie looked at her wristwatch. "About four?"

Caldwell nodded, turned away from Maisie and raised his hand. A black police motor car moved from the place where it was parked and approached at a snail's pace.

Maisie half-turned to go back into the mansion where her first-floor office was housed. "Don't worry,

Inspector, I'll keep you posted all the way along. And I will find the killer."

"I know you will, Miss Dobbs."

"How do you know?"

Caldwell put his hat back on. "Because you're a terrier, Miss Dobbs. You might not be quick, and you might not go about it like I would, but you never let go. Now then, you go and get your teeth into his story. See where that leads you."

Maisie waved and made her way back up the stairs to her office. Caldwell was right, she wouldn't let go. She couldn't, because fifteen minutes earlier, when she'd turned from the window and looked into Pramal's eyes, she had seen the open wound across his soul that the death of his sister had inflicted upon him. And Maisie Dobbs could never turn away from such an entreaty.

"Now then, before we begin, Mr. Pramal, would you like more tea, or have we soaked you?" Maisie smiled and nodded to Billy, who pulled the chairs into a circle. He had already allowed for Sandra to join them.

"No thank you, Miss Dobbs. I have had sufficient refreshment."

"So, you returned to India after the war—did you remain in the army?" Maisie made small talk while

Billy and Sandra took their places, both with notebooks ready.

"For a while, yes. I left the service in 1920, and I am now a civil engineer with a company in Bombay, though I spend much time in other places, mainly working on water flow—irrigation, for example—and bridges."

"Sergeant Major Pramal was an explosives man in the war—tunneling and laying explosives. Not very good for the heart, that. Takes a very calm man to do the job of blowing things up," added Billy.

Pramal smiled. "I am pleased to be the recipient of your respect, Mr. Beale, and I understand addressing me by my army rank is ingrained in the soldier when he sees the medals, but I am happily no longer in the service of the King and Emperor."

"But you wear your medals with much pride, Mr. Pramal," said Maisie.

"They have their uses—for example, when I wanted to be heard at Scotland Yard. There are men there who might have passed me in the street, looking the other way, but if they've had military training—which many have—it remains locked in the memory, so they could not help but accord me respect when they saw my medals. In a few hours with your police force I think I was saluted more than at any other time since the war."

Maisie smiled. "We are grateful to you, Mr. Pramal." She paused. "Now then, this is how we go about our business, especially in an initial conversation with a new client. Though we could easily read through a series of reports provided by Inspector Caldwell, we conduct our own interview first. You may already have answered questions, and I realize there is much you cannot answer, but this helps us. The reason we are all sitting here is that we all listen in different ways, and something I miss might be noticed by either Mr. Beale or Mrs. Tapley."

The man pressed his hands together and bowed again. "I am grateful for your attention. Please ask your questions."

Maisie began.

"Let's start with Usha. How old was she?"

"My sister was twenty-nine years of age, last birthday, April 15."

"How long had she been in England?"

"She sailed with the family approximately seven years ago. It might be more. Sometimes it seems only yesterday, but at other times I can hardly remember her features."

"Do you have the name of the family who brought her here? What about an address?"

"The Allisons. Lieutenant Colonel Allison, his wife, and three children, who were then—if my memory serves me well—two, four, and six."

"He was an army man?" Billy interjected.

"Not at the time. He was a civil servant, with the British foreign service, as far as I know, though his army achievements were sufficiently impressive for him to continue using the form of address to which he was entitled. His wife advertised for a governess for the children, so my sister applied and was accepted for the position. She was a trained teacher, Miss Dobbs. She was with them for almost two years before they left to return to Great Britain, and she came with them."

"I see. Did she want to come here? How did she feel about the journey, about leaving her home?"

Pramal sighed, and Maisie remembered her father, at a time when her mother was so ill, taking more money from the savings tin to go to yet another doctor. He'd slump into the chair after carrying her mother upstairs to bed. "It's the telling of it all that wearies us, Maisie. They look at you, these doctors, and you can see that not one of them is thinking any differently from the others, as if they've all read the same book. But you keep on going, trying to find the doctor who's writing a new book, not just taking his knowledge out of the old ones." Pramal, too, seemed tired of the telling.

"Usha was a headstrong girl, Miss Dobbs. We are a well-to-do but not a wealthy or aristocratic family such as you might find here, though the war allowed me to achieve some measure of, well, professional stature. My father was broadminded, and believed in the value of education for a woman. But perhaps that was the downfall for Usha—she did not want to be married, not at the time, and the fact that our mother was dead did not help matters; a young woman needs a mother to prepare her for womanhood, you see. Suitors were arranged, but she turned them away. My father did not insist and soon her chance was gone. She relished the thought of coming to Great Britain, and accepted the position knowing full well that she would leave her country, though I believe she expected to return. You see, she had plans."

"What plans?"

"Usha wanted to found a school for girls. Not rich girls, but girls with promise who wouldn't otherwise go to school, or who had had their education curtailed. She wanted to save money, and perhaps to find a sponsor, someone who would enthusiastically support her endeavors."

Maisie rubbed her forehead. "Mr. Pramal, tell me what Usha was like. I want to know who she was, how people saw her."

The man nodded, brought his hands together in front of his face, and then to his sides, grasping the chair as if for support.

"As child, clever and headstrong, questioning, and sometimes a bit of a know-it-all. She saw no division in people—no, that's not true, she saw division, but she ignored it. She would touch a leper. She was very—I am not sure that I am explaining this well—she was very much a touching person. If she stopped to talk to a neighbor in the street, she would reach out—" Pramal moved as if to touch Maisie, to demonstrate his sister's way of being, but drew back his hand.

"Do you mean like this?" Sandra spoke up and touched Billy on the arm. "How do you do, Mr. Beale? Isn't it a lovely day?" She swept her hand around the room, as if the sun were shining through the ceiling.

Pramal nodded and smiled, his face at once alive as if the memory of Usha had become sharper. "Very much so. And there was no intention in her touch, except to . . . except to . . . except to connect with that person, like one electrical wire to another. And no matter how many times reprimanded by my aunts and cousins, by friends of my mother who had tried to guide her, she would just laugh and do things her way. Her spirit was quite without discipline."

Maisie was still looking at Billy's arm, at the place where Sandra had placed her hand and, for a glimpse in time, seemed like another person. *A spirit without discipline.*

"Do you have a photograph of your sister?" asked Maisie.

"Yes, here—I brought one for you." Pramal reached into his pocket and brought out a brown-and-white photograph, a portrait of a woman with large almond-shaped eyes, high cheekbones, and lips slightly parted, as if she were about to laugh, but managed to stop herself. Her hair seemed oiled, such was the reflection in the photograph, and though Maisie could only guess at the colors of the sari, she imagined deep magenta, a rosy peach, perhaps rimmed in gold, or silver. She touched the dark place on her forehead where Usha had marked her skin with a red bindi, and at once she felt pain between her own eyes. She handed the photograph to Billy.

"She was a beautiful girl, Mr. Pramal," said Billy.

Pramal nodded, as Billy passed the photograph to Sandra, who frowned as she studied the image.

"What is it, Sandra?" asked Maisie.

"Nothing, Miss." She shrugged, handing the photograph back to Maisie. "No, nothing—she just looked sort of familiar, that's all. But then they all—no, it's nothing."

"May we keep the photograph?" asked Maisie.

"Indeed. I have others."

"Tell me what happened when she arrived here—where did she live?"

"I would send letters to this address, in St. John's Wood." Pramal pulled a piece of paper from his pocket and gave it to Maisie. "This is the address. Later, she wrote that I should send my letters poste restante to a post office in southeast London."

She nodded. "Where was she living when she died? Have the family been in touch?"

Pramal shook his head. "My sister was given notice within a few years of disembarking here in Great Britain. She was cast aside by the family, with nowhere to go, no money except that which was owed her. I did not know this until a long time afterwards—she did not want to bring shame on her family."

"But what happened to her?"

"She found somewhere to live—in an ayah's hostel, in a place called Addington Square. That's probably why I was not given an address—she didn't want me to know where she was living, and I think she also would not have wanted anyone else intercepting her correspondence."

"Addington Square's in Camberwell," said Billy. "But what's an ayah's hostel?"

"It's where women live who were servants," Sandra interjected, leaning towards Pramal. "They call them ayahs, don't they? Women who look after the children—they do nearly all the work so the mother doesn't have to lift a finger. They come over with the family, and when the family doesn't need them anymore, that's it—out on your ear in a strange country with nowhere to go." She looked at Maisie. "We talked about this problem at one of our women's meetings—terrible it is. At least there are a couple of hostels for the women, though it doesn't stop some from having to work as—"

Maisie shook her head. Sandra had become involved in what was being talked about as "women's politics" and would not draw back from confrontation. It seemed to Maisie that she had found her voice since the death of her husband—but on this occasion, she did not want Sandra to describe the ways in which a homeless ayah might be pressed to make enough money to keep herself.

"So Usha found lodgings in an ayah's hostel. And you had no knowledge of her situation until—when?" asked Maisie.

"Until about nine or ten months ago. I have a family, Miss Dobbs, so I did not have sufficient funds to pay for her immediate passage home—and she told me she had almost enough, so was planning to sail at the end of the year." He paused. "You see, she wasn't only saving to come home—she wanted to bring enough money to open her school. She said she could earn better money here in London than in all of India, so she remained."

Maisie could see fatigue in the lines around the man's eyes and—as much as he fought it—knew it was in his backbone.

"Mr. Pramal, here's what I would like to do now. I will be visiting the Allisons, and also the ayah's hostel—I am sure we can find the address, if you don't have it to hand. In the meantime, I think it best that you return to your hotel and rest. We should like to reconvene tomorrow morning—would nine o'clock suit you?"

"Indeed, thank you, Miss Dobbs."

Maisie stood up, pushing back her chair. Sandra returned to her desk, and Billy stood ready to escort Mr. Pramal to the front door.

"May I ask if you have satisfactory accommodations while you are in England?" asked Maisie.

"A small hotel, Miss Dobbs. It's inexpensive, close to Victoria Station. I was staying with an old friend, but I did not want to inconvenience the family any longer."

Maisie nodded. "Please do not hesitate to let me know if the hotel ceases to be comfortable. I am sure I can arrange another hotel, with help from Scotland Yard."

Pramal gave a half-bow, his hands closed as if in prayer. "You are most kind." He turned to Sandra. "Thank you for the tea, Mrs. Tapley."

Billy extended out his hand towards the door and left the room with Pramal. While Sandra removed the tea tray, Maisie walked to the window again, where she watched Billy bid farewell to the former officer in the Indian Army. As if he couldn't help himself, Billy saluted Pramal again, and was saluted in return. Each recognizing a war fought inside the other.

Chapter Three

"I always thought women in India were sort of tied to the house until they married," commented Sandra, while marking the name "Pramal" on a fresh cream-colored folder. "Then we had this woman—a visiting lecturer—come along to talk to the class last week. She's been standing in for someone else. A doctor, she is—not medical, but of something else; history, I think, or perhaps politics. It was a history class anyway. She was talking about imperialism and about Mr. Gandhi, and what was happening in India, and how it would affect Britain. Very sharp, she was. Kept us all listening, not like some of them."

Sandra continued talking as Maisie looked down at a page where she, too, had marked a name: Usha Pramal.

"Not that there was any reason for her not to be intelligent, mind," Sandra went on. "But you know, I was surprised to see an Indian woman there, teaching us. She was very, very good—better than most of the men, I have to say."

"It seems Usha Pramal was of her ilk—her brother's description reveals an educated woman with an independence of character," said Maisie. She looked up. "Do you have her name—your lecturer? I think I might like to see her, have a word with her; she could have some valuable information for us, perhaps, regarding Indian women here in London."

"She'll be giving the lecture tomorrow evening. I've forgotten her name now, but I can find out when I get there."

"Thank you, Sandra." Maisie paused. "If it can be arranged, I would like to meet her—at this point, I think any information will be useful, even if it is removed from the case, but it could shed light on how Usha Pramal might have lived. I fear more time has elapsed on this case than I would have wanted. Evidence will be thin, and we'll be dependent upon the opinions and observations of people who might well have worked hard at forgetting whatever they knew about Miss Pramal. We need to draw in as much background information as we can."

Billy returned to the room, smiling at Sandra, then at Maisie. "Nice bloke, eh?"

"Yes, a very good man I think, Billy," said Maisie, standing up. "Let's all take a seat by the window and get a case map started. I'll be bringing back more information after I've seen Caldwell this afternoon."

Billy took a roll of wallpaper, cut a length, and unfurled it upside down across the table, where he and Sandra pinned it in place. The wallpaper had been given to them by a painter and decorator friend of Billy's, who often had surplus from his paper-hanging job. Maisie placed a jar of colored crayons on the table— some of thick wax in bold primary colors, others fine pencils in more muted shades. She took a bright red wax crayon and wrote *Usha Pramal* in the center of the paper, circling the name. This was the beginning, the half-open shell in what would become a tide pool of ideas, thoughts, random opinions; of words that came to mind unbidden; and of threads connecting evidence gathered. Some of it would make sense, though much of it wouldn't, but eventually something on the map, often one small buried clue, would point them to the killer. And a terrier could always find something buried, if she'd caught the scent.

"Billy, we need to find the exact point on the Surrey Canal where the body was discovered. I'll get more information from Caldwell; however, in the meantime, I don't want to depend upon it, so would you go down to Camberwell, find out where she was found on the canal. Talk to anyone who might have witnessed something— remember, people would love to forget this, so carefully does it." She sighed. "Mind you, on the other hand, there are probably a few gossips who'd enjoy nothing more than a good old chin-wag about a murder. In any case, could you also find out about movements on the canal that might have taken the body along. I believe timber is transported back and forth to the works there, from Greenland Docks or Rotherhithe—can you find out and ask around? See if any of the dockworkers saw anything of interest to us, or if anyone knows someone who did?" Maisie pushed back her chair, and went to her desk, where she took a camera from a large desk drawer. "Use this. There's film in the box, and it's easy to operate—heaven knows, if I can take a photograph, anyone can! I have a neighbor who has a darkroom in his flat, so he'll get them developed for us, and he's quite quick about it." She handed the box containing her pawnshop purchase across the table to Billy—a Number Two C Autographic Camera, manufactured by the Eastman Kodak Company. "Study the instructions for a few minutes. I think it will help us to have some photographs of the area."

Billy nodded. "Right you are, Miss. We should use this a lot more, I can see it being handy for our cases."

"Keep it in your desk drawer—I can always grab it if I need it. Anyway, back to Usha Pramal: though we'll have names later, Billy, root out what you can about the boys who found the body—they were messing around along the canal path, probably getting up to harmless mischief. Now they'll probably have nightmares for years, poor little mites. Anyway, Billy, you're a father of boys, so you will know how to deal with them."

"It's our girl who's going to need dealing with, I can see it coming already. Nearly a year old and breaking hearts already."

"They always say that about the girls, but it's the boys who break the hearts," said Sandra.

"Not if I've got anything to do with it—no one will break my little girl's heart."

"I'm sure they won't, Billy," said Maisie, turning to her secretary. "Sandra, you said you thought you might have seen Miss Pramal before—have you had any recollection?"

Sandra shook her head. "I wish I had, Miss. At first I thought I might have seen her—and I'm sorry I nearly said it in front of her brother, but they all sort of look the same, when they're from somewhere else like that. You know, your Chinese, your Indians. I'm sure you can see the differences if you live there and you're used to the faces, but when you only see them now and again, you can't always tell. That sounds really terrible, but, well, I think a lot of people get confused like that."

Maisie sat back in her chair, tapping the crayon on paper, creating a series of dots. "You know, that might be something for us to bear in mind—what if Usha was not the intended victim? What if someone just got it wrong, and thought she was another person?" She looked up at Sandra. "It's a sad reflection upon us, if we're that insular. After all, we've all nations under Britain's roof and it's not as if we're short of people from other continents, here in London." She leaned forward and wrote "mistaken identity?" on the wallpaper, circled the words and then linked them with a line to Usha's name.

Sandra spoke again. "It's not that I go to many places in a day—I go from here to Mr. Partridge's office, or the house, or I go to classes at Morley College, or to Birkbeck—and I go back to my flat. I think I've only ever been to Camberwell once or twice, even though one of my friends I share the flat with goes to the art college there." She frowned, then looked at Maisie, her eyes wide. "Hold on a minute—I think I know where I saw her. Well, it might not have been her, as I said, but . . . about four months ago, must have been in May or thereabouts, my friend asked me to go with her to one of the lectures; open to the public, it was. The talk was all about colors and how things feel—textures, and that sort of thing. The lecturer had people helping him—it was all very interesting, I must say—and he was showing pictures these different artists had painted, and their sculptures, and what have you, and then he talked about color and places, so she—if it was her—came onto the podium with this pile of saris, all these lengths of silk in different colors, and she opened one up after another, and draped them over her arms. I remember her standing there, like a goddess, she was, clothed in all these colors. Your eyes could hardly stand it."

"And you think this assistant was Usha Pramal?" Maisie picked up the photograph, now some years old and torn at the edges. She handed it to Sandra.

The young woman frowned, and began to nibble the nail on the middle finger of her left hand. "Oh, dear—I can only say it looks like her, because I remember the woman smiling, really smiling, as if she'd turned into a butterfly. My friend was thinking the same thing, because she whispered in my ear, 'She's a Camberwell Beauty, if ever I saw one.' You know, the butterfly, the Camberwell Beauty?" Sandra paused. "I couldn't swear on the Bible in a court of law, Miss, but I am halfway positive that it was her."

"Any chance that your friend will remember the name of the lecturer?"

"I'll ask her tonight."

Maisie nodded, and was about to put a question to Billy when Sandra spoke again.

"I remember him as if it were yesterday, though I couldn't tell you his name."

"Why? What was it about him that stuck in your memory?"

"You could tell he'd been wounded, in the war. There were scars on his face, and he had a bit of a limp; used a cane."

"That's a fair description of almost all of us who went over there," said Billy.

She shook her head. "Now I'm remembering—and I still don't know for definite if it was her. But I remember the way he was talking, and he ran his hand along one of the saris she held over her arm, and she smiled this big smile at him. Then afterwards, he was helping her to fold the saris as we were all filing out—and it was slow going, what with people stopping to talk and picking up their things; the line was moving like treacle off a cold spoon. When they'd finished, the Indian woman went to shake his hand—which I thought was very bold of her, I mean, to hold out her hand like that. He looked at her hand as if it were something very precious he was being offered, and at the point where their fingers touched, she took his hand in both of hers. Then, when he turned away—the Indian woman was by now talking to some women that my friend said were students studying embroidery—he looked at his hand and rubbed it, as if he'd touched something warm." Sandra looked at Maisie, frowning. "I don't understand that, how one minute you can be sorting things out in your brain, looking for something you've lost, then the next thing, the memory comes rushing in."

"It might be to do with the color. I remember Maurice telling me that it opens up another part of the brain. Recalling all those saris and the explosion of color was the key that unlocked the treasure chest with that particular memory." She turned to her assistant. "Billy, remember that. Remember the color. I'll ask Caldwell about the sari Usha was wearing when her body was discovered—we can get some similar fabric. It might help people remember."

"I'd better be off then, Miss. Got a lot to do today."

"Any luck with that other case, the missing boy?"

"Not a lot yet, though I spoke to his teacher and apparently he had a great interest in the sea. I hate to think of it, but if I was that age and I wanted to do a

runner, I might try to jump on one of them ships setting off from the docks."

"Well, keep on it, just in case. " She looked at her
notes, then at Billy and Sandra. "Right then, let's have
a discussion after our meeting with Major Pramal
tomorrow morning. We should have a lot to add to the
map for Usha Pramal by then."

Sandra began putting the crayons away and folding
the case map. "Funny name, isn't it? Usha? Does it
mean anything?"

Maisie nodded. "Most names from the subcontinent
mean something—just as English names have a mean-
ing, or French names. And that's something I remembered, when you were talking about the woman with
the saris. I remembered—it was years ago now, when
I was studying with Maurice—learning about different mythologies. Hindu mythology was a subject all on
its own and could keep you busy for your entire life, I
think. But I remember Usha. She was the goddess of
the dawn; she was considered to be the Daughter of
Heaven."

"Right, Miss Dobbs, sit yourself down. Sorry I can't
offer you a cup of tea, but we don't have time for that
sort of thing." Caldwell looked at Maisie. "On account
of the criminals."

"Not to worry, Inspector—I had my fill this morning, and I am sure we kept you from the brink of thirst."

Caldwell rolled his eyes, a mannerism that seemed to be the inspector's signature reaction to almost any comment with which he had no truck. He pushed a folder towards her. It was a folder that had been previously used for another case or two; the edges were frayed and torn, and as she opened the cover, she could see a series of names crossed out inside the flap.

"Commissioner cut your stationery allowance?" asked Maisie.

Caldwell sighed. "I shouldn't be mentioning it to you, but it's the bean counters, coming round and checking how we're using everything from a pencil to a pin." He nodded towards the notes in Maisie's hands. "To tell you the truth, I feel sorry for the woman. Even the examiner said she was a beauty. Taller than some of them. Bob Carter was in India, with the army, and he said she would have been of a higher caste, or with a bit of Anglo in her, he thought. But there again, she was living in that home for servants."

"It might have been the only place for her to go—she had been taken on as a governess. How long had she been dead when she was discovered?"

"About twenty-four hours, according to the post-mortem report."

"Had her body been brought to the canal? Were there any signs of her death along the canal path? The summer's been dry for the most part, so there would have been blood on the ground if she'd been shot nearby."

Caldwell shook his head. "I had men walking up and down that path looking at the dirt and gravel until they couldn't move their necks for a week. Nothing."

"So, she was carried there?"

He nodded. "I would have thought so."

"Not easy to lift, a dead weight," said Maisie.

"Unless there were two doing the carrying."

"Were there distinct footprints?"

Again, Caldwell shook his head. "Someone was very careful, I reckon. Could have shot her next to the canal, so she just fell in when the bullet hit her."

Maisie sat back and regarded the inspector, the way he fiddled with a piece of paper on his desk and avoided meeting her eyes. *He feels guilty,* she thought. *He didn't do the job as well as he could have, and he knows it.*

"What else did you discover? And I know I could read all this, but what might you have found out about Usha Pramal that you were keeping from her brother?"

Caldwell sighed. He looked up at Maisie, then came to his feet to stand alongside the small soot-stained window through which sun would never shine into his office.

"We have evidence to suggest she was a prostitute."

Maisie frowned. "Are you sure?"

"We talked to people in the area, and from all accounts she was seen with men."

"I'm seen with men, Inspector, but I hope no one thinks ill of me."

"But not her sort. It's not on for them, is it? Seen going into houses to see men."

"Are you sure? Was she seen going into a house to see one man, but five people saw it? Or was she really seen going into different houses?"

The detective sat down again. "I admit, a bit of doubt crept in. She was never seen out at night—we talked to the warden at the ayah's hostel, and she said Miss Pramal was always in of a night. Rules, you see. But she was out during the day. According to the warden, she always had some money—not lots, mind, but she had some sort of work outside what was organized for her. Most of them work as cleaners, anything they can get." He paused. "And there's no two ways about it, a lot of these women who were given their marching orders by the people who brought them over here *have* ended up on the streets, especially down by the docks. They find their own kind there, see. Lascars—Indian sailors."

Maisie chewed the inside of her lip. "Poor souls probably didn't have much choice. What kind of people would bring a young woman from her home—so different from this country—then cast her out when they no longer had need of her services?"

"They didn't all do that. When I spoke to the warden, Mrs. Paige, she said a fair number had their passage paid to go back home. And there's cases of these ayahs' getting a new job straightaway and coming right back again with another family."

"Then why is there an ayah's hostel?"

"Well, you've got a point there, Miss Dobbs. Mrs. Paige and her husband—churchgoers, they are, very religious—said they felt they had to help these women. Started when Mrs. Paige came across an Indian woman begging on a street corner, so she got talking to her and realized what had happened—lost her job, and had nowhere to go. She brought her home, gave her room and board in return for work, and she discovered that there were more who needed that sort of help. Of course, they couldn't keep them all, it gets expensive, with so many mouths to feed, so they went to their vicar, scrounged every penny they could from their fellow parishioners, and they turned their house into a hostel. They had the room after all, it's a big house. They've got enough beds to accommodate twelve women on three upper floors. The Paiges have the ground floor, turned it into a nice flat for themselves."

"That's very generous."

"Like I said, they're religious."

"I'll see them as soon as I can."

"Of course you will."

Maisie looked at Caldwell. "What's happened on this case, Inspector? You started off according to the book—a quick glance here tells me you began everything in line with correct procedures—securing the area where Pramal was discovered, conducting a search along the canal, speaking to associates, locals in the area who might have seen the woman. Then very little follows."

He shrugged. "It went cold. We hit a brick wall with nothing new coming in, and there were other cases pending. Life's not getting any easier around here, you know. There were no relatives banging on my door every day, and word came from a bit higher up to leave it alone and get on with more pressing cases."

"And a gunshot wound to the head is not pressing? Was the bullet identified?"

"Went straight through the skull, out the other side." He sighed. "And no, we couldn't find it. There is a best guess, though—Fred Constantine, the pathologist on the case, said he could well be off his mark, but he couldn't help but think it was a Webley Mark IV revolver. Standard issue to British officers in the war."

"And officers from Empire armies."

"Yes. And Empire armies."

"And it needs a practiced hand, I seem to remember," said Maisie. "Otherwise it jumps as it's fired."

"That's right. Good little pistol—had one myself. But in the war we kept our eyes out for a Luger, if we found a dead German. Nice little prize to get yourself, that." Caldwell shrugged.

"But you had to relinquish your pistol when you were demobilized, didn't you?"

"I did. Yes. But you know as well as I do, Miss Dobbs, not all were handed back, and anyone who wants to arm themselves will find a way."

Maisie nodded, lifted the folder, and placed it in her briefcase. "I'll go through this and get in touch if I have any questions."

They stood at the same time, the two chairs being pushed back making a scraping sound across the floor. They shook hands.

"I'll get my sergeant to see you out."

"Thank you, Inspector Caldwell."

Caldwell reached forward and opened the door for Maisie to depart the room.

"I'm sure it's all in here, Inspector," said Maisie, tapping the document case where she had placed the file. "But can you tell me exactly when Mr. Pramal was informed of his sister's death?"

"As soon as we got the details from the Paiges. I sent a telegram to the police in Bombay, and they found him quite quickly—working somewhere else at the time, he was."

"And then he came over straightaway?"

Caldwell nodded.

"And now he's staying in a hotel here. That can't be much fun."

"Well, he was with an old mucker, from his army days," said Caldwell, summoning his sergeant with a wave of his hand.

"He told me he lodged with a friend for a short time."

"Yes, he did, Miss Dobbs," said Caldwell. "And he is very well thought of, according to Mr. Singh—that's his friend. He said the Sarn't Major's men would have done anything for him, in the war. Anything."

Maisie nodded and smiled, holding her hand out to Caldwell. She would find out herself if Usha Pramal's brother was no longer staying with the friend who would do anything for him, simply because it became an inconvenience.

Maisie looked at her watch. Billy and Sandra would both have left the office by now, so she decided to make her way back to Ebury Place and the mansion where she lived—though she still thought of it as "stayed"—with James Compton. Compton was not her husband, or her fiancé, though he was open about his desire to be married to Maisie. Her friend Priscilla Partridge, whom she had known since she was seventeen years of age and a new student at Girton College in 1914, continued to press her to make up her mind; yet even she knew that Maisie's foot-dragging was due to not one but several threads of reticence. The difference in background between Maisie and James was one, despite the fact that Maisie was now a woman of considerable wealth following the death of her longtime mentor, Dr. Maurice Blanche. Maisie had a successful business, and had worked hard to establish herself as a professional woman—she did not relish relinquishing that independence to become a society matron. James Compton had promised her that he would not expect such an outcome, though it was already clear he was not happy with the risks inherent in her work. But more than anything, Maisie had established within herself a strength, a sense of her own worth, and an independence. At the same time, though she had long recovered from the wounds of war—wounds of both body and mind—there were times when the ice still felt thin beneath her feet, and she retained a fear that she might crash through into the cold waters of her most terrible memories if events conspired to make her fall. She feared that in marrying she might give up that essential part of herself, the resilience that kept her skating above the ice. Fortunately, Maisie was not the only woman of her day who had chosen a looser relationship than marriage might have offered, and she knew that, for now, James Compton's love for her and his fear of losing her outweighed his need to be married—and more important, to produce an heir to the Compton estate.

"Miss Dobbs, welcome home." The butler, Simmonds, held out his hand for Maisie's coat, which she slipped from her shoulders. He handed the coat to the maid as he continued to address Maisie. "Viscount Compton has telephoned to say he may be a little late, and would you please dine without him this evening."

"Oh, I see—yes, I think he had some visitors from abroad at the offices today. I daresay he's taken them to his club." She pulled off her gloves and unpinned her hat, which the maid reached out to take from her; the presence of a maid assigned to her service was something that still occasionally took Maisie by surprise. She handed the hat and gloves to the young woman. "Thank you, Madeleine." She turned back to the butler. "In that case, I think I'll just have something on a tray in the library. Soup with some bread and cheese would be just the ticket."

"Cook has prepared your favorite, Miss Dobbs— oxtail soup."

"Thank you, Simmonds. In about half an hour."

"Very good, Miss Dobbs." He gave a short bow.

Maisie made her way upstairs, pleased that the staff had finally become used to the fact that she abhorred being referred to as "mu'um" or some other strangled form of "madam." She had uttered the word often when she herself was a member of the belowstairs staff in this same grand mansion, and did not care to be addressed in such a fashion.

James had taken her to task, pointing out that she was making the staff feel uncomfortable, but Priscilla had told her that she shouldn't worry about it, observing, "You know your trouble, Maisie—you care too much."

After supper, she set her tray to one side, then moved to an armchair close to the open French windows that led into the gardens. Michaelmas daisies danced in the cool air, contrasting with the burnished colors of autumn leaves waiting to loosen and fall, and their green neighbors yet to change. And she wondered about Usha Pramal, a young Indian woman, far from home, yet always smiling. She wondered about her independence of spirit, and how that might have upset those who knew her as a girl—a girl who, like Maisie, had lost her mother at an early age. She closed her eyes and brought to mind the scene described by Sandra, at the lecture she attended in Camberwell. It wasn't the image of colorful silks draped across Usha's dark skin that drew her attention, but rather Sandra's description of the lecturer's reaction to the woman's touch when the lecture had ended, as if a precious element remained on his skin.

Yes, she would see the man as soon as she could, she would find out what it was he felt in his hand. She wasn't sure why, but she thought his might be valuable information, an insight to what it was that Usha Pramal carried inside her, and perhaps something of her essence.

She's a Camberwell Beauty, if ever I saw one. Maisie reflected upon Sandra's recollection of her friend's description of the murdered Indian woman. She walked over to the stacks of books in the library, a library that had grown over the years—though it had seemed full to overflowing even in the days of her girlhood, when she would steal downstairs at night to read and read and read, in an effort to quench her thirst for learning. She knew this library like the back of her hand. She ran her fingers over the spines of books and soon found what she was looking for. It was a tea card book, a collection of palm-size cards from boxes of tea, pasted in by James Compton when he was just a boy. "Butterflies & Moths of the World" was inscribed in his childish handwriting. She flipped through until she reached the one she was looking for: *The Camberwell Beauty.* She had simply wanted to look at an image of the butterfly, curious, for she could not remember what it looked like. It wasn't a butterfly often seen in Britain, let alone London. More accustomed to the climates of Asia and North America, it was the discovery of two of the butterflies in Coldharbour Lane in Camberwell in the mid-1700s that led to the local name. With soft wings of deep purplish red decorated with small blue dots and rimmed by a yellow border, the butterfly was at once elegant and mystical. Maisie felt her skin prickle when she read the more common name for the Camberwell Beauty: the Mourning Cloak. It was not a clue, not an element of great import to her investigation, but there was something in the picture before her that touched her heart. That something beautiful was so bold, yet at once so fragile.

Chapter Four

"I promise, I won't be home quite so late this evening, Maisie." James Compton cut into a slice of toast, spreading it liberally with butter and marmalade. "It was that meeting with Tom Hollingford, you know, the architect working on those houses we're building in Bromley. It just went on and on, and at the end of the day, it was all about apple trees."

Maisie placed her table napkin beside her plate and glanced at the clock on the mantelpiece. She wanted to leave for the office and prepare for the meeting with Usha Pramal's brother. "Apple trees, James?"

"Well, you know the entire area was once apple orchards—all down to Henry the Eighth and his desire for an abundant supply of fresh fruit in days of yore. Anyway, what we are trying to do is retain at least one apple tree in each garden. Keep a bit of the past lurking in the present. And it's proving to be a bit of a pain in the neck. Hollingford wants to just plough the whole lot in, though I believe we should keep as much as we can—it's good for public opinion. We don't want to be seen as a raze-and-build firm, and there are some very big contracts, here and overseas, that will come our way if we get it right. It's always so much easier when permission to build goes through the local council without too much ado, and that's more likely to happen if people are happy about what's going in."

Maisie stood up, leaned forward, and kissed James on the forehead. "Keep the apple trees. People will thank you for them."

"Shade in summer and fruit in September," said James.

"Yes," said Maisie. "And a tree is always handy for tying one end of the washing line."

James laughed. "I never thought of that."

"No, James, you would never have thought of that. Now then, I must go. Stick to your guns, James."

As she left the room, Maisie reached out and took an apple from the bowl on the sideboard buffet. "A cox's orange pippin is so much nicer than apples from foreign parts," she added, closing the door behind her.

"**Mr. Pramal,** you must be quite busy, with the various arrangements that have to be made. I didn't think of that when I asked you to come back so soon." Maisie held out her hand to the chair made ready for Pramal. She nodded to Billy and Sandra to join her; Pramal waited until the women were seated before taking his place.

"Finding the truth of my sister's death is the most important thing I have to do at the moment," said the man, his head bending forward as a mark of respect.

"May I ask what arrangements have been made for her . . . for her funeral?"

"We have had to do our best to honor her in our way, Miss Dobbs. So, as soon as her body is released to me by the authorities, Usha will be cremated. I will take her ashes back to India with me, and a ceremony will follow. It is most important that she is laid to rest in a proper way."

"Of course." Maisie nodded to Sandra, who was to take notes. "Now then, let's get down to work. "We asked you some questions yesterday, but I feel it might have at first been difficult for you to speak in front of Detective Inspector Caldwell."

"He is a prejudiced man. He does not like the color of my skin, the sound of my voice, or the fact that I know he has not done his job. So much for the illustrious Scotland Yard. He wants me on a ship. Gone. And with my sister poured into a glass jar, safely in my suitcase."

Maisie looked at Pramal, and felt the power of his grief and anger.

"Major Pramal—"

"Miss Dobbs, as I pointed out yesterday, I am no longer a member of His Majesty's Imperial Armies, so I do not deserve to be addressed as any sort of major. I do not seek to be known in this way. I have enough memories of the war, so would rather be the mister I was before I first came to this country."

"Of course, Mr. Pramal. I also served in the war, so it is a habit of acknowledgment I am given to slipping into when I see medals worn with pride." She paused, glancing at Billy. "But I understand the importance of leaving the past behind, and your reasons for wearing your medals in front of Caldwell."

Maisie thought Pramal had an attractive face, with a hint of European expression, though he moved his head as he spoke with the light cadence of his fellow countrymen. His hair was neat and oiled, combed back with a parting to one side. His eyes were like his sister's—the shape of almonds and the color of dark chocolate. His skin was clear, barely lined, yet his hands were the hands of one familiar with manual work. She imagined him overseeing construction, physically moving iron and brick, clambering over the site of a new dam or bridge, demonstrating to workers exactly how he wanted a job done. She saw him talking to his foreman, and never giving in to the urge to remove his jacket, or open his stiff collar and loosen a tie from its perfect position. It was as if he were intent on being the perfect King's subject.

"It was clear from our conversation yesterday that you made a request for the case to be referred to me. I should have asked at the time, but—where did you hear of my services?"

"From Dr. Basil Khan. Of Hampstead. I knew of Dr. Khan from my great-uncle. They were young men together."

"They were?" Maisie leaned forward. "I confess, I sometimes forget Khan was a doctor—I have only ever known him as 'Khan.' "

Pramal smiled. "He is—as you probably know—from Ceylon; however, as far as I know, he came to Bombay in his youth. He was a medical doctor, but it was not his calling. Instead he went to live in the hills, in Sikkim. Then he went away, and it was years before anyone knew where he'd gone. All over the world, everyone said. My uncle is no longer with us, but I remembered his story, and that Dr. Khan now resided in Great Britain. So I came to him in my time of sadness. He told me that you would help me." Pramal smiled.

"What is it?"

"He said that I must look beyond your youth. But you are not as young as I thought you would be."

Maisie smiled. "I don't know how to take that. To be fair, I was very young when I first met Khan—not yet fifteen years of age—so he probably still considers me a girl."

"No, Miss Dobbs. He said you were a wise woman."

Maisie blushed, opening the file she had collected from Caldwell. "I only hope I don't disappoint you, Mr. Pramal. Now then—" She turned over a page. "Can we talk about Usha coming to England? She was a governess, and never employed as a maid, or a nurse to the children?"

"That is correct. There was already an ayah, who looked after a younger child and undertook general housekeeping, though she did not accompany the family to England. The Allisons were very well positioned, you know. They wanted a governess who could teach English, French, who could read with the children and who could also give them lessons in arithmetic."

"Did they make any promises regarding her future employment?"

"They said that she would be looked after, that she would be with the family until the youngest child had finished her education—then she would have her passage paid to return home. The boy was destined for a boarding school, but I believe it was intended for the young ladies to learn at home and then attend a school in London before being sent to Switzerland. That is the way with these people."

Maisie looked up. Billy caught her eye and raised an eyebrow, while Sandra held her gaze for a second longer than a glance.

"Mr. Pramal, may I ask—it seems quite common for families to bring an ayah with them from India, but not a governess. Am I right?"

Pramal sighed. "Yes, you are correct, but my sister was a highly regarded young woman, who matriculated from her college with top marks and first-class references. She was well versed in the English language and literature—she was tested many times. And she had learned French as well—not a common language to learn in my country."

"From my notes here, it seems that she was given notice to leave her employment with no financial assistance, apart from that which was owed her. Can you account for this?"

"Usha did not tell me about what had happened. In her letters she seemed as happy and content as she had ever been."

"If I may risk overstepping the mark, Mr. Pramal, I would like to return to a point we discussed yesterday—would Usha not have been betrothed to be married at some point?"

Pramal shook his head. "I wish she had, but as I explained, my father indulged her following the death of my mother. My aunts tried to advise him in the most very strong way, but he allowed her to turn up her nose at every suitor. And if I am to be perfectly honest, there were not many suitors—a family soon learns when a girl is too headstrong for their son. It is not desirable, and it comes with a reputation. I believe that if my mother were alive, Usha would have been a different person—but . . ."

"But perhaps not."

Pramal shrugged. "Perhaps not."

Sandra held up her pencil, as if she were a student in class.

"Have you thought of something, Sandra?" asked Maisie.

Sandra blushed, and at once Maisie wondered if she felt less than confident in her classes when called upon to speak or to answer a question.

"Well, yes." She cleared her throat. "Mr. Pramal, I just wondered if any of Miss Pramal's suitors might have gone away feeling, well, slighted in some way. If they and their family tried to bring about a, um, a betrothal—is that how it is?—well, a boy might have had a bit of a chip on his shoulder when she turned down a proposal."

Maisie nodded her agreement. "Mr. Pramal?"

Pramal sighed. "My friend, Mr. Singh, he was in love with Usha once. She made it clear to my father that she would not accept any approach from his family. And there was another man who called upon her, though most unsuitable. An Englishman. He came to the house one day. Usha was very furious with him and asked an aunt to send him away. I—"

Maisie looked up from a note she was making. Pramal had stopped speaking, and was now shaking his head.

"Mr. Pramal?" Maisie leaned forward, to catch his eye.

"I—I had a suspicion at the time—though I never proved it, of course. But I wondered if Usha had already been seen out with the Englishman, without a chaperone. He was a young man, not long in India, and I would say he was a very naive boy—a civil servant, working in the shipping office, or perhaps he was some sort of diplomatic person—I can't remember now. It was soon after he came to our home that she decided to accept the position of governess. She worked for the family for a while before they sailed to England. I never saw the man again, and doubt he ever saw Usha."

"Do you know his name?" Maisie held her pen ready above the index card.

"I really don't remember—in fact, I am not sure that I ever knew. You see, I was not at home then, and did not visit often, because I was new in my position and working very hard to establish myself. I heard that he was a very ordinary young man with nothing to commend him. It was most discourteous that he should call to see Usha without an invitation from my father, or even one of my aunts, standing in for our mother. Such a lack of respect. He had much to learn about India."

"Before we leave the subject of Usha and her suitors, do you think there's anyone else we should know about?" asked Maisie.

"As I mentioned, there was my fellow officer, with whom I stayed for a short while here in London. He is married now. Our mothers were close and our fathers had business together—there was at one time a hope that he and Usha might join the two families. It would have been a source of joy, but she was not to be persuaded."

"Mr. Pramal. Please, correct me if I am wrong, because I have not been to India and my experience of your way of life is rather limited, but everything you have told me about Usha points to the fact that she very much sailed against the wind, that she—for want of a better phrase—took liberties. How was she not vilified in the community . . . didn't people talk?"

Pramal smiled as tears rimmed his eyes. "Ah yes, indeed, Miss Dobbs, that should have been the case. But you see, Usha was beautiful and loved, and ever since she was a child—a very precocious child—it was as if there was a young goddess in our midst. She carried with her an eternal sunshine, you know. She was one of those people who walk along the street and everyone notices them; it's as if they are the source of all brightness."

There was silence for a half-minute.

"Well, excuse, me, Mr. Pramal," said Billy. "But someone didn't like all that brightness, did they? In fact, someone would have had to hate it enough to kill her, or she would still be here. You've got to have given someone a right upset, to get a bullet through your skull, if you don't mind me saying so."

Maisie looked at Billy, shocked at his tone, then turned back to Pramal, her voice modulated to soothe in the wake of her assistant's words. "Mr. Beale has a point—we are now down to who might have wanted her dead, and we might well get to some answers through asking why rather than via any other route." She held up her closed palm, opening each finger in turn as she listed possibilities. "Usha was likely killed for one of the following reasons: One—she had offended or upset someone to the extent that they lost their temper, or they premeditated her murder. Two—she knew something about someone that cost her life. Three—it could have been a random attack, possibly the result of prejudice. Four—mistaken identity. A decade ago London saw some of the worst violence, based upon the color of a person's skin, ever to take place on this soil; that sort of tension can linger, especially in these difficult times. Five—someone loved her too much and wanted to punish her for it." She held up the opposite forefinger. "Six—envy. Someone was envious of her."

Sandra half-raised her hand again, but put it down as she asked another question. "Mr. Pramal—what do you think might have been the reason for your sister's death?"

Pramal shrugged and sighed. For the first time his military bearing seemed to have abandoned him. "If I was to guess, I would say that you have a point with each of your suppositions, but I believe Usha was killed because someone was afraid of her."

Maisie, Billy, and Sandra were all silent, waiting.

"Yes, *afraid*." Pramal went on. The previously tear-filled eyes now seemed calm, but resolute. "Usha had a power inside her—it is almost beyond me to explain it. A goddess on earth, that's what people said about her, even when she was a small child. You see, Miss Dobbs—" He looked at Sandra and then Billy, acknowledging them. "You only had to watch her walk. She did not take small steps. No, my sister could stride. Everywhere she went, it was with some purpose."

Billy returned to the office following Pramal's departure, joining Maisie at the table by the window, where the case map was spread out.

"Billy, Sandra's taken the cups along the hall. Before she gets back, I wanted to talk about the meeting with Pramal—you were very quiet, and then you snapped at him. It was a fair observation, to a point—but what caused you to speak in that tone? The man came here for help, not to be addressed in such a manner."

Billy shrugged and slid down in the chair. Maisie thought he resembled a recalcitrant schoolboy.

He shook his head. "I dunno, Miss. He just sort of started to get on my nerves—all this business about her being some sort of fairy godmother. All mysterious. I just didn't believe him, that's all."

"Go on—that's not enough."

Billy looked at Maisie. "There's something not right about all of this. I'm not like you, Miss—not your sort that gets lots of feelings about things. I take it all as I see it, as a rule. But I just started to feel like I was listening to someone stringing me along."

Maisie nodded.

"What do you think, Miss?"

"Again, I think you have a point, but I think there's more to it than that. I think—and we may all be well off the mark here—I think he's floundering. I think there might have been some serious discord in his dealings with his sister, even at a great distance. We can't prove that, but we can find out more."

"Aw gawd, Miss, I can't understand half of what them people say—I can't go out there and talk to Indians."

"Don't worry. I have the names of the boys now—that's your job. Find out all you can about the boys who discovered the body."

Billy took a sheet of paper from Maisie. "I feel like the Pied Piper, what with that other boy on the loose."

Maisie looked up. Billy had returned to work following a serious injury while investigating the death of another man earlier in the year, and she felt he needed some sort of encouragement to inspire him. So to underscore her confidence in him, she had handed him the most recent case to supervise. The opportunity was presented when a man named Jesmond Martin came to see Maisie with a view to retaining her services in the search for his missing son. Fourteen-year-old Robert had walked away from his school—Dulwich College—in early July and had not been seen since. Asked about the delay in contacting Maisie and his reason for not previously alerting the police, Martin explained that the son was well able to look after himself, that he did not want his son to fall afoul of the police, and that he had also wanted to give the boy a chance to come home on his own. To deter the school from approaching the police, Martin had informed them that the son was now at home and he had withdrawn him from the school's roster of pupils.

After the meeting, Maisie decided that it would be good for Billy to be in charge of an investigation—especially as he was the father of boys. Now she wondered if it was such a good idea.

"When we're done with this, let's talk about that case, shall we? See where we are with it."

Sandra returned to the office. She placed the tea tray with clean crockery on top of a filing cabinet, and when Maisie beckoned to her, joined them at the table.

"What about the issue of prejudice?" asked Maisie.

"You never know what people will do, do you?" said Sandra. "I mean, when there are lines of men looking for work, people marching on London from up north, thinking we've got it easy down here—and they soon find out Londoners are in the same boat, don't they?— well, it makes it difficult when you find out there's paying work going to people who don't even come from here."

Billy made a sound that drew the attention of both Maisie and Sandra, an exhalation of breath demonstrating his disdain. "Prejudice? Let me tell you, if people here can be prejudiced against their own, you can bet your life they can be prejudiced against someone else." He leaned forward. "My mate told me what it was like, after the war—he came home at the beginning of 1919. And just because the war had ended, it didn't mean it was suddenly all cushy over there in France. No, a lot of them men were still covered in mud, blood, and rats' you-know-what by the time they stepped off a train at Waterloo." He shook his head, his eyes narrowing. "Because I'd been wounded in Messines, I was sent back here to Blighty in 1917. But one of my mates was over there until a good three months after the Armistice. He told me that they got off the carriages and were told to stand at ease while they were awaiting orders. So they all sat down on the platform—blimey, they'd been on their pins for long enough and it was obvious where they'd just come back from. Then along came these commuter types, all top hats and creases in their trousers. 'These men are a disgrace,' said one of the toffs. Then another went on about how the soldiers were nothing more than tramps. Now *that's* discrimination—when you look down your nose at the very men who fought to make sure you could still go to work in your tidy, warm office. That's the trouble with people—they cherish their comforts, but they don't want to know where they come from. The ladies like their cheap Indian cotton bedspreads, but they'd turn their noses up at the women who sit there doing the weaving for next to nothing." He folded his arms and sat back in his chair.

There was silence for a few seconds, during which Maisie looked at Sandra, and motioned with her head towards the door. Sandra nodded.

"I think I'll just nip across to the dairy. What with all that tea drinking, we've run out of milk."

"Right you are, Sandra, thank you. Remember to reimburse yourself from the petty cash."

When Sandra had left the room, Maisie sat for a while, waiting. She watched Billy as he leaned forward, gazing at his feet. During the attack that had led to his absence from work, he had sustained serious head injuries, though they had healed sufficiently for him to return to work. At first it had seemed that all was well—life had calmed down at home for Billy, and their two boys seemed to be putting their mother's difficulties behind them. Doreen Beale had become mentally unstable following the death of her youngest child, a girl named Lizzie. It was a psychiatric condition exacerbated by Billy's ill-health. But in the past few weeks Maisie had noticed a new pattern of behavior in Billy. His moods could change in a matter of seconds, from happy-go-lucky one minute, to morose and argumentative the next. That his war wounds still troubled him on occasion was obvious, but it was rare for Billy to lose his good temper. His respect for Maisie had never been in question—she was the nurse who had helped save his life in the war. Now she felt a confusion at the center of his being—in the way he sat, in his facial expression, and in the moods of melancholy laced with anger that rendered him as volatile as a grenade without a pin.

"Don't think I don't know, Miss. Sandra went out so you could have a word with me."

"She has been here long enough to know that you're not yourself, and that I would want to talk to you about whatever's troubling you." Maisie's voice was soft. She was once more careful with her words, as if weighing them for their potential to inflame the situation. Billy was distressed enough already.

"I don't know why you have me here, to be honest." Billy folded his arms across his chest.

Maisie did not miss the move, knowing he was protecting his heart.

"I have you here because I trust you, Billy. You know that." She paused. "Now, perhaps you could describe what happened when you became agitated towards the end of our meeting here with Mr. Pramal, and when you became short-tempered with Sandra."

"I . . . I don't know." Billy's hands moved, one to either side of his head. "I don't know, Miss and it's—oh, nothing," He folded his hands in front of his chest again.

"It's not nothing. Your well-being is not nothing." Another pause. "Do your best, Billy. Try to describe what happens."

"Oh, Miss, all that describing business. I don't know. I just need to pull up my socks and not let you down. I got a bit angry, that's all it was."

Maisie was silent, watching Billy. His foot, drawn back against the chair; his heel tapping. Tap-tap-tap-tap. The agitation was mounting again.

"Yes, you got a bit angry. But that's not all it was. What went through your mind?"

"Well, I just want to snap, don't I?" His voice was raised. "I just want to say, 'Miss, I can't do this job anymore, because I can't keep my thoughts in my head.' " He pressed his fingers to his temple. "I've hardly done anything on that case about the missing boy, because

I don't know what to do next. I can't remember what comes after I've seen people; how I'm supposed to put it all together. I look in my notebook and I panic, because I don't know how to get from here to there. I don't know how to join the dots anymore." He choked back his tears.

Maisie stood up and, as if by instinct, rubbed his back, as a mother would a child in distress. She stepped away as he regained control.

"And what with Doreen, and the baby—the boys are getting bigger, especially young Billy—who's a bit full of himself. Getting on for twelve he is now, and more like a walking mouth. Knows everything, all of a sudden. And what kind of father am I? Gammy leg, gammy mind."

"You're a very good father, Billy. Your boys look up to you—I've seen the respect they have for you." Maisie paused, thinking. "Billy, I think you came back to work too soon. I think you've overdone it, and it's caught up with you. Here's what I want you to do—go home early today. Take a few weeks rest—the weather is still very nice, why don't you get the family away down to the coast? I'll not expect you back here until next month, or later, if you don't feel up to it."

"What about the missing lad?"

"I'll deal with it. And the Pramal case. I'll ask Sandra if she can work some extra hours here in the office." Maisie nodded towards the telephone. "And I think you should see that neurologist again. Are you having headaches?"

Billy nodded.

"I seem to remember you saw Dr. Patchley; he was brought in by Dr. Dene after he examined you. If you like, I could find out his address and telephone number—would you like me to?"

Maisie continued to speak with care, not only because Billy seemed so fragile, but because she had been taken to task in recent months by Priscilla, who suggested she'd overstepped the mark in helping others.

"I'll get in touch, no need for anyone else to help me with that," said Billy. "I just need to know how to get to see him."

"I'll find out now, before you leave—you can telephone from here if you like."

Maisie lifted the telephone's black receiver and dialed Andrew Dene's number at Guy's Hospital, where she spoke to a clerk and scribbled the information on a slip of paper.

"Here you are." She placed the paper on Billy's desk. "I have to nip down to collect the post. You can telephone now. Sooner rather than later."

Billy nodded. "Thank you, Miss."

Maisie stepped towards the door and left the office, but stood outside to listen before making her way downstairs. She heard Billy lift the receiver, heard him dial the number and speak to a secretary. She knew only too well that a Harley Street neurologist would cost a pretty penny. But there were ways to diminish the cost—she would make an important telephone call herself, as soon as he left to go home. And Billy would never have to know.

Chapter Five

Addington Square in Camberwell had seen enough years to have housed the gentry, the well-to-do, the less well off, and, indeed, those who were struggling to stay afloat in turbulent times. Its residents over the centuries reflected the shifting fortunes of an area that was once filled with successful merchants, but which nowadays was home to a mix of students, academics, the more successful market traders, the poor, and those seeking to improve their lot. The properties were mainly of Regency and Georgian stock, and the fact that there was no uniformity to the buildings enhanced, rather than diminished, the character of the area. The Grand Surrey Canal, built in the early 1800s, brought with it a flurry of construction, which added Victorian housing and effectively completed the square, which was named after the then Prime Minister, Henry Addington.

Maisie parked her motor car close to the address she had been given for the ayah's hostel where Usha Pramal had been living at the time of her death. She looked around the square before lifting the brass door knocker and rapping three times. Some moments later, the door of the brick Georgian terrace house was opened by a young Indian woman wearing a sari of olive green cotton with a wide border embroidered in a medley of pale green and yellow threads. She wore her long jet-black hair in a single braid, and as she stood on the threshold to greet Maisie, a cluster of thin silver bangles on her wrists jangled when she pushed a stray hair behind her right ear. Maisie noticed that she was wearing a silver crucifix.

"Yes? May I be of assistance to you?" The woman's smile was broad and welcoming.

"I'd like to see Mr. or Mrs. Paige, if I may. Are they home?"

"Mrs. Paige is here. Please come in." She stepped aside, and held her hand out to one of two ladder-back chairs situated on either side of an umbrella stand in the entrance hall. "Please wait—I will fetch her." The woman bowed her head and walked on tiptoe towards the door at the end of the passageway. It seemed almost as if she were dancing, so light was her step.

While waiting, Maisie regarded her surroundings. Dark cream wainscoting ran along the bottom half of the walls, above which wallpaper with a design of intertwined red geraniums had been hung without matching the pattern. She thought that if she looked at the wall for long enough, she would become quite dizzy, so strong was the sense that the bricks were moving underneath the paper. She looked at a collection of photographs on one wall, of a series of very British-looking adults clustered together in places other than Britain. In one they were seated at a table under a palm tree, in a second together in front of a series of mud huts. There was one of a church minister holding his hand up to the heavens while talking to a group of dark-skinned children, all seated with legs crossed and each one appearing to hang on his every word. A crucifix hung on the wall.

"Good morning. I'm Mrs. Paige." A short woman with a round face and hair tied back in a bun stood in front of Maisie, her hands clasped in front of her middle. She wore a flower-patterned day dress with the low waist that might have been fashionable some ten years earlier, though the fabric seemed to pull across her middle. Her face was unlined, and her cheeks rosy red, as if she had been sitting in the sunshine without a hat.

"Mrs. Paige, please forgive me for imposing upon you without notice; however, I wanted to see you at the earliest opportunity." Maisie held out a card. "I have been retained by Mr. Pramal to look into the death of his sister, Miss Usha Pramal, who I believe resided with you."

The woman appeared agitated, looking at the card without taking it, and wringing her hands together. "Well, yes, but . . . but my husband isn't here, you know."

Maisie nodded. "I see—but perhaps you could spare me five minutes or so. I have just a few questions for you, Mrs. Paige."

"Oh, all right then. Come with me."

Mrs. Paige led the way into a front-room parlor. It was a dark room, revealing a sensibility that was somewhat old-fashioned, even by the standards of those who were slow to change or who had little money to do so. A picture rail painted in maroon gloss that had lost its shine framed the deep-red, embossed wallpaper. A table set next to the bay window had a plant on top with leaves that had grown out to the point of diminishing natural light that might otherwise have illuminated the room. Ornate plasterwork on the ceiling seemed oppressive, as if it were bearing down on one's head, and heavy cloths on tables and across chairs lent the room a funereal feel.

Paige led Maisie to the table, where she pulled out two dining chairs carved in a manner that would have made them at home in a church.

"Please sit down. Would you like tea? I can summon the girl."

Maisie shook her head. "No, thank you, Mrs. Paige."

"I've already had the police here, weeks ago. Not very nice at all, what with the neighbors getting nosy. We've had it hard enough, looking after these women, you know. This is a good area, after all." Paige nodded as she finished the sentence, and Maisie thought this might be a habit.

"You have been most benevolent, Mrs. Paige. I have heard about your work—how you gave room and board to women far from home who have been abandoned by the very people who should have looked out for them."

"We're doing God's work, Miss Dobbs. The women here have all toiled for those far wealthier than us, you know. We give them a roof over their heads, and we find them jobs so they can earn their way back to their people. We ask only that they work hard, keep themselves and their rooms tidy, their conduct above reproach, and that they follow the word of the Lord." She nodded again.

"I see. Very commendable, Mrs. Paige." Maisie paused. "I wonder if I might ask about Usha Pramal. How long was she with you?"

"Let me see. Three years it was, perhaps four. Yes. No, now I come to think about it, it was more like four years ago she came to us—1929. She arrived on the doorstep without a place to go, so we took her in. My husband and I live only on this floor, and we've given over the upper floors to our lodgers. They generally share three to a room, but Usha was one who had her own room, as did a couple of the others, of longer standing. We haven't had as many through as we once had, so there's a bit more space now. More families coming home from India without bringing the ayahs, you see. And fewer families going out there. There's been some trouble over there, you see—uprisings. There isn't the respect that there was, not for us, you know."

Maisie nodded. Yes, she did know, but didn't want to have a conversation about politics—not yet, anyway. "Did you know that Usha Pramal was not brought here as an ayah, but a governess? She was a well-educated woman."

"So they said, the police, but she never let on. Of course, I noticed that she had books, and could read English very well. She probably went to an English missionary school."

Maisie shook her head. "No, she was a graduate of a well-regarded ladies' college in Bombay."

Paige seemed surprised, but said nothing.

"Where did she work?" asked Maisie. "You said you found work for the women who live here."

"Mainly as cleaners, maids, that sort of thing. Miss Pramal worked for two employers, as an extra maid for cleaning."

"May I have the names of her employers?"

"The police didn't ask for all this, you know."

"But I am working with the police, Mrs. Paige—you can telephone Detective Inspector Caldwell of Scotland Yard if you have any doubts. And I would like to know who Miss Pramal was working for."

Paige patted the back of her bun, then fingered the crucifix at her neck. "Right you are." She sighed, and seemed to slump a little. "You see, it's sometimes hard enough to find work for the women here. People are so . . . so . . . so difficult. Of course, I can understand it, looking at it from their point of view. But we vouch for these women, and we teach them to be Christians and not pagans, so that should stand for something. We do our best for them."

"I'm sure you do, Mrs. Paige. The names?" Maisie had an index card and pencil ready.

"The main ones were Mrs. Baxter of Birchington Gardens, in Kensington, and Mrs. Hampton, of Colbourne Street, also in Kensington. I'll find the addresses for you when you leave." As if to underline her point, she looked at the clock. "There's also been others over the years, but, as I said, those are the ones she worked for most of the time, over the past few years."

"Well, that's a start. Thank you," said Maisie. "Now, tell me about Miss Pramal's comings and goings. Did she leave on time? Arrive home on time? Can you tell me about her interests, where she went when she had time off?"

"She went out by seven in the morning. That meant she was at her job in time to wash up after breakfast, clean the stove, scrub the kitchen floor, then work her way up through the house. There was generally a house-keeper and a cook, plus a parlor maid—two maids with Mrs. Hampton—so she wasn't needed until eight, and she was there until three or four, generally, depending upon how much laundry there was to do, and any mending and ironing. She was with Mrs. Baxter on Tuesdays and Thursdays, and Mrs. Hampton on Mondays, and of course, they often needed extra help after guests on a Saturday and Sunday—and then on Wednesdays and Saturdays, plus Sunday morning on occasion. If the women didn't have work arranged for a certain day, it seemed that something temporary always came up—an inquiry about tidying a house before or after a party, perhaps, or lending a hand cleaning a sickroom. There's always jobs to do here, or at the church."

"Like Cinderella, wasn't she?"

Mrs. Paige seemed to swell with self-importance, checking her posture and drawing her shoulders back before answering. "A good day's work for her money. And all the women came to church for Sunday evensong—and we studied the Bible two evenings a week with them, and had prayers before bedtime and lights out, so I can tell you she was always in on time."

"And what do you think she was doing to be found in the canal? Was it a place she usually walked? Was there anyone locally who had been seen with her?"

Paige reddened. "I'm sure I don't know. We thought her life might have been taken somewhere else and then she floated here—that river has tides, you know."

Maisie nodded. "My grandfather was a lighterman on the water, so I do know—very well, in fact. Mind you, I think it might be somewhat fanciful to think she floated home to Camberwell." She paused. "Do you have knowledge of any associations, anyone Miss Pramal might have been seeing?"

"Do you mean men?"

"No, I don't. I mean anyone—men or women."

Paige shook her head.

"How about the other women living here? Were they all friends? Did they know her well?"

"Well, they're all from India, so I suppose . . ."

"Mrs. Paige, I think Miss Pramal's level of education indicates that she might have been somewhat frustrated by her work. What do you think?"

"I'm sure I don't know—we do our best for the women. As I said, they have a roof over their heads, and meals. And we save their money for them, so they can go home again."

"You save their money? How? Did you collect wages from them?"

Paige became flustered, patting her bun again, and then picking an imaginary piece of fluff from a sleeve. "I'm sure I mustn't discuss money matters without my husband here. He looks after the accounts."

"I'll talk to him about it, then. In the meantime, may I see Usha Pramal's room?"

"I—well, it hasn't been touched, you know, not since she was found. We thought it best to wait until the brother arrived from India so he could collect her belongings. The police told us not to move anything, anyway, until further notice."

"That's very thoughtful of you. I am sure Mr. Pramal would be grateful to you for keeping her personal effects in the order she left them. In any case, I would like to see the room—could you let me have a look?"

The woman sighed. "Come with me, then."

She led the way towards the staircase, stopping alongside the banister.

"Wait here a minute. We'll need the key."

She was gone for a couple of minutes, during which time Maisie heard her voice echoing through the house. "If you know what's good for you, you'll get the floor a bit cleaner than that!"

Maisie wondered if this was an example of how the women who had come seeking refuge were generally treated. Soon she heard Mrs. Paige approaching, huffing as if the exertion of collecting the key had taken her breath.

"Follow me," she instructed, rubbing her chest.

Maisie made her way up two flights of stairs in the woman's wake, until they reached the top-floor attic room.

"Had this all to herself, she did. Here we are." Mrs. Paige unlocked and opened the door. The room inside was dark and shadowed. She stepped towards the heavy faded velvet drapes and drew them back. At once sunshine streamed in through the window, catching dust motes in broad shafts of light.

"And I wonder why the carpets fade, what with all this hot sun. I had to tell her of it many a time, she was always leaving the curtains wide open. I shan't draw them back like that again. It rots the carpets, the sun."

"Please leave them—I'll close them when I leave. If it's all right with you, Mrs. Paige, I'd like to spend a few moments here in Miss Pramal's room on my own. Just to sit for a while, and look around me."

"I don't know what my husband would say, but—well, all right. Come down when you're ready—but don't be long, because I don't want to have to come all the way up these stairs again."

"No, I won't be long. I just want to look at her books, try to gain an understanding of her character."

The woman tutted, and turned away from Maisie, closing the door as she left the room.

Maisie sighed. At last. Now she could take time to see what Usha Pramal had left behind of herself. Looking around the room, Maisie took account of the low ceilings and sloping attic beams, of the small iron-frame bed to the right of the room, under the eaves. In the corresponding alcove to the left, a series of shelves were filled with books and small ornaments. Four framed photographs on top of the chest of drawers to the immediate left of the door were, Maisie thought, of family members—she would look at them in detail in good time. To the right, behind the open door, stood a wooden washstand with a marble top and tiled back, on top of which was a bowl and ewer of flower-patterned china. The carpet was threadbare—*nothing much to protect there*, thought Maisie—and there was no source of heat that she could see. She hoped she might find an electric heater, for this room was doubtless freezing in winter.

Maisie stepped further into the room, towards the window, where two small wicker armchairs had been placed at an angle suitable for conversation between confidantes. The wicker was unthreaded in places, and the chairs bore the wear that one would expect to see in garden furniture; they had doubtless done duty outside before being brought into the house. Folded blankets served as cushions, and were probably snatched back on winter nights as Usha Pramal tried to stay warm in her bed under the eaves.

The window commanded a view that Maisie thought must have been balm for Usha: a square filled with flowers in spring, and trees in blossom. The assortment of houses seemed bold against branches still bearing the green flush of late summer, though in winter the barren bark would seem stark and cold. What did Usha think, Maisie wondered, as she looked from this window out to the street below and to the houses across the square? What did she think of these people, after having lived in a house with family—her father, brother, and aunts. Perhaps this place became something akin to home for her, and the women her sisters.

Usha Pramal's reading choices were as broad as they were deep, with books on philosophy, on French and English literature; there were novels and one guide-book to London, which was worn and well-leafed. And to her surprise—the Paiges must have been either ill-informed or not ones to pay attention—the small ornaments were in fact statues of Ganesh, Vishnu, and Shiva, gods from a more familiar realm. And there above the alcove with the books was a single framed drawing of Christ on the Cross. It occurred to Maisie that Usha Pramal had kept all doors open in her com-munications with the divine—and she wondered to what extent she went through the motions of following the Paiges' Christian beliefs.

The bed was covered in simple plain white sheets that seemed a little gray. A single blanket was topped with an Indian cotton bedspread in a red, yellow, and blue paisley pattern. It appeared somewhat worn, but Maisie thought there was comfort in that. She sat on the bed, feeling a little like Goldilocks in the baby bear's bed. Placing her bag on the floor beside her, Maisie slipped off her shoes so that her feet could touch the carpet beneath. With her hands on her lap, she closed her eyes.

This was what she had wanted to do, to sit in the room that had been Usha Pramal's refuge, yet even with the woman's belongings about her, she realized there was no sense that it was ever a home. And as she placed a hand on her chest, she felt enveloped by a deep yearning. At once she took a short breath, so sudden had the feeling touched her—it was as if, inside this room, Usha Pramal had given in to her sense of estrangement. Maisie felt tears pressing against her eyelids, as if through her the dead woman could weep the tears of loneliness, tears that expressed an ache for the place that was her home. She opened her eyes, and rubbed away the tears that had come freely. She had not taken due care. She was in the home of a woman who was now dead, who had died alone, far from those she had loved. Maurice would have cautioned her, *Take care, Maisie. You are sensitive to the essence of one who has passed—do not assume that this field is benign. Protect yourself.*

Maisie lay back on the bed. She felt weary. Worry about Billy, about Sandra, and now this case had at once made her so tired, she felt as if she could close her eyes and sleep. She pressed her arm into the bed to lift herself and felt something solid against the point of her elbow. Sitting up, she turned and pushed down upon the bed with both hands. The horsehair mattress was firm, but at this very point, even more so—and lumpy. She had been in the room ten minutes. Soon Mrs. Paige would be calling up the stairs, or sending the Indian girl to find her. She stood up, rolling back the covers so she might with speed make the bed again, and then lifted the bottom sheet to reveal the mattress. Along one side, instead of stitching, a series of pins held the seam in place. She removed them, setting them on top of the white drawn-back sheet. Now she could reach into the mattress. Her fingers were busy, feeling among the fibers to find something she knew had been hidden by Usha Pramal. Soon she touched a cord, which she pulled. She gasped as she realized the cord was attached to a scarlet velvet drawstring bag, which she drew out to inspect. And there was no mistake, it contained a significant amount of money. She reached in again, and found another bag, then one more, secreted in the hair of a long-dead horse.

Stairs creaked, and a voice called out. Maisie moved with speed, sliding the bags into her document case. She replaced the pins, tucked in the bottom sheet and remade the bed.

"Miss Dobbs?"

Maisie slipped on her shoes, stepped out of the room, and looked into the deep blue-brown eyes of the young woman who had answered the door when she arrived at the house. Her head was to one side, and she smiled.

"Mrs. Paige asked me to come find you. Is everything all right?"

"Yes, indeed. Such a lovely room—but I bet it's cold in winter."

She laughed. "The whole house is cold in winter—but Usha used to come to my room when there was a frost. She had nothing above her head except the roof; no loft, nothing to keep her warm. But my room has a fireplace, and we bought coal with our spending money—Mr. Paige sells us a pennyworth at a time."

"He doesn't just make up your fire for you then?"

Another laugh. "I wish Usha were here—she would find that very funny."

"Did you know her well?"

The young woman shrugged. "We came from different families—different backgrounds—but we found some company together. She helped me with my lessons, you know. I learned to read and write at school, but she read books I could not understand, so she helped me."

"Do you work outside this house—I'm sorry, I should have asked your name."

"My name is Maya Patel. And I do work outside the house, every day, but my employer did not want me to come today—he has had to leave London at short notice."

Maisie heard Mrs. Paige call up the stairs, telling Maya Patel to escort Miss Dobbs to the front door, as she was seeing the grocer about the delivery. When they reached the door, Maisie turned to Maya Patel.

"Would it be possible for me to speak to you—alone—at some point soon? It's about Usha."

The young woman looked down, and nodded. "Yes, I think I should like to speak about Usha."

"How might I find you? I don't think I can come back here in a hurry."

"I will be at my second employer's house tomorrow afternoon until four o'clock. I can meet you at St. Pancras station—near the entrance. Would half past four be suitable?"

"Of course. Half past four then, at St. Pancras."

Maya Patel nodded. "And please, Miss Dobbs, take care of Usha's nest egg. She worked very hard for her money. We see hardly any wages from our work. It was her passage home, you see, and more important, for her school. She wanted to build a school for poor girls.

'If I have to teach in the streets, I will, Maya,' she said. And she meant it."

Maisie looked at the young woman, into sweet eyes of light and dark that could see with such clarity. "Don't worry—I will see that her money goes to the right place."

After collecting her jacket she waved to Maya Patel and made her way along the road to her MG motor car. And as she placed the case into the back of the car, using her jacket to cover the valuables, she looked down at her blouse. A single black hair, long and shining like polished ebony, perhaps caught from the bedclothes when Maisie searched Usha Pramal's room, had draped along the length of her sleeve.

Chapter Six

The French doors leading to the gardens at 15 Ebury Place had been left ajar. Though past eight o'clock, the light still seemed dusky outside; coal fires had not yet been burned in earnest, so there was little evidence of the yellow pea-souper smogs that would envelop houses and streets as winter approached and colder evenings drew in. James Compton reached for Maisie's hand and held it in his own.

"Can we talk, Maisie?"

Maisie felt a tension in her spine. She anticipated a conversation she had avoided for some time, and thought that she might now have reached a cul-de-sac, a place of no escape from what might be another painful dialogue. When she turned, it would be to face the truth of James' intentions.

"Yes, let's talk, James." She smiled, and squeezed his hand.

Following an initial courtship filled with promise, Maisie had felt doubt about the future of her relationship with James Compton. James had pressed her to scale back her work—unfairly, she thought—after he had taken possession of the newly refurbished mansion, where Maisie had rooms and where she was considered mistress of the house. She was unwilling to exchange her business for marriage, for her work represented a steadfast rock that had grounded her through the journey of recovery from the wounds of war, especially those lingering in her soul. It often seemed that an inner dialogue intersected with the task in hand, so when she came to the close of an investigation, it was with a deeper sense of knowing about herself—and a humble understanding of how much more there was to learn. Where might she find strength if she relinquished her work?

Yet on the other hand, she loved James Compton, in her way. He, too, had suffered in the war and had battled memories that kept him awake at night. He had rebuilt his life, and now wanted to forge a future with Maisie at his side. Their courtship had floundered in recent months, though both felt they were on a more even keel. However, as Maisie had discovered to her chagrin, James had been drawn into the plans of powerful men who were preparing for the possibility of another war. With Germany's new chancellor, Herr Adolf Hitler, diminishing the freedoms of so many people in his country—and with intelligence to suggest a stockpiling of weapons and the training of young aviators in direct contravention to the agreements made during the 1919 Peace Conference—there were those of James' acquaintance who were making plans to prepare Britain for another conflict. John Otterburn was one such man. Having started his career as a newspaperman, the wealthy self-made Canadian now lived in England, where his success in the print industry had afforded him large mansions in London and Surrey—and a good deal of influence in the highest quarters. Such power had brought him into contact with one man in particular—Winston Churchill—who was languishing on the hinterland of British politics. Otterburn supported Churchill's prediction that in another war with Germany, the fight for Britain would be in the air. In secret, Otterburn was bankrolling the design and testing of new military aircraft—and had recruited James Compton to his cause. James had been an aviator in the war, and for him, flying represented a passion. His loyalty to his country was without question. Yet Maisie had discovered that Otterburn was also ultimately responsible for the death of an innocent man in a case she was investigating. Otterburn's position rendered him untouchable, and she was deeply affected by her inability to bring him to justice.

"I know I might sound like a scratched gramophone record, Maisie, but I want to talk about us," said James.

Maisie nodded. "Yes, you're right. We've danced around it before—me more than you, I confess. I think it's time."

She could see the tension in James' face, the small vein that throbbed at his temple, the muscles in his neck, taut with apprehension.

"I know you hate me to talk about John Otterburn—and I absolutely understand your position—but I'm afraid I have given my word. I have promised to be in Canada in about six weeks. I'll be in Toronto, at the Compton Corporation head office there, but I will also be back and forth to Otterburn's headquarters. We'll have some time for a little flight testing this year, before the weather closes in, but still, there's a lot of work to do with the draftsmen and engineers through-out the winter months, until we can resume aircraft trials again next year. I'm not sure whether I'll be back for Christmas, Maisie."

"Yes, I see. Who will take care of the Corporation here, in London?"

"That second cousin of mine, Jonathan Compton—frankly, the families aren't close, but he's worked for the Corporation for years and has been groomed to be my number two. He's a bit older than me, actually. My father brought him into the company during the war, when I was in the Flying Corps—sensible idea, after all, you never knew when I might have had a particularly bad landing."

Maisie rubbed her forehead with her free hand; James still held the other.

"So, we're down to the crunch, Maisie." He picked up his wineglass, then set it down again without taking a sip. "Will you come with me? Will you marry me and come with me as my wife?"

Maisie felt light-headed. This was not a new question, or an unexpected proposal. But it was time to give an answer.

She rubbed her forehead again, back and forth.

"Well?" James looked at her intently.

"Oh dear." She caught her breath. "James, let me tell you something. I have been thinking about traveling. I have never been anywhere really—apart from France—and I think I need to go overseas. But not to Canada; not yet, anyway."

"This is the first you've said about it. Where do you want to go? I mean, we could go together. We could plan a tour, then make our way out to Canada. A long honeymoon—though not the best time of year for shipping, I'll grant you. We could—"

"James. James, stop." She paused. "Here's what I think I must do. I cannot consent to marriage at this point, because I want to follow in Maurice's footsteps. It's a journey I think I must embark upon, but I don't know when. I've just taken on a couple of new cases, and Billy isn't well; he never recovered from those injuries he sustained during our last murder case. I've told him to take at least a month, and if I am honest, I don't think he should return." Maisie could hear herself, the speed of her words, as if the velocity of her explanation would mollify James. "He needs another job, something more regular. And then there's Sandra, and—"

"Maisie—" James leaned forward, forcing her to look at him. "Maisie, shhhh. Here's how it is. As I said, I'm planning to leave in about six weeks. You can give me your answer at the last minute if you like. Or you can join me later. Your choice, but you know my intentions."

"All right. Yes . . . I see."

"And I might be able to help with Billy. Just give me a little time to talk to Jonathan and some of my staff."

Maisie smiled. "Oh James, thank you."

He pushed back his chair and came to kneel at her side, taking her in his arms. "I love you, Maisie."

She nodded, her eyes downcast. "And I love you, James. I love you."

Sandra stood up as soon as Maisie opened the door to the office and stepped into the room.

"That Caldwell has been on the telephone, he wants to speak to you."

Maisie went to her desk, set her briefcase down beside her chair, and pulled off her gloves. "If we're not careful, we'll be calling him 'that Caldwell' to his face! Did he say what he wanted?"

"Only to give him a call—a 'bell,' he said—as soon as you showed your face this morning. And those were his words, not mine." Sandra lifted the receiver, adding, as she began to dial, "Oh, I've found out that Miss Pramal's former employers, the Allisons, are presently in Italy, and are not expected back until Sunday." She looked up at Maisie as the call was answered, changing her tone to speak to the Scotland Yard operator. "Miss Maisie Dobbs to speak to Detective Inspector Caldwell, please." She smiled at Maisie and held her hand over the mouthpiece. "This'll get him going, me doing the calling for you. Shows him you're important."

Maisie shook her head. "Sandra, I do think you're setting up a vendetta here."

Sandra smiled at Maisie as she began to speak once more. "Ah, good morning again, Detective Inspector Caldwell. I have Miss Maisie Dobbs on the line for you, per your request." The sweetness of her greeting was laced with just the hint of a sarcastic edge. She handed the receiver to Maisie.

"What's the matter, can't get your finger in the dial of a morning?" said Caldwell.

"Good morning to you, too, Inspector. I have just come from an early meeting, so Mrs. Tapley placed the call for the sake of speed—she said you wanted to speak to me with some urgency."

"Murder is an urgent matter, in my book."

Maisie felt her smile deflate. "What's happened, Inspector?"

"I understand you recently spoke to a Miss Maya Patel."

"Yes, when I visited the ayah's hostel—we were to meet again today."

"Well, you won't be meeting her at all, I'm afraid— her body was found by some dockers early this morning, round the back of a warehouse, not far from the canal. Doesn't look like she was dumped, we reckon she walked there."

"What was the cause of death?"

"A bullet, Miss Dobbs. Same as the other young lady—straight between the eyes."

"Oh, dear God."

"At least it was quick, Miss Dobbs. At least it was quick, not like some of them I see. Anyway, can you come to the Yard?"

"I'm expecting Mr. Pramal here at any moment."

"Right then, just the man I'm looking for—I'll come to you." There was silence on the line for a second or two.

"Caldwell?"

"How long do you want with him before I get there?"

"About forty-five minutes or so. And thank you, Inspector. I appreciate your forethought."

"Might as well show a bit of willing. After all, Miss Dobbs, we're in this one together. Getting to be a habit."

Maisie walked to the window. She'd been due to meet Maya Patel at half past four, at St. Pancras station. How much of a coincidence was there to connect Patel's death with her knowledge of Usha and the fact that she had welcomed the opportunity to meet with Maisie and perhaps confide in her? She wondered what connections might exist between the dead women, beyond secrets shared in their accommodations. She suspected that, if they had been in their own country, they might not have encountered each other, but here they had been brought together by the common experience of exile.

The bell rang, announcing the arrival of a visitor. "That'll be *Mr.* Pramal," said Sandra.

Maisie escorted Usha Pramal's brother to the office and offered him a seat in front of her desk. She brought her chair to the side, so that the desk did not form a barrier between them. Pramal declined tea, so Sandra remained at her desk.

"Mr. Pramal, I have some news to report, and as you can imagine, more questions. First of all, the disturbing development, and I am very sorry to have to break this to you under such circumstances. Another resident of the ayah's hostel, a friend of your sister, has been murdered, and at this point it would seem that she was killed by a single bullet to the head. Detective Inspector Caldwell will be here at about ten—as you would imagine, he wishes to interview you; however, he has been most gracious, and not entirely following protocol, by allowing our meeting here to go ahead."

"I suppose I am among the suspects." Pramal's anger was barely disguised, the words delivered without meeting Maisie's eyes.

"I believe that if you were a prime suspect, you would not be here in my office, but at Scotland Yard. Having said that, be prepared for Caldwell to be somewhat confrontational—it's his way, and he has a murder to investigate."

"It's a pity he didn't get a bit more confrontational when he was investigating my sister's death, wouldn't you say, Miss Dobbs?"

"Your frustration is warranted, Mr. Pramal. But let us not waste time going over old ground. Maya Patel has been killed, and she was due to meet me later today. I am assuming she had some crucial information to impart, and in a way she already has." Maisie paused, allowing her words to filter through Pramal's temper. "I visited Usha's accommodations yesterday, and discovered something very interesting, which I must tell you about. Hidden in her mattress—not a terribly safe place, but no one else had looked, clearly—I discovered a considerable sum in savings. I have taken the liberty of depositing the monies at my bank, in a box under lock and key."

"Usha had money?"

"Easily enough to return home, I would say, but I spoke to Miss Patel long enough to establish that Usha was remaining here to earn a sum sufficient to achieve her ambition of founding a school. It seems they had confided in each other."

"But this Miss Patel, she was just an ayah—she doesn't sound like someone my sister would confide in."

"From our conversation yesterday, it would seem that Usha thought nothing of flying in the face of convention, and if she considered Maya and her fellow ayahs less than herself, she would not have remained, or would have returned sooner. I believe she and Maya Patel might have found comfort in their friendship, especially so far from home."

"Yes, of course. You are right, Miss Dobbs. My comment would not do Usha justice."

"Let's move on—Caldwell will be here shortly. Mr. Pramal, I am interested in the two men who had a romantic interest in Usha—your fellow officer, the gentleman with whom you lodged upon first arriving here, and also the young man whom you said had inappropriately courted your sister in India." She looked at her notes. "First of all, have you had any recollection at all, of the man who had declared his love for Usha?"

"As I said yesterday, Miss Dobbs—I don't know that I ever knew." He frowned, as if trying to agitate his memory. "I only know that he was most pressing in paying her attention. And my aunt said it was clear the whole event had distressed Usha—she clearly reciprocated his affection, which was most worrying, but at the same time felt embarrassed by him, and by his lack of respect. You see, it is not usual for a man to come to the house without an invitation, and any approach of this kind would of course be discussed with his family, who would accompany him if serious intent to propose marriage was on the cards. Courting might be the British way, but it is not ours. And I must explain, although Usha might have done things her own way, she would not have wanted to bring that sort of gossip to the door, and would have been very circumspect if she were seeing this man outside the house. She would have kept it secret. It was one thing for people to think she was a free spirit and tut-tut here and there, but she would not have wanted a serious slight against the family in connection with her moral code. A line was crossed."

"Yes, I understand, Mr. Pramal. But what about Mr. Singh?"

"Oh, Singh was like so many—head over heels at first glance, but Usha showed no interest whatsoever, and to be frank, teased us both, because of course I would have welcomed him as a brother. He's very happily married now, though, and living here in London."

Maisie nodded. "Yes, I plan to visit Mr. Singh—please do not be alarmed, it's just that he might have some insight that has evaded you, being her brother. Do you know if she kept in touch with him, when she came to London? Or why she did not call upon him when she found herself thrown out by her employers?"

Pramal smiled. "Pride. Usha would have been too proud to have done that, though Singh and his wife have told me that, once she was settled, she came to see them. But she never told them about her change of circumstances."

"Yes, I can imagine her being like that." She looked at her notes again. "And just to keep you apprised of our progress, Mrs. Tapley reports that Usha's former employers are on holiday in Italy, but will be home soon. I will visit as soon as they return to London. In the meantime, I have another question regarding Usha. My visit to the ayah's home revealed that your sister was left with precious little money from her daily work—which was as a cleaner in two mansions. Miss Patel informed me that Mr. Paige took most of the wages and saved them on behalf of the girls, so that they could one day return home. If that is so, then there should have been money coming to you from that quarter—have you received word regarding the funds?"

Pramal pressed his lips together. Clearly the thought that his sister was engaged in menial work was painful to him.

"I have received nothing."

"I thought not. I'll ask about it. However, there is the matter of this money saved in the mattress. That being the case, I wonder, how do you think she might have been able to earn and put by such a tidy sum?"

"Are you suggesting—?"

"I am not suggesting anything, I am asking a very good question. Your sister had saved a considerable amount, and though it was over a period of some years, it still mounted up. Maya Patel was going to tell me more and now she's dead. So, if you could offer me anything you know about Usha that might help me establish where the money came from—it might well be the key to finding her killer."

Pramal folded his arms, and as he moved his hands, Maisie noticed an obvious yellow stain on his fingers—he was a man who smoked cigarettes and, surprisingly, given the tension caused by her questions, had not asked if he might light one.

"She was a teacher, so she might have taken on private tutoring."

"Her free hours were limited, but it's a possibility," allowed Maisie.

"And she . . . no, nothing. There's nothing else."

"What were you going to say, Mr. Pramal? Was there something else?"

Pramal fidgeted in his chair. Maisie felt Sandra looking at her, and looked back. She indicated the clock to Maisie—Caldwell would ring the bell soon. The moment might be lost.

"Mr. Pramal. What else might Usha have done to earn money?"

He shook his head. "I can't imagine that she would have, but—"

The bell above the door sounded. Sandra pushed back her chair.

"Let him wait, Sandra." Maisie held up a finger. The bell rang again. "Mr. Pramal?"

Pramal took a deep breath. "She touched people."

"She touched people? I know you said she was the sort of person who might set her hand upon the arm of another when speaking with them—but you don't mean that, do you?"

"It was not something she ever would have done outside our family, and never with men—never, ever, would she have touched a man. But if one of the women was in pain, if she had an ache—in the feet or the shoulder, anywhere—my sister would gently rest her hand on the place, and the pain would be soothed. She could leach away pain and suffering."

"Ah, I see. Yes, I see," said Maisie.

The bell rang once more. Sandra stood up. "Miss?"

Pramal spoke. "Do the police know about my sister's savings?"

"No, I have not told them."

"They were incompetent in their investigation. Please do not give them that piece of information."

Maisie looked at Pramal and nodded, then glanced at the clock. "I shouldn't let him wait on the doorstep any longer—it might be difficult for you if he's built up a bit of a temper."

"Then my temper will be a match for his, Miss Dobbs. I have nothing to fear from Detective Inspector Caldwell of your esteemed Scotland Yard."

Maisie had no questions for Pramal throughout the interview, and Caldwell's inquiries were predictable, asking if Pramal knew Maya Patel, where he was at the estimated time of her death—which had been established as early the previous evening—and if he knew of a friendship between his sister and Maya Patel. Caldwell asked Pramal if Usha had ever mentioned the other young woman in letters. There appeared no doubt that Pramal had never met Maya Patel, and had no knowledge of her until Maisie informed him of her death. But like so many others, Maya Patel had been touched by Usha Pramal, and had died for it.

Chapter Seven

Addington Square was bathed in sunlight when Maisie arrived at the Paige residence that afternoon. She'd taken the opportunity to walk around the area first. There was common ground behind Goodyear Place, a somewhat less salubrious street adjacent to Addington Square, where children played with a large retriever dog, running to and fro, catching a ball, then throwing it to each other as the dog gamboled between them, as if hoping to snag the prize. Providing an additional distraction for the youngsters, the canal was also close by. As a working waterway, it wasn't a comforting place to meander, though Maisie could see how young boys might be drawn to the path, perhaps to call to the men on the timber barges, or to skim stones across the dark water.

Mr. Paige answered the door when Maisie called, and was soon joined by his wife in the parlor, which seemed to lose none of its dour character on a bright day. Maisie thought Paige rather matched the sense of emptiness in the room, with his drawn pallor and hollowed cheeks suggesting a sour nature rather than physical deprivation.

"Thank you so much for seeing me, Mr. Paige," said Maisie. "I am sure you have had a lot to deal with, given that the police will have already been here to talk to you."

"There was a constable on the street, in front of the house, until an hour ago, but mainly they came and went this morning. It's all very distressing, I must say." Paige looked at his wife, who was sitting on a straight-back chair next to his.

Mrs. Paige sniffed into her handkerchief. "They were both good girls, Miss Pramal and Miss Patel. They did their work without complaint, they studied the Bible, and they never gave a moment's trouble."

Maisie nodded. "Are there other women here at the moment?"

"There were three more in residence—we've room for more, but as I said, numbers have dropped off. The police thought they would be better off at another house—a safer place, they said. Apparently they've found them lodgings somewhere across the water, not far from a police station, but I don't know which one. I dread to think what the neighbors might say—and all we ever wanted to do was some good for those less fortunate. There might have been a bit of gossip about what we did here, but once people knew our ladies were courteous and kept themselves tidy, there wasn't much talk at all."

Maisie suspected that Mrs. Paige might be the daughter of a vicar, or at least brought up in a home with parents who observed the tenets of the church with an intensity that bordered on the oppressive; she had a sense that the woman's religious belief was something deeply ingrained. As she spoke, she clutched the plain silver cross worn around her neck, and her diction revealed a person not originally from southeast London. Her husband, though, seemed as if he were from a family of tradespeople, perhaps having chosen missionary work following a reigniting of faith. If she allowed her mind to create a story for him, she would say he had been affected by a charismatic man of the cloth who had visited the area when he was at an impressionable age, possibly in his early twenties, perhaps at a time when he was enduring a period of self-doubt. While he spoke well, there was the occasional pronunciation that suggested a childhood spent in the local borough. The couple had likely met later than one might expect of a youthful romance, and then forged a bond based upon wishing to do the work of the God they worshipped, with the ayah's hostel being the culmination of that work.

Mr. Paige was a lean man, with clothes that made him seem taller and thinner than he was. Gray trousers were topped with a gray shirt, navy blue tie, and maroon sleeveless knitted pullover; errors in the cable suggested a homemade garment, and that Mrs. Paige was an easily distracted knitter. Paige's hair was cut very short at the back and sides, as if he were newly conscripted into the army, though the weathering at the nape of his neck indicated a man who was used to being in his garden.

"Had anyone ever shown a grudge towards the women?" asked Maisie. "I know the police will have asked that question, but I must press it upon you again."

Husband and wife shook their heads at the same time. Paige answered. "We do good work here, Miss Dobbs, and our women don't have much time to go out meeting people, though they are over the age of consent, so they can go for a walk or to the library if they want, when their work is done. You see we have rules—about lights out and being here for Bible study—so they don't have too much in the way of loose time on their hands. And in general they don't have a lot of spending money. Our intention is to get them back to India when their savings allow it—and of course, we want them to go back with something, so that they're not destitute when they disembark from the ship."

"I understand that you thought Miss Pramal often had more funds than her allowance might suggest, Mr. Paige. Can you account for that?"

Paige shrugged. "She seemed to have more money at times, but when I asked her about it, she just said she'd always been like a mouse with crumbs, saving them up in her hole."

Mrs. Paige interjected. "Miss Pramal sometimes had a bit of lip on her. She could say something without being obviously cheeky, but when you thought about it, you knew she meant it. As if we only gave them the crumbs off the table, and that she slept in a hole. She could be like that, though most of the time she kept herself to herself. Went to the library a lot. And she and Miss Patel would go out together, on a nice evening, just for a walk. Miss Pramal liked to walk. She liked to wander along busy streets, especially on a hot day when most of us would want to be inside in the cool—she said it reminded her of home."

Maisie nodded. She knew that feeling. She remembered during the war, in France, there were days, in spring especially, when she'd wake up and believe she was at home in Kent. There was perhaps a scent on the air, the sound of birds calling—a song short-lived before the cannonade began again. And she would be reminded of walks alongside the streams that ran through the Chelstone Manor estate, when the pungent smell of wild garlic would waft up with every swish of her skirts. And then she would remember, again, that she was not home at all, and the ache of longing would rise within her.

She pressed on with her next question. "When I came before, I think you told me, Mrs. Paige, that you were the first recipients of the women's earnings, and you gave an allowance—pocket money for essentials— each week. Would you explain that to me again? You said that Mr. Paige was in charge of those accounts."

Paige cleared his throat. "We're not wealthy people, Miss Dobbs. Our house was left to my wife by a distant relative, which was indeed a blessing from the Lord at a time when we were newly arrived in Britain follow- ing two years of missionary work in Abyssinia. I also received a small bequest when my father's business was sold—he had several hardware shops; the largest was on Rye Lane. Neither my brother nor I wanted to take it on—we weren't the best of friends—so it was sold. It allowed my brother to purchase a smallholding in

Kent, and I was able to continue with our work here. As well as offering a home for these poor women abandoned by their wealthy employers, we do God's work by taking food down to the docks, where men stand looking for a job."

"That is kindness indeed, to share your good fortune with others. But what about the ayah's savings?" asked Maisie.

"We obviously took money to reimburse us for offering lodgings—these women would not have found landlords willing to rent to them—and for their general keep. And they tithed to help with our work. Each woman's wages was divided in three—one third for the lodging, one third tithing, and one third for them—out of which they would be given ninepence each per week."

"It would have taken many, many years to save for passage home to India."

"And in the meantime, they have a roof over their heads, food on the table, and sustenance from the Holy Spirit."

Maisie nodded. "I'd like to return to the fact that Miss Pramal gave you the impression that she had more funds than she might, considering the allowance she was given from her wages. If she was earning money elsewhere, what do you think she might have done to accumulate the funds?"

Mrs. Paige sat up taller in her chair, her hands in her lap. Paige folded his arms. He shook his head. "I really don't know, Miss Dobbs. She helped with Sunday school at church—she was good with children, as you might imagine—though there was no financial recompense for that, obviously. And our Reverend Griffith thought very highly of her. Always spoke well of her work."

"Did she go to church every Sunday?"

They both nodded. "All the women do," said Mrs. Paige.

"You've not asked us much about Miss Maya Patel, Miss Dobbs," said Paige.

"Not at the moment, no. I believe that her life was taken because she knew something about Miss Pramal that someone else did not want her to know. Or it could be even simpler."

"What do you mean?" asked Paige.

"It could be as obvious as the color of her skin."

Maisie asked to see the room allocated to Maya Patel and was taken upstairs by Mrs. Paige. Maya had made fresh curtains from sari silk lined with plain cotton muslin. The medley of bright colors brought a freshness to the room, which was otherwise plain. There was a wardrobe in the corner, a washstand alongside one wall, and a small chest of drawers next to the bed. The bed itself was narrow, and as Maisie pressed down upon it, she could feel that it was old and poorly upholstered, and definitely not conducive to a good night's sleep.

Mrs. Paige lingered by the door as Maisie walked around the room. There was a sadness within the four walls, and she thought the room might have been both a cell and a retreat. It was a place Maya could come to that she had done her best to make her own, yet at the same time, an incarceration of sorts in a country that had, in truth, abandoned her. The Paiges had clearly helped the women, who might otherwise have had nowhere to go at all, and Maisie conceded that there were a lot of folk who would love to have a room in a house in Addington Square—but still she felt the discomfort, not least because there was a dark side to the Paiges' generosity: in control of money, and what grown women were allowed and not allowed to do. Was such a regulated life to the benefit of women alone in a country so different from their own? Perhaps. She could not argue with the fact that the vulnerable were always easy prey, whether women, children, or, indeed, men. But how long would it have taken to afford a passage back to the land of their birth? At the rate of recompense allowed by the Paiges, it would take a very long time.

"Thank you, Mrs. Paige." Maisie turned away from the room and smiled at the woman, who she thought was nervous. She allowed for the fact that the woman had suffered a difficult day—a second one of her charges found murdered, the invasion of her house by police, and now additional questioning.

"Did the police take much from the room?"

The woman shook her head. "I don't know that they took anything. She didn't have much, poor girl."

"Letters?"

Again, a shaking of the head from Mrs. Paige. "I don't remember her getting any, even after all these years. I think that's why she depended upon Miss Pramal so much—Miss Pramal was like family to her. I think she looked up to her, to tell you the truth, and I heard Miss Pramal saying that when she went back, well, she'd take Miss Patel with her."

"Is that so? Do you think she would have?"

"Oh yes. She wasn't one who struck you as the sort to make promises she had no intention of keeping, Miss Dobbs."

Maisie nodded. It seemed there was little more to be revealed by a couple who were reaching the end of their tether.

"I'd better be going now," said Maisie.

The Paiges stood at the threshold to see Maisie on her way. She thanked them for their time and for accommodating her questions, especially when there was so much to trouble them. As she put on her gloves, she asked a final question.

"I'd like to speak to the Reverend Griffith. Where might I find him?"

Paige pointed across the square. "If you go across there onto the next street, then a couple of houses on the right, you'll see a blue door with his name on a brass plaque on the wall alongside; that's where he lives. He might be at the church, or even out visiting parishioners."

"I'll take my chances, then."

"He'll speak very highly of Miss Pramal, you know," said Mrs. Paige.

"Did she do a lot for your church, beyond teaching Sunday school?"

"He sometimes asked for her to go with him when he went to see a woman patient who was poorly. He said she brightened up a room, what with her silk saris. He said it made people feel better."

"And there was no discrimination?" asked Maisie. "After all, you said that people sometimes talked about your offering a place of refuge for the women here."

"Well, when she was with the vicar it was different. No one would have said anything to him. He had a regard for her, you see."

Maisie nodded. "Thank you. You've been most kind." She turned to leave, but as the Paiges were about to step into the house, she looked back as if forgetting something. "Oh, one last thing, Mr. Paige. Could you tell me how much longer Miss Pramal would have had to wait until she had enough saved for her passage to Bombay?"

Paige looked at Maisie for more than a few seconds before answering. "She could have sailed three months before she died, Miss Dobbs, but I think she wanted to wait for Miss Patel. She didn't seem in a hurry to leave, even if she did feel like a mouse with a few crumbs."

Maisie left Addington Square and walked in the direction of the canal. Though it was far from being the loveliest walk in London, she could imagine Usha Pramal and her friend Maya Patel meandering close to the waterway, and then on the streets in the neighborhood where they lived. Had Usha ventured farther afield, to the bustling markets and shopping streets on this side of the river? Was it a certain wanderlust—a desire to be in places where people swarmed, where the teeming activity reminded her of home—that had taken her into a thoroughfare where she might not have been welcome? More to the point, what did Maya Patel want to tell Maisie? She had jumped at the chance of a meeting across the water—in a busy station, among strangers, many from overseas, and among whom she might not be recognized—but she had been silenced before her secrets could be shared. *This time yesterday, she was alive*, thought Maisie. She imagined her smiling, walking along, her silken sari flapping in the breeze on the warm September day, not knowing the very fragility of her future. But someone was watching her. Someone with a gun in his hand. *His* hand? Yes, it would have to have been a man, wouldn't it? After all there was that kickback, wasn't there? A man had the strength to handle a gun like that, especially if he'd learned to use it during the war. Maisie walked back towards the square. She felt as if she were looking at Usha Pramal through a kaleidoscope. Whenever she thought of her, a myriad of colors seemed to flash into her mind's eye, but they changed with every turn, creating a new and complex pattern. And at the center, she could see the woman's eyes looking back at her, waiting for her to find her way to the truth. Now she must find and talk to the man of the cloth who thought so highly of Usha Pramal.

The Reverend Colin Griffith was at home when Maisie arrived at the house. It was not the vicarage—there was a vicarage in Goodyear Place, but it accommodated the Church of England minister. Instead,

Griffith lived in another home similar in architectural style to the one owned by the Paiges in Addington Square. And Griffith's church was not the local "C of E," or the Congregational Emmanuel Church with its tall spire pointing towards heaven; his flock met in a community hall not far from the square. It appeared Griffith may have founded his own church. Maisie wondered how local parishioners—those for whom churchgoing was a regular event—might choose between places of worship, as there were several in the immediate area. Her question was answered when Griffith came to the door. A bright smile, deep blue eyes, and silver-gray hair on a man who seemed only a little older than Maisie combined to render his appearance almost angelic and engaging at the same time. He wore no priestly garments—on this day not even a white clerical collar—and might have been taken for a teacher in a boys' boarding school.

"Yes? How may I help you?" His smile became broader, and Maisie at once revised her opinion of the content of his sermons. In speaking with the Paiges, she had imagined a grim-faced paternal figure, promising all manner of ills if one did not follow scripture to the letter. Griffith appeared friendlier than she had expected, and she suspected that what he had to say to his parishioners might leave them feeling quite uplifted.

"My name is Maisie Dobbs." She handed him a calling card. "I'd like to speak to you about Miss Usha Pramal and Miss Maya Patel, and other women the Paiges have brought to church."

Griffith studied the card. Maisie could see his smile lose some of its vitality, like a ripe fruit weakening on the vine.

"The police have already been here, you know." He placed a hand on the doorjamb, as if to protect his home.

"Yes, Reverend Griffith, I know. I am working alongside Scotland Yard, but also more specifically on behalf of Mr. Pramal, Miss Pramal's brother. He has come a long way and is very anxious to know why his sister might have incurred such hatred that someone would take her life. I thought you might shed more light on her character and on those who knew her."

He removed his hand. "Yes, of course. Come in, won't you?"

Griffith stood back to allow Maisie to enter. He closed the door and walked past her to lead the way along a passage, then out to a room overlooking a walled garden behind the house. Ivy-clad stonework gave a sense of being held in place. A mature rhododendron had grown to quite a height in one corner, and the garden was a pleasing mix of hardy perennials and other blooms that would have been considered weeds if they were gracing a hedgerow, but which seemed equally at home among the cultivated plants. Griffith held his hand out towards a low slipper chair uphol-stered in faded purple velvet. He pulled a wheelback chair away from a desk and sat in front of Maisie.

"I only rent one floor—I have this, which is a sort of sitting room cum study, plus my bedroom, and a kitchen. Having the garden flat helps; it gives me an extra room on a fine day."

Maisie looked around at books piled on the floor, at a black typewriter on the desk, and the half-finished document lodged next to the platen. A wastepaper basket was filled with crumpled sheets of paper.

"Not having much luck with Sunday's sermon, I'm afraid. It usually comes right about half an hour before I'm due to leave for church, otherwise I'm sort of like a mad aviator, flying directly into the sunshine."

Maisie smiled. "Yes, I can see that. Have you taken to the air, Reverend Griffith?"

He gave a half-laugh. "Well, apart from being three inches from the ground before every service, yes, I have. When I was in Africa I went up in an old bone-shaker a few times."

"Is that where you met Mr. and Mrs. Paige, in Africa?"

"No, but we have mutual friends, others who have been involved in missionary work among the tribal peoples. I was there for a year, and that common experience brought them to my ministry here."

"So you are used to bringing a Christian faith to those from other parts of the Empire."

"Just Africa, Miss Dobbs."

"Tell me what you thought of Miss Pramal."

Griffith sighed and rubbed his chin. "Miss Pramal was a very vivacious young woman. Always had a greeting for everyone, even if—and I hate to admit this of my parishioners—even if they were not so energetic in their response to her approach." He paused. "People in London, as you know, are used to seeing faces of another color, of hearing another language spoken, and are tolerant of those differences—to a point, until that other color, creed, or language goes where it hasn't set foot before, and then there's a snigger here, an unkind word, a greeting left hanging in the air without response. For Miss Pramal, such—what could I call it? Such *discrimination*—" He left the word hanging in the air for a second or two, as if it might be superseded by a better word. "Such discrimination," he went on, "did not affect her at all; it was water off a duck's back. Which is why she was so good with Sunday school— children say all sorts of things that aren't terribly nice, and Miss Pramal would never react, never reprimand. She would simply smile, perhaps make a child laugh, and then she would remind them of scripture, that there is no greater commandment than you should love your neighbor as yourself."

"Did she give any impression of having friends, associations outside her work and her immediate neighbors in the ayah's hostel?"

He shook his head. "Miss Dobbs, I saw Miss Pramal when she came to church on Sunday morning for the first service of the day, after which she remained so that she could take the children into the back room for Sunday school while their parents were here for the later service. Then she went home. Mr. and Mrs. Paige ensured the women were brought together for prayers in the home, and for Bible study. They were generally present in church for Sunday evensong. I doubt she had the time to do much else in the way of establishing social contacts."

Maisie nodded and looked out at the garden, which, although it was a fine day, seemed a little soporific, as if it were tired of summer and was ready to slip into an autumnal nap before enduring the frostbitten days of winter.

"Have you any idea why Miss Pramal and Miss Patel were murdered?"

Griffith seemed to flinch at the word. *Murder* was not part of his usual vocabulary. It came to Maisie's lips far too often.

He shrugged and looked down at his hands, which to Maisie appeared almost unnaturally unblemished, as if opening books had been the extent of his life's work.

"I cannot imagine why anyone would want to kill another person, Miss Dobbs. I never went to war. I have never lost my temper. I have only love for my fellow man, so I have no other answer for you." He rubbed his hands together. "But there are people who will trample flowers into the ground, who will beat dogs, and who will exert a terrible cruelty upon children. None of this do I understand, but I know it exists. And in my ministry I do what I can to banish evil from the little world I inhabit here in London, in the hope that the ripples of peace, of the word of the Lord, will gently go out further and further until they reach the far edges of humanity here on earth. No, I cannot imagine how anyone could take the life of a bright shining star such as Usha Pramal."

Maisie stood up and looked down at the vicar, who came to his feet. He turned away to put the chair back in front of the desk, though not before Maisie was able to see his pained expression.

At the front door, Maisie extended her hand. "Thank you, Reverend Griffith. I am grateful for your time—you were obviously busy with that sermon."

Griffith's grip was firm when he took her hand. "I think you've given me some food for thought, Miss Dobbs. I think it's time to pull out a sermon about us all sitting at the feet of the Lord, who pays no mind to color, creed, or to youth or age."

"May I return if I have some more questions?"

"Of course. Anything I can do to help."

Griffith smiled once more as a beam of sunlight haloed his silver-gray hair.

Maisie waved as she went on her way, and pressed her palms together to re-create the sensation she experienced when she shook the Reverend Griffith's hand. Although it was soft, almost like a woman's, there had been a catch against her hand when they touched. A shaft of rough skin ran along the V formed by the outer edge of his right forefinger and the inner flesh of his thumb. This part of his hand had worked hard—perhaps against a spade in the garden, or a broom in the house. She couldn't imagine that lifting a chalice would cause such a callus. But she wondered whether the repeated handling of a weapon might. It was not an idle thought, but a secondary consideration when she realized that the Reverend Griffith had misled her. He had most certainly been to India—a photograph on the wall above his desk attested to the fact that he had even been transported by an elephant, seated as he was on the giant beast, both he and the mahout with broad smiles for whoever was behind the camera.

Chapter Eight

M aisie returned to the office to find a message from Sandra in her clear, slanted handwriting. The ink had been pressed dry with blotting paper, and Maisie considered how different the message was from those left by Billy, whose almost childishly formed letters bore splatters of ink unless he wrote with a pencil. His messages, however, always contained details of key importance to the case. Sandra's words were equally informative.

I have addresses for the boys involved in the discovery of Miss Pramal's body and will be at Albany Road school when they come out this afternoon. Two of the boys go to the school, so I will ask one of the younger children to point them out to me, as the infants' classes generally end before the juniors. I've also found out the name of that lecturer who addressed the women's meeting. Her name is Dr. Chaudhary Jones. I've left an index card with her address in south Kensington. She is married to an Englishman, who is also a professor. I've been told he's at the Imperial College of Science and Technology. I remember when she started her speech, she made us all laugh when she said she didn't want to give up her maiden name when she married because with her skin she could never see herself as just Jones. She said that her husband was a wonderful man, who often introduced her as "The Mrs. Quite Lovely Just Jones." She said she would never have married him unless he'd been that sort of man, and that no woman should ever marry unless they had a husband who would put them on a pedestal.

Lucky *Mrs. Just Jones*, thought Maisie. She sat back in the chair and stared out of the window across the room. She had to admit to herself that James was such a man. Yes, he had wanted her to forgo her work, but not because she earned money or had her own business, but because he feared the outcome of some of her cases, which often took her into dangerous territory. Her own father preferred not to think about it, knowing his headstrong daughter was adamant about keeping her job, even though he hated to consider what might happen if she crossed paths with the wrong person at the wrong time. "We can all do that, Dad," she'd argued. "We can all cross paths with the wrong person. Wasn't there an old man hit over the head for the tuppence in his pocket, in Tunbridge Wells, of all places? He was walking down the street in the middle of the day, not even at night." Frankie Dobbs had conceded to her argument and rarely mentioned his worries.

James Compton was a Mr. Jones. James was a dependable man. A man who would put her on a pedestal and call her *Mrs. Quite Lovely Dobbs-Compton*, if that would please her. But she wouldn't be a Mrs., would she? Marriage to James would come with strings attached; strings that tied her to a long history, to a big house, to the kind of people she did not always care for—though his parents were an important and much-valued part of her history, and she had great affection for Lady Rowan in particular. Having the Compton name would tie her to a different kind of life. She sighed. But hadn't that happened already, to some extent? Had not the wealth inherited from Maurice set her apart from others? Or had it simply been a different sort of apart, for hadn't she created a moat around her separateness years ago? In fact, if she was to be honest, being with James had helped soften the edges around the protective circle of her own making. She had found that some of those people she thought too wealthy to be aware of those less fortunate were indeed philanthropic with their time and money—not all, granted, but more than she might have imagined. And there were people she'd been introduced to who had welcomed her into their group, not simply because she was with James, but because they had a generosity of heart and could see the same in her. Did her money make a difference? Yes, she allowed that it obviously made a difference, not least because she knew she would not have had access to such company if she had been simply an educated, very fortunate woman who had been born in Lambeth.

She set down the note, rubbing her eyes. Priscilla had always said that Maisie saw all the gray areas. Now she was seeing even more of those gray areas, along with some stark black and white. Her education and her work with Maurice Blanche had set her at the foot of the mountain. His money—her money now—had allowed her to ascend almost to the summit in terms of her place in society and the company she kept, though she felt as if she wandered back and forth a lot, if only to remember the strength in her roots.

Mrs. Quite Lovely Just Jones. She wanted to meet this woman, and not just to ask her about her life in London, or about the way she was perceived as a woman whose complexion, whose mode of dress, of speech—or the luster of her hair and the deep red bindi smudged upon her forehead—conspired to set her apart. She wanted to ask for her help in understanding a culture that was as complex as the patterns at the edge of a wedding sari. She wanted to know how this woman could hold on to the Chaudhary in her while embracing the Jones.

Maisie picked up another file left for her by Sandra. Oh dear. She had almost forgotten Billy's case of the missing boy, which she had committed to working on in his absence. She opened the file. And as her eyes took in the pages of notes, she realized the extent of the damage Billy had sustained when attacked and left for dead that spring. Words not formed, unfinished sentences, numbers of houses without full addresses. Hurried scribbles, an ill-executed sketch of the front of a building. A map with no address and nothing pointing to a significant location. But not the usual format of notes, with a date listing an address, a name, a list of questions answered, facts discovered, points to act upon, another clue, another step towards the successful closure of a case, towards an invoice submitted and payment received. There was nothing to continue, nothing to suggest that work of any substance had taken place. She would have to start from scratch.

Maisie leaned forward with her head in her hands. She would have to visit Jesmond Martin again so that she could create a new plan for the inquiry. They had met when he first came to the office to discuss his son, missing some weeks by the time he'd contacted Maisie. Should she invent a story to account for the lack of progress? Or should she simply tell the truth, that during a previous investigation, her assistant had been left for dead by thugs in the pay of a powerful man—and she placed blame for Billy's breakdown firmly at the feet of that particular man. Should she tell him she'd left the case in Billy's hands, trusting—hoping—that he could manage on his own.

"Oh Billy, how I have failed you," said Maisie aloud.

It was on the way home through traffic thick with motor cars, exhaust-belching omnibuses, clattering trams, and high-stepping carthorses that Maisie began to list what she knew about the life and death of Usha Pramal against elements of the case still to be discovered. Yes, she had to interview the friend at whose house Usha's brother had lodged upon his arrival in England. She was eager to discover the name of the young man who had courted Usha in India, in her younger days. Had he returned to England? And had she chosen to work away from home as a governess to avoid contact with a man she might have loved, but who was an unacceptable suitor? From the information Maisie had garnered thus far, Usha was not one to allow family disapproval to stop her doing what she wanted, and imagined her swatting away the warnings of a cluster of interfering aunts as if they were annoying midges flying around her head on a warm summer's eve. But she drew the line at being humiliated by the actions of a young man who did not appreciate the customs of her country or was too impulsive to believe they might apply to him.

"Do you think your Billy could come to the office to meet Bob Wilmott—he sorts out taking on staff and so on—for an interview next week?"

Maisie was standing by the window, looking out at the carefully tended shrubs, colorful late-blooming roses, and flower beds filled with chrysanthemums, asters, and her favorite daisies. She'd always loved the simple flowers—primroses, bluebells, and daffodils in spring, wild roses in summer, and all manner of daisies in autumn. Her thoughts were on the other side of the river, close to Addington Square; she was thinking about the Reverend Colin Griffith and his unruly yet colorful garden.

"Sorry, James—miles away. What did you say? About Billy?"

James set down his drink, stood up from the armchair, and came over to her. He put his arms around her waist and kissed her on the neck. "I do believe I've been talking to the wall for the last fifteen minutes. I asked about Billy Beale."

"Au contraire, James—I may have been a bit distracted, but I believe I heard the words 'Your Billy.' "

"Figure of speech. Now, what do you think? Could he come in?"

Maisie paused, considering the question. "Here's what I think—this shouldn't come through me. I think it's best if your company's usual protocol were followed."

"We're always snitching good people from otherwise worthy employers."

"That's not what I mean, James, and you know it." She turned to face him, but did not move from his arms. "And I would suggest it's best to wait a little while. Billy's been under the weather. Then it would be a good idea if Bob Wilmott wrote to Billy, or telephoned him at his home, and asked him if he would be interested in coming in to discuss an open position. Billy knows that I've talked to you in the past about a job, so it won't come as much of a surprise, yet, it would be better for his self-respect if he thought the actual landing of a job was up to him."

"Well, it would be anyway, Maisie. If Bob or anyone else he would be working with didn't think he was up to it, he wouldn't be taken on. All we've done is open up the path to get him to the station—we're not buying the ticket and putting him on the train."

Maisie nodded. "Bob should be the one to get in touch, not me. I'm more than willing to give a reference—it will be a very good one, and completely honest. I think this would be a fine opportunity for Billy. Heaven knows I will miss him terribly, but I have to think of him first, and what's best for his future and the family."

"Oh, I think that whether he comes to work for us or someone else, you'll always make sure his future is bright."

Maisie shook her head. "That's something I have come to learn the hard way, James. You can send out your army to stop an invasion on the horizon, but sometimes it comes from a completely different direction. That's what happened when their little Lizzie died. I tried to help them, tried to keep them from going under, but look what happened—so much befell that family, and most of it came from within: Doreen's illness, for example." She sighed. "I don't want to meddle. I just want them to be settled and content. Working for me is making Billy far from happy, if I am to admit it. He is a man of dutiful intentions and great loyalty. He will do well at the Compton Corporation, of that I am sure."

"And if you are sure, then I am sure your reference will take him in the right direction."

Maisie nodded, allowing James to hold her close.

"Let's make it an early night, shall we? I probably won't be home until late tomorrow—a meeting with your most unfavorite person."

"Otterburn?"

James stood back as, resting his arm across her shoulder, he led her towards the door. "I know you've told me that the less you know about all this, the better it is all around. But there are some people he wants me to meet in connection with our work in Canada. Scientists. An engineer, a materials man, and a physicist who's apparently top of his tree when it comes to aerodynamics and speed. He's a bit of a boffin. I just nod my head like an intemperate donkey when he chimes in, though he is a very good sort indeed. He tries to make it all seem very easy, as if I were one of his less able students."

Maisie stopped as they reached the door. "What's his name?"

"Oh, you don't really want to know that—and it's more than my life's worth to say."

She rolled her eyes, though she felt no sense of humor at his tongue-in-cheek reply. She knew only too well that little stood between Otterburn and the level of security surrounding his interest in the marrying of aviation and defense of the realm.

"I spoke to a couple of those boys, Miss." Sandra was waiting for Maisie when she came into the office the following morning.

Maisie removed her hat and took a seat at her desk. "Go on, Sandra, I'm all ears."

"A right pair of ragamuffins they were, too. Freddie Holmes and Sidney Rattle. Both of them nine years old. Freddie had a right shiner on his left eye as well, as if he'd been in a nasty playground scrap."

"Did they tell you anything?"

"A couple of penny dippers did the trick. Boys that age have a sweet tooth—they'd probably sell their grandmothers' souls for a bag of toffees. Anyway, there's this little gang of them—and not all the same age; there's a couple of older lads, they're both twelve or so; one of them's got a job at the market, so he gets home early, and the other one has a habit of sciving off school; eventually they all get together when the younger ones come out of school."

"And they go along the canal?"

"Oh, they get up to the things that boys will—you know, collecting conkers, playing a game of football in the street, teasing the girls while they're playing with a long skipping rope, all waiting their turn. But the canal draws them—they throw stones, call out to the men working the boats, sometimes cadge a lift up to the lock. And they poke around with sticks, looking for treasure—their kind of treasure."

"What did they say about finding Usha Pramal?"

"They said they saw a big silk bubble, so they tried to reach it with sticks and stones, and then eventually it moved closer. And then it turned, and at first they thought it was a log, but suddenly one of them shouted, 'It's a body. It's a dead body.' "

"Then what?"

"The two younger started screaming, and one of the older ones went for help, while the other sort of held the body steady with sticks. The boys admitted they were both as sick as dogs."

"I'm not surprised," said Maisie. "Those children will be living with that memory forever."

"Oh, you know boys—they'll be telling the story time and time again, adding a bit here, them being the big heroes of the day."

"Did they see anything else? Anyone in the area they'd not seen before, that sort of thing?"

"These two didn't. The older boy came back with a couple of policemen he'd come across—their usual beat turned out to be a bit unusual that day."

"It sounds like the boys managed to get a good look at the body—though it would have been in a poor state having been immersed in water. I wonder if they recognized the victim—did they say anything about knowing Miss Pramal?"

"I'm glad you asked that, because when I put that question to them, young Freddie said he knew it was Miss Pramal, because she'd helped his nan with her rheumatism."

"Helped his nan?"

"Yes, he said his nan has hands like claws, and pains in her back and legs, and that his mum had asked the Indian woman to come round to the house."

"Did he say what she did?"

"His mum turfed him out, so I'll probably need to talk to her—oh, I mean, only if you want me to, Miss."

Maisie was thoughtful. "Here's what I think is best. Why don't you continue on with interviewing the boys—you've done well, and you can obviously get them talking to you, which is no mean feat. Boys of that age can be a bit of a handful—I know from my godsons; they're very boisterous at times. I have several inquiries to make today, but perhaps we can go over to Camberwell together—I'd like to visit a parent or two, if I can."

Sandra beamed. "Oh, thank you, Miss. I've to put in a couple of hours with Mr. Partridge this afternoon, but I could go at about five, before my class at Morley College at half past seven."

"Perfect."

Parking the car outside the end of terrace mansion in Hampstead, Maisie sat for a few moments to compose her thoughts. She had come to this house many times over the years that had passed since Maurice had first brought her to meet Dr. Basil Khan. He was known only as Khan, and to Maurice he was a mentor, a man who had guided him when he faltered, though at the time Maisie could never imagine Maurice becoming unbalanced when he stepped onto life's uneven ground. She sat in her motor car and remembered those earlier days, when she was awed by Khan's silence, by his demeanor, and not least by the white robes he wore and the spartan yet graceful room in which they always met. She once wondered if heaven itself might look like that room—all white, with muslin curtains that billowed, candles that soothed, and many cushions placed on the floor for those who came to see a man so wise that visitors traveled from far and wide to be touched by his presence. When he was in conversation with callers, whoever they were, they were on the same level. Never mind if a man was wearing a bespoke suit from his Savile Row tailor, or the woman a day dress of the finest silk. They had come to seek the counsel of a simple man in white robes who asked them to join him on the floor, so that he might better see them. Yet Khan was blind.

Sitting in silence, Maisie stilled her mind and quieted the voices asking their questions. She wanted to know about Sergeant Major Pramal. In their meeting, when Usha Pramal's brother had mentioned Khan, Maisie realized that in her mind she had absolved Pramal of any wrongdoing in the case of his sister's death. Given that he was so far away, he could not have been directly responsible for her murder—but on the other hand, he was not yet cleared of complicity in the crime. Maisie wondered if she should temporarily disengage her trust in Khan, though she knew he thought highly of her and would not have sent a man to her who might have had a hand in the taking of another life. Unless, of course, in this one very rare instance, Khan had not seen the truth.

She remained in the MG, the passing traffic barely denting her quieted mind as she prepared for an audience with the man her beloved Maurice had turned to in times of doubt. Soon she took a deep breath and left the motor car. She unlatched the heavy iron gate and made her way across the courtyard to the front door. It opened at the very second she raised her hand to grasp the bellpull.

"Miss Dobbs. Welcome." A young man dressed in a long white tunic and white linen trousers bowed before her, his hands together as if in prayer. "Khan sent me. He said you would be here soon."

Maisie put her hands together and gave a short bow in return. "Thank you. Would he be able to see me now, or shall I wait?"

"Oh no, no waiting. He wishes to see you at once."

She slipped off her shoes, leaving them on a bench at the side of the door, and followed the young man across the hexagonal entrance hall and into Khan's inner sanctum.

Khan sat by the open window, as was his habit. The fine white curtains flicked back and forth, twitched by the breeze, which in turn seemed to move the heavy scent of incense around the room so that it never seemed cloying, but was carried gently on the air.

The young man plumped several cushions on the floor for Maisie to sit as Khan turned to face her, his hands outstretched.

Maisie took his hands in her own. "Khan, you knew I would come."

"Of course. You have questions for me, and rightly so, for I have sent you a problem, a maze to be negotiated, I am afraid."

She drew breath to respond, but he held up his right hand. "No, let us speak of you first. Do you still grieve?"

"Of course, Khan. I miss Maurice very much, though the pain is not so sharp—instead it catches me when I least expect it. When I see his handwriting on a card, or when I want to hear his voice directing me."

Khan nodded, and as he moved his head, a long white strand of hair fell forward. He did not reach to touch the hair, but ignored it, as if the distraction had not happened.

"Those are reminders, my child. Each time you see his penmanship or hear his voice in your head, it is as if he is here with you, and in your soul you will know his advice for you."

"I wish I could be as confident. Sometimes I feel that, with passing time, I am losing him, losing all that he taught me."

Khan laughed. Maisie thought it sounded like a chuckle, a sound that might come from an amused child, yet this man was of a great age. His mind, though, was as sharp as a freshly honed knife.

"You will never lose him, Maisie Dobbs, for he is as much part of your mind, of your work, as your skin is part of your body."

Maisie drew breath to speak again, but Khan posed a question.

"Now, what of you? Where are you on life's road?"

"That's a very good question." She paused. Khan made no movement to hurry her. "I want to go overseas, Khan. And I think I want to travel to India. And the strange thing is that it isn't inspired by this case—your referral of Mr. Pramal to me. I had decided long before he first came to me that I wanted to travel. You see . . ." She faltered, searching for words. "You see, that's the missing link. I have followed Maurice into this work, and I have been so very fortunate to be the recipient of his wisdom, of his deep knowledge. Yet he learned so much through a breadth of experience, not least in much time spent abroad, often living in simple circumstances. I have read his diaries and I have, in a way, seen those places in my mind's eye. But it does not replace the desire to see, to feel, to smell another country." She rubbed the place at the nape of her neck where she'd been wounded by shelling when she was still no more than a girl—she had lied about her age to work as a nurse close to the front lines of battle during the war. "And now this . . . this case. The Indian woman whose life was taken so violently, to be followed by the death of her friend, Maya Patel, in exactly the same manner."

"It should come as no surprise, Maisie. You invited that country into your life, so do not marvel that it has come to you."

"It is a very cold trail, Khan. You have recommended me, yet I do not know if I will be successful. I am only asking questions the police asked before, I am sure. If a loose thread remains, I will be hard-pushed to find it."

"Then do not press so hard upon the fabric." Khan put out his hand and grasped the curtain as it flapped. Holding the material with one hand, he reached forward until he felt Maisie's right hand. "Here." He pressed her hand firm upon the fabric, holding her fingers and running them back and forth across the muslin. "What do you feel?"

"Just the curtain."

"Do you feel the pattern?"

"There is no pattern."

"Oh, but there is. Now, feel the pattern." He took her fingers, holding them gently upon the white fabric. So light was her touch that she could barely feel it beneath her skin. But then, as she closed her eyes, she began to feel a movement, like tiniest ripples across a pond, and then something clearer. A slub in the weave, a thread proud against her fingertips. Khan smiled. "Ah, you feel it?"

"Yes."

"Do your work with a light step. Run your fingers across the weaving of knowledge you've gathered. Then you will be successful."

Maisie sighed. "Murder is never a light touch, Khan."

"No, it isn't. But truth buried for a long time can be trodden down by a heavy footfall. Step lightly." He stopped speaking and breathed deeply. "You would like to know about Pramal, Usha's brother?"

"Yes, I would," said Maisie.

"I knew the children's father when he was a boy—though at my age anyone much younger than I seems like a boy. He lost his wife when his daughter was quite young, and in her he saw his wife incarnated. Such was his love for Usha that he indulged her with freedoms she might not have otherwise encountered. He treated her as older than her years. I know this because he wrote to me about his children. He held his son in high esteem, and was full of praise for his service in the war. But though he had not a favorite among his children, Usha was favored—and if Maurice were here, he would ask you to see the distinction."

"I know—and I do," said Maisie.

"But Usha's brother has assumed the responsibility of the father, and he has come to find the person who took his sister's life, and to see that she is laid to rest, that her soul does not suffer. He was not confident in the work of the authorities here, so he wanted to know whom he should task with this challenge. Yours was the only name I could give him."

"I have a question, Khan, and I know it will sound clumsy and disrespectful. But I must ask it."

Khan smiled. "I will save you from using a heavy hand, Maisie Dobbs. I will tell you now that I who am never shocked would swear that Pramal would never have lifted a finger to bring an end to his sister's life. I would have misjudged him greatly if that were the case."

Maisie nodded. "Thank you, Khan. It is time I took my leave—you must be tired."

There was no answer, and she realized that the old man's eyes were closed. Coming to her feet, she stepped away from the cushions and towards the door. When she looked back, she noticed that Khan was still holding on to the curtain, his finger and thumb running across the raised threads with the lightest of touches.

Chapter Nine

It was some two years earlier that Maisie had first asked James about the possibility of a position for Billy with the Compton Corporation. Canada was on her mind then, as she wondered how it might be possible for the family to emigrate with some sort of work and accommodation already in place. Billy's dream had been to embark upon a new life in Canada—but was it still a dream for him? Since moving from the dark streets of Shoreditch to a new house in Eltham—helped by Maisie—Billy had seemed more settled, though the move had not been without problems in the wake of Billy's attack. Now she wanted to see him settled in a job with more regular hours and less risk. And she also wanted to know that he was not without work when she left, for as time went on she was gaining confidence in her decision to close the business and depart, bound for the kind of adventure that had been the making of Maurice Blanche.

For Billy to secure a new position, he must be well. She tapped her fingers against the steering wheel, and upon hearing the horn from another motor car, she pulled over into a side street and stopped the MG. She wanted to think.

When Billy had gone through a breakdown of sorts some four years earlier, she had sent him down to Chelstone, to live with her father and help with the horses on the estate. The fresh air, the slow pace of life, and the down-to-earth counsel of her father had worked magic with Billy. Doreen and the children had visited, and during his sojourn amid the rolling hills of the Kent countryside, Billy had found a measure of peace and had come to know himself again. Could that magic work a second time? Could Billy and the family return to good health following a break from their new house? The children might have a bit of trouble at the local school—their rich Cockney accents would mark them as outsiders—but she was sure they could weather it and make friends in short order. But would they welcome her interfering in their lives again? She could imagine Priscilla taking her to task about it. Then again, perhaps she should ask Priscilla—some of her ideas were on the unpredictable side of fantastic, but on the other hand, when it came to families, she had a strong practical no-nonsense streak that Maisie envied. Yes, she would talk to Priscilla.

Now it was time to return to the office, to collect Sandra and visit the homes of two of the boys who had found Usha Pramal's body. It was as she slipped the MG into gear that she realized she did not know the name of the person who discovered the murdered Maya Patel.

"Let me see," said Caldwell. Maisie could hear him turning a page. "Yes. Here we go. It's not as if I've forgotten the name per se, but it's one of them names that sounds as if it's backwards. Martin Robertson. No fixed address at the time, though he has one now and we've asked him not to move. He's a laborer living in digs, getting work where he can, mostly on the river. Seventeen years of age."

"Martin Robertson?"

"That's it."

In repeating the name, Maisie identified the sense of familiarity upon hearing Caldwell's words. *It's one of them names that sounds as if it's backwards.*

"Can you tell me the circumstances of the discovery, Inspector? Was he alone, and was it he who alerted the police?"

"Well, as it happens, he wasn't alone. He was with another bloke, a—wait a minute." Papers rustled again. "Sean Walters. Irish lad come over here to find work. Robertson saw her first and Walters ran for help."

"What does Martin sound like, when he speaks?"

"Funny question, Miss Dobbs. You know something I don't know?"

"Not sure—but can you tell me what he sounds like?"

"Sounds like your ordinary south-of-the-water lad to me. Why?"

"I'm not sure. It could be nothing. A coincidence, perhaps."

"I hope you'll tell me if it's important, Miss Dobbs. I know how you can keep things to yourself."

"I will. I just don't want to be wrong."

"All right then. Now, this won't get the eggs cooked, me talking to you all day."

Maisie held the receiver for a second longer, the continuous tone sounding after Caldwell had ended the call without so much as a swift "good-bye" to bracket the conversation.

Martin Robertson. She picked up the folder pertaining to the missing boy, the case she had given to Billy. Robert Martin. Son of Jesmond Martin, a stockbroker living in St. John's Wood, and his wife, Miriam. But this boy was not yet fourteen. She looked at the date he was missed from his boarding school, Dulwich College. One week before Usha Pramal's body was discovered floating on the canal. And Dulwich was only a bus ride from Addington Square, and the Grand Surrey Canal.

Maurice had taught Maisie to trust coincidence. He warned her that such things happen in an inquiry, as if the time and thought put into a case drew evidence in the same way that tides were affected by the proximity of the moon. Coincidence was the way of their world, and many a case depended upon the timely entrance of that serendipitous event. Maurice had taught her so much—and much that she doubted. He had told her that cases reflect each other, and that certain lessons come in threes. A case might mirror the one before, perhaps in the relationship between suspects or in the nature of their work. The victim of a new case might have something in common with another.

She flicked the only readable page in the Robert Martin file: notes taken when she and Billy had first seen the boy's father. Not the mother. Just the father of a missing son. She had found missing sons and daughters in the past, had seen parents relieved at the discovery—and on at least one occasion equal relief when she reported that the trail had run cold. Billy should have made regular telephone calls to their client to report on progress, though Maisie doubted he had done so. Yet she had not received an angry telephone call from the anxious father awaiting news. Was he so busy that he did not have time? Did he trust them to find his son without learning of their progress along the way? Could Jesmond Martin have been going through the motions of looking for a lost son, but with no true commitment on his part? Yes, she had known that before, a man making a promise to his wife, but lacking the conviction himself. She rubbed her neck and walked across to the filing cabinet and pulled out the rolled Pramal case map, which she unfurled across the table and pinned to keep it flat. But her thoughts were still on the man who had come to her because his son was missing.

He had made an appointment for late afternoon, explaining that he could not come earlier due to his work, which demanded his undivided attention from an early hour. She had not asked for an explanation, but Jesmond Martin seemed keen to establish his credentials as a busy, important man. He was like so many of his kind who worked in the City, as if they had been issued with a certain attitude along with a uniform. Martin wore a dark pin-striped suit, removed a top hat upon entering the room, and carried a briefcase that had without doubt been expensive at time of

166 • JACQUELINE WINSPEAR

purchase and was now worn around the handle and the corners and along the top flap. A brand-new case at his time of life would have pointed to only recent success, whereas the age and wearing of good leather proved to be a badge of honor among businessmen of his ilk. He had given details of his son's disappearance in a tone devoid of emotion, yet when Maisie looked at his eyes, it was as if she was staring into a well of sadness. She remembered wondering what walls of division might be at the root of family discord, and whether an argument—perhaps one of many—had inspired the son to leave his boarding school. Jesmond Martin showed no embarrassment or regret when he explained that his son, Robert, had been missing for several weeks; in fact he exuded an air of indifference as he spoke. He informed Maisie and Billy that he had at first expected the boy to return in good time and saw no reason to alert the authorities. And there had been only a brief mention of a poorly wife. Would she go as far as to say the father appeared cold? In fact, she found herself feeling rather sorry for him, for she thought he had an affection for his son that had been scarred in some way, perhaps by discord as the boy formed his own opinions of the world and no longer followed the lead of his strong—and, it would seem, opinionated—father.

If Robert Martin was indeed the boy who found Maya Patel—and until confirmed, the guess was tenuous, at best—how might it be related to Usha Pramal? She shook her head, and wrote in large letters, *Robert Martin—Martin Robertson?* and drew the names together in a large red circle. Martin Robertson was not a police suspect, so she had to be careful. She would have to make another call to Caldwell to gain an interview with the lad. Before turning the page she took out a photograph of Robert Martin, in his Dulwich College school uniform. "He looks barely able to wear long trousers," she said aloud. She remembered asking for a recent photograph, not an old image from earlier in the boy's childhood. "The features can change so much in these years, Mr. Martin," she'd said. And they could, to be sure. But one aspect of a person's looks rarely changed—and that was the eyes.

Maisie noticed that Sandra was clutching the passenger seat when she approached Tower Bridge. The evening was already drawing in, and motor car headlamps lit up the road as they crossed London's most famous bridge.

"Are you all right, Sandra?"

"Yes, thank you." She continued to grip the seat. "I just haven't been in many motor cars, and the last one was a lot bigger than this. I'm more used to buses, or the trains. But I prefer buses. Not going under the ground." Her eyes were focused straight ahead.

"Well, perhaps it would help if I gave you a few driving lessons—you'll enjoy it."

"Oh, I don't think so, Miss. No, I don't think I will."

Maisie had been pleased with Sandra's report on her "little chat" with the two boys she'd seen outside the school. She had encouraged them to tell her how scared they were when they saw Usha Pramal's body, and that they'd both had bad dreams ever since. She'd asked them if anyone else had seen the body, and she'd discovered that they hadn't seen any strangers in the area either before or after the flash of green-slimed peach silk had caught their attention. Both boys lived at home with their parents, as would be expected, and both had paper round jobs before school in the morning, and quite far from home, considering the area; they were mainly delivering to bigger houses just off the Old Kent Road. If the boys had work to do after school—looking after the younger ones, perhaps, while the mother went out to an evening job, and before the father came home—they had little time to skim stones across the canal. Sandra had asked how friendly they were with the older boys, and learned that they all lived on the same street. "So we're a gang," said one of the boys. Sandra had asked them about their "gang" and discovered that it was just the four, a little group of boys who had been in and out of each other's houses for years, whose mothers chatted over the garden fence or while hanging out the washing. They might well grow up to marry each other's sisters or cousins, because that's how it was on the streets; people who had lived cheek by jowl with each other, who had seen babies born, and who had gathered when one of their own passed away, were like a clan. Only a moonlight flit with parents who couldn't pay the rent took the children away from friends who were like family. Would they lie to protect each other? Yes, without a shadow of doubt, they would lie.

The two older boys lived on opposite sides of the street, just a few doors away from each other. Before they alighted from the MG—which was surrounded by a clutch of children almost as soon as Maisie parked on the street—she turned to her secretary.

"Look, let me talk to the father and mother—or whoever's at home—and you have one of your chats with the boy. You seem to be very good with the youngsters. I really want to know exactly what they saw, who they saw, and if there was anyone new around lately. These boys are on the streets before and after school, and they hear their parents talking, too. They'll close ranks if ever someone from the street is fingered for a crime. But no one suspects the boys of anything, and as long as they've done nothing wrong, I believe they'll talk to you as easily as the younger ones."

Maisie emerged from the MG at the same time as Sandra closed the door on the other side.

"Right then, who wants to earn a penny?"

The hands shot up, all the children focused on Maisie.

"Good. There'll be a penny each for looking after my motor car—not a scratch, not a bump, and no bits hanging off when I get back. All right?"

"All right, Miss," they said in unison.

A baby screamed from within the house as Maisie rapped on the rough and splintered door of the Flowers' house.

"Tony! Tony! Get off yer bum and see who that is at the bloody door. And wipe your sister's nose while you're at it." There was a pause. "I don't bleedin' care what you're doin'—and don't whine that it's always you. I don't care who it always is, but I want you to answer that door—and if it's old man Walsh, tell him I'll pay him next Friday."

Maisie and Sandra looked at each other.

"Sometimes," said Maisie, "the time you choose to call upon someone is not necessarily the most convenient time for them."

"You're not kidding, Miss."

"Don't worry. I'll slip into my best local vernacular," said Maisie.

The door opened. A boy, tall for his age, Maisie thought, pulled his arm away from his runny nose. "What d'yer want?"

Sandra stepped forward. "Tony! I've heard all about you from your gang of friends; they say you're one of the best. You look after everyone, don't you?" Her accent had changed. Maisie thought she sounded like Enid, with whom she'd shared a cold bedroom at the top of 15 Ebury Place, oh so long ago. Enid was always trying to improve herself, and had developed an incongruous posh edge to her Cockney accent. Maisie's local dialect had never been as pronounced, though it was noticeable enough at the time. But it had changed gradually in those early years while taking her lessons from Maurice, so that, like a piece of fabric gently warmed and fashioned into a hat, her diction had taken on a new shape, a new roundness with distinct turning points, so that by the time she went up to Girton College, she might have been taken for a clergyman's daughter. But more important, she could put it on when she liked; years of blending with those of a higher station meant that she could assume the clipped tones of the aristocracy if it helped her

172 • JACQUELINE WINSPEAR

gain information she wanted. But now, in this street, losing the odd "h" in pronunciation might not be a bad thing—and it seemed that Sandra had the accent down pat.

"So, what if I do?" asked Tony Flowers.

"My friend just wants to talk to you, if that's all right with you," said Maisie. "It's about the Indian woman—and don't worry, you're not in any trouble. We want you to help us, that's all. So, can I go back and have a word with your mum while you help out Mrs. Tapley here?"

Tony kicked at the front tiled doorstep, which his mother had clearly tried to keep tidy with Cardinal polish.

"All right, then." He turned into the passageway behind him. "Mum! Mum!" he bellowed. "Mum, there's a woman here to see you. Not the bailiff. About the Indian woman."

"Well, I can't come out there now, can I?" his mother screamed back.

Maisie nodded at Sandra and crossed the threshold, stepping over toys in the passage while making her way to the back of the two-up-two-down terrace house, which smelled of boiled cabbage.

"Hello, Mrs. Flowers. Thank you so much for letting me come in to see you."

"Where's that boy gone now?" The woman looked up from nursing her baby. She seemed thin and harried, her hair gathered up by a scarf tied at her crown. Many poor women were known to feed the breadwinner in the family first, and themselves last, after the children, and Tony Flowers' mother seemed true to type. "Sorry and all that, but the scrap's got to have something before I go out to my job. Never a spare moment."

"Tony's with my assistant, Mrs. Flowers. I've come to see you about him finding the Indian lady, in the canal."

"Not that again. We already had the police round here. People don't like seeing police come to a door, do they?"

"They certainly didn't where I come from. In Lambeth."

"Well, you'd know, wouldn't you? So, what do you want with me, then?" The baby stopped suckling, and without looking at her child, Tony Flowers' mother rested the baby against her shoulder, pulled her underclothes and blouse back across her breast, and patted the little girl's back.

"I wonder what Tony told you about it all," asked Maisie.

"Just that they saw something in the canal, and when they tried to find out what it was, turns out it was one of them Indian women. Been shot, she had, right there." She stopped patting the baby's back for a second and touched the middle of her forehead. "Had terrible nights at first, he did. I'd hear him screaming, waking up the other kids. I thought it would go on forever. His father said he'd have to get a bit of backbone, otherwise if he ever saw what he saw in the war, well, he'd end up loony."

"Did he ever say anything about seeing anyone else that day—or even in the days before he and his mates found the body?"

Mrs. Flowers looked towards the window, almost as if she could see beyond the glass, which she couldn't due to the film of soot on the outside, and condensation on the inside. "I'm trying to think—it was weeks ago now, and what with all I have to put up with, it's a wonder I remember yesterday, never mind a month or even a fortnight gone." She sighed. "It was well before that, but I do remember Tony being late coming home, and because I had to get to work, I went up the road towards the canal—as you've cottoned, that's where these boys go to get up to no good. Anyway, I saw them in the distance, and called out to Tony, and he came running. Now, when I looked at them, the boys in the distance, the sun was in my eyes, and you know how it is in the afternoon—it can blind you, it can, when it's bright. Well, I could have sworn I saw five boys together, not the usual four—and them four are like that, you know." She held her hand away from the baby's back again, and twisted her forefinger and middle finger, like the base of a vine. "Thick with each other, they are. But anyway, he came along, and I gave him a piece of my mind, and I said to him, I said, 'Who's your new mate then?' And he said, 'Oh, no one.' 'No one?' I said. 'Funny no one with two legs, a head, and two arms, eh?' She leaned towards Maisie. "I don't want my kids getting into trouble, Miss— what's your name?"

"Maisie Dobbs."

"Well, like I said, I want my four to keep away from trouble, because trouble will find them round here, no two ways about it. Yes, you don't have to look far for trouble, because it's waiting for you. That's what I say." She looked at a clock on the mantelpiece. One hand was broken in the middle and the glass cover was cracked. "Blimey, I'd better be off—got to get down to the soap factory. We might not have much, Miss Dobbs—but by heck we're clean in this house." She stood up, and Maisie came to her feet. "Here, hold her a minute." Mrs. Flowers gave the baby to Maisie and ran along the passage, yelling at the top of her voice. "Tony. Would you come in here and watch this baby now!"

The baby rested her head against Maisie's chest, and closed her eyes. Not a cry or a whimper. She closed her eyes and began to sleep. Maisie walked towards the door, and along the passageway, remembering, at that moment, the comfort she felt when she held little Lizzie Beale years ago. Now this child's soft downy hair was under her chin, and as if she could not help herself, Maisie kissed the top of her head.

When she had thanked Mrs. Flowers and pressed a sixpence into Tony's hand, she nodded at Sandra. They were ready to leave. Mrs. Flowers had taken the baby from Maisie, handed her to her son, and rushed into the house to grab her coat and a rather battered hat.

"Oh, Tony," said Maisie, as she distributed pennies to the children gathered around the MG—a group that she could have sworn had grown larger since they first parked the motor car. "Tony, before you go in, what was the name of the other boy who sometimes came along by the canal?"

Tony rolled his eyes. "Oh, him. He's not in the gang. Not one of us lot."

"But what's his name?"

"Marty. Said his name was Marty."

"Was he around much?"

Tony Flowers shrugged. "Sort of. Said he didn't know anyone much, so he just sort of followed us along the canal, or down the market, which is where we go of a Saturday morning sometimes."

"Do you know where he lives?"

The boy shrugged. "Nah. He's just around sometimes."

"Is he older than you?"

Another shrug. "Dunno. Reckon he works on the docks somewhere."

"What makes you think that?"

"His hands. Got all that hard skin, when you look at them. You know, like he's been picking up heavy boxes all day."

"You don't shy away from a bit of hard graft either, do you, Tony? Your hands don't look too soft."

The boy blushed and shrugged as he held the baby tighter. "Gotta get her in now."

"Yes, I think she looks like she needs a nap. But Tony, do you know if your friend is in? Sydney Rattle, along the road?"

"Nah. He's just got another job. Nights. His mum found it for him, so he works days, then goes out again after his tea. Won't be back until late. Only comes out with us on a Saturday afternoon now."

"Can I come and see you again, if I need to?"

Tony Flowers shrugged again. "S'pose so."

"And if you remember anything else about Marty, would you try not to forget?"

He nodded. "Yes, Miss. I'll remember."

"Tony," asked Maisie, her voice lower, "did this Marty scare you?"

Another shrug. "I dunno, Miss. He wasn't like us. He was different."

"Thank you, love. I bet your mum thinks you're a real diamond. Here, buy yourself some sweets." She slipped another sixpence into his pocket. He blushed again, nodded his thanks, and took the baby back into the house.

Soon Maisie and Sandra were back in the motor car, driving towards the Elephant and Castle and Waterloo Bridge.

"How did you know there was another boy?" asked Sandra.

"His mum mentioned it."

"But he never told me there was anyone else."

"It was how I asked. He'd just had the baby put in his arms, so although he is protective of his little sister, he's also a bit softer on the inside when he's holding her. And I didn't ask him if they'd seen anyone else, I just asked the name of the other boy—I didn't give him a chance to say there wasn't someone."

"Oh, of course." Sandra paused, as if committing what Maisie said to memory. "So, I wonder, why did the younger ones lie?"

Maisie sighed. "It could be that they wanted to protect their group, or that they don't like saying anything without the older boys there. Or they might be embarrassed—perhaps Marty has something that marks him as different, for example. If he's that much older than them their parents would get suspicious, especially if he's an outsider. He could have some information on them that they don't want to go any further—perhaps he saw them getting up to some mischief that the local bobby won't be too happy to know about."

"What's your guess, Miss?"

"I would say that on the one hand these boys feel sorry for him—he might be lonely, perhaps—but he's not like them in some way. He's an outsider. And I think they're also scared of him. Perhaps he has a confidence that they don't, and instead of knowing about something they've done wrong, he might be one of those youngsters who eggs on the others to get up to more serious mischief, calling them names and intimidating them when they don't. But I could be completely wrong, and I might be thrown by putting two and two together and getting five, which is why everything goes on the case map. But tell me about your conversation with Tony."

"Much like the chat I had with the younger boys—nothing more, nothing less, though he is older, and seems more thoughtful. He sounded brotherly towards them, as if he looked out for them."

"That sums up the children here, growing up together. They probably fight like cats and dogs at times, but they protect each other as well."

"What's next, Miss?"

"I'm going to see Jesmond Martin, the father of the missing boy. I'll ring from the office and go over there this evening, if I can. In any case, there's a lot of catching up to do on that inquiry as it is."

"Do you think Billy will be all right, Miss Dobbs? Will he come back to work?"

"Let's wait and see, eh?" Maisie felt a catch in her throat as she spoke. She took a deep breath. "In any case, did you manage to find out the name of that lecturer, at the art college?"

"I'll have it tomorrow morning—seeing my friend at class this evening."

"Oh, do you want me to drop you anywhere, Sandra?"

"Just by Charing Cross, that would do well enough—but only if it's not far out of your way. Thank you."

Some twenty minutes later, as Maisie pulled away from Charing Cross Station, she looked back at Sandra. Her glance came at what must have been an inopportune moment, for it was just in time to see Billy emerge from the station, smiling as he limped towards Sandra.

Maisie returned to the office and made the call to Jesmond Martin, which was answered by a housekeeper, who informed her that Mr. Martin was not yet home from work, and in any case was expecting guests this evening. Maisie left a message that she would like to speak to him as soon as possible, and wondered if she might call at his office—she asked the housekeeper to pass on a message at her earliest opportunity, requesting he call her in the morning. Having made that call, and another to Mr. Pramal's hotel, she picked up the receiver one more time.

"Maisie, darling," said Priscilla as soon as she heard Maisie's voice. "Are you coming to supper soon? The boys so want to see James again. Directly I tell them you're coming, they'll be camped out on the stairs waiting for him, wearing aviator goggles."

"Yes, we're looking forward to seeing them, too, but I wondered, Pris—have you got a moment this evening, if I come over now?"

"Drinks at the ready, Maisie. Three quarters of an hour, then?"

"About that—and a cup of tea would be just fine."

"For you, perhaps, but not me!"

Maisie smiled and shook her head. "In a while, Pris."

"Crocodile. See you then!"

———————

It seemed to Maisie that Priscilla's sons were all growing up faster than ever. The eldest, Thomas, was almost as tall as his mother, and the youngest, Tarquin, had lost the babyishness of earlier years, despite still being without the front teeth he'd lost in a spat at the first school he'd attended upon the family's move from Biarritz back to London. The contretemps with another boy—possibly due to his coloring; Priscilla's sons were tanned by the Riviera sun, and all had her rich dark-copper hair—resulted in his brothers diving into the fray to protect their younger sibling. This act of loyalty—or wanton pugilism, according to the headmaster—led to their suspension and subsequent transfer to another school, one for the sons of a more international group of parents.

"Mummy's in the drawing room, Tante Maisie," said Thomas, who had greeted her with a kiss to each cheek.

"Is Uncle James with you?" asked Tarquin, looking down the steps towards her motor car.

"I'm afraid not—but he'll be with me next time."

"Excellent!" said Timothy. He was looking at Maisie through a pair of large goggles, while wearing a leather aviator's cap.

"You look like the Red Baron, Tim," said Maisie.

"No, not me. I'm going to be like Captain Albert Ball."

"Let's hope not," added his older brother. "He came off worse after a bit of a spat with von Richthofen, you know."

"Well, I'll be him before he went down, then," said Timothy.

"And I'll be better than both of you, because I'll be Uncle James," said Tarquin.

"That's quite enough of that!" Priscilla's voice silenced her sons. "You'd better set a course for upstairs right now. Where's Elinor? Oh lummy, she's still out on her half-day. All right. Tom, you're it—I don't want to hear one single scream, or a ball hitting the wall. Elinor will be back in half an hour, and she will report to me if my sons have not acted like the sort of gentlemen that will make their mother proud. And your father will be home in an hour, so let that be a warning."

The boys ran upstairs, and Priscilla greeted Maisie. "Not that their father is good for any discipline, and they know it. Come on, let's go and have a drink."

Maisie thought they must look like bookends, each taking up one end of the sofa, with shoes kicked off and knees drawn up. Yet they were bookends only to a point—Priscilla was a woman of easy elegance, and even at home in London she often seemed to have arrived fresh from Paris. On this day she was wearing a white silk blouse with navy blue silk trousers and a wide cummerbund-style belt. Her hair was pulled back in a chignon, bringing an even bolder look to her face— Priscilla had deep brown eyes, high cheekbones, and a nose that on another women might have seemed long, but on Priscilla added to the impression of a personality to be reckoned with. But Maisie knew Priscilla's Achilles' heel—the memory of her beloved brothers lost in the war, and the dreadful fear that she might lose her sons. And she knew Priscilla had often dulled that fear with alcohol.

"What news? You sounded worried," said Priscilla.

"I am. It's about Billy."

"It's been about Billy for a long time, hasn't it, Maisie?"

"I need your advice."

Priscilla sipped her gin and tonic, holding it close to her mouth for another sip as she spoke. "I love it when you ask for my advice; it makes me feel quite clever."

"I wouldn't be asking if you weren't quite clever," said Maisie. She put her drink on the side table, though she had yet to lift it to her lips. "I think Billy needs a break from London, even from the new house. He wasn't well enough to come back to work, and frankly, I think he's having some sort of breakdown."

"That poor family—what with Doreen, and now Billy. It's not surprising that he's having trouble—he's had to have backbone enough for both of them for a long time." She sipped again, then, still holding the glass, rested it on her knee. "I know this seems harsh, but she's not the first to lose a child, and she won't be the last. I've as much compassion as the next woman, but as far as I'm concerned, she has to buck up."

"We're all different. I do feel for her."

"And so do I. But life goes on. Her husband needs life to be a bit lighter if they are to come through these setbacks, grim as they are."

"Yes, you're absolutely right, which is why I'm here. When he had something of a breakdown about four years ago, he went down to Chelstone for the summer, to work with my father. With everything that's happened, and—"

"And the fact that if you try to mend the broken fence again, it will be one time too many."

"Exactly—you said yourself that I shouldn't interfere. So, I wondered if, well—you see, I think the risks involved in more recent cases have told on him. There are late hours, and that attack has laid him very low. He would go to the ends of the earth for me, I know that, but I just don't want to send him on that sort of journey anymore. There's the possibility of a job at

James' company, but in the meantime, I thought some fresh air and a different place would do wonders for them all."

"Maisie, you can't save Billy by proxy. I have a feeling that you are about to inquire if I need more help at the house, and if I could speak to Mr. Alcott and ask him about taking on some more help, now that the gardens will have to be sorted out, the leaves raked in a few weeks, and the gardens generally put to bed for the winter."

Priscilla often referred to her family's country home as "the house." She had inherited the estate after her parents' deaths during the influenza epidemic following the war. For a while she found shallow solace in a round of parties in Biarritz—until she met the very solid Douglas Partridge, who had given her a reason for living once more.

"Well, I thought it might be a good idea, what with one thing and another," said Maisie. "But talking about it aloud, well, it wasn't so bright, was it?"

"Not really, but on the other hand, you don't come up with bad ideas very often. It's not right, and besides, he'd know, and more to the point, Doreen would see your fingerprints all over the idea." Priscilla put down her cocktail on the table adjacent to her side of the sofa, and picked up her cigarette case and a long ebony-and-white cigarette holder. She proceeded to push a cigarette into the holder. "There's more to it, isn't there," said Priscilla. She lit the cigarette, inhaled, and blew a perfect smoke ring upwards.

"There wasn't, until this evening." Maisie took up her drink and sipped.

"Go on."

"I have a feeling that Billy might be having some sort of romantic affair with Sandra."

Priscilla's eyes widened. "Oh, that'll rock the bloody boat. I can see the whites of Doreen's eyes already."

Maisie nodded. "I know. Me too."

Chapter Ten

"Maisie, I wonder if we could talk about going to the Otterburns' tomorrow evening. I really don't want to go alone." James set down his teacup. "I know how you feel about the man, but—"

"James, I am not sure that you do know how I feel. I just don't want to be in his company. Every time I see Billy, every time I think of how he was left for dead, I think of John Otterburn. And while I think that his efforts to bolster our country's air defenses are—as you say, 'visionary'—I cannot be in the same room as him." She paused, seeing the disappointment on James' face. She reached for his hand. "Look, perhaps another time, in a neutral place; at someone else's party might be an idea. We're bound to cross paths with him and Lorraine soon enough."

James sighed. "Oh, I can't say I blame you, Maisie. I just feel better with you at my side."

She smiled. "And I like being by your side, James—just not tomorrow evening."

He shrugged. "But you don't like being by my side enough to marry me, do you, Maisie?"

"That's not fair, James. We're enjoying ourselves, aren't we?"

"I'm sorry," said James. "You're right, that wasn't fair. We had an agreement, and all is indeed well." He set his table napkin beside his plate and looked at his watch. "Now, I must get to the office—a busy day ahead. And you?"

"Yes, a very busy day. I'll . . . I'll see you later, then."

"See you, my love." He leaned forward and kissed her on the cheek.

"James," said Maisie, pushing back her chair. "How about we spend this evening at the flat—I'll cook for us. Just the two of us, no fussing from Simmonds. One of our indoor picnics. I'll think of something special, not just the usual soup and crusty bread."

He took her in his arms. "I rather like soup and crusty bread. It's warming."

"About seven then?"

"Lovely—I'll let Simmonds know he can stand down this evening."

Mr. Ramesh Singh was at his shop in Commercial Road when Maisie called.

"Ah yes, I am very pleased to see you, Miss Dobbs. My friend Pramal told me to expect your visit." He looked up at the door. "I had better close up shop for a few minutes while we are having our conversation."

Singh flipped over the sign that told customers the shop was closed—he had pinned an extra note with the words "Open again in half an hour." Maisie thought it interesting that he did not specify when the half an hour would begin. He was a tall man, and well built— Pramal had an energetic wiriness about him, whereas Singh looked as if he were content with his life, and enjoyed many evenings sitting with his family over a well-provisioned table. He dressed as she would expect any ordinary working Englishman to dress, and would not have been surprised had he put on a flat cap before leaving his shop. His black hair was short and combed back from his face, save for one small clump of hair that would not be tamed and fell into his eyes every moment or two. She suspected Singh might have a good sense of humor, and enjoyed sharing a joke with family and friends—she could imagine him teasing children and making fun of the womenfolk as they bustled about their business, though such mockery would be in good heart.

When she was settled with a cup of tea in a small room behind the shop, Maisie asked Singh about his friendship with Pramal.

"It is of many years, since we were boys. We went to school together, then later, to war together, so he is indeed like a brother to me, though I returned to this country after the war, and ended up marrying here. I remain here for the love of a good woman, as you English might say."

"You met your wife here?"

"Indeed. My very British wife—and please do not seem surprised, Miss Dobbs. I am not the only man from your Empire to marry a British woman."

"I'm not shocked, Mr. Singh—though I wonder, if you don't mind me asking, if you are subject to any prejudice?"

"As I said, I am not the only one, though obviously we do not number in the thousands—indeed, there are only about seven or eight thousand people from India living here in Britain. That is beside the point, though. Do other people matter? Yes, I suppose they do, but we have managed, and we know others in our little community of Anglos and Indians, and it has been for some years now that we have been married, so people are used to us. And our children."

"I understand that you once held a torch for Miss Usha Pramal."

"Oh, I did, most definitely! And so did many others, though none were good enough for Usha. Even her brother despaired of her and said she would bring shame on the family if she went on as she did—not that she was bad, no, never bad. But she was willful, you know. Very willful, and her father was powerless—he loved her so very much, and saw his poor dead wife in her eyes. Pramal always said that if his mother had been alive, Usha would have been a different person, but I don't know—that particular leopard had very distinct spots."

"I do not want to offend, but I'd like to know if she had ever upset you in any way?"

Singh shook his head. "Not at all. No, that's not true. It was clear that she had no intention of accepting an offer of marriage between us, so my family and hers did not discuss the possibility; it saved face—as you English might say—all around."

Maisie nodded. "Yes, I understand. Did you know about the young man with whom she'd exchanged affections? He was an Englishman, according to Mr. Pramal."

"I knew something about it, though Pramal would not have discussed it with me. He would not have wanted the man's appearance at the house to have ruined her chances in the future."

"But I thought they might have seen each other outside the house, without a chaperone, perhaps."

Singh seemed thoughtful, and at once Maisie saw a certain sadness in his eyes, as if he were in mourning.

"Usha was like a butterfly, Miss Dobbs. Flit, flit, flit, from this flower to the next, taking nectar and tasting sweetness. She saw the very best in everyone, and I never knew her to be without a smile or a good word for one and all. If she saw this man outside the house, it was with innocence, not a plan, and she would never have wanted a reputation with men to be brought home to her doorstep. Can he be blamed? Yes, he should have known better, though he had not been in our country long—as far as I know—but still, he should not have put her in that position, even if he was in love with her."

"How do you know he was in love with her?" Maisie leaned forward.

Singh smiled, despite eyes that had now filled with tears. "Because everyone loved Usha, Miss Dobbs. No one could fail to love such a person, so perhaps he had no choice but to follow her, and that led to his disrespect of her position." He sighed. "Usha was truly the daughter of heaven, you know."

There was a moment's silence before Maisie spoke again, her voice soft. "Do you have any idea why someone might want to kill her, Mr. Singh?"

He leaned his head forward to rest on his hands, made into a fist in front of his face, with fingers laced. "On the one hand, I could not imagine taking such a precious life—and I speak as a man who took precious life in the war, and of that I am not proud." He paused. "But I can only think that she was killed because someone loved her very much and either could not stand that love, or someone else couldn't."

Maisie nodded, inhaling his words as if they were the spices that gave fragrance to air in the room. She looked around her, and for the first time since entering the shop, she took in the many jars and boxes on floor-to-ceiling shelves around the room. Jars filled with color and fragrance she had never experienced, and boxes exuding aromas that teased her senses, along with an exotic redolence seeping from sacks on the floor.

"Mr. Singh, do you think a man could kill for such a love? Do you think he could take the life of one so adored?"

Singh sighed audibly. "I do, Miss Dobbs. I think that one so precious might drive a person—man or woman—to distraction. You see, no one could ever own Usha—it would have been like trying to catch a summer's breeze to put it in a bottle and clamp down a stopper. Children would follow her, you know—as if they could be wrapped in her essence while walking in her wake. That is who she was." He shook his head, as if to banish images in his mind's eye. "I would have married Usha, had I thought I would be accepted, but fortunately, I didn't. I fell in love with a very wonderful English lady and was saved the turmoil of being a slave to the unattainable."

As if on cue, the door opened, and a woman entered the room. She was of average height and, arguably, average appearance—if she had been wearing a skirt and jacket, with a hat, gloves, and leather shoes, she might look as if she were a countrywoman on her way to church to arrange the flowers for the Sunday service. Instead, this English woman, with her pale complexion and blue eyes, with her dark-blond hair drawn back, would attract a second look wherever she went. The sari of deep blue seemed iridescent, and the dark red bindi appeared larger on her white forehead, as if it were a more defiant hallmark of the culture she had adopted upon her marriage. She saw Maisie and bowed, her hands clasped together.

"I see my husband has offered you tea, Miss—"

Maisie stood up. "Miss Dobbs. Maisie Dobbs. I'm honored to meet you, Mrs. Singh."

The woman's eyes sparkled. "Oh, let's not stand on ceremony, eh, Miss Dobbs. Surprised, yes, but probably not honored—I don't think I have ever warranted any honors, except the honor of being married to a very good man. Are you sure you don't want another cup before you go?"

"Um, well—no thank you very much. One cup was enough—I sometimes think I could easily drink my weight in tea." She gathered her gloves and turned to Singh. "Thank you for your time, Mr. Singh. It was so kind of you to close the shop for a while—in fact, I think I might make some purchases; those spices are quite heady."

Mrs. Bess Singh introduced Maisie to the spices, herbs, and different kinds of flour in the shop, to the pickles and chutneys she had never before tasted. The pungent ajmud—celery seed—seemed familiar, though the cardamon seeds teased her with their freshness, along with jeera—cumin seed; jethimadh—licorice powder; and one she loved, dhania—coriander. A large jar of turmeric caught her eye—she remembered Mrs. Crawford, the cook at Ebury Place, using turmeric in a stew. Her attention was drawn back and forth along the array of colors and textures, and she was delighted by the vibrant yet delicate threads of saffron in a crystal container. Allspice was familiar, along with cloves and peppercorns, but she was fascinated by their Indian names: kabab chini, lavang, kali mirch. As Bess Singh weighed out a small pouch of dried ginger to add to a collection of small blue-paper pouches collected on the counter in front of Maisie, she began to speak.

"I knew Usha, you know."

"Did you?" Maisie was quiet, watching the woman twist the top of another blue paper pouch and replace the glass jar on the shelf. She turned around, and spoke while collecting the pouches and putting them into a larger paper bag. "She was very striking, but it was not so much her looks that attracted people— and you've probably heard all this, I daresay. It was her *way*, how she moved, and how she sort of claimed the street when she walked along. And I confess, when I first knew her, she'd come here to the shop to see Singh when she came over to England with the family." Maisie noticed that the woman referred to her husband by his surname. "Well, I wasn't sure about her, to tell you the truth," Bess went on. "Though I liked her well enough. She reminded me of those flowers you see at Kew—have you been to Kew, Miss Dobbs?" She did not wait for an answer. "Well, they've got a plant there, with a large, very beautiful flower—but if you chanced to put your finger near the petals, it would take your finger off. You can watch it—it eats the insects drawn to its beauty and fragrance."

"I've heard of plants like that—from Polynesia, or Indochina, somewhere like that."

"That's what Usha reminded me of, you see. People were drawn to her beauty, and if she touched a person—and she was one of those people who touched, you know, when they talk to you, or meet you in the street—they went off looking as if their arm had been blessed, or their cheek, or their fingers. But if people became too close, she could clam up. Singh told me about that young man in India—she shut him out, never spoke to him again, by all accounts. And he wept at her door, to the point where even her aunts thought something should be said to him, to help his broken heart."

"Oh, I see—I didn't know it was that intense," said Maisie.

Bess Singh nodded, pulling up the silk of her sari so her head was covered. "According to Pramal, yes, it was."

"And no one seems to know the man's name," said Maisie.

Bess Singh looked at Maisie, then added, "There's remembering with an outsider, and remembering with family, no matter where you come from—so really, someone might know the name, but they won't say any more about it. It would have been embarrassing, you see, disrespectful. It brought some talk to the family's door—it might have been unfounded, but it was talk all the same—and they wanted Usha to be settled in a marriage. They'd have wanted her to be accepted into a good Indian family—and to get her out of the house to be another man's problem, though they all loved her very much. And as I said, you couldn't help being drawn to her—she came up to you, fluttering around you, paying attention, her eyes only for you, and you loved her."

Maisie nodded. Again, much of the description was familiar—it was a hallmark of her work to hear repetition. But among the stories told and retold, there was often that little thread, that new slub in the fabric of a tale she had not noticed before.

Maisie left the shop clutching her collection of spices, nuts, herbs, and some onions, along with a scribbled recipe for a dish called Mughlai Biryani—she had been promised it would be unlike anything she had ever eaten before. Walking along to her motor car, she began to reconsider the two conversations. That Singh had loved Usha was without question, though it was the kind of youthful love that a person might have for the unattainable—a love that had at one time been searing, yet sweet. It might have been a love that inspired tears, and at the other extreme, intense joy should a smile be bestowed upon the admirer by the one who is loved. But that love had been superseded by marriage to another, and with it had come a deeper, perennial love. Maisie could see the respect that Singh and his wife had for each other. Without doubt, their union represented a road that had been difficult, though they'd had each other on the journey, and it seemed the couple—and their children—had been accepted in the community.

Maisie thought Singh was right, that Usha could well have been killed by someone who loved her very much. And it would appear that everyone who met Usha Pramal fell in love with her, almost as if she had cast a spell upon them. But new light had been thrown onto the dead woman's character by Bess Singh—Usha could turn her back on an admirer if that person came too close, close enough to feel the snap of indifference to his deepest feelings. Maisie thought Mrs. Singh spoke very much from the heart—after all, she had loved Usha Pramal, too, though it might have been an affection that was against her better judgment.

"Oh, good, so Mrs. Chaudhary Jones can see me this afternoon—excellent." Maisie looked at the card

Sandra had just handed to her. "Not far from Imperial College. If I can make an appointment to see Mr. Martin, I will go on to his house immediately afterwards." She picked up a pen to make a note in her diary. "Anything else, Sandra?"

"Yes, here's the name of that lecturer, at the art college in Camberwell. "Dr. Harry Ashley. He lectures at the Slade, too, but apparently he has an office at the college. Shall I make an appointment?"

Maisie was thoughtful. "No, I'll try to catch him on the fly—does he have hours when he sees students?"

"According to my friend, he's generally there in the mornings until early afternoon, between eleven and one."

"Right, I'll make a point of seeing him tomorrow morning, if I can. In the meantime, could you call Jesmond Martin at his office. I had it in mind to go later this evening, but I can't—and I would really like to see his wife as well. Would you ask if I can see him at his home, around five-ish. He might be able to leave his office early, which means I can get on back to the flat after we speak. In fact, I might well go over to his house without prior consent; I think I need to take that chance."

"It's all as good as done," said Sandra. "Anything special on this evening, Miss?"

202 • JACQUELINE WINSPEAR

"I'm cooking. Something rather different, so I'll need some more time. Indian food."

"Is that what that smell is? Indian stuff?"

"Yes, it is. I think it's very nice."

Sandra crinkled her nose and shook her head as she picked up the telephone receiver. "I think I'd prefer sausage and mash, myself."

Maisie looked across at her secretary, a young woman whom she admired for her tenacity—Sandra had risked her life and freedom to find the man behind her husband's death in a so-called accident. Not only was Sandra an employee, but there was a connection of mutual regard and friendship, though the difference in age and experience, and the fact that Maisie was Sandra's employer, ruled out the same sort of deep emotional bond between women of the kind shared by Maisie and Priscilla. Maisie wondered whether she should mention seeing Sandra and Billy—after all, she might be wrong, there might be nothing more to their meeting than friendship, a companionship that had grown from working together. On the other hand, there was something in the way they moved towards each other that suggested to Maisie a closer connection. She sighed. Should she let such a thing run its course? She had to concede that there was a thread that drew them together—Sandra had lost her husband, and though Doreen was still very much alive and at home with the children, her psychological well-being caused her to detach from her husband, to go into a shell, leaving Billy isolated.

No, she would leave well enough alone. For now.

To the south of Imperial College, a terrace of grand mansions had been divided into apartments for teaching staff and made available at a fixed rent. Maisie had knowledge of this already, as she had attended an art class not far away, and the teacher—a vibrant Polish woman who always wore clothes of clashing colors in every hue—had her studio on the top floor of a similar mansion, and paid only a peppercorn rent given the fact that she was also a teacher at another London college. Dr. Jones and his wife lived on the second floor of a mansion, not far from Princes Square. It was a fine day with a slight nip in the breeze, and Maisie enjoyed the walk from the motor car to her destination. She remembered delighting in the Saturday classes with Magda, and the sense of freedom she felt when working with color. Her life had seemed so very gray at the time—perhaps it was the lack of light in her heart—and the hours spent in Magda's studio with a motley assortment of people she might never have otherwise met elevated her, gave a spring to her step as she was leaving. Stopping to look around her, Maisie remembered the day she'd bumped into James Compton, her hands still bearing the stains of dyes used to color raw yarns. He'd taken her for a meal, and then calmly told her that her face was speckled with colored spots. They'd laughed together, and she remembered that feeling of lightness, of a sense that there was a connection between them. She touched her stomach, where butterflies seemed to have gathered. Sometimes it seemed as if the past bound them—that deep understanding of what it was to go to war, to see life taken on such a scale and so violently—yet it was also the past that threatened to tear them apart. Those interludes of joy, of lightheartedness, of forgetting everything but the good fun they were having, were the best of times, and she acknowledged that she would grieve for his company if he were gone from her life forever. She pushed the thought aside as she arrived at the address for Dr.—Mrs.—Chaudhary Jones.

A young woman in a well-tailored pale blue wool barathea costume answered the door. The jacket was cut to enhance her slenderness, with a narrow belt around the waist. The skirt came to mid-calf, with kick pleats to allow freedom of movement, and her shoes were plain black with a strap fastened with a patent button.

"Miss Dobbs. Dr. Chaudhary Jones is expecting you. I am her assistant, Layla."

The young woman held out her hand to Maisie, who smiled, shook the proffered hand, and stepped into the entrance hall. Maisie had been somewhat taken aback when the woman first answered the door, for her features suggested she was of Indian origin, yet she wore the garb of an Englishwoman. They reached the door to the apartment, which had been left ajar, and Layla led Maisie along a wide corridor, past several closed doors until she reached an open door to the right. She knocked lightly and stepped in, indicating that Maisie should follow her.

"Amma, Miss Dobbs to see you."

The woman before Maisie was seated behind a desk piled high with books, and framed by light from the open window behind her. Another desk across the room was neater, with only a pile of papers on each side of a typewriter.

"Thank you, my dear," said Dr. Chaudhary Jones, as she stood up and stepped from behind her desk to greet Maisie. She nodded to the young woman, who left the room. It had not taken the young woman addressing Dr. Chaudhary Jones as "Amma" for Maisie to see the familial connection. Though Layla's skin was lighter, her eyes a greenish hazel rather than dark brown, Maisie could see the mother in the daughter. The older woman was dressed in a sari of deepest olive with a pale green border decorated with golden thread. She wore no jewelry except for small hoop earrings and the ring on the third finger of her left hand. A small pile of silver bangles had been set to one side on the desk—most likely put on this morning, they had become a hindrance as the woman was writing. Her hair was drawn back in a bun, with the strands of gray around her hairline adding to an overall impression of worldly wisdom rather than narrow experience.

"Thank you very much for agreeing to see me, Dr. Chaudhary Jones."

The woman smiled at Maisie, and took her hand. "It is a pleasure, Miss Dobbs, though I confess, I was intrigued by your secretary's description of why you wanted to see me—you are a psychologist and investigator, and you are looking into the death of an Indian woman. And in suspicious circumstances. My gosh, I thought, what have I done?"

Maisie smiled. "Nothing at all. I know it must have sounded a bit cloak-and-dagger, but I wanted to speak to an Indian woman who could give me some information—a picture, if you like—of the lives of other Indian women here in Britain, especially London."

"I see. Well then, sit down and let's have that chat." Chaudhary Jones extended her hand towards the chair in front of her desk, and returned to her place.

"Your daughter is very striking, Dr. Chaudhary Jones."

"I know. A beautiful daughter is the delight of young motherhood, but when they reach womanhood, it is a worry. She gets her mind from her father, though— she's a student here at Imperial, though he is a physicist at heart, while she is studying microbes."

"Do you mind me asking—I see you in a truly beautiful sari, yet your daughter is dressed as if she was a professional woman in an office."

"She *is* a professional woman in an office when she's working for me, and she prefers to wear the same clothes as other young women, plus it's easier when she's in the laboratory. But she dresses in the sari for special occasions, and for supper. Her father likes to see her in the sari, actually, whereas I don't really mind—as long as she works her brain, I don't worry too much about the clothes."

"That's a bit unusual, if you don't mind my saying so."

"I suppose some people think we're an unusual family. But if you want to find out more about Indian women, you should start by knowing that the stereotype doesn't reflect everyone, though it might give an impression of the majority. Now, tell me about this young woman—I'm curious."

Maisie described Usha Pramal as best she could, drawing upon the descriptions she'd received from those who had known her—or perhaps known only a facet of her character.

"Oh, my, she *was* a butterfly, wasn't she? But what a daughter to have, I would say—a bit of spark never hurt anyone, and can take a woman far, unless it causes her to burn out too soon. But she had ambition, with her plan to start a school. Yes, a good daughter to have."

"Dr. Chaudhary Jones, I confess, I am very confused. On the one hand, here I am with you—a highly educated woman with her own professional status, married to an Englishman, with a daughter who is also a scientist."

"And a son who is a writer of poems, in India."

"Really?"

"Yes, I despair of him, though to be a poet is an honorable thing."

Maisie went on. "I have met an Englishwoman married to an Indian man, and I have passed Indian women in the street who seem to adhere to what you referred to as a stereotype. Amid all this information, I am trying to get an impression of Usha, of who might have taken her life, and to underpin my investigation, I want to gain an understanding of how her life might have been here, of what kept her here when she could have returned to India months before she died."

"Oh, the grand dilemma. Trying to put India in a little box—a country with goddesses as revered as gods, and where women are at once downtrodden and highly educated. My gosh, it sounds almost like Great Britain, does it not? You might not have had goddesses, but you've had your share of warrior women, haven't you?"

"I see your point."

"Yes, and I think you might have seen it before you came here, but you were intrigued because I represent the picture not always acknowledged." Lakshmi Chaudhary Jones rested her elbows on her desk and her chin in her hands. "In a nutshell, though we have traditions to honor, there are many very educated Indian women—women who are powerful in both their families and their villages, and indeed in the country, though you might not always hear their names. The same is true of Great Britain. Let me give you some names to think about. Bhicoo Batlivala—her father owned a woolen mill, and she was from quite a privileged family; however, she was highly educated and became a barrister here in England. You've doubtless heard of Sophia Duleep Singh, a brilliant woman, and a most forceful suffragist. Twenty-three years ago she was with Emmeline Pankhurst and Elizabeth Garrett Anderson, marching to Parliament on Black Friday— and she the daughter of a maharajah! Then there's another one—Bhikaiji Rustom Cama—she is a firebrand. Seventy-one years of age now, but she has made her voice heard, whether it be for home rule in India or equality for our sex. I could continue, I could tell you about the Indian women who have studied medicine, science, law, and so on, in this country—some have remained and others taken their precious intellectual and academic gifts home to India."

Maisie leaned forward. She took a breath as if to ask a question, then sat back again.

"I think you want to ask me if a woman such as your Usha Pramal could have been killed by one of her countrymen, someone who did not like the way she walked, or her presence in a church, or her confidence. You want to know what I think."

"I do, yes, that's one thing."

"I think that is entirely possible. Of course I do. There are British men who would do the same—you know that, Miss Dobbs. Why do men kill prostitutes, for example? And please do not worry—I am a woman of the world, and the woman's place in the world has been the subject of my work for a long time. A man might feel the urge to physically assault a woman who has power over him—whether that power breaks his will in some way, whether it causes acute unease, or whether, for example, he is shamed by the darkness of his shadow. And of course a savage assault can lead to death—for both of them."

"Yes, I understand that very well."

"I'm not a psychologist like you, Miss Dobbs, but I would say that you're looking for someone—and don't rule out the fact that it might be a woman—who was fearful of the shadow that emerged when they saw Miss Pramal."

Maisie nodded.

"So, how else can I help you, Miss Dobbs?"

"Tell me about your country, Dr. Chaudhary Jones. Tell me about India, and why you left. Do you miss your country? And how do you keep . . . how do you keep a connection with your . . . your heritage, when you are married to an Englishman and living here in Britain."

Lakshmi Chaudhary Jones smiled, left her desk, and opened the door.

"Layla! Layla, would you bring us a nice cup of tea. And some of those biscuits your father likes. Thank you!"

She turned back into the room.

"I think a little chat between women calls for a cup of tea, don't you?"

It was over an hour later that Maisie left the apartment of Dr. Chaudhary Jones. Layla accompanied her to the door.

"Thank you, Layla," said Maisie. "Your mother is a remarkable woman."

"Yes, she is." The young woman paused, smiling at Maisie. "But she's just like any other mother, really."

"Oh, I don't think so," said Maisie.

"I know so. She's already putting away little baby clothes in anticipation of becoming a grandmother— and she's not looking to my brother to give her that exalted status."

"All in good time, Layla."

"Not any time, Miss Dobbs. Not for me."

Maisie bid the young woman good-bye, and walked out into the mid-afternoon sun. Her smile was short-lived, though, as she thought back to Lakshmi Chaudhary Jones' words. *I would say that you're looking for someone—and don't rule out the fact that it might be a woman—who was fearful of the shadow that emerged when they saw Miss Pramal.*

Chapter Eleven

The Martin home stood on a leafy street in St. John's Wood. Most of the houses were just visible behind tall hedges and seemed to be of Georgian architecture. Maisie's destination, though, a grand house built in the later years of Edward VII's reign, was inspired by an architectural style favored by wealthy merchants in Tudor times, but with a front door on the corner of the house, rather than at the front. Above it a square bay window seemed to jut out with self-importance, as if it were an afterthought added by a builder anxious to put his stamp on the dwelling. Maisie could see swags of fabric behind the windows, and thought the interior might be quite dark. She wondered if it would have been too dark for a boy growing up, and reminded herself that Priscilla's light and spacious home where few rules seemed to reign over the lives of the Partridge boys was the exception; the windows on so many houses were still lined in the heavy fabrics favored by a generation that came of age when Victoria was queen.

Having parked the MG in front of the house, she walked up to the front door, gravel crackling beneath her feet with every step. She suspected Mr. Jesmond Martin used the local St. John's Wood tube station to travel into the city—though he might also have a chauffeur, she saw no sign of a motor car.

When she pulled the bell at the side of the front door, there was nothing to indicate anyone was at home. No sound came from inside the house, no shuffle of an old housekeeper, and no commanding step of a butler, nor even the rushed footfall of a harried maid, bustling along the hallway wiping her hands on a cloth and shouting, "All right, all right, I'll be there in a minute." She rang the bell again.

"Who's there?" A moment later the call came from outside.

Maisie stepped back and looked around her.

"Up here. Look up."

Maisie looked up at the square bay window, which from that angle seemed even more of an afterthought, as a child might slap an extra piece of clay onto the side of a model house. A nurse—she presumed it was a nurse, for she wore a white dress and apron, and the same kind of cap that Maisie had worn in the war—was looking down at her from an open window.

"Oh, hello," said Maisie. "I'm here to see Mr. Martin. My name is Maisie Dobbs, and I have an appointment."

"Oh, yes. Yes, you. Well, he telephoned a little while ago to say that he had been kept at his office and wouldn't be home until later. He said you must have your secretary make another appointment to call."

"I see." Maisie paused. "I wonder, could I have a word with you—or are you busy?"

The nurse drew back into the room, then leaned out of the window again. "Well, all right, but I don't know what you might want with me—who are you anyway?"

"I've been asked to conduct an investigation into the disappearance of Mr. Martin's son."

Maisie could have sworn the woman rolled her eyes.

"You never know what he's going to get up to next, that one—mind you, it's not as if I could always blame him. He can be a bit of a tyke, a real thorn in his father's side, though. Look, she's gone down now, so I can spare a few minutes."

She's gone down? thought Maisie as she stepped back onto the front doorstep to await the nurse's arrival.

The door opened, and the nurse, her face flushed and with a few strands of strawberry blond hair escaping from her cap, stood back.

"Nurse Wilkins," she introduced herself. "I live in. There's a daily, who leaves at half-past three, and then there's the cook, who's as deaf as a post, so she wouldn't have heard you. Won't you come in?"

Maisie stepped across the threshold into an entrance hall decorated in a baronial style. A wide wooden staircase swept to the upper floor in front of her, and to the right was a reception room with the door open. To the left a hallway led, she assumed, to other rooms and, possibly, the kitchen staircase. Nurse Wilkins made no move to invite her into the reception room, nor did Maisie expect such a breach of employer trust. She was somewhat surprised to be asked into the house at all, but suspected the woman might be lonely for company.

"Thank you so much for your time, Nurse Wilkins. I wanted to find out a little more about Robert—we have a possible lead as to his whereabouts, but of course some more information would be useful."

"Robert. Nice boy at heart, I suppose, but he can be a handful. I think it was all high jinks really, him running off. And his father has a very strong thumb, if you know what I mean." She pressed her thumb into the center of her forehead, to illustrate her point that

Mr. Martin was a firm disciplinarian. "I tell you, she hasn't had a sparkle in her eye since that boy left." The nurse raised her thumb towards the ceiling.

"You mean his mother, I take it."

"Yes, though she's been like that since he was a nipper, so I was told. And only young, she was, when she had him."

"What's wrong with her?"

"Gets terrible heads. Has to be in the dark, and can't have strange smells in the room, or loud noises—one squeal out of the boy could start her off when she was younger. And she gets sick with it, can't keep a thing down."

"Does she have times of respite from this illness?"

The nurse shrugged. "She does sometimes, but I can't take her out, because it would start her off again."

"Oh, poor woman. I am deeply sorry for her. Those sort of headaches can be debilitating. How is she treated?"

"It's been one doctor after another. I know that, like I said, light from the window and loud noises can start her off again, and so can smells—she can't abide scent, won't have it in the room. And apparently, she used to love her Shalimar, once upon a time."

"And she lies there all day?"

"She has powders, to make her sleep."

"What a terrible life. And does she see much of her husband, when he's home?"

"He comes up for a visit, when he's home from his office, and on Sundays he goes out, Saturday nights, too. He has a club, and he has his shooting parties. Always took the boy with him, so he wasn't able to see his mother much either, what with school. And then he went to boarding school. It was just before the summer holidays that he went missing, as you know."

"Yes, I know—but Mr. Martin didn't call the police, and didn't even come to me immediately."

"I imagine he thought Robert would come home."

"He'd absconded before then?"

Nurse Wilkins nodded. "A day or two here and there. Probably off with his friends, shooting apples."

"Shooting apples? Did he own a gun?"

"I don't know how he was with a gun, but he was a bit of a Robin Hood with a bow and arrow. You had to watch yourself, if you were out in the garden; never knew when one of them arrows might go whistling past your ear." The nurse smiled. "But even though he's tested me beyond measure at times, I'd like to think Robert is a good one, at heart. He loves his mother, so I'm surprised he left, in that regard."

"Did anything else happen? Did he have an argument with his father? Or do you think he was having trouble at school?"

Nurse Wilkins shrugged. "He and his father weren't exactly best friends—well, you don't expect them to be, do you? After all, one's the father and one's the son, so they're not pally, though I thought Mr. Martin tried to do his best with the boy, you know, keep him in line, but at the same time not be brutal with it." She was thoughtful. "Mind you, it wasn't long after that Indian woman stopped coming that he went off."

"Indian woman? What Indian woman?"

"Lovely girl, Miss Pramal. Started coming in to help the maid, just a day or two each week—not for long, mind. Anyway, one day she came into the room to clean, and asked me what was wrong with Mrs. Martin, and I told her and she said, 'May I see her?' Now, normally, I would have put a stop to that, no two ways about it. But it was the way she looked at her, really tender, as if she had a sympathy for the woman. So, I asked Mrs. Martin, and to tell you the truth, I don't think she'd've cared either way. Miss Pramal goes up to her, takes her hand, and says she's going to touch her on her temples." Wilkins placed the tips of her fingers on either side of her head. "Just like this."

"Did it have any effect?"

She nodded. "Her headache was gone in an hour. And Miss Pramal said she had something that would help. Next time she came, she crushed up these spices and grains to make a sort of paste, then she poured hot water on and gave it to Mrs. Martin to sip. I swear, that woman started to get better. And young Robert noticed it, too—he started staying longer with his mother, making her laugh. And he has a laugh on him, that one—it could raise the roof. It was a joy to see them together. To tell you the truth, I thought it wouldn't be long before I was out of a job."

"So, what happened?"

Nurse Wilkins shook her head. "I reckon it was down to the fact that Mr. Martin used to live over there, in India. He found out what was happening, and he didn't like it at all. You would have thought he'd be pleased, what with his wife getting better, but he wasn't at all. I reckon he didn't like the fact that the lad was so close to his mother, and he certainly didn't like the fact that Miss Pramal had helped her. It's a wonder I didn't lose my job, too, for allowing it all to happen, but not everyone wants to work alone all day in this house, and just a sad, moaning woman for company."

"Did he tell Miss Pramal to leave?"

She nodded. "Yes, as far as I know, he did—though I could be wrong. There was a dust-up with the boy, too, so I reckon that didn't help matters. It was strange, because I thought Mr. Martin quite admired Miss Pramal. She might have been an Indian woman, but she was one to look at—she sort of drew you to her, no matter what you thought of them before. But I saw him looking at her a couple of times—he usually wasn't here when she came to clean, but he works from home in his study on the odd occasion. And when he looked at her, I could see she had that effect on him, too. Trouble is, I don't think he liked it at all." Nurse Wilkins looked at the clock on the mantelpiece. "Oh, look at that, I'd better get on. I must take some broth up to her."

"Thank you, Nurse Wilkins. I am grateful to you for your time—and your honesty."

"I hope it doesn't get me into trouble."

Maisie shook her head. "Not to worry. This is between us. I do have one question, though."

"Yes?" said Wilkins, reaching for the door handle.

"What do you think Robert thought of Miss Pramal?"

Wilkins smiled and rolled her eyes. "Puppy love, I would say. A boy with his head in the clouds. Of course, she walked on water as far as he was concerned, because she'd helped his mother. But you could see he had a bit of a schoolboy crush. She was beautiful, after all. Like a princess, really. Now then . . ."

"Of course. Thank you. Thank you very much."

As she reached the hedge, she turned, and looked back at the house. A woman with long gray hair stood at the window, her hands pressed against the panes, her face filled with despair.

Maisie couldn't get the image of Mrs. Martin out of her head. Trapped in her room, her hands against the windowpanes, and the look on her face. She might have been one story above Maisie, but for a second her expression of distress was as clear as day—and it was wretched. Maisie felt an anger towards Jesmond Martin, whom she suspected might be a controlling bully—then checked herself, knowing that if Maurice were there to offer counsel, he would admonish her for jumping to such a conclusion based upon a limited opportunity to observe.

Following the original meeting, when Jesmond Martin had asked for assistance in finding his son, Billy had put forward the idea that perhaps Martin just didn't like the police. Maisie had then turned to Sandra, who sighed and looked at Maisie with an air of resignation and, she thought, some annoyance. "I'm not saying this just because I didn't like Mr. Martin—and I can't help it, Miss Dobbs, I didn't like the man. And I'm not saying it because of my political views. But I think he came to you because you're a woman, and he reckons a woman couldn't be a good detective, and a woman won't be able to find his son. I don't think he wants that son of his found, if you want my opinion."

Maisie had nodded, while Billy had raised his eyes and sighed deeply, a common mannerism when he heard something a bit controversial, or "near the mark" as he would say.

"That's an interesting observation, Sandra," Maisie had responded. "But what do you think might have inspired such feelings?"

Billy was the first to speak. "He might've been jealous of the boy. Or he might've been jealous of his wife. Could be that he was good at all the manly sort of things, like taking the boy shooting, but when it came to just having a bit of a lark, he was too much of a stuffed shirt."

"Enough to see a boy of fourteen leave home and not know where he is?" asked Maisie.

"I'd been out at work for two years by the time I was fourteen," said Billy.

"Me too," added Sandra. "And my father certainly didn't expect to see me but once a year."

And then the moment Maisie now regretted. "Billy, if he thinks a man could do a better job, which is why he came to a woman, why, we'll give him a man—and one who knows boys better than Sandra and me put together."

She had thought he would be pleased, and he seemed genuinely so at first. It was later that his fear of failure had been so devastatingly played out. But she was now fairly certain that Sandra had made a good point. Perhaps Jesmond Martin had not wanted his son found, or at least, not for a while. Not only did she wonder why, but she found that she was not as surprised as she might have been to find that Usha Pramal was, for a short time, part of the Martin household.

Usha Pramal was still on her mind as she cut into a clutch of herbs, then crushed seeds and measured spices according to the recipe given to her by Mrs. Singh. She felt at once as if a spark had lit the kindling under her senses. Her skin tingled when she leaned over the bowl and breathed in the fragrance. The different aromas seemed like ribbons twisted and tied together; though each hue was distinct, a brash new color had been created. It felt alive, this color, as if it were a person.

In two separate pans she fried onions and the whole spices, adding a ginger and garlic paste to the mix, along with crushed almonds. Juggling the pans as best she could—she wondered just how many frying pans an Indian cook might need—she set aside the cooked ingredients and turned her attention to the meat. She boned a fresh chicken, putting the carcass in a sauce-pan with water to draw the stock, perhaps to make a soup for another day. Having cut the flesh into smaller pieces, she began to place them in a large cast-iron frying pan into which she had poured an oil called ghee, also purchased from the Singhs' shop. When the chicken was golden brown—and the smell of cooking had well and truly penetrated her flat—she began to blend the ingredients together, turning down the gas burner to a mere simmer.

"There," said Maisie. "That should do it." And she smiled, pleased with her efforts thus far.

Concentration on the task at hand had once again transported her to thoughts of leaving England. She would not be gone for long, perhaps a few months—six, at the outside. Or perhaps a year. That was a nice, rounded length of time; time enough to truly be a traveler and not a tourist. Some specific plans for that part of her journey were emerging; there was something she wanted to accomplish. And then Canada, perhaps. Certainly, when James described the broad, unforgiving landscapes, she was intrigued—but would that interest sustain her? As she stirred the simmering chicken, she realized, again, that it was James' love for her and hers for him that he imagined would sustain them both—but would it? She reached for a small pot of cream—she could not find the yoghurt specified in the recipe but thought this would do—and used a penny to twist off the lid and poured in half, sweeping it into the deep yellow mixture and enjoying the change in color and texture as it merged until there was a lighter golden hue, like morning sunshine bringing everything alive.

That's what they would be together. *Blended.* Not two, separate; but two, becoming more united with the years. And there was a comfort in the thought. Perhaps, like a complex dish, they could retain their separateness—leaning over the pan, she could still distinguish turmeric and cardamom—but be part of something else, something stronger together. Priscilla was probably right—she simply had to let go. She would not fall; she would not be left alone, grieving. She would not fail to be able to provide for herself— she was well provided for anyway. And she would not lose herself, because in truth, James loved who she was and he would not want to see her become less than the Maisie Dobbs to whom he had given his heart. But still, there was that niggle holding her back, the sense that this was a promise that would change everything.

"I could always be Mrs. Dobbs-Compton," said Maisie aloud. And she began to laugh. Never had anything sounded so preposterous.

"Hello! Anyone home?" James called out, having let himself into the flat—he had held a key since the early days of their courtship.

"Just a minute, I'm in the kitchen." Maisie turned the gas dial down a notch, took off her apron, and went to greet James.

"What on earth are you cooking? Your flat smells like a Delhi dining room."

"Good, that means I'm not doing too badly."

James enfolded her in his arms. "Even your hair smells of curry. What's for supper—as if I didn't know! I brought a bottle of wine, but now I think I might have been better bringing ale—doesn't curry taste better with beer?"

"I don't think it's too strong—I've tasted it, and Mrs. Singh, who owns the shop where I bought the seeds and spices, promised that it's a dish fit for a king—well, if you're a Mughal ruler."

"What's it called?"

Maisie shook her head. "Mughlai something-or-other. She gave me the basic recipe and most of the ingredients, though I had to make do with a substitute here and there."

"Well, it's certainly teasing my taste buds."

James poured wine for them both and lingered by the kitchen door while Maisie served the cooked chicken over a bed of saffron rice. "You're supposed to sort of mix it all together and use a different rice, but I liked the look of saffron, and I thought I'd just do it differently."

"Always your own way, Maisie." James raised an eyebrow, adding, "So, is this practice for going to the far-flung reaches of Kashmir, or something of that order?"

"Kashmir? Now, I hadn't thought of that—isn't that where they have lovely houses on the water? Houseboats, aren't they?"

"And problems with the locals, and spitting cobras, no clean water, and—"

"Have you been there, James?"

He shrugged. "No, but I would quite like to go."

She lifted the serving plate and nodded towards the door. "Supper is served, and if the maharajah doesn't want it dropped on the floor, he'd better move out of the way quickly, and sit down."

"Mmmm, this is very good, Maisie," said James, tucking into a mouthful. "I wonder if we can get the cook at Ebury Place to adopt this sort of recipe."

"I think that would be pushing it a bit. Think how much she had to stick her neck out to do that Pavlova—mind you, that was her idea, but I think it taxed her a bit."

James set down his fork, picked up his glass and raised it to Maisie. "This is lovely, Maisie. My favorite supper—anything you choose to put in front of me in this flat, just the two of us." He took her hand.

"Yes, it is lovely, isn't it?"

A silence descended upon them, and Maisie thought they were both probably thinking the same thing—would it be such a leap to marriage? Although it was more likely that James was probably wondering why she couldn't yet accept his proposal. And at that moment, she was wondering the same of herself.

"Will you stay here at the flat tomorrow evening, while I'm at the Otterburn party?"

"Yes, I believe I might. I've been thinking of asking Sandra if she would care to join me for supper. We may work in the same office, but we don't have time to talk about, well, how she's doing in that shared flat with the other girls, or her courses."

"Or if she's seeing anyone," added James.

Maisie sighed. "She's still in black, James."

"Yes, I know. But she will find someone, in time."

"I don't know. She might have an admirer or two."

"Good, she shouldn't wear those widow's weeds forever."

"Yes. That's right."

"I think I'll probably be seated next to the Otterburns' daughter, Elaine, tomorrow evening. Apparently, she and her fiancé ended their courtship a few months ago—John said that, thankfully, he hadn't spent much on the wedding, because Lorraine was in the early throes of going mad arranging everything. Now I think they believe I have the names of other eligible London bachelors in my address book, and can initiate introductions to Elaine—who, I might add, is probably quite a handful for whoever takes her on."

"Is she?"

"Well, independent, certainly—and such a good aviator, very much her father's daughter. But on the other hand, she's easygoing, likes to laugh and have fun. She lights up the room that one, but of course, she's twenty-one, perhaps twenty-two now, as far as I know, so her mother thinks she's on the shelf."

"Heavens, what does that make me?"

James laughed, then continued to talk about John Otterburn. It was when he spoke of Otterburn's friend Winston Churchill—the man whose beliefs and plans Otterburn was secretly supporting, by putting money into the design and testing of agile aircraft suited to combat in the air, rather than in the destruction of what lay below—that Maisie saw a deep respect and regard in his eyes, a loyalty and commitment that would take him across an ocean to be of service.

"Since Churchill's speech in August, about Germany's rearmament, John has been like a man possessed," said James. "Elaine and Johnny—his son—will also be flying in Canada, so heaven knows when he thinks he will be able to find a suitor for his daughter. But that's by the by. In the meantime, I think no one could be blamed for being worried about Germany."

"I know. I've seen things in the papers I never imagined I might see. So I know why you have to go—you don't have to persuade me, James. I do understand. What was it Churchill said? That there was grave reason to believe Germany was seeking to arm herself, despite the treaties signed in Paris."

"Oh, he's got Ramsay MacDonald's number. This government has put forward ideas about allowing Germany to be on a par with France, in terms of armament—and they've been encouraged by our friends across the Atlantic, too. But Britain has to be as strong as possible—as he said, and I swear, I believe this will go down in history, 'Britain's hour of weakness is Europe's hour of danger.'"

Maisie reached for James' hand. "That's why I understand why you have to go to Canada, James. Truly I do."

James nodded. "Yes, I know." He paused. "But you do know, India's not looking much like a picnic at the moment."

"I may not go to India. Who knows, we may be trying Polynesian dishes next."

"Give me a chance to digest this one, eh?"

Later, with James sleeping soundly beside, her, Maisie looked out at the night, though no stars could be seen through a thick blanket of low cloud. Foghorns blasted along the river, starting loud, then echoing into the distance. *Where will I be by Christmas?* And the fact that she could not answer both thrilled and scared her at the same time. She would be leaving not a place that she disliked or people she could stand no longer, but instead she would be—perhaps for a short sojourn, perhaps for longer—leaving everything she loved most. She thought of all those in the world who were moving beyond the boundaries of their everyday lives, and upon whom the stars stood sentinel each night. There were the many Jews leaving Germany, bound for a new life in Palestine—some sixty thousand over the next six years, according to newspaper reports of the recent Haavara Agreement. A world away from the streets of Munich or Hamburg or Berlin; families were trying to find a place for themselves in a barren desert. And look at the people who had teemed into her own country. Gypsies from Bohemia, who had brought color with their flouncing skirts and stuttering language. Maltese grocers and purveyors of Italian coffee. There had been Indian sailors—lascars—who had remained in Britain when their ships docked, many to marry Englishwomen and merge into life on the streets of London. And there was Usha Pramal and Maya Patel, women who had come to another land with trusted employers, only to find themselves cast out. People leaving home with hope in their hearts. That's what she clutched, a hope in her heart that "abroad"—a place in itself—might be the final step in bringing her home to herself. It was only then, she knew, that she could stand alongside another, could perhaps consider and accept James' proposal and be his helpmeet, wife, and lover, for life.

She remained awake for some time, consideration of the case in hand merging with thoughts about what life might hold. She could almost hear Priscilla offering advice. "You know, the trouble with you, Maisie, is that you think too much." But there was one element in all this that Maisie knew Priscilla would light upon and chew over, and that was the small, almost inconsequential mention of a certain Elaine Otterburn, who would be seated next to James the following evening, at a supper given by her parents. Yes, Priscilla would not like that at all, and Maisie could almost hear her saying, "Never mind convention—you tell James immediately that you've decided you'd love to come to supper, and perhaps Mrs. Otterburn could make a last-minute seating arrangement. I'd keep Miss Elaine Otterburn well away from James, Maisie." And on this occasion, as if Priscilla had actually been in the room admonishing her, Maisie thought her friend could be right.

Chapter Twelve

It was at breakfast that Maisie asked James if it wouldn't be too much trouble for her to come along to supper at the Otterburns' that evening after all.

"Oh, that's wonderful, darling—thank you for changing your mind. I'll have my secretary call the Otterburns; I am sure they will be thrilled you're able to come." James leaned forward and kissed Maisie on the cheek. He sat back. "But how are you feeling about John Otterburn?"

"The same, James, but I also appreciate that he is part of your plans for the future—in fact, that he is directing your plans for the future, so I should perhaps not be so, well, dismissive of his importance in your life. I can't bring myself to hold him in any regard, though."

"Fair enough, Maisie. But there are many men—and women—who do things in a time of war that they wouldn't dream of doing in peacetime, and all for the common good."

Maisie looked at James, and for a second she knew she would remember his words forever, along with her reply.

"But, James, we're not at war, and this is supposed to be a time of peace."

And with that, she wondered how she would ever get through the evening, and was already half-regretting her decision.

Once again Maisie drove in the direction of Camberwell, in good time to be at the School of Arts and Crafts to see Harry Ashley during his tutorial hours—she hoped he would be in his office, and with some luck there would be only a short queue of students waiting to see him, paint-splashed or with dried clay under their fingernails.

The morning was fine, with sunshine pressing through a dense morning mist, and just a nip in the air to remind London that winter would draw in on that mistress of disguise, the Indian summer, soon enough. She parked the MG close to the college and neighboring gallery, its design typical of so many public buildings constructed during the reign of Queen Victoria, when a certain bold grandeur proclaimed the wealth of Britain at the center of a burgeoning Empire. Above the ground streets had been torn up to provide an architectural legacy intended to stand for hundreds of years, testament to a golden age, while in the subterranean depths of London, fetid rivers had been pushed underground and now formed part of a labyrinthine sewer system designed by a civil engineer, Joseph Bazalgette, to last several lifetimes.

Maisie made her inquiry at the main porters' desk, and was directed to a corridor of rooms on an upper floor. Stepping along the hallways and up the stairs brought back memories of a past case in which she took on the guise of a college lecturer. Being deprived of the schooling she so loved at twelve—and all of her classmates then had left the dour black school buildings at the age of twelve—had doubled her hunger for learning. Now she'd had that education, and had even taught in a college—but she always felt something of an excitement to be among students.

The door was slightly ajar as she approached, so she could already see Harry Ashley. He was a man in his early forties, wearing dark gray corduroy trousers, a gray shirt, and a sleeveless woolen pullover in a Fair Isle pattern. He wore scuffed leather brogues, and on his desk, Maisie could see a pile of fabrics, some pieces of pottery, and a collection of books and papers. He was poring over a handwritten note.

"Mr. Ashley?"

As he turned, Maisie saw the livid scar along his jawline, a line following bone that had, at one point, been reconstructed.

"Yes?"

Maisie smiled. "May I speak to you for a few minutes? My name is Maisie Dobbs." She extended her hand, and it seemed that he looked at it for a second before reaching forward with his own. "I am working on behalf of Mr. Pramal, the brother of Miss Usha Pramal."

"Miss Pramal? Usha? Is she all right?"

Maisie looked at the man, at his eyes, in particular. Was he genuinely inquiring about Usha Pramal? Or was it a feigned surprise, meant to deflect her inquiry?

"May I sit down?" asked Maisie.

"Oh, yes—yes, of course. I'm so sorry, forgetting my manners." He pulled a pile of papers from a chair and brushed across the seat with his left hand—which Maisie noticed was claw-like, though he could, she noticed, wield a pencil with some dexterity.

"So, is Usha all right? I haven't seen her in a long time."

"Mr. Ashley, I am afraid I must inform you that Miss Pramal is dead. In fact, she was murdered."

Ashley looked at her without speaking, as if he had watched every word form in letters and leave her mouth. Maisie could see that for the teacher, time had been suspended, and her words seemed to linger in the air above them. *Miss Pramal is dead. In fact, she was murdered.*

"Mr. Ashley?"

Ashley started, jolting himself into the present. "I'm so sorry, Miss . . . Miss . . ."

"Dobbs. Maisie Dobbs. And it is I who must apologize—I thought you would have known."

He scraped back the chair and walked the three steps his small cluttered room allowed, and then back again. Maisie noticed he walked with a slight limp. He ran his fingers—his good fingers, from his right hand—through his hair, and then sat down again.

"I . . . I am shocked. I had no idea." He rubbed his chin, his thumb worrying the scar back and forth. "Mind you, there's no reason why I would know. I haven't seen anyone who knows Usha for ages, so why would I be told? Was it in the newspapers?"

"Yes, but not in such a way as to catch the eye readily."

He shook his head again. "Don't read them anyway, if I can help it. And I'm in my studio much of the time, or at home—I'm in digs near Russell Square."

Maisie nodded. "So you come out by bus every day?"

He shook his head. "Not every day. I only lecture a couple of days a week here, and I also teach privately—mainly using oils. Here I teach a course that's sort of a mix of anthropology and art, so we do a lot with textiles, and with pottery, looking at rock art, that sort of thing. There is an emphasis on craft here and Usha assisted me with a couple of lectures for the embroiderers, though other arts students came along, because it was all about color and how they could be blended, what they mean in different cultures, that sort of thing." Ashley had been folding and unfolding a piece of paper as he spoke. Now he paused, crumpled the paper, and looked at Maisie. "How did it happen? Who killed her and how did it happen?"

"It was very quick, I would imagine, Mr. Ashley. She was shot." Maisie touched the place in the middle of her forehead where, if she had been an Indian woman, a bindi would have been smudged in red.

"Oh, God, what— I mean . . . who would have done that to such a sweet girl?"

"That's what I am trying to find out. I thought you might be able to help me."

"Me? I hardly knew her, Miss Dobbs."

"But she helped you here."

He nodded. "Yes. She brought along some lovely examples of the sari—her Indian friends helped and gave her some to help illustrate my lecture."

"But how did you know her, Mr. Ashley?"

"I was introduced by a friend—well, I say 'friend,' but more of an acquaintance, really—who said she would be a good person to talk to about the sari."

"I see—who was your friend?"

"Oh, he lives not that far from here, near Addington Square. Colin Griffith—or I should say, Reverend Griffith."

"Oh, yes."

"Have you met him?"

"I have, indeed," said Maisie. "He was introduced to me by Mr. and Mrs. Paige—not in person, but they owned the house where Miss Pramal lodged, on Addington Square."

"Very good chap, and thought highly of Usha, I must say."

Maisie allowed a silence to linger for just a second more than was necessary, and watched as Ashley fidgeted, then scratched the back of his wounded hand with the fingers of the other. As he did so, Maisie noticed a bracelet formed of some sort of cord had slipped forward on his wrist.

"That's an unusual bracelet—forgive me for mentioning it, but I have never seen anything like it before." Maisie leaned forward.

"Oh this?" said Ashley. "Yes, I suppose it is unusual." He extended his wrist towards Maisie, so she could better see the knots on either side, and how the bracelet could be adjusted to a smaller or larger size. "It's made of elephant hair. Apparently, they were originally made in Africa, but this one came from India."

"Well, I never," said Maisie with a feigned enthusiasm, though she was not really taken with the piece. "Where did you get it?"

"Oh, this came from Griffith. He was in Africa— just after the war, I think—then went to India. He knew how to construct these things, and with the right hair, he made a few of them himself, and gave me one because I'd helped him out, running an art class for his Sunday school children. I rather liked it—never been anywhere that exotic myself—" He blushed. "Unless of course you count the Dardanelles. So it seemed rather fascinating to me."

"That is interesting. Perhaps that's why Reverend Griffith liked Miss Pramal's company—she helped with Sunday school, too, I believe—it probably reminded him of India." Maisie smiled. "I wonder when he was there—do you know?"

Ashley shrugged. "Gosh, from what he's told me, I would say about eleven or twelve years ago. He was only in Africa for a year, as far as I know, then had a couple of years back here in England before trundling off to India. I don't think he was doing missionary work there, though. No, I think he was a civil servant or something like that—he's talked about the work being really tedious, and how much he hated the humidity, and that he would rather have remained in East Africa. I think that's why he left, actually."

"And how did you meet him, if I may ask?"

Ashley sighed. "I was . . . I was still in hospital for a few years after the war. Nothing seemed to work. My leg was gammy, my hand was gammy, and my mind wasn't up to snuff, all that sort of thing. He'd just returned from Africa and was a volunteer visitor to the hospital—in Richmond, on the hill there, above the river."

Maisie felt a shiver, felt the room move slightly out of kilter. Was it just for a mere feather's weight of time, or did Ashley notice?

"Do you know where I mean, Miss Dobbs?"

Maisie smiled; it was a quick smile, a smile of acknowledgment. Ashley nodded, as if understanding.

"You know it. I can see that."

"Yes, I do. I've been there, as a visitor," said Maisie.

"I thought you had, the way you looked when I mentioned it." He paused. "I'm so sorry."

"Yes. Thank you. And so am I. For you. That you were there."

"That we were all there, Miss Dobbs. I'm sorry that we were all there."

"Did you know a man named—?"

Ashley stopped her. "Don't ask. It's gone. Past. Please don't ask, because I don't want to remember."

"Yes, of course. It's best, isn't it? We struggle to get so far along the path, don't we?"

He nodded and smiled. "And we're so easily dragged back again. Anyway, I first met Colin Griffith there, where he was working as an orderly—I believe he had been a conscientious objector in the war, not that I have any issue with that. I think by the time the fighting was over, a fair number of people had a lot more time for those who'd put their foot down about the war. Anyway, I think Griffith must have gone to Africa not long after the Armistice. I didn't meet him again until this past year, and I don't know him that well, as I said."

Maisie asked a few more questions, and learned that, following the introduction by Griffith, Usha Pramal had met with Ashley just once before the two lectures, and never saw her again afterwards. It was as Maisie was leaving that Ashley added a personal reflection.

"She had an aura about her, Miss Pramal. It was as if . . . as if she was powerful and strong, and she knew it. But not in an overtly pushy way. She just knew she had something that others didn't—a sort of self-possession." He paused, sighing, then went on. "I don't know how you do your job, or what knowledge makes a difference, but there are people who don't like that presence, especially in a woman."

Maisie waited, for she felt he had more to say.

"I know this sounds as if I'm a cranky art teacher—and you know, perhaps I am. Perhaps that's why I came back to art, after the war—it's a license to be a bit strange, after all; I sometimes think people expect it, so the fact that I am different doesn't matter. And I've felt different, ever since the war." He rubbed his damaged hand. "But the thing is, in all my experience as an artist, I have found that there are people who want to destroy beauty. Is that because it's beyond them? Is it because beauty represents something they cannot have, or is not inside them? I have seen children destroy flowers growing alongside the canal. Of course, you can say, 'That's just children for you.' But I don't believe it at all—I believe there is some pain, something untoward in certain people—certain communities, even—perhaps it's anger, a sense of dis-possession or disenfranchisement, and they have to destroy that which brings joy, and love."

Maisie nodded. "I think you're right—but do you think that someone might have taken the life of Miss Pramal for this reason?"

He scratched his head with the curled fingers of his lame hand. "I hate to say it, but I think so. Yes, I think so, from what I have observed of the destructive nature of man. Perhaps there is nothing more unattainable than the beautiful outsider, so perhaps someone, some-where, wanted to end a sense of their own ugliness by taking the life of the beautiful thing that gave weight to those feelings." He shrugged. "It's just all so very sad." He looked up at Maisie. "I don't know how you do your job, truly."

She looked at Ashley, into his eyes. "Sometimes I don't know either. But at the end of the day, I do my job so that people like Usha Pramal have a voice. I cannot bring back their beauty to this world—and even the most ragged soul was once beautiful, Mr. Ashley. But I can stand up and find out the truth. Sometimes I'm successful and sometimes not. But I do my best."

He nodded again. "I take my hat off to you, Miss Dobbs. Every time I see art desecrated, I want to strangle the person who did it."

Maisie smiled. "Oh, I sometimes feel like that, too. But I also know that inside the perpetrator of a crime, inside the destroyer, there is often a work of art that has also been ravaged."

She bid good-bye to the art teacher, who stood at the threshold of his office, his hands in his pockets, his head bowed. And she knew she had just met another person whose heart had been touched by Usha Pramal.

But who had taken her life? With each interview, with each new nugget of information, and as her knowledge of the woman and her life took shape, she felt that Truth was playing games with her, as if she were being led through a forest by a sprite who sped in and out of trees saying, "Over here." And behind each tree, under each leaf, there was just a little more to go on, but nothing that pointed to a killer.

As she walked to her motor car, the mist having lifted and the sun breaking through white clouds puffed with gray, she wondered again if Ashley had ever seen Simon at the convalescent home in Richmond—Simon, the young army doctor wounded alongside Maisie when the casualty clearing station in which they struggled to save lives torn apart by war came under enemy attack. He had been her first and most special love, yet he had lingered for years in a netherworld of existence, brain injured and shell-shocked, before finally succumbing to his wounds. She had struggled to put memories of their love and the terror of that war behind her, and now she wondered if this man before her, himself battling wounds long after the war had officially ended, had ever walked past Simon's wheelchair placed in the conservatory. Had he perhaps sat alongside him, close to the window where leaves of so many green and luscious plants were reflected in his blank, unseeing eyes, their shimmering almost creating the myth that there was movement somewhere in his mind? And she wondered if, in going away, in leaving this country, she would expunge that final vapor of the dragon's breath. Oh yes, the dragon. Priscilla had described their memories of war as being like a dragon that lived deep inside. The dragon had to be kept quiet, had to be mollified; otherwise he could breathe fire into the most ordinary of days. If a journey overseas could slay that dragon once and for all, she could not wait to be on her way.

She would go to see the Reverend Griffith again now, and return to the street where children played hopscotch and cricket on cobblestones in threadbare shoes cut down from old footwear meant for adults. And she would draw up the list of people she still wanted to see, and those to whom she would pay another visit. There were more statements to collate, more information to add to the case map. She had met many men in the police force who maintained that the killer is present early in an investigation, that in the hours after a murder, the name of the man or woman who took the life of another is there written among the names of so many suspects. There was some truth in that assertion—Caldwell always said that you should keep your eye on the person who found the body—but on the other hand, though the link might be there, the chain could lead anywhere; it could be far away or hidden in the shadows. A group of boys found Usha Pramal, and two young dock-workers discovered the body of Maya Patel. And as Priscilla often told her, pinning down boys was a bit like herding cats.

"Miss Dobbs! A pleasure to see you once again—have you good news regarding your investigation? Will someone be brought to justice for taking the life of dear Usha?"

Maisie thought the greeting was just a little too effu-sive, though Reverend Griffith, she realized, always seemed to be on tiptoe, enthusiastic to a fault—which, considering the competition for congregation in the area, was hardly surprising. Only a small percentage of the community attended church, and she'd already seen quite a few places of worship vying for their allegiance.

"Just a couple more questions, if you don't mind—have you a moment?"

Griffith led her into his sitting room cum study, where, once again, it appeared he was struggling to compose a sermon, evidenced by the many crumpled pieces of paper in and around a wastepaper basket.

"I see you looking at the fruits of my labors this morning, Miss Dobbs. Let me assure you, I waste not, want not and each discarded sheet has seen both sides penned from margin to margin. To be honest, I write the sermon, but in most cases, I say what's on my mind anyway. I might as well not struggle and just allow the muse to inspire me on the day, but sermon preparation is part of a vicar's life, and if the bishop thought I'd ad-libbed my way through the Sunday service hoping for a gentle whisper in my ear from the likes of Polyhymnia, that dear goddess of the sacred word, he would be appalled. And I might be in terrible trouble."

Griffith held out his hand toward a chair; Maisie took her seat, followed by the vicar, who relaxed back into his chair.

"I've been having a word with Harry Ashley. I'd heard that Miss Pramal had helped him with a lecture on color and texture, so I thought he might know her. He said you had suggested he speak to her."

"Yes, that's right. I know Harry from his time in convalescence, as he's probably told you."

Maisie nodded. "Reverend Griffith, I believe that, having returned from Africa, you went on to work in India for several years."

He nodded. "Did I not tell you that? I'm sorry. Perhaps I said that I was a missionary only in Africa. Besides, I wasn't in India that long, a matter of just a few years. And don't mind my telling you, I didn't like it at all. I suppose I was spoiled by Africa—I loved my first missionary work in British East Africa, so taking on the job of a government scribe in India probably wasn't a very good decision."

"I suppose you didn't come across the Pramal family while you were there."

Griffith laughed. "Oh, come now, Miss Dobbs. That would be like a visitor to London asking if you happen to know their cousin who lives in Shetland—not very likely, is it?"

"I see your point," said Maisie.

"It's a common error, though, among those who haven't wandered beyond this sceptered isle."

Maisie blushed, feeling the criticism inherent in his comment. She was not beyond a retort of her own. "Do you think your experience of India, limited though it was to the civil service, contributed to your understanding of Miss Pramal?"

"My true calling has given me a certain understanding and tolerance that others might not have, and it was clear that Miss Pramal was an intelligent woman. I thought there might be some talk among the parents regarding her work with the children at Sunday school, but I was surprised—the children were enchanted with her and she knew her Scripture, so there were no complaints." He paused and leaned forward towards Maisie, his elbows resting on his knees. "Look, I know you are turning over every leaf, stone, pebble, and fluttering piece of paper left on the ground in your quest to find the killer of Usha Pramal, but I really don't think I can help you, Miss Dobbs. If you find yourself at a dead end, then that is perhaps because there is nothing here. I have struggled to find a reason for the death of such a lovely creature on God's earth, and have come to the conclusion that the person might be long gone, that it was likely random."

"And her friend, Miss Patel?"

He scratched his head. "Oh yes, I had forgotten about that. Well, in any case, I really can't help you—I wish I could offer you more."

It was as he lifted his hand to his head that Maisie saw the black woven bracelet on his wrist.

"Oh, you have an elephant hair bracelet."

"This? Yes, I made it myself—in fact, once I learned, I made quite a few. This one is from an Indian elephant, though—"

"These bracelets are usually from Africa, aren't they?"

"That's right. To the African people, the elephant is a sort of link between heaven and earth—the knots represent different things, and one like this has two knots, for the bond between earth and nature. If I was wearing this on my right hand, you'd have to be worried, because it would mean I had killed the elephant myself. In any case, it is said that wearing the bracelet protects the wearer from all manner of ills."

Maisie nodded. "Why do you wear it? As a man of the cloth, do you not feel protected?"

He smiled. "As a man of the cloth here, in this place, I am always thinking of ways in which to be of service to my parishioners, especially the younger ones—to be honest with you, anything to steer them away from trouble. In places of want, there's always a criminal element ready to prey on the young. So, I do my part to keep them busy, especially boys who are coming up to working age; eleven, twelve, thirteen."

"And how do the bracelets play a part?"

"I give each boy one of these—so they're in my gang, if you like. Gangs offer the change of belonging to something, and I just want to make sure it's the right sort of gang."

"What do you do?"

"First, what I don't do—I don't ram the Bible down their throats, but I can teach in all sorts of ways. I've taken boys out to the country, to fish—then I can slide in a story about Christ and the fisherman. I have taken them across the river—some have never been to see Buckingham Palace, or the Changing of the Guard. That's a perfect place to introduce the story of the eye of the needle. And I set them up with games—there's that land that edges down to the canal, so I've taught them how to build a fire without matches or paper, and how to build a camp. The self-sufficiency gives them confidence, helps them to see beyond the boundaries of their lives here, on the streets. We can talk about Jesus and his disciples, and the bonds between friends."

"And you all have these bracelets."

He shrugged. "Better than all having a weapon, isn't it, Miss Dobbs? Or a prison record in common to show allegiance."

"Yes, of course. However, I wonder, do you meet on the same day each week? Or is it a monthly arrangement?"

"The boys' club meets on the first Wednesday of the month, in the church hall at seven o'clock in the evening."

"And do the same boys come along each time?"

"Generally, though some drop in and out, dependent upon whether they're needed at home. Most of the mothers like it, but some of the fathers tend to tease the lads—a bit of jealousy, perhaps. We plan our adventures throughout the month at the Wednesday meeting."

"Have you seen anyone new in the past few months, someone not from this area?"

"I try not to ask too many questions, Miss Dobbs. The parents in these parts are suspicious of questions, and so are the children. I've noticed newcomers from outside the area, but I just get on with welcoming them to the fold."

Maisie looked at Griffith's hands again, and considered the rough skin on his right hand. "Do you shoot, Reverend Griffith?"

"That's not a question a vicar has to answer every day of the week, and I do hope you aren't suggesting I took the life of Miss Pramal."

Maisie shook her head. "I'm just interested, if you don't mind."

"Actually, I do. But not living things, not God's creatures, bright and beautiful, great and small. I confess that, when I was in Africa, I accompanied some acquaintances on a safari, and what I saw sickened me. But I am not against shooting lumps of clay flying through the air, and I have discovered that, given the chance, my boys rather like it, too—it gets rid of the frustrations of being a young boy in a man's world of work in the factories, the docks, the market, or down the sewers."

"You allow the boys to shoot?"

"All very organized, in fact, I approached some local businessmen—the wealthier ones, not the greengrocers and suchlike—and asked for their help. They're men who engage in that sort of recreation, and one by one I tugged on their conscience, so that once a year I organize a charabanc down to Surrey where the boys can have some fun and learn clay pigeon shooting."

"I thought there were shooting schools in London," said Maisie.

"Yes, there are, and shooting of clay targets has been popular for years—you may remember the first open shooting championship was held in London about six years ago. But not for lads from this part of the world, I'm afraid. And it does them the power of good to get away from their home turf, if only for a day."

"Were any of them a good shot?"

Griffith shook his head. "That's a bit transparent, Miss Dobbs. Why not ask if I thought any of them could have killed Miss Pramal, if only they'd have had the weapon and the ammo?" He sighed. "To tell you the truth, they were all over the place, shots going everywhere but at the target. There were a couple who showed talent, who had a good eye."

"Do they enjoy it?"

"For the most part they see it as a lark and a chance to let off steam."

"I won't keep you any longer, Reverend Griffith. I would like to ask you one question, though—what kind of shot are you?"

"Sadly, Miss Dobbs, I am an excellent shot. I have no idea where the talent came from, for I do not practice in any way, but I always hit my target spot-on—and even with a Webley. Pity the same could not be said for my sermons."

Maisie smiled and held out her hand, wondering whether to ask just one more question, one she felt would nip at her if she didn't.

"I'll leave you in peace then. And best of luck with your sermon." As she shook his hand, she noticed that his clerical collar seemed just a little askew. "I must ask, however—how on earth did you know that Usha Pramal was killed with a Webley?"

"After the boys discovered her body, I thought it would be wise to have the entire club in here, to talk about matters of life and death—perhaps try to circumvent the nightmares that would inevitably follow finding the body, and the tales that would be told time and again among the lads. I encouraged them to talk about it, about what they had seen and so on, and one of them mentioned that it was probably a Webley. I don't know where he got the information, but he seemed knowledgeable. I suspected he had overheard the police."

"Which one was it?"

Griffith stared out at the garden as if he regretted the ungoverned comment, then turned to Maisie. "I'm sorry, but I really don't remember."

Chapter Thirteen

M aisie thought she might be able to take a guess at the name of the boy who had identified the gun that killed Usha Pramal and Maya Patel. And it wasn't one of the local boys she had in mind. Instead of making her way back to Fitzroy Square, she stopped at a telephone kiosk and placed a call to the office to inform Sandra that she would not be in until after lunch, as she had changed her plans and was going directly to Scotland Yard.

"Oh, just as well you telephoned, Miss Dobbs. Detective Inspector Caldwell called this morning, with some news. Apparently, that lad—the one who found the body of Maya Patel—has absconded. They couldn't hold him anyway because he hadn't done anything, but as you know, he was in new lodgings. Now he's gone."

"Just as I was going over to get permission to see him."

"He's important, isn't he?"

"And not only because he found Maya Patel. I'm very anxious to see him."

"Miss," said Sandra, "I hope you don't mind me saying this, but I think it might be an idea to go into Miss Patel's room again. I don't think she was killed because she was an Indian woman, though it might seem like that. I reckon she knew who the killer was— and that was why she wanted to talk to you."

Maisie nodded, pushing the door of the telephone kiosk ajar—she always felt trapped in such small places. "Yes, you're right, Sandra. Here's an idea: Leave as soon as you can and take the Underground to the Elephant and Castle Station. I'll collect you and then we'll go back to Addington Square and see if we can view Maya Patel's room together—another pair of eyes might see something I've missed. What do you think?"

"Just one moment, Miss. Would you hold the line?"

Maisie frowned. Why did Sandra want her to hold the line? Her question was soon answered.

" 'Lo, Miss."

"Billy! Billy, what are you doing at work? You should be at home, digging your garden or playing with your boys."

"I had to come into the City this morning. But what I thought was that if you want, I could look for that boy—the one who found Miss Patel. I've got a few hours to spare, so I could ask some questions, have a sniff around."

"The police have already done that, Billy—and I think you should go home."

"I'm a bit bored, Miss. And it's only one afternoon, ain't it?"

Maisie sighed. "Billy, I have to put my foot down. I am concerned for your health and I want you to get well. I know you want to help and I know you have a good idea, but you must go home."

"All right. I'll go home and dig the garden."

"It'll do you good. Now, I must speak to Sandra again."

As the receiver was passed between the two, Maisie heard Billy mutter something and Sandra giggled.

"I'll see you at the station, Sandra. Make sure you have a bite to eat before we leave, won't you?"

"Oh, Billy brought in some sandwiches, and we're just finishing them with a cup of tea before he goes off again."

"Right you are. Half an hour."

Maisie smiled, a brief smile, as if Sandra could see her. But she didn't feel very much like smiling. She felt like a child who was being instructed by her teacher to sit on her hands to stop her fidgeting, and she knew she was fidgeting because she wanted to stop whatever was going on between Billy and Sandra—which might be nothing, of course. On the other hand, it could be something. And she had no right in the world to interfere.

Built in 1890, the Elephant and Castle Station was a grand Arts and Crafts–style structure designed by Leslie Green, who had been the architect of so many London Underground stations. Sandra emerged from the terra-cotta and white building and ran towards Maisie's MG, taking her place in the passenger seat. They were soon on their way along Walworth Road towards Addington Square.

"I hope there's someone home when we get there," said Sandra. "Those remaining Indian women are all somewhere else now, aren't they?"

"It's a chance we have to take, though Mrs. Paige doesn't look like someone who goes out visiting much, unless it's to church, or to a women's meeting." Maisie paused as she changed gear to turn a corner. "And speaking of women's meetings, how are you getting on with your society?"

"Once a week, Miss Dobbs. We're working hard to get equal pensions for women. And next week we're going to a lecture by Ellen Wilkinson."

"Red Ellen? She lost her parliamentary seat a couple of years ago, didn't she?"

"Oh, she'll be back. I'm positive about it. Anyway, I'm looking forward to hearing what she has to say."

"That'll be something to remember, Sandra—she's a firebrand. I like her."

Maisie could see that Sandra was a little more relaxed in the MG now, more used to being in a motor car.

"I bet it was nice to see Billy again today. The office is probably quite quiet when I'm not there," said Maisie.

"Oh, there's always a lot to get on with, and as soon as we're back I've to go over to Mr. Partridge—luckily, he's seeing his publisher again today, so he doesn't need me until about three."

"I'll drop you at his office, if you like." Maisie paused again. "Do you think Billy looked well?"

"I thought he looked better, Miss. Not completely well. But better."

"It's probably lovely for the family to be together a bit more. I bet Doreen is grateful to have him at home." Maisie felt the clumsiness in her words.

Sandra looked out of the passenger window. "Hmmm."

"Do you not think so, Sandra?"

"It's not for me to say."

"Not for you to say what? Come on, you can tell me what's on your mind."

Sandra turned to face Maisie, who was keeping her eyes on the road. "I think she's a weak woman. I know all about them losing their little girl, and no one can tell someone how to get over that sort of thing, but I know what it's like to lose someone, too—and so do you, Miss. But you don't drag everyone else down with you, not to my mind. And that's what she's doing to Billy. I think she should pull her socks up."

Maisie cleared her throat, now wishing she'd kept a lid on this particular Pandora's box. "Sandra, I think you have a point, but at the same time, I have worked with people who have psychiatric illnesses, and it's not always as clear cut as that. You and I have been fortunate, we have been able—to a point—to get on with things. We know that you throw your line out to a rock somewhere, and pull yourself through the oncoming tide to the next landing place. Someone suffering as Doreen has doesn't have the strength to do that, so she can only thrash around in the current, trying to get to the rock."

"But she's taking Billy down. If you look at it like that, Miss, she's got her hands around his neck and she's pulling him down while he's swimming for both of them—and look at him." Sandra folded her hands in her lap, her color heightened by the strength of her words.

"Sandra," said Maisie. "Perhaps you've become a little too close to Billy—to his problems—so you can see only what's happening to him, rather than how they are coping as a couple. They've had some very difficult times, but they will come through it, if given the chance. He could not leave Doreen, ever. He's too good a person. So they will make their way together. And soon, I believe, things will get much better for them. It's hard for people to leave everything they love, you know, and Billy loves his family very, very much."

Maisie slowed the MG, and parked by the side of the road, knowing Sandra's eyes had filled with tears.

"Oh, Miss . . ." Sandra began to weep almost as soon as Maisie put her arms around her. "I've made a fool of myself, making up to a married man, and me a widow. I thought I was doing well, you know, I thought I was getting over it all, what with my college and these new friends I've made. But I realized—" She choked as she took a handkerchief from Maisie. "I realized I was becoming a different person. If Eric was here, he wouldn't know me. He would wonder who I was. And I do miss him. I miss us coming home to each other, being there, and then knowing, when he went down to work in the morning, that we would come home to each other again. Now I have all this coming and going, and learning, and working, and it's all very well, but there's no being with someone at the end of the day. Someone to talk to, to have your tea with, to go out to the picture house with or to walk out with. There's all the others, but not the one. And having that one is special. That's what I think." She wiped tears from her eyes. "And when my Eric died, when I heard him calling and I ran down the street to hold his hand as he was bleeding to death, I knew it wasn't the pain in his body that was hurting most. No, it was because he was leaving me and he was trying to hold on to me. I know he really loved me. He really did."

"I know, Sandra. You were made for each other, anyone could see that. But think of it like this, that he is never far, in your heart. I know those words are thin, but you have been such an honor to his memory, and he loved you so much he wouldn't want you to turn back. You can't, Sandra. Just think of how proud he would be, how much he would love you for everything you're doing—even going to see Red Ellen."

Sandra laughed through her tears. "Oh yes, we'd have a giggle about that, a right bellyacher."

"And let's let Doreen and Billy get through this together, just the two of them, if we can."

Maisie slipped the idling motor car into gear again, and pulled out into traffic.

"You're a fine one to talk, Miss. The reason Billy came up to town was because he'd been asked to see someone at the Compton Corporation, in the City. They've offered him a job. Not starting yet, apparently, but in November, when they've had some work done on the offices and some other sorting out. It's to do with office security, from people using the telephones to keeping an eye on who comes in and out. They said it's a new position, and he'd come highly recommended."

"Did he say he'd take the job?"

Sandra nodded. "He said he'd hate to leave you, leave the business—he thinks a lot of you, Miss, says that without you, he'd be nothing—but on the other hand, it's regular hours, no evenings, no Saturday afternoons or Sundays. He said Doreen would like it."

"I confess, I recommended him for a position, but I didn't know the fine details. I'm sure he'll tell me all about it. It'll be a good job for him—and you'll see, everything will calm down in the family, once they have a regular routine."

"Leave in the morning, and come home to the ones you love at night," added Sandra as they parked outside the Paiges' house in Addington Square. "It's what keeps people going, that."

Mrs. Paige sighed when she saw it was Maisie at the door.

"I really don't know what I can do for you, Miss Dobbs. This business has cast a dreadful pall on Mr. Paige and me, and we were only trying to do good—and now these terrible deaths have started our neighbors talking, and I don't know what it's all coming to."

"I know, Mrs. Paige. It must be very difficult for you. But may we come in? This is my assistant, Mrs. Tapley—she sometimes comes with me to see people, if that's all right with you."

"You might as well come into the parlor."

Mrs. Paige led the way into the small room, and they were soon seated.

"I'm interested in Miss Maya Patel, and wanted to ask some more questions. You've said that they were very friendly, she and Miss Pramal, but I was wondering if you ever noticed anything, well, amiss, in the friendship." Mrs. Paige seemed confused, the creases between her eyebrows deepening as she listened, so Maisie continued. "For example, you told me that Miss Pramal was a very ebullient person, always smiling, one for whom each day was a reason to smile. Was Miss Patel the same, and if not, what do you think she thought of Miss Pramal?"

"I see what you mean," said Mrs. Paige. She cleared her throat and began to gather the fabric of her dress into a concertina at her knee—making tiny pleats with her busy fingers, then pressing the material flat and gathering it again. "I will say this—and I might have mentioned it before—but I think Maya Patel was in thrall to Miss Pramal. It was as if she were some sort of handmaiden, that's what I thought when I saw them walk down the road together, to church, say. I think they knew a lot about each other—just like most women, they talked, and they must have spoken about personal matters. They become quite close, our ladies here. I can only imagine that the ones the police have put up in other lodgings must want to come back, because this is their home, isn't it?"

Maisie thought that while the house wasn't exactly like home, it was likely something of a comforting refuge for women who had been cast out by their employers.

Sandra cleared her throat, as if gathering courage to speak; it was a habit Maisie had noticed and thought might diminish as she gained confidence. She imagined her waiting until the last minute to ask a question following a lecture at college.

"Mrs. Paige, had you noticed any change in the women in the days before Miss Pramal was murdered? Did one or both of them seem more, well, morose? Unhappy? Or even sunnier than usual?"

"I didn't see them as much as you might think, Mrs. Tapley. The women went out in the morning, to work; they came back in the evening or the afternoon—if they were in early, the time was their own. They had jobs around the house here, and at night we had our supper and some Bible study—and I'm a busy woman, I can't go looking at the women, wondering what they're thinking." She began pleating the fabric of her dress again. "But I remember saying to Mr. Paige—must have been a month before Miss Pramal died—that she didn't seem very happy, and we put it down to one of her jobs. And as for Miss Patel, she hadn't been herself since the murder, which is understandable."

"Could you tell us about the job that you think caused Miss Pramal's unhappiness?" said Maisie.

"We put an advertisement in the paper every now and again, so we have cleaning and household jobs lined up for the women, and there was an inquiry from a housekeeper over in St. John's Wood, needing a bit of extra help for a short period of time—it was for spring cleaning, not last year, but the year before. Miss Pramal went over there, and I don't think she liked it much. I put it down to the journey, but on the other hand, our women can't expect to get their jobs around the corner. All the same, she stayed on there for a good while—not a regular day every week, but as and when needed. I asked Miss Patel about it, if Miss Pramal was unhappy, and she said it was the sick woman at the house making it awkward. Well, you know how they can be about sickness—very funny, to my mind. No wonder there's all them Indian students at St. Thomas' Hospital, learning to be doctors, I mean, they've got to take proper medical practices back over there, haven't they? What with putting their bodies in the Ganges River to float off to heaven—thank the Lord we were able to bring the Bible to our ladies."

Maisie glanced at Sandra. Mrs. Paige had been more forthcoming than at any other time.

"Do you have the name of the customer, Mrs. Paige?" asked Maisie.

"I can check in my books."

"While you're doing that, might we have a quick look in Miss Patel's room again, and Miss Pramal's quarters, too?"

"You might as well—you'll have to take yourself up there, though. I'll have to trust you."

Maisie and Sandra made their way up the stairs.

"You know who the customer is, don't you, Miss?" said Sandra.

"I'm quite sure I do, because I spoke to the sick woman's nurse. I had to inquire further of Mrs. Paige—it wouldn't seem right if I hadn't asked the question. Here we are, this is Maya Patel's room."

Maisie opened the door, and for a moment the two women did not move, but stood on the threshold looking in.

"It's as if no one ever lived here," said Sandra. "I mean, there's things, bits and pieces, but there's no feeling of her, is there?" She stepped into the room, though Maisie did not follow. "A room should tell you something about a person, shouldn't it? I think this room tells me that Maya Patel tried hard to make things comfortable for herself. She wanted things soft—and from what I saw of that woman downstairs, and the way she worked these ayahs, it was far from restful here."

Maisie could see that there was little more to be gleaned from a search of Maya Patel's room—the Indian woman had taken any confidences shared, any secrets told, and kept them to herself. Now only supposition would draw back the veil on the motive for her murder—unless she found the killer and a confession revealed why her life was taken. Closing the door, Maisie pointed to the staircase, and they made their way up to Usha Pramal's attic room.

Following Maisie into the room, Sandra picked up the small statuette of Ganesh. "For a churchgoing woman, she hadn't left her true beliefs far behind, had she?"

"I think she knew it was important to her employers, to learn the Bible stories, and she was a sharp, intelligent woman, good enough to teach Sunday school.

But she was not going to leave her culture far behind."
Maisie looked around the room. "I don't see anything
new here. My guess is that both Usha and Maya knew
the Paiges would come into their rooms on occasion, so
they wouldn't leave anything out that was important.
I know Usha concealed things." She turned to Sandra.
"Usha saved a fair amount of money that she hid in
this room—I discovered it, almost by accident. I don't
know exactly how she earned that money, but I suspect
she had a talent—skill, gift, call it what you like—for
easing pain, by touch and by blending various herbs and
spices. I remember Dr. Elsbeth Masters—you remember her, she was the one who treated Doreen; I worked
with her once, years ago—well, she was brought up in
Africa, and she once told me that as a child she had
seen the local native women use simple herbs picked
from among the grasses to cure something as dreadful
as cancer. Dr. Masters is a fine physician, but she said
she knew that much valuable, timeless knowledge is
being lost from so many places around the world where
missionaries—and doctors—have settled. I think Usha
was probably doing something that came quite natu-
rally to her, but she also had something else, and that
was the willingness to touch someone who was sick."
Maisie looked out of the window, partly to prevent
Sandra from seeing the tears that had welled up in her

eyes. "I remember, when I was a nurse, a man—he had been terribly wounded in the war—saying to me that people don't touch you when you're mutilated, when you're sick, even those who love you most. Perhaps that was Usha's gift, that she had no fear of touching people, no sense of propriety even in her own country. Remember . . ." She turned to Sandra. "Remember her brother saying how much it distressed his family, that she would touch people, would be too forthcoming, simply in greeting."

Sandra nodded. "What a maze this is, Miss Dobbs. A real web to unravel."

They both searched Usha Pramal's room, and Maisie ran her hands across the mattress again, just in case. She had a sense that almost all the clues she would find in this case were already in her possession, and alone they might not be enough. But she was about to be given a name, and knew already that it would be Jesmond Martin.

After they had descended the staircase and had been given the slip of paper confirming the name she had known would come up once again, she asked one more question of Mrs. Paige.

"I know that any monies belonging to Miss Pramal will go to her brother, however, you must also have savings put by for Miss Patel, too. What will you do with them, as no next of kin has been identified?"

"We'll give it to the Reverend Griffith, of course. The church always needs money, and those women have much to thank the Lord for, so the money goes to the Lord."

Maisie nodded. "Well, thank you, Mrs. Paige. Thank you very much." As she stepped out across the threshold, Maisie turned to Mrs. Paige. "Such a nice afternoon, isn't it? Is Mr. Paige out walking, taking advantage of the weather before it turns?"

"Probably. He said he was going to see Reverend Griffith, but he likes a walk, especially along the canal. He walks there almost every day."

"I see, well, it's a good day for it. Thank you, Mrs. Paige."

Maisie started the MG as Sandra settled in the passenger seat. Before setting off, they both looked at the house belonging to Mr. and Mrs. Paige: a place of refuge for women who were so far from home.

"What do you think, Sandra?"

"Well, I'm only a beginner at this, but I would say she didn't have anything to do with the deaths of those women, but I don't think her motives for having them there have been completely altruistic—is that the right word?" She didn't wait for an answer. "Anyway, I don't think they're as much do-gooders as they look. I would say that they've set themselves up nicely, on the work of those women. They've given them a roof over their heads, I'll grant you that, but they've looked after themselves, too. And I bet this Reverend Griffith doesn't get as much as they say—probably just a few extra coppers on the collection plate. Or maybe he's in on it as well, and does all right."

As they crossed the river, Maisie added another thought to their discussion. "One glaring gap in all this is the Allisons. When did you say they were due back from their holiday?" asked Maisie.

"On Sunday, according to the housekeeper. So you should be able to see them on Monday."

"Good. And in the meantime, I would like you to visit the two women who employed Usha Pramal: Mrs. Baxter and Mrs. Hampton. Confirm the terms of employment—hours, wage, and so on—and just ask a few more questions to see if they noticed anything out of the ordinary in the weeks before Usha died. Did she turn up for work on time? Was she working to her usual standard? Frankly, Sandra, we both know that most of these employers don't notice a thing about the staff, so you might see if you can ask a few questions of anyone who worked with Usha. There's not a moment to lose now. I'm going to try to see Jesmond Martin tomorrow—and wouldn't it be good news if Billy had found the boy? I have a feeling that not only is he the son we've been charged to find, but he's also this 'Marty' the boys have talked about."

"Two birds with one stone then."

"Two birds with one stone," said Maisie. "Just like Usha and Maya—two women killed with one gun. Except that boy might not know as much as we're hoping he does."

With Sandra dropped at the office of Douglas Partridge—somewhat later than she was due at her second job—Maisie returned to the office, which was late-afternoon quiet. She pinned out the case map and added some more information, linked a couple of statements she'd penned onto the sheet of paper, and ballooned in a separate color. Like those stones across a river, they would soon lead her across the waters of ignorance to knowledge of Usha Pramal's killer, she hoped. And there was something else playing on her mind. Now she had made the decision to close her business, to leave London, Kent, and—perhaps only for a while—James, she thought it would probably be best if she began to make firm her plans. If she was going to go, she had better get on with it; rather like tearing a dressing from a wound, she must make her arrangements and simply go, as soon as this case was closed and all ends tied. It seemed as if Billy's immediate future might be settled, so now she must think of getting Sandra placed in another job, and of talking to Frankie—leaving her father, even for a sojourn of a few months, might be one of the worst decisions she had ever made, at his age. But she knew he would be the first person to say she should follow her dream. He had always, without exception, been her greatest supporter, even considering the part that Maurice had played in her life.

She scribbled a letter to Mr. and Mrs. Allison for Sandra to type the following day, and jotted a plain postcard to Mr. Pramal at his hotel—there was no telephone at such a small establishment—asking him to please get in touch so she could keep him apprised of her work thus far. A telephone call to Detective Inspector Caldwell informed her that, no, the boy they knew as Martin Robertson had not been found, though Caldwell was somewhat more sanguine about the lad's disappearance, saying it was probably the shock of finding a body and then having to deal with the police. "His sort don't like the boys in blue much, even when we're not out to sling them in clink."

Maisie had sighed, though Caldwell's droll comments had come to amuse rather than annoy her.

Maisie realized she had been delaying her departure from the office. She had been fiddling with small tasks, pinning papers together that really did not need to be pinned, or filing papers that would usually be put on Sandra's desk to attend to the following day. But she had made a late commitment to go to the Otterburn house for the supper party, and go to the house she would, no matter how much unfinished business she might have with the man in question.

James was already home by the time Maisie pulled into the mews behind the Ebury Street mansion. Forsaking protocol, she entered by the kitchen door, told the servants—all of whom stood to attention as she entered—that they should take no notice, she was in a hurry, before proceeding to run up the back stairs to the floor where her rooms were situated. She knew she had crossed a boundary by doing such a thing, but since coming to live at the house—and she lived there most of the time now—she had pressed against boundaries more and more, mainly, she realized, to escape a sense that she might suffocate under the weight of expectation. Now the servants, all of whom were fairly new employees, would know that Maisie was very familiar with the hidden stairs and entryways that were the exclusive domain of downstairs staff.

A navy blue box with gold ribbon binding had been left on her bed; the gift seemed almost too exquisite to open.

"Well, aren't you dying to look inside?" James stood behind her, a whiskey and water in one hand, and already almost dressed for their outing—his shirt was open at the neck, with cuffs unlinked. He ran his free hand through blond hair silvered with gray, and smiled.

"Oh, James, what have you done?"

He came to her and held her to him. "Spent money wildly and lavishly on the woman I love—oh, what a sin."

"James, I—"

"Oh, do just open it, Maisie. Can't you for once accept a gift without admonishing the person who loves you enough to want to surprise you, to give you wonderful things?"

She smiled and carefully loosened the satin ribbon, which ran through her fingers as softly as if it were warm cream. The box was sturdy, though the lid came off with ease to reveal sheets of the finest gold tissue paper. Maisie gasped as she slowly lifted a dress in silk of the darkest violet, with silver threads added just so, that to wear the dress would be like being part of the night sky above.

"I thought it matched your eyes," said James.

Maisie held the dress against her and walked to the bevel mirror in the corner of the room. With long sleeves and a boat neckline—the cut accentuated her fine collarbones—the dress was draped in the bodice and from the waist fell in a slender column cut on the bias, to just above the ankle. A narrow belt in the same fabric with a silver clasp put a delicate finishing touch on an exquisite gown.

"Oh my. Oh my goodness, James, this is so gorgeous. I can hardly dare to wear it."

"Dare you will, and"—he looked at his watch—"in forty minutes we should be on our way or we'll be late. Drink while you're changing, my love?"

She shook her head. "I daren't. I might spill some. Oh dear, what will Priscilla say? Perfect, just perfect, and it's not even one of her cast-offs." She laid the dress on the bed and went to James. He held her in his arms. "Thank you, James—you've spoiled me and I don't deserve it."

"I love you, Maisie."

"And I love you, too," said Maisie. And she knew, in her heart, that her words were true. She loved James, and realized that there was something in what Sandra had said about having someone to come home to. And it didn't depend upon a new dress.

Though she usually shunned assistance from the maid who had been assigned to help her personally, Maisie summoned Madeleine to help her dress—she was so scared that she might spoil the new gown. Her hair had grown longer, so she thought she might wear it pinned up for the evening. Madeleine proved to be an expert hairdresser, her nimble fingers fashioning a braid from ear to ear that brushed against the nape of her neck. When she had finished, and before Madeleine helped her into the new garment, Maisie used a mirror to look at the braid. She touched the skin under the woven black hair.

"Are you sure you can't see my scar?" asked Maisie. "I wouldn't want it to show."

Madeleine came closer, frowning. "What scar, Miss Dobbs? I never saw no scar."

Maisie turned and took the girl's hand in hers, causing her to blush. "Thank you, Madeleine. You're a dear."

Maisie stopped to make one final check in the mirror before joining James. Her high cheekbones were enhanced by her hair being drawn back, and her eyes seemed deeper as they reflected the color and sheen of the gown, which fitted perfectly. She already owned a pair of black satin shoes, which would do nicely, and matched the black clutch bag she would carry with her. She would not take a wrap, as she had nothing to complement the dress—and the evening was not too cold in any case.

"I think that will do, don't you, Madeleine?"

"You look really lovely, Miss—like one of them film stars you see in the picture books."

"Oh, you lovely girl. When I am bleary-eyed at the end of another working day, I will remember what you've said, and it will buoy me up."

As she reached the door, the maid spoke again. "Miss, if I may ask, what scar were you talking about? Did you have an accident?"

Maisie smiled. "I was a nurse, in the war. I came home wounded . . . I was caught in the shelling, you see. But if you can't see it, that's a good sign—it means it's almost gone."

Chapter Fourteen

The party at the Otterburn mansion was much as Maisie expected it to be. A gathering in one of the grand reception rooms, much shaking of hands, effusive hellos, and champagne cocktails served as if the flow would never end. She was relieved to see Priscilla and Douglas Partridge among the guests, and Priscilla was doubly delighted to see her.

"I didn't know you were coming," said her friend. "I thought you had begged off this one."

"I changed my mind." Maisie sipped champagne from a crystal flute engraved with an *O*—as a self-made man, Otterburn did not have a coat of arms, so he used his initial to underline ownership of luxury.

"Probably just as well," said Priscilla, nodding towards a young woman wearing a clinging white backless gown peppered with sequins, her cropped hair closely curled, as she made her way towards the group.

"James, it's so good to see you again," she said, lifting her lightly rouged cheek to his, and pressing her red lips together to kiss the air.

James blushed and stepped back. "Hello, Elaine. Lovely to see you, too." He turned to Maisie, his hand at the small of her back, and introduced her to John Otterburn's daughter, making it obvious with his tone and the way he touched Maisie that they were a couple.

Elaine Otterburn smiled at Maisie and offered her hand. "Lucky, lucky lady!" She turned to greet Priscilla and Douglas, whom she had met before, and then said she must be off to do the rounds. She smiled again, as if turning on a switch, then turned away, waving to a young man who had just entered the room.

"Whew, she's a streak of lightning, that one," said Douglas.

"But a damn good aviatrix, despite appearances," said James. "Though a bit too forthcoming, to my mind—but then, she's young."

"Not that young," said Priscilla, raising an eyebrow as she turned her attention to Maisie and began to recount the latest escapades of her three boys.

As Priscilla was speaking another couple entered the room and immediately garnered the attention of almost all present. Heads turned, then turned back again; women seemed at once less colorful than they thought themselves to be, and there was a split-second hush that propriety ended quickly. The learned scientist Raphael Jones had arrived, with his equally learned wife, Lakshmi Chaudhary Jones, resplendent in a sari of iridescent golden silk, with a deep burgundy border, embellished with delicate beading depicting a series of butterflies. Maisie had never seen anything so beautiful, and knew the sari had been handmade for Mrs. Chaudhary Jones; the butterflies must have been her own idea. However, it was James who surprised Maisie.

"Oh, good, there's Raff." He turned to Maisie, Priscilla, and Douglas. "Come on, I'll introduce you— Raff is an extraordinary physicist and engineer, an expert on flight, velocity, maneuverability of aircraft, that sort of thing. Not met his wife before, but heard a lot about her—she's just your sort, Maisie; very intelligent, an academic herself, I believe. Hello—Raff!" He waved, and they moved towards the couple, who were both drinking water with a slice of lemon.

The couples exchanged pleasantries following introductions, though Lakshmi Chaudhary Jones took the opportunity of an approaching footman to turn to Maisie. While passing him her empty glass, she whispered, "Let's not tell them we've met; probably better for you, Maisie, given your work—which I am sure everyone knows about, even if they'd never say a word to you on the subject."

Maisie nodded and smiled. She liked Mrs. Chaudhary Jones; she was indeed a thoughtful woman.

Soon supper was announced, and the guests took their places along the seemingly never-ending table. Fortunately, Maisie was seated next to Douglas on one side, and a well-known journalist on the other, and James was between Priscilla and Mrs. Chaudhary Jones. Elaine Otterburn was positioned well along the table, between the young man she'd greeted so effusively earlier and her mother's brother, whom Maisie had had the poor fortune to be seated alongside at a supper earlier in the year—he was a drunk. Later, when Lorraine Otterburn stood to indicate it was time for the ladies to withdraw, leaving the men to their port and cigars, Maisie saw James step away from his chair and move towards Otterburn. Raphael Jones followed. Now it was clear. Lakshmi Chaudhary Jones' British husband was the scientist working with Otterburn to develop the aircraft that he believed would be the answer to Britain's defense prayers.

Thoughts spun through Maisie's mind while sitting with the women, on occasion nodding in agreement as the conversation buzzed back and forth. Though she went through a process of reflection at the end of a case—originally instigated by Maurice, when she was his apprentice, wherein each place of note in the investigation was visited, as if to exorcise remaining ghosts of the inquiry—the emotions wrought by certain cases lingered, and she felt the weight of them in the drawing room she had previously visited in the midst of a major case at a time when she had been powerless against the might of John Otterburn and the moral dilemma presented by his actions. He had brought about the death of a man in order to keep secret certain plans that would be to the advantage of Britain in a time of war, which he anticipated would happen within just a few years. The knowledge that she might never forgive herself for her failure to bring Otterburn to justice was once more brought to the forefront of her thoughts. And now she wanted to leave. She wanted to leave the room, leave Otterburn's house, and she wanted to leave her country. But was it really her desire to see new lands and experience other cultures that drove her to seek adventure abroad, or was she running from frustration and failure? Perhaps it was as Dame Constance had counseled. *Pilgrimage to the place of the wise is to find escape from the flame of separateness.*

Her deliberations led her back to Usha Pramal, and she wondered again what painful experience she might have been running from, and what she was casting away in leaving her home for an unknown land so many miles away. Maisie was convinced it was ultimately her past, not the way she conducted herself in the present, that had brought about the woman's death—and that of her loyal friend.

"You seemed to enjoy the party more than you thought you might, Maisie," said James as they drove home some hours later.

"Well, Priscilla and Douglas were there. And I like Lakshmi Chaudhary Jones. I like her very much."

"I thought you would." He laughed. "And what about Elaine Otterburn? I think John ought not to depend upon her doing much flying in Canada, the way she was hanging on the every word of that chap she was sitting next to just before we left."

"Perhaps not, James. But isn't it supposed to be a woman's prerogative, anyway—to change her mind."

Though it was dark inside the motor car, she knew he was smiling.

Maisie was somewhat surprised to find Billy at the office when she arrived in the morning.

"Billy, how are you?"

"I'm all right, Miss. Not so bad, anyway," he replied. He was tapping his fingers on his desk.

Maisie set her briefcase on her desk and continued speaking as she removed her gloves and hat. She was aware of the tap-tapping of Billy's fingers, and thought he seemed agitated.

"I've just remembered, Sandra's with Douglas Partridge this morning, isn't she?"

"That's right, Miss. I thought I'd pop in to tell you something I think might be important on this case— it's about that boy, the one who's missing."

"Billy—you're supposed to be resting." Maisie pulled up a chair in front of Billy's desk. "All right— what about him?"

"Well, I think he's dossing down somewhere near where them women were found—well, Miss Pramal in particular. Got a feeling he's not far from Addington Square somewhere."

"What makes you think that?" asked Maisie.

"I was over there yesterday. I know you said to go home, but I had a right bee in my bonnet about it, so I ended up going across to Camberwell. It must've been after you'd been to Addington Square, because I didn't see your motor car anywhere. Miss, I could have sworn I saw him, walking along near that field over the back. It was a boy who fitted his description anyway—mind you, I'll admit that his description fits a lot of lads of that age. Anyway, I took the chance and came up on a really early train this morning, to have another look. I reckoned that, if he was sleeping rough, he would come out before anyone else was about—them kids with their great big dog, for instance. Or I thought perhaps he'd stay over there, keep his head down. But I didn't reckon on seeing what I did."

"Billy, you're supposed to be resting, enjoying time at home with your family, digging your garden." She leaned forward. "What did you see?"

"Miss, there's only so much digging a garden of that size will take, and I thought I could lend a hand with the case. Anyway, I was walking along—and by then there were a few people about, so it wasn't as if anyone would notice me because I was the only bloke on the street—and when I got to the street that leads onto the square, Goodyear Street, or Place, or something, the door opened from one of them houses, and a man stood on the doorstep, looked around—of course, I stayed back, behind a tree—and then this lad came out and ran along the road." He took a breath and wiped his brow. "I reckon the fella might have been a vicar or a verger or something, because he left after the boy had gone, and he went down the road to his church—if you can call it a proper church."

"Well, that's a turn-up for the books." Maisie leaned back in her chair, folding her arms. She looked up at Billy. "I don't think I'm surprised, to tell you the truth—but of course, it might not be him, and the Reverend Griffith might be offering refuge to a helpless young man in all innocence—that's part of his ministry, to be a source of comfort to those less fortunate. We have to give him the benefit of the doubt—though I believe you're probably right." She paused again. "Billy, you're all in, what with getting up at the crack of dawn and all that walking around yesterday. I was worried about you then, and I'm worried now—and not about you being bored! Would you go home, please, and rest?"

Billy looked at his hands, then brought his attention back to his employer. "I've decided to take that job, you know. At the Compton Corporation. The money's fair, and it's regular. Doreen's pleased already; after all, I won't get much grief from a broken telephone, or a clerk who's nicking drawing pins, will I?"

Maisie smiled. "I think you're right—you've made a good decision."

"One thing that bothers me, Miss. What about the house? I mean, you own that house of ours, Miss, and I'm paying you rent. If I'm not working for you, can we stay there? Is that all right, I mean?"

"Oh, Billy, of course you are staying—it never entered my head that you wouldn't. In fact, I wanted to talk to you about that—but perhaps not yet. I'll just put the word in your ear to consider. I was thinking that it would be a good investment for you—for the future—if your rent were to go towards payment of the house. That would mean you would own the house one day, and it would be yours. I can give you the original purchase price, and we'll take it from there—proper papers drawn up, so no concern on that score."

"Oh, Miss, that's an awful lot, ain't it? I mean, to go from Shoreditch to a semi-detached house in Eltham is a big old leap, eh? And, well—"

"Have a think about it. Talk to Doreen. You wouldn't be paying any more than you are now, and you would be on the way to owning your house. And you can take your time—I have no other plans to sell the house. It's your home."

Billy took a while to answer. Maisie allowed him his silence, while at the same time wondering whether she had overstepped the mark again.

"Thank you for the opportunity, Miss, I really appreciate all this. And I know Doreen will. She'd love to think we might own the house—and do it on our own."

"Good. Think about it. Now then, Billy—you go home."

"Miss—"

"What is it, Billy?"

"What're you going to do? Will Sandra be working for you, taking my place?"

"No one can take your place, Billy. Ever. But I have some plans of my own—and no, don't ask, I've no thoughts about getting married." She paused, taking a deep breath. "I believe I might close the business for a while. I haven't told Sandra yet, so keep it under your hat. I have some things I need to take care of."

"Is it to do with Dr. Blanche?"

Maisie sighed. "Yes, I suppose it is. I am going to honor his memory, in a way. Do something he would have liked me to do."

Billy nodded and smiled. "Well, good on you, Miss. Good on you for doing it, whatever it is."

"I'll keep you posted. Now then, you go on home."

"You will get on the old dog and bone if you need me, won't you? This ain't a straightforward case, is it?"

Maisie laughed. "Come on, Billy—when did we ever have a straightforward case?"

"Yeah, you've got a point. I suppose there was that one embezzlement . . ."

Maisie telephoned Jesmond Martin at work, and he grudgingly agreed to see her, though he asked her to come to his office, rather than to his house, later in the day, as she would have preferred. She also left a message with the Allisons' housekeeper, confirming that she would like to call on Monday afternoon— yes, she knew it was short notice considering they would only just have returned from holiday, but this was an urgent matter in connection with a police investigation. Maisie hated bringing Scotland Yard into the equation, but she knew there were times when her position as an independent inquiry agent was not quite enough to gain a crucial meeting. If asked, she knew that Caldwell would cover for her. Her Friday was taking shape. Jesmond Martin, followed by another trip over to Addington Square—this time with her stout walking shoes. Now there was one more call to make before she left the office. But the telephone began to ring as she reached for the receiver.

"Fitzroy—" She had no time to repeat the exchange number before the caller started to speak.

"Maisie, love, is that you?"

"Dad! Dad, what's wrong? Are you all right?" Maisie felt her heart begin to beat faster. It was unusual for her father to initiate a telephone call—Frankie Dobbs had never quite become used to the telephone she'd had installed in his cottage following a serious fall he'd suffered some years earlier. On hearing his voice she was immediately fearful that something dreadful had happened.

"Nothing wrong, love. No, nothing wrong. I just wondered if you were coming down here to Chelstone soon."

"I was just about to telephone you, Dad—I was planning to drive down tomorrow morning. I thought I'd give Mrs. Bromley a call next, to let her know. Are you sure everything is all right?"

"Right as rain, love. I'll see you tomorrow then. And don't worry—I'll let Mrs. Bromley know you're on your way; I daresay I'll be seeing her today."

"That'll save me a moment. And I'll be arriving about midafternoon."

"That's all right then. Will Mr. James be with you?" Frankie tended to refer to James as "Mr. James"—he was not at ease with the fact that Maisie was romantically involved with the son of the family by whom he was employed. Maisie knew his discomfort came from a sense of not knowing quite where he stood; Frankie Dobbs was a man who liked a certain order, though he also thought his daughter was worthy of more than James Compton. Maisie always felt that Frankie doubted James, and had he shared his feelings would have said, "I'd like to see more fiber to him, that's all." Frankie was still a man who respected work with the hands before toil behind a desk.

"Yes, he probably will—though he will obviously be with his parents for the most part."

"So, tomorrow then."

"All right, Dad."

"Mind how you go, in that little motor of yours."

"I will, Dad. Not to worry." Maisie smiled as she replaced the telephone receiver, but at the same time she remained a little unsettled. She could count on the fingers of one hand the number of times her father had picked up the telephone and dialed her number. She didn't think it was an idle curiosity about her plans for Saturday and Sunday that inspired the move.

Jesmond Martin's office was in the City, close to St. Paul's Cathedral. Maisie loved the City, the smell of the centuries that seemed to rise up from the pavement, waft along alleyways, and linger in ancient doorways. The tall, narrow building that housed Jesmond Martin's office had recently been treated to a scouring, but would soon be soot-stained and dark once more. It pleased her, though, to see the effort made.

She could not account for her preconceived notion that Martin worked for a larger concern, and was a little surprised to see him supported only by a secretary and two clerks. His offices comprised two rooms.

The outer office seemed dour, with oak floors in need of some polish, and three heavy desks. Only the secretary had a telephone, and from the open ledger on her desk it appeared the clerks had to request permission to place a call. Several slightly more comfortable chairs—still straight-backed, but with cushioned seats—were positioned a few feet away from the secretary's desk, and Maisie was directed to make herself comfortable while Mr. Martin was informed that she had arrived. The secretary knocked on the door at the far end of the outer office, and stepped inside to speak to her employer. Two minutes later, Maisie was summoned.

Jesmond Martin was a tall, thin man with angular features and narrow shoulders that seemed slightly rounded. Maisie wondered if years of trying to protect his heart had led to such a development, or was it simply close work over a desk late into the day? He could once have been a handsome man, one who attracted the attention of women—girls, then—for his eyes, though sad, seemed as if in earlier years they might have been full of life and joy. It was a fleeting impression, but when Maisie looked at those eyes, she thought of an empty fire grate in the cold of morning, after the warmth and light of the night before. Lines stretching to his temples and around his mouth spoke of disappointment and perhaps the strain of observing his wife's decline along with the more recent disappearance of his son. She had not noticed these elements before, when they first took on the case, but perhaps they were more evident when he was at work.

Jesmond Martin remained standing behind his desk as Maisie stepped forward. He held out his hand towards a chair for her to be seated.

"Miss Dobbs, good of you to call. Do you have news of my son? My wife is not a well woman, and his continued disappearance is having a detrimental effect on her well-being. She waits every day for news, and it has been some time." He stood until he had finished the sentence, and then sat down at his desk, his hands clenched on top of the blotting pad in front of him.

"I think we might have a good lead, Mr. Martin. I will get straight to the point: I believe your son might be living under an assumed name—though one similar to his own—and in rough circumstances."

Martin did not seem surprised, though he shook his head and leaned back in his chair. "I just don't understand. I have done everything I can for that boy. I have raised him to the best of my ability, and he has the love of his mother—what could have caused this? Who has influenced him?" He resumed his former position, hands clasped atop the blotting pad. "He must be intercepted and brought home at once, Miss Dobbs.

If I have to order another agency to bring him to his senses, I will."

"Another agency won't be necessary, Mr. Martin. We have come this far; however, I am afraid I must ask some more questions. You see, to all intents and purposes, there was no undue influence upon your son— if I have identified him correctly. He left school of his own accord and moved into lodgings in Southwark. From there he was well situated to gain work on the docks—he is young and fit, tall and strong for his age, and he would not be paid the same as a grown man, so he was hired by the day."

"Working on the docks? But my son is a gentleman, he would not—" Martin had clasped his hands together with such force that his nails left an impression on his skin. "If he wants to work, then so be it—a suitable position could be found for him. Naval rating might do very well; a spell at sea if he wants a harsher life—his has clearly been too soft for him thus far."

"I know this is very troubling for you, Mr. Martin, but there is more. If we have identified him correctly, then he is also sought by the police. I should add that I have not suggested his identification to my contacts at Scotland Yard, in case there has been an error."

"The police?" Jesmond Martin pressed his hands on the desk as if to lever himself to stand.

"Please let me finish, Mr. Martin. A young man fitting your son's description, and living under an assumed name that appears to be derived from his own, was the first to find the body of a woman murdered close to the canal. He has not been implicated in her murder, and he was with another worker when they came across her remains. He was taken to alternative lodgings by the police—for his own protection; this is a difficult case as the woman was not English, and it was the second such murder in several months. And this information, as you might imagine, is highly confidential."

"My son would never murder—"

"I'm not saying he would, Mr. Martin. This is simply by way of information regarding a young man we believe to be your son. Let me continue." Maisie cleared her throat and coughed. The room was musty and a fine sheen of dust seemed to linger in the air.

"Would you like tea, Miss Dobbs?" Martin's manner changed, becoming solicitous.

"A glass of water would suffice, if you don't mind."

Martin rang a bell on his desk, whereupon his secretary entered the room, and he requested a glass of water for the visitor. They did not continue speaking until the woman returned, and Maisie had taken several sips to soothe the irritation in her throat.

"The weather is strange for this time of year, isn't it?" said Jesmond.

"Yes," replied Maisie. "Drier than usual." She cleared her throat again, took one more sip, set the glass on the desk, and went on. "Now, back to your son. He is not under suspicion, though he is a most important witness. It is possible he ran away again to avoid being sent home. Which brings me to a point of some delicacy." She looked at Martin, at the large eyes that now seemed filled with melancholy, at the hunched shoulders and the gray, lined skin at his temples. How old was he, this man who seemed as if he was beyond fifty, though at the same time could be much younger, yet hardened by tragedy? She had seen that very look in the war, in the faces of men marching back from the front, their eyes telling of terrors seen and friends lost. Had this man seen the front lines of battle? But then, not all wars were fought with guns and shells; sometimes the charge came from another quarter. Life itself could provide an onslaught enough to diminish the spirit and challenge the soul, and surely seeing a beloved wife suffer was such an engagement, with many conflicts to endure.

"I know we asked you this question before, when you first came to us, but can you think of any reason why Robert might have run away? Of course, I understand

302 · JACQUELINE WINSPEAR

his mother is quite infirm, which must be terribly difficult for him, but it has been this way for several years now, has it not? I wonder what might have happened to change his perspective?" She chose her words with care. "When you were late returning for our previous appointment, at your home, I had the opportunity to speak to your wife's nurse, and she described Robert's love of his mother and his commitment to her, so I am surprised he left in such a way."

Martin shrugged. "He might have reached some sort of crisis, Miss Dobbs. Men have been known to experience moments of weakness."

"But he is not a man, is he?"

"Almost. Man enough to know what he is doing."

Maisie saw the anger rising, and at once felt as if she were on uneven ground.

"Mr. Martin, I must draw your attention to a compelling coincidence in this whole matter. I did not mention it at first, as I wanted to gain an impression of your son, yet this is a crucial element in terms of his continued disappearance. Though it is to his credit that Robert—the young man we believe to be Robert—and his companion sought help as soon as they discovered the remains of the young woman, I should add that her name was Miss Maya Patel, late of Addington Square."

"I don't know any Maya Patel. Nor does my son."

Maisie waited a second or two longer before replying.

"But you do know Miss Usha Pramal, I believe. Wasn't she a member of staff in your household until several months ago?"

Jesmond Martin picked up a fountain pen and pulled off the lid, which he then pressed home again. "Miss Dobbs, I am a very busy man. I arrive at my office early, and I leave late. I have to consider not only my wife's health, the extra expense of her condition and a full-time nurse, but my son's education and future. I am not a wealthy man in the way of earls and kings, but a man who has to work hard for every penny— and I have a necessary staff here to consider, too. The housekeeper is responsible for all matters concerning the running of the household—I simply pay the bills. I do not know the name of every person employed in my house, small though it may seem by baronial standards. My first consideration is my wife and my son. There you have it." He threw the pen on the blotting pad and leaned back, his arms folded.

"Of course, and I understand that completely, Mr. Martin; however, we have been given a remit from you to find your son, and this is part of our investigation. I am sure you understand that some distress might have inspired him to run away. Miss Usha Pramal was not only a member of your household, albeit on a very ad hoc basis—I am sure you would recall her in time, as she was a person most beloved by all who knew her, and I understand much admired by your son, especially as she helped your wife to gain some freedom from the pain and distress she suffered due to those dreadful headaches."

"Oh, you mean that bloody woman and her potions." Martin unfolded his arms and once again rested his hands on the desk, fingers splayed. "I am a fair man, and broad-minded, but I could not have it. I just could not have it, a woman assuming the role of physician with no respect for my wishes and for the health of my wife. I could not allow such insubordination to continue. I admit—I gave orders for her to be dismissed at once."

"Despite the fact that she helped your wife?"

"I don't think that's true—it was all in her mind."

"But it helped—she was free from pain, I understand."

"Miss Dobbs, I was not aware that my instructions to find my son included express permission to interrogate my staff and—it would seem—harass my wife."

"Mr. Martin, I feel I must tell you that in my business I am often responsible for several cases at once—like you, I have a staff to support my work. But when two quite different cases intersect, it adds another dimension to my investigation, and I am probably more exacting in my questioning of those involved."

"What do you mean?" Martin was staring at Maisie now.

"Maya Patel was the second murder of this type, as I mentioned. She was killed by a single shot to the head." Maisie touched the middle of her forehead. "The first was Usha Pramal."

Though it was slight, Maisie could not fail to notice Jesmond Martin blink several times in quick succession.

On the way back to her office, Maisie thought about the meeting with Jesmond Martin. What was his history? And how might she discover more about him? Could Robert Martin really be the "Martin Robertson" who had discovered Maya Patel, and who might now be living rough close to the place where Usha Pramal was discovered? According to his father, and subsequent corroboration from his school, Robert Martin was fourteen years of age. Usha Pramal was still in India when he was born, so a connection could be ruled out there. But what of his mother? What of her past, and could there possibly be any thread to link her to India?

Chapter Fifteen

Mr. Pramal's hotel was a dreary narrow building close to Victoria Station, and of the same age, built to accommodate temporary visitors, travelers awaiting the next boat train, or those who needed a few hours sleep before moving on—and sometimes those few hours sleep might have been in the company of a woman who claimed a few shillings for the pleasure of her warmth and comfort. This was not a good hotel, but it was likely cheap and money was probably very tight for Usha Pramal's brother, especially if he had a large extended family to provide for at home.

A man and woman were arguing in the small foyer when she came in. The man, who was standing behind the counter with arms folded, appeared to be waiting for money.

"If you want ten per bloody cent, what does that leave me with?"

"Ain't up to me, love. It's the guv'nor," said the man. "If you want to make a bit here, then you've got to pay your way. That's the rules. There's always round the back of the train sheds, if you want it like that—then you don't have to pay no one, do you? Mind you, you don't get as much, so it's down to what you want at your back—bricks or a mattress, call it like you want it."

"You bleedin' tyke." The woman threw a couple of coins at the man, then turned and stormed towards Maisie.

"I'd find a better class of place, if I were you, love." She looked Maisie in the eye and wagged her finger. "That bleeding crook over there'll take the lot."

Maisie stood back to allow the woman to pass, then made her way to the counter, where the man was placing the coins in his waistcoat pocket.

"I must apologize, madam. The previous guest was not of our usual class, and did not recognize a lady." He inclined his head. "May I help you?"

"Yes," said Maisie. "I wonder, do you have a guest here by the name of Mr. Pramal?"

"Indian chap?"

"Yes, that's right. I understand he has been staying here."

"He was here. I signed him in myself. I served in the war alongside their sort, so I don't mind them about. Mind you, when the guv'nor came in he had other ideas, and said he had to go."

"He was asked to leave the hotel? But why?"

The man reddened. "Well, miss, I didn't think I would have to explain, but there are some who have a different opinion of them, you see." He ran a finger around his face to indicate the color of Pramal's skin. "It wasn't me, like I said—I know a good man when I see one. But the bloke who owns this hotel has his moments, and he had one when he saw Mr. Pramal."

"Mr. Pramal was a Regimental Sergeant Major in the war. He fought for our country—and your employer treated him like dirt? When he allows women like . . ." Maisie stopped herself. "Do you know where he went?"

"He said he was going back to his friend's house. Very proud man, Mr. Pramal. When he came in, he said he didn't want to stay with his mate, putting him out indefinitely, which is why he came here." The man scratched his head, ruffling hair that Maisie thought was rarely washed. "But too good for this place, he was, if you ask me. Just went out in the morning, and came back at night, to his room. No messing around, never saw a woman coming out of there."

"Thank you." Maisie turned to leave, and then turned back, placing a sixpence on the counter. The man swept it up into his weskit pocket with a quick nod of the head.

Instead of returning directly to the office, Maisie walked along Buckingham Palace Road, past the Royal Mews and the Palace, and on towards Green Park. The afternoon remained fine, though a light breeze was swirling early autumn leaves along the street. Peddlers passed with their barrows, offering sweets, fruit, and ices. Taxi-cabs and buses blew exhaust fumes into the air, so Maisie drew her scarf over her nose and mouth. Once in the relative peace of the park, she chose a bench under a tree to simply sit and think.

What was evading her? Something obvious was there, hidden in plain sight—she could feel it, but she was missing the point. She'd allowed herself to be distracted by her own ambition. It was now a visceral feeling deep within her, the urge to be gone, to be somewhere else, a place other than this, and now. She wanted to beat her own path, and as time went on she wanted a physical distance between her and the past eighteen years, since 1914, even more.

Was that how Usha Pramal felt? Had she taken the position with the Allisons because she wanted distance?

Distance from her family, from expectations, from her life in India? Or did she simply want distance from a love who had, without anticipating the outcome of his actions, humiliated her in front of her family? Family was important to Usha Pramal, and though it seemed she took pleasure in upsetting the familial status quo with her mercurial manner, there was a line she would not cross. And though she wanted to return to her beloved country, she remained. Was it only to gather more money with which to make her dream of establishing a school for girls from poor families come to fruition, or was something else keeping her in London? Did she feel responsible for Maya to the extent that she would stay? Yes, Maisie thought she would; from what she understood of Usha, she was kind in that way.

Maisie watched as two women walked past pushing prams, their babies sitting up against mounds of pillows, reaching out to each other and chuckling in the sunshine. The innocence of the scene led her to wonder again who had the skill to take the life of two women, both of whom unwittingly wore the perfect target that would allow someone to kill with precision. And who had the necessary moral and emotional bankruptcy to do such a thing?

Threads, threads, threads and not one leading to a viable picture in her mind of who could have killed

Usha Pramal, and why. She was frustrated by her lack of insight. Perhaps she had not paid enough attention to Maya Patel. She asked herself again: What did Maya Patel know that could have led to her death? Was it simply because she was an Indian woman? If so, then the police did well to remove the other ayahs from the Paiges' house. But Maisie didn't think it was so. Maya Patel demanded more attention. It occurred to her that the missing link was someone not known to her—yet. But a new plan was forming in her mind.

Big Ben rang the hour in the distance. It was now two o'clock in the afternoon. She had time to collect the MG, drive to Camberwell, and, if they were there, visit the Paiges just one more time—assuming they would see her. She knew she was testing their patience. And afterwards, before the sun set, she would, she hoped, have time to stroll across the common land where a young man might be sleeping rough. Would she visit Reverend Griffith? Perhaps. She wasn't at all sure about the respected man of the cloth, and whether she should wait to pay another call when she had more information to hand. The image of bound elephant hair kept coming to mind. She did not care for the clumsy knotting of an animal's hair, and she wondered if that was a prejudice, a valuable clue, or intuition. But she felt the esteemed reverend might worship more gods than just the One.

Maisie parked the car across the road from the Paiges' home, went to the front door, and knocked. Soon heavy footsteps could be heard approaching; it was Mr. Paige who answered.

"Oh, not you again."

"Mr. Paige, I am afraid it is me, and I beg your pardon for dropping in without notice once more, but I was not far from here, and I thought you might be able to help me."

The man made no move to invite Maisie inside the house.

"I suppose we can speak here just as well as anywhere." Maisie looked back and forth down the road. "No neighbors seem to be walking this way, though I am sure I saw a few curtains twitching."

Paige's face darkened. "Come in, then." He closed the door behind him and led Maisie into the parlor. "My wife isn't here—she's doing flowers for the church this afternoon—she likes to make sure it looks welcoming for Friday evensong."

"Tell me, the Reverend Griffith's church isn't C of E, is it? Nor is it Baptist or Methodist—though I see you use the old community rooms, but he doesn't seem very much of that type of minister."

"No, you're right. We just refer to ourselves as 'the Church of a Greater God.' I'm not sure where the

Reverend Griffith gained his theological credentials, but he is a most caring vicar, of that I am sure—and he fills our church with goodness."

"Of course, yes. I'm sure he does." Maisie paused, putting the information about Griffith to one side in her mind, as if moving a saucepan to another burner on the stove—it was not to be forgotten, but could simmer while her focus was on the main reason for her call. She looked at Paige, noticing the tension in his shoulders as he awaited her question. "Maya Patel intrigues me as much as Miss Pramal. Mr. Paige, I know the women had become close, so I am asking once again if you noticed anything different in the weeks preceding Maya Patel's death."

Paige shrugged. "She grieved more than any of us, but that's to be expected. At first she didn't want to go back to the church, saying that our church had done nothing to protect Miss Pramal, that our God was not their God. Of course, our Christian hearts went out to her, and we knew it was shock speaking. Reverend Griffith called to see her, and she refused, which was very embarrassing, I must say—and that's when I felt it had to stop, that her wailing had to come to an end. It wasn't Christian, having a sound like an Indian banshee howling throughout the house."

"There are those who believe it's best to grant sadness a very loud voice—she had lost her best friend, the nearest thing to family she had. But tell me, how did you stop her?"

"I had Griffith come in and take the devil out of her, like he did in Africa."

"You did?" Maisie felt a revulsion for the unfolding story—a disgust she knew was evident in her expression.

"The good man lay his hands on her head and prayed, and as he prayed she screamed and wept until it was out of her—the demons that had come from Usha Pramal and taken her thoughts."

"You believe Miss Pramal had demons? Could you explain why?"

"Oh, she was a good person on the face of it—as we said, all our women here kept good hours and were not out at night. They weren't that sort. But there was a side to Miss Pramal, you could see it in her eyes. She wasn't afraid of anything."

"What should she be afraid of? If she kept good hours and wasn't out at night? What reason was there for fear?"

"The power of the Lord, of course. She had no fear—and though she went to the church and helped with the younger ones in Sunday school, you could see she wore her own power, as if she thought *she* were something special, sent down to earth."

"I see." Maisie paused. "Were you afraid of what you perceived as her power, Mr. Paige?"

"When you have the Lord on your side, you're not afraid."

"Do you know anyone who might have been afraid of Usha Pramal?"

"I can't answer that question, Miss Dobbs. I'm not other people, but I am sure others saw what I saw and what the Reverend Griffith saw. Mrs. Paige and I talked about it, how that demon of superiority had to be fought and banished."

"Hmmm. But nothing was done about it, from a church point of view—your church, that is?"

"It was done for us. Not that I favor what happened to the poor woman—she was a human being, after all. But someone didn't like her, did they?"

"And what about Miss Patel? I haven't heard her spoken of in the same terms."

"I don't know what happened to her. As I said, though, I have my suspicions that Miss Pramal upset someone—and it isn't right that they took her life, but I am not here in judgment. The Lord will judge us all, in the end."

"Do you think Miss Patel lost her life by association? Or did she have knowledge, do you think, about the murderer?"

"I don't know. I want to put it behind me—behind us—and continue doing God's work among those who have no god or too many gods. That is all I ask, for my wife and I to be allowed to plough our land and sow our seeds of faith."

"And the money you took from the women lodgers will buy a lot of seeds, will it not?"

Paige reddened. "I don't know what you mean."

"Oh, I think you do, Mr. Paige. You've been fleecing your lodgers for years, and telling me that Usha Pramal had the money to leave months ago does not throw me off the scent—she probably had the money to leave years ago. She might have acted like a goddess, in your estimation, but she was a good worker, and people liked her, didn't they? They liked her disposition, and I would hazard a guess that there were some who liked the fact that she made them feel better, especially the elderly who suffer aches and pains, and those who were ill. I bet there were quite a few down the years who wanted her to come to them, but that was too much power to give to one person, never mind the money it drew in. I have a good mind to bring in the police to look at your books."

"They don't care, Miss Dobbs. It's only a few destitute Indian women we've kept in this house, and if we didn't look out for them, who would? As far as the police are concerned, they're off the streets."

"You may be right, but I have other contacts beyond Scotland Yard—people in high places charged with ensuring nothing goes amiss in our relationship with the Indian subcontinent. And your little charity here is very amiss—unless you clean up your accounts." Maisie had chosen words to instill fear in the man, and it had worked. All color had drained from his face. "Now then," she continued. "You can start by going through your ledger and giving me what was truly owed to Usha Pramal and Maya Patel."

"And what will you do with it?"

"I'll give Miss Pramal's money to her brother, and Maya Patel's along with it, to contribute to a fund that Miss Pramal started."

"A fund? What fund?"

"For the training of ambitious young goddesses in India. What else?"

"I must ask you to leave."

Maisie stood up, aware of her mounting anger, which was close to boiling point. "No. I would like to visit Maya Patel's room one more time, and Usha Pramal's as well. I will be long enough for you to run your finger down a few lines of numbers and come to a figure acceptable to me, and you will give me the money to take away—or does the Reverend Griffith have it?"

Paige folded his arms and looked away. "I can get it for you."

"Good." Maisie turned away, as if to walk towards the staircase. She looked back. "I have never said this in all my years in this job. I am usually very circumspect in my manner with people such as yourself. You haven't killed someone, Mr. Paige, but you know how to take a life. And you sicken me. You, with your twisted ideas of God, sicken me."

"You, what do you know of God?"

"I know when He is truly present in someone's heart."

As she made her way up the staircase, Maisie did not feel the recrimination she might once have felt for allowing her emotions to gain the better of her. She heard Paige walk towards the back of the house—his heavy footfall echoed up through the stairwell. She knew she would get the arrears in wages due to the dead women. Then she had to find Pramal, to tell him about the money and more about Usha's personal savings; funds she had earned by mixing spices to cure headaches, or by taking the arthritic hands of the elderly in her own, until her youth and strength rendered them painless, if only for a short time.

Usha Pramal's room at the top of the house seemed hollow without her books and other personal belongings arranged on shelves—they had been gathered and placed in a box by the door; Maisie would have them collected and given to her brother. There was now barely any sense that she had lived in this room in the eaves of a Georgian house so far from her beloved home. Maisie closed her eyes and at once saw the image of a woman with fine features, her olive-brown skin and almond eyes rimmed with kohl; her stride full as she walked tall along the street, her sari caught by a summer's breeze.

Maya Patel's room had also been emptied of her belongings—just her Bible remained in a cupboard by the bed. Maisie took out the leather-bound book, and noted it was a type with each gospel indented. A ribbon had been laid through the book of Exodus. She suspected the room had been cleared with some speed, probably only the day before; perhaps the police had finally given permission. It was interesting that no one else had noticed the marked place and gauged its potential importance. In pencil, lines had been drawn through one of the Commandments, indicating that Maya Patel had considered what it meant to possess graven images of any other deity considered to be at home in heaven above, and had found it wanting. She had circled two others of the Ten Commandments: Though Shalt Not Kill and Thou Shalt Not Commit

Adultery. Maisie took the Bible, placed it in her bag, then looked around the room once more and stepped towards the door. She smiled. What would it mean to the Paiges if they knew that a woman named Maya—a queen, no less—had been the mother of Gautama, the Buddha? Maisie, who had been reading more books about her chosen destination of late, also remembered that Maya was the goddess of illusion, which she thought interesting. She believed Maya Patel had been keeping a secret for her friend Usha Pramal. And it was beginning to dawn on Maisie what that secret might be.

Paige was waiting for Maisie at the bottom of the stairs, a well-filled envelope in his hand.

"Here you are, Miss Dobbs. Everything owed to Miss Patel and Miss Pramal, with an explanatory note pertaining to the amounts held on account for them." He held a book with another piece of paper laid out on top. "You can sign for it here."

Maisie did not rush to count the money, and took her time in checking the amount on the receipt. She signed the paper, and asked for a second copy to be produced, for which she had to wait while the rat-tat-tat of a typewriter disturbed an otherwise silent house. She took a certain pleasure in making Paige work to be rid of her. He returned ten minutes later.

"Good, this is progress, is it not, Mr. Paige? I do not expect to darken your door again, though I will send a messenger to collect the remaining belongings of your two late residents." She turned to leave, but as Paige was about to close the door, she called to him. "By the way, Mr. Paige—just as an aside, did you know that the name Usha means 'daughter of heaven'? I thought you would find that interesting."

He slammed the door, and Maisie went on her way, though she could have sworn she felt a silken breeze alongside her hand as she walked.

Having hidden the envelope under the seat of her MG, then donned her walking shoes, Maisie locked the motor car and set off towards the common land behind Addington Square. As she was striding through the knee-high grass, she saw a group of children playing, a large golden retriever bounding around them, chasing sticks and generally trying to keep some sense of order among his charges. She waved to the children, who stood still and watched her approach. They were a motley group, the three girls in summery dresses and cardigans that looked as if they had been passed down a few times, while the two boys—clearly they were all siblings—held sticks with which they hit out at the grass. The dog stood in front of the children and barked.

"What a lovely dog you have," said Maisie as she approached.

"His name's Nelson. He looks after us," said the eldest girl.

Maisie could see now that the dog's coat hid the fact that he probably lived on scraps from the table and little else, and though the children were as well turned out as a harried mother with little money could keep them, they all seemed as if they could do with a good meal.

"Do you play here a lot?"

"After school, before my dad gets home and only when we've done our jobs in the house and the garden so he can have a bit of peace."

"I see." Maisie could imagine the mother giving her children tasks and errands to keep the house quiet when a hardworking father returned from work, and perhaps shouting at them to allow him a "bit of peace."

"Have you seen anyone camping here?"

The children looked at one another.

The eldest boy looked at his siblings. "Well, there's sometimes tramps, people who've got nowhere to live and no money. But it's cold at night 'cos of the river. There's other places what are better." He pointed beyond the field. "Like under the railway arches, that's where a lot of tramps are."

"Oh, I see. So you haven't seen a boy here, a bit older than you, living out, camping?"

They looked at one another again, as if to see who might know the answer. Then the taller of the girls spoke, pointing into the distance. "We're not supposed to go over there, because our mum can't see us from the bedroom windows, but there's trees—see them? And under the trees all the grass has gone flat, like there was someone sleeping there."

"But we was a bit scared to look," said the youngest boy.

"No we wasn't." The eldest boy shoved his younger brother. "We ain't scared. None of us is scared."

"No, I should think you're all very brave, and you have a good big dog, don't you?"

"He's braver than all of us. He barks at that funny vicar, the one what comes over here sometimes."

"Oh, does he?" said Maisie. "That's a really brave dog!" She smiled upon the retriever, who was now laying in front of the children, somewhat less on guard, but still with his eyes on Maisie. "Why's he a funny vicar?"

"My mum says he comes from a church that's not right. She says that it's not your C of E, so she won't have anything to do with it," said the older boy.

"But we don't go to church anyway," added a younger boy. His middle sister nudged him.

"So, you come over here all the time, then. You must know this place very well." Maisie looked at the children, especially the older boy and girl.

"We don't get told off over here, and me mum says we could get killed on them roads, if we play on them. We aren't allowed near the canal, though. It's too dangerous," said the girl.

"It most certainly is dangerous, so it's best you and your dog play right here," said Maisie. "Well, I think I'll go and have a look by those trees."

"On yer own?" asked the middle girl.

"Yes, on my own."

The girl's eyes grew, and she pressed a finger to her lips. "You better be quiet then, in case you wake the giant what lives there."

"What giant?"

"Joey said there was a giant, and if we didn't behave—"

"I did not!" said Joey—the older boy.

"You did," said the older girl.

"Look, let's not have a row about it—I'll look out for anyone bigger than me. It's probably time for you all to be getting home." She pulled half a crown—a small fortune for the children—from her purse. "Here, stop at the butcher's and get your dog a bone—in fact, he should give you one for nothing, but if you have to pay, don't give more than a farthing for it and make sure there's meat on the bone. Give the rest of the money to your mum. Be sure to tell her it wasn't a nasty man who gave you the money, but a lady who you helped. All right?"

"We was told not to talk to strangers," said the smallest child, a girl.

"Then you were told right. Keep that dog fed and his coat shining, and don't talk to any more strangers today." Maisie moved to walk away, and waved to the children. "Bye!"

She did not look around, but could feel the group watching her as she made her way towards a clump of trees with low-hanging branches, a mixture of willow and birch, and with buddlea growing up here and there. Upon reaching the spot described by the children, it was easy to see what they meant—the grass was flattened, as if someone had been sleeping there. Maisie stepped around and in between the trees, then noticed a mound of grass at the foot of a birch tree. Investigating further—something the children had probably been scared to do, despite the brashness of their talk—she discovered a knapsack and blanket had been pushed in between the twin trunks of the tree and covered with grass. She looked around, then at the foot of the tree. She pulled out the knapsack and unbuckled the flap. Inside was a jacket, a woolen Guernsey-style pullover, and a water bottle of the type used by soldiers in the war. The name on the inside of the knapsack, clearly marked in indelible ink: Captain Arthur Payton. Maisie sat back on the grass, and looked around again. Who on earth was Captain Arthur Payton? Was she so completely out of her depth in this case that she had never come across a Captain Arthur Payton? Or on the other hand—why should she? A boy named Martin Robertson had discovered Maya Patel's body, and he might never have been here and might have nothing to do with Jesmond Martin. This could be the hiding place for a man who had no work, perhaps a man wounded in the war and with no roof over his head except the sky. She looked up as tiny leaves fell from the birch trees. She didn't need a dog to let her know that she could well have been barking up the wrong tree from the very beginning. And now it was getting later, and on a Friday. So much of the precious information she needed to uncover would have to wait until the following week. Surely records had to exist for Arthur Payton. And while she was at it, for Jesmond Martin, too.

Chapter Sixteen

Maisie and James drove to Chelstone together, stopping on the way in the village of Westerham for lunch at an inn. It was a pleasant interlude, with James detailing plans for his travel to Canada, a journey that was fast approaching. Ostensibly, his absence would be only for a month or two—he expected to be home at Chelstone for the Christmas holiday, though he spoke of his dread of spending the festive season without Maisie, if she indeed chose to leave England at the same time.

"I can't believe that this time last year the builders were working on Ebury Place. I was so excited about us spending our first Christmas together there—and we just scraped in, didn't we, though the upper rooms weren't all finished."

"I know, James, and it was a lovely time—waking up in a house that seemed so familiar, yet new and important, then driving down to Chelstone on Christmas morning. I like the feeling of driving home for Christmas on the very day."

James nodded. "Wonder where you'll be, come December."

Maisie reached for his hand. "Let's not become sad, James. Wherever I am, I know I will have Chelstone, snow, and you in my thoughts, even though I may be in sunshine or showers."

"You're excited about it, aren't you? I can see it in your eyes: a different sort of sparkle I haven't seen before."

Maisie smiled. "I am a bit, though scared, too—it's a strange feeling, embarking upon something so new, so deliberately different. And I haven't booked my passage yet."

"You'd better get a move on then, Maisie—I would do it on Monday, if I were you."

"You too, I would have thought."

"Yes, me too." James looked out of the window. "We'd better be on our way. It's looking like rain and I'd like to be home before the clouds open."

James came into The Dower House with Maisie and had a cup of tea in the kitchen. He had become more

used to Maisie's informality at the house—sipping tea
in the kitchen while Mrs. Bromley, the housekeeper,
buzzed around, cleaning and cooking. Even though
they had just had lunch, James was able to polish off a
few homemade ginger biscuits, a favorite treat.

"You're light on your toes this afternoon, Mrs.
Bromley," said James.

"Am I, sir? Well, it's a nice day and there's a lot to
be done." She set down a pan, and turned to James
and Maisie, untying her floral apron and retying it
around her body, with a knot at the front of her waist.
She pressed her hand to her hair, which—Maisie
noticed—seemed to be tied back in a different style,
which framed her face more favorably. "Now, I think
I will just pop into the conservatory and plump up the
cushions—they do settle so, and I know you like sitting
in there first thing in the morning, Miss Dobbs." Mrs.
Bromley dashed from the kitchen.

"Nice day?" said James, shrugging his shoulders as
he looked across at Maisie. "It's pouring with rain out
there, and it's getting dark."

"She is acting a bit strange, isn't she? Sort of jumpy.
I'm glad she's staying here this evening—she likes to
go back to her cottage in the village most nights, but
stayed on because she knew we were coming home
late."

"Perhaps your father knows what's wrong with her—they are quite pally, after all."

"Gosh, I hope she's not working up to telling me she's leaving, just when I need her most to keep an eye on the house. Maurice left her very well provided for, so I've always felt very fortunate that she wanted to stay on. I don't know what I would do without her."

"Speaking of your father—he usually walks up to see you as soon as he hears your motor car in the driveway. Wonder where he is."

"You know, why don't you drop me off at the Groom's Cottage when you go down to the manor. It'll save me walking down the hill. I want to see if he's all right."

Maisie collected the cups and set them in the large, square sink. She called to the housekeeper on her way out.

"Mrs. Bromley! I'm just popping down the lane to see my father—we'll both be back later. All right?"

"Yes, Miss Dobbs. Mind that weather, won't you?"

"Not such a 'nice day' now, is it?" whispered James as they left the house.

It was hardly any distance down to the Groom's Cottage, but Maisie was glad to be taken by car, as the rain was coming down even harder now. Frankie Dobbs had heard the motor car's tires on gravel, and came to the door, his lurcher dog, Jook, at heel.

Maisie kissed James on the cheek, stepped from the motor car, and ran towards her father.

"Dad, I've missed you!"

They both waited on the step, waving to James as he reversed out of the lane and turned his motor car towards the manor house.

Frankie put his arm around Maisie. "It's lovely to see you, girl. Come on in out of this rain."

Soon they were in the kitchen, where Frankie put a pot of tea and two mugs on the table.

"Oh, Dad, I just had a cup up at the house. Mrs. Bromley had made James some of his favorite ginger biscuits. I thought he would demolish the whole plate."

"Is that so. Well, she makes nice biscuits."

Maisie looked at her father and noticed his hand shake as he reached to lift up his mug.

"Dad, is everything all right? Are you ill?"

Jook sat up from her bed—an old eiderdown folded in the corner—and came to Frankie's side. She lay her head on his knee.

"Dad, there's something you're not telling me, but it's written on your face, and even Jook can tell you're upset. Come on—no secrets between us."

Frankie's once-jet-black hair was liberally threaded with gray now, and his face told of a life lived through good times and bad. Having suffered the death of his

332 · JACQUELINE WINSPEAR

beloved wife when Maisie was still a girl, he had struggled with the responsibility of preparing her for womanhood, and in his despair decided that the best place
for her was in service—and so Maisie went to work in
the Ebury Place mansion of Lord and Lady Compton.
It was while a lowly kitchen maid that she found solace
in the library. Being discovered in that book-lined
room by her employer in the early hours of the morning
had been the catalyst for enormous change in Maisie's
life—though she would never forget her roots.

"It's like this, Maisie . . ." Frankie's voice tailed
off. Jook whimpered and looked up at him, her head
cocked to one side.

"Dad, if there's something wrong with you, I want
to know now. I can get the very best doctors, you know
that, it doesn't have to be like Mum, you know. Things
are different now—"

"I'm getting married."

"You're getting married?" Maisie leaned towards
her father. "Married?"

Frankie looked up at his daughter while resting
a hand softly upon his dog's head. "I've asked Mrs.
Bromley if she would do me the honor of becoming my
wife."

Maisie noticed how Frankie had squared his shoulders to give her the news. "Oh, Dad—were you scared

to tell me?" She took his free hand in hers. "I am shocked—but I am very, very happy for you. Come on, let me congratulate you properly."

Maisie pulled away her hand, stood up, and leaned over to embrace her father as he sat at the table. "You've been alone for so long, Dad. Mrs. Bromley has given you your old laugh back—and it's been a joy to hear."

Frankie began to laugh, and as his delight was evident, so was the bittersweet memory of his long-dead wife. "I'll never replace your mother, and I'm not looking to do such a thing—not at our age, anyway. And Brenda—Mrs. Bromley—her husband died years ago of a terrible stomach infection when they'd only been married a year, and because of the distress of it all, she lost the baby she was carrying. So she went back into service to keep herself—she reckons that it was only when she went to work for Dr. Blanche that she started to feel like she belonged somewhere again." He paused. "Anyway, so what with one thing and another, and us having our lunch and a bit of supper together every day, and a laugh about this and that, it seemed a nice thing for both of us, you know, to have someone to rub along with when the days get shorter."

Maisie felt a lump in her throat. "I know what you mean, Dad. And I'm glad of it. Truly I am." She sat back in her chair. "I hope you'll get married soon, though. Because I've some news of my own."

She could not fail to see the look of optimism when she spoke, so she was quick to put to rights any foregone conclusions her father might have. "I've decided to spend a bit of time abroad, traveling. I'll be going on my own, but that's all right. I will be safe and there's more and more women traveling alone now—the world's getting smaller. I want to see more of other places. I've read Maurice's diaries and it's given me a hunger to see more of the world."

"I don't know about that, Maisie. I never liked it, you going off in the war, and I don't like it now—you never know what you might come home with; they have terrible diseases abroad, what with all that strange food."

Maisie took her father's hand again. "Don't you worry, Dad. I was a nurse, remember? I know all about diseases, so I reckon I'll be all right." She changed the subject to divert her father's concern. "I think we should put Mrs. Bromley—Brenda—out of her misery. She's been blushing like a schoolgirl since I walked into the house, and now I know why. And let's talk to the vicar tomorrow—see if we can get everything arranged and the banns read so you can be married before I leave. I'm not going to miss my own father's wedding."

"All right, then. Put on your mackintosh and rubber boots, and we'll walk up the hill to your house." Frankie stopped a moment to catch his breath, his hand on his chest. "This is a fine state of affairs, eh, Maisie? Me asking your housekeeper to be my wife. I don't know what sort of position that puts you in."

"I'm sure we can find a way through it all, Dad. Will you live here at the Groom's Cottage?" Maisie passed her father his coat.

Frankie nodded. "I like it here, and so does Brenda. We'll keep her cottage in the village, on account of the fact that we might like it later, when we retire."

"Then we'll see if she still wants to work for me, and if she does, I'd be happy—I need good staff to look after the house while I'm away—and it would be even better having family in charge." Maisie reached down to pat Jook. "And you should mind your *p*'s and *q*'s, old girl, you're going to have a mistress who'll keep you in check." Maisie turned to her father again. "Well then, let's go and have a toast to you and your bride—I'll just telephone the manor."

"James?" said Maisie as soon as he picked up the telephone. "James, I've at least solved one mystery. I know why Mrs. Bromley was at sixes and sevens. Come up to The Dower House—oh, and could you bring a bottle of champagne?"

"What are we toasting?"

"My new stepmother-to-be."

"Your what?"

Maisie laughed. "Lovely, isn't it?"

That Saturday and Sunday were two of the best days Maisie had ever spent at Chelstone. It seemed as if everyone's spirit was elevated by the news of two elders in their small community finding love and companionship. Staff on the estate commented that even Lord Julian was seen to smile consistently—not that he was known as a sourpuss, but he gave the impression that he was the sort of man who squirreled away his lifetime quota of smiles lest they run out too soon. The local vicar was consulted on Saturday, and it was planned that the banns would be read for three Sundays commencing the following week. Maisie's skin prickled with goose bumps when the date was set—if all went well she would be sailing within days of her father's marriage. But she was content in the knowledge that he would be alone no longer, and that he had found a place in his heart for new love.

Maisie and James traveled back to London on the Sunday evening, with Maisie thankful that, to his credit, James did not use the announcement of an impending wedding to press Maisie on the subject of their relationship. They both knew that things were going along well as they were, and that the future, at this point, would remain a mystery to them both—with the exception of their respective plans to leave England.

Tomorrow she would have a busy day—there would be a visit to see the Allison family at Primrose Hill, then on to see Mr. and Mrs. Singh, where she hoped she would find Pramal.

The Allisons lived in a spacious Georgian house that seemed as if it would be more at home in the country—though, indeed, Primrose Hill had been as rural as the south downs when the mansion was first built. Maisie was shown into a drawing room at the back of the house, with a deep bow window overlooking long lawns mowed to striped perfection and framed by borders of vibrant shrubbery. It was a most calming scene, with three children—two girls and a boy—throwing a ball and running from an energetic cocker spaniel. How very similar and at once different when compared with the family she found playing in the fields behind Addington Square. This dog was groomed and well fed; the children wore good clothes and sturdy shoes. They seemed to be having every bit as much fun as their less fortunate counterparts, and were doubtless loved equally.

"Miss Dobbs," said Allison, entering the room. He held the door open for his wife.

Maisie looked back from watching the children to be greeted by a well-dressed couple, who showed none of the strains of travel just a day earlier.

"Ah, Mr. Allison, Mrs. Allison—so good of you to see me and without very much notice." Maisie held out her hand to the man and his wife in turn, and was invited to take a seat by Mrs. Allison, a slightly built woman with reddish-blond hair.

"We understand it's about dear Usha," said Mrs. Allison. "The police came here—when was it, Gerald?" She turned to her husband, then back to Maisie. "A couple of months ago—yes, that's right. We were completely shocked to hear of her death, and in such a terrible way—a gunshot."

"We couldn't believe it—she was such a likable young woman. That sort of prejudice is just not on, really. She was an educated woman, not some . . . some flotsam and jetsam just off the boat."

"It was a terrible death no matter who she was," said Maisie, reaching into her document case for an index card upon which to make notes.

"Yes, quite," said Allison. "But how can we help? Please, let us know what we can do to assist you—your note of introduction said you were working on behalf of her brother." Allison rubbed his chin back and forth, as if only just realizing he had not shaved that morning. Maisie thought he must be tired following the long journey from overseas.

"That's right—he wanted an independent investigation, so he came to me. I should add that I also work closely with Scotland Yard, so there is no conflict of interest, and they are supporting my inquiry in every way possible."

"Glad to hear it," said Allison. He ran a finger around the edge of the cravat at his neck, as if he could not believe he had been so remiss in his personal care. "As far as I'm concerned, they did precious little in the first place."

Maisie was taken aback by his words. She was gaining an impression of the couple's deep affection for the dead woman, which was at odds with her understanding that Usha had been turned out by the Allisons without due warning or sufficient financial assistance.

"I wonder if you can tell me something about the relationship between your family and Usha Pramal. When did you first meet her? And when did she join your family as a governess? If you could start there—and please, I must apologize if you've already answered these questions, but everyone hears things differently, and I might gain an alternative perspective than the policemen who interviewed you before."

"Oh, they were in and out within, what, dear? Ten minutes, all told?" Allison looked at his wife.

"At the outside, dear, definitely. We talked about it, wondering how deeply they were looking into it. I mean, once they told us why they were here, we thought, definitely, we must help in any way we could—and we thought we were in for a few hours' worth of questioning—didn't we, my love?" Mrs. Allison turned to her husband. "You were very angry, weren't you?"

"I was, actually. I thought the police were letting us all down—after all, we're dealing with a very tricky situation over there in India at the moment. Another ten years and I'll be surprised if we're over there at all, what with one thing and another—and even though it's a small case on the world stage, it's the sort of thing that, if the Indian press got hold of it, it would be all over the place and the next thing you know, you'd have the Mahatma strolling half-clad into Scotland Yard, with a flower-throwing entourage behind him."

"Um, yes," said Maisie, though she thought Allison's prediction melodramatic. "I wonder, when did Usha first come to work for you, and how did you find her?"

"Ah, yes," said Allison. "It must have been about eight or nine years ago—yes, we came back in 1926—I went into the civil service following my military discharge, and we were sent out there for a few years. And a few years was quite enough, I can tell you. Our children were quite young—in fact, the youngest only a matter of months old when we left."

"I never made the journey back here to have my children, Miss Dobbs. Most of the women do, you know—it's safer, but frankly, all that time at sea is just dreadful."

"Yes, I would imagine it is." Maisie turned from Mrs. Allison to her husband. "So, how did you make Usha's acquaintance?"

"Recommendation from a colleague. He realized we wanted someone who was not your run-of-the-mill ayah, but a proper governess—and I won't beat about the bush here, we were able to take on Usha Pramal for just a bit more than you would have paid a semi-illiterate woman who knew how to change a baby's napkin. The older two were ahead of themselves in their reading, and she—blessedly—had a good accent and could also speak French and German. Of course, she had a bit of that up and down lilt, but the children loved her—and we considered ourselves very fortunate that she wanted to travel. You see, she didn't have to work, not with her father being quite well off, as far as they are there." Allison rubbed his chin again, worrying at a particular area of stubble. "Apparently, she wanted to get away—lost love, that sort of thing. A man had come calling for her without paying attention to the protocols of Indian family life—the blithering idiot. Makes things very hard for all of us, a complete disregard for the natives."

"The natives?"

"Figure of speech, Miss Dobbs. Too many years in foreign service. Luckily, I'm no longer a diplomat, though I travel a fair bit."

"A diplomat? Really? Well, that is interesting." She paused, smiling at Allison. "So, Miss Pramal returned to England with you—and you were living here at the time?"

"No, we rented a house in St. John's Wood for a while, then bought this when my husband was assigned to another branch," said Mrs. Allison. "We wanted to settle down a bit, give the children a permanent home—my father was also a diplomat, and I didn't want them to have the same sort of upbringing, though I must say, I got to see a lot of places, as a child and young woman."

"I see. You were living in St. John's Wood, and then something happened and you asked Usha to leave your employ."

The Allisons looked at each other. Mrs. Allison spoke first, followed by her husband.

"But, Miss Dobbs, you have been misinformed. We did not nor would we have asked Usha to leave our employ."

"Our children adored her. They thought the world of her and they learned so much—they were well ahead by the time they went to school."

"I thought . . ."

Allison shook his head. "No, we were astonished when she said she was leaving, truly shocked. We offered to book passage back to India for her, so she wouldn't be left at a loose end if she really was that homesick, but she declined. She gave no explanation, save for the fact that it was time for her to leave."

Mrs. Allison continued. "I confess, we were a bit put out—weren't we, Gerald? I mean, she was working for us, but we weren't treating her as if she was some sort of common skivvy—she was a much-valued employee."

"She had more or less sole charge of our children, for heaven's sake!" added Allison. "You were very upset by it all, weren't you, Margaret?"

"The children wept, I wept, and I think the dog almost wept. You see—this may sound very odd, but well, here goes—we were entranced by her. The children never had a cold or any of the illnesses other children seem to come down with, from the moment she came to work for us. She made them lovely drinks each morning—nothing you would have found an English governess or nanny making—and they loved them. Spices and fruit and all sorts of things, and they were the healthiest children we knew. But more than anything, you see, we thought she loved them—and then she went. Gone. Just like that." Margaret Allison snapped her fingers.

"I know this happened some time ago, but I wonder if you can remember anything about the day she said she was leaving. Was it an ordinary day? Or were the children doing something different, out of the normal routine?" asked Maisie.

"I was probably at work—darling, do you remember?" Allison turned to his wife.

"Oh dear, let me see." Margaret Allison scratched her forehead. "Well, after breakfast, Usha usually began lessons with the children—she always liked to make it a happy time for them, she said they remembered things if there was a game attached to it, which seemed to work very well, so I had no argument with her on that point. After lessons, if the day was fine, she would take the children for a walk and they would come back with all sorts of treasures—a fallen chestnut, or a leaf, perhaps an insect in a glass jar."

"And she generally walked around the area where you lived—did she ever take a bus anywhere, for example?"

"Good lord, no," said Allison. "We were all for children having lessons in a fairly unconventional manner, but to go out on a bus? No, that sort of thing wasn't really on."

"I see. And where did you live in St. John's Wood?"

"Alwyn Gardens. A lovely house, wasn't it, Gerald?"

"Rather cramped, I thought, but it sufficed for a while until we found this one."

"Which is perfect," said his wife.

"If I may come back to Usha," said Maisie. "What can you tell me about the day she gave notice of her intention to leave your employ?"

"I was out for most of the day," said Margaret Allison. "And I returned after tea with friends. The children were in the nursery, and all was well. It was all according to the usual round for the day—Usha bathed the children, read them a story, then they were allowed to read quietly until their father and I came up to say good night. Usha knocked on the door of the drawing room—we were having drinks, if I remember rightly. She came in and said straightaway that she had decided she wanted to leave, that it was nothing to do with us or the children, whom she loved, but she said she had been offered another job and would be leaving the following morning—she specifically wanted to leave before the children were up, so she wouldn't have to say good-bye to them."

"Then what happened?"

"We were shocked, of course. I mean, we had treated her more than fairly. She could not have found better employers here or in India," said Allison.

"You were very angry, Gerald."

"Darling, you were rather angry yourself—it left us in the lurch." Allison turned from his wife to Maisie. "My wife was alone with the children all morning until we were able to cover Usha's absence. Mind you, despite the hard feelings at her news, we paid her in full and also gave her a bit extra."

"Did you have any reason to believe she was lying, or was scared?"

"I only thought it was so out of character, and it occurred to me that she might have had some sort of shock."

"What made you think she'd had a shock—did she seem scared?"

The couple looked at each other; then Allison spoke. "She was jittery. Nervous. It was as if she had to act with speed."

"Did you ask her whether she was all right, whether she was under some sort of strain?"

"Of course we did, Miss Dobbs," said Margaret Allison. "I mean, we deserved more of an explanation, after all we'd done for her. But she just said she was anxious to leave as soon as possible so as not to upset the children. She said that she had made her decision, so now she had to act."

"I see." Maisie looked at her hands, then back at the Allisons. "Is there anything else you noticed before all this happened?"

The couple looked at each other, and shook their heads in unison.

"No, not at all," said Allison.

"And you never heard from her again," said Maisie, as a statement to be confirmed, or not.

"No, we never heard a word from or about her until the detectives came to ask if she had worked for us and when she had left our employ."

Maisie nodded. "Right. You've been very kind to allow me so much of your time, especially when you must be so tired from traveling."

"We wanted to help. Usha may not have left our house as we might have wished, but we would have wanted only the best for her. Please, if you have occasion to communicate our condolences to her family, we would appreciate it," said Allison.

The couple accompanied Maisie to the front door, the housekeeper closing it almost in silence as she stepped out into the tree-lined street.

Usha Pramal had left her employers—with whom she had been happy, despite their lapses in "diplomacy"—one day following a walk around the area of St. John's

Wood. The question of who she might have seen that day to have inspired relinquishing a satisfactory post as governess might be easily answered if one were to consider the obvious coincidence—that Jesmond Martin and his family also lived in St. John's Wood. But if Usha had reason to leave upon seeing him—or perhaps his wife—why on earth would she have returned to the area to become a cleaner at his home? Unless she could not avoid the situation.

Chapter Seventeen

Maisie left the Allisons intending to go straight to St. John's Wood, but soon checked herself. Precipitous decisions had not always served her well; reconsidering her options she came to the conclusion that a visit could do more harm than good at this stage of the case. No, one step at a time. Before speaking to Jesmond Martin again, she should have more information to hand. First, she would visit the Singhs, as planned, to see Pramal. Then she would go back over her work and darken the Paiges' doorstep one more time—she knew they would be furious, but she had to take the chance. And while in the area, she wanted to have another conversation with the Reverend Griffith. There was something there, a missing link in the chain of information. It might not be a key to the final door, but it could help her beat a path to the lock. Finally, she knew she was drawn to the common land behind the square, to see if the elusive Martin Robertson was still camping out—if it was him, after all. The name in the knapsack had thrown her—completely new names at this stage in an investigation suggested a crucial point missed early, rather like a dropped stitch in knitting discovered only when a garment was almost complete. At this juncture she would expect all names to be on the case map, with only the correct order of relationship between them awaiting a final nugget of information.

Mrs. Singh welcomed Maisie into the shop, but informed her that Mr. Singh and Mr. Pramal had gone out to the market. The two women talked about vegetables and fruits in season, and how they might be added to autumn dishes. After receiving another recipe from Mrs. Singh and purchasing the requisite herbs and spices, Maisie engineered the conversation back to Mr. Pramal, and asked Mrs. Singh why she thought her husband's friend had moved from their home to the hotel in the first place—after all, wasn't the community a tight one, where a warm welcome to lay down one's head would always be found?

"Oh, he could have slept here, we'd have made room above the shop, but he didn't want to. He said he didn't want to bring misery to the house, that it was bad luck and would cast a pall over our roof." She sighed as she weighed and measured spices into small indigo paper bags, then twisted the ends closed before placing them in a large jar. "I think he might have wanted more peace and quiet, to think. He is grieving for his sister, make no mistake, Miss Dobbs." She stopped weighing the rich golden powder, and looked up at Maisie. "And if truth be told, there was something else, though I hate to admit it. I think it might have been me being here. His best friend now married to an Englishwoman. And though it's not unheard of—as I told you before, there were many lascars off the boats who stayed and married locally—it wasn't something he entirely approved of. I don't think he believes I'm good enough for his friend." She coughed as a fine cloud of dust rose from the counter. "I do beg your pardon, Miss Dobbs."

Maisie had stepped back, feeling the same irritation in her nose and mouth. "No, not at all. That's quite pungent powder you have there."

"Does you the power of good, too, this one—it's a blend of several spices. Clears the head."

"I see," said Maisie, feeling as if she were, indeed, breathing a little easier. "But you were telling me how Mr. Pramal might not have approved of the union between you and Mr. Singh."

"Yes, that's right. I think he thought my husband could have done better." She smiled at Maisie. "And perhaps he could, but he's got me—and Pramal can see now that we do all right, me and Singh." She pointed to the bindi in the center of her forehead. "You can tell I give it my best. I get on very well with people around here, now they're used to me."

Maisie nodded. "Mrs. Singh, you seem to know a lot about all these spices and herbs." Maisie held up her hand towards a series of shelves filled with jars of spices. "Can you cure ailments with these powders and petals? Do you think they really help the body, or do you think it's all in the mind? Could it be that because people believe in the cure, then it works?"

Mrs. Singh set down the ornate silver spoon she was using to measure the powder onto a small weighing scale. "That's a fair question, Miss Dobbs, and one I would have asked myself, but you know, we all have our cures, don't we? I thought of that when I was first told to put a little of that powder—the deeper yellow one over there—into my food each day. I was told it would help the pains in my shoulders, where I wrenched myself carrying shells at the munitions factory in the war. Oh, it would play up on a cold, damp day and give me trouble. But it helped all right, and if I forget to put a little sprinkle in my soup, I know all about it again after a few days. I don't believe there's any mind over matter there. And think of us, you know, the English. You can go anywhere in this country of ours and find the locals use something they pick themselves for their ailments, whether it's comfrey, peppermint, or a sprig of rosemary. My mother swore by a cup of her own ginger beer for a digestive upset, and if you had a bee sting, she'd stick an onion on it and tell you to hold it there. Then there was my father: he said that if you cut yourself, a little sprinkle of gunpowder in the wound would sort out any poisons festering in there. It's the same sort of thing—it's just that we're letting doctors and their pills and medicines wipe out our memories of what we can do for ourselves; there's no money for them in it, is there? But that's not happening so much in a tight little community like this. Mothers teach their daughters, and it goes on down the family."

"I was a nurse, in the war, and I suppose I became used to the medicines, and I saw how they saved lives," said Maisie. "Mind you, the French soldiers carried garlic juice to cleanse their wounds and prevent sepsis, and we used it sometimes, too."

"There you are then," said Mrs. Singh as she screwed a top on the jar.

"I expect Usha knew how to use all these spices and herbs to heal a sick person," said Maisie.

"Now it's interesting you should say that, because Mr. Pramal has always said his own mother was acknowledged as a local doctor, though she wasn't trained, not like our doctors are trained. But people came to her when they were sick, and she would treat them, and they would leave her what they could afford—I suppose it was often a bag of vegetables or something like that. They said she had a gift, though I've often wondered why she couldn't save her own life, but then I've never asked the question either. I don't know that Usha was able to learn much from her—after all, she died when the girl was very young—yet Usha definitely knew how to mix the spices and add what was needed to take away pain. That was what she was good at, whether it was touching someone or mixing up a drink—taking away pain was her specialty. But she wanted to be a teacher, so she never saw people at her home, like her mother had before her."

"I see, that's interesting," said Maisie.

Mrs. Singh turned to her. "Now, don't you go putting Usha on a pedestal, you know. There's many a woman I know, living on these few streets here, who could do the same thing. Like I said—we may be forgetting our old ways, but they're not. I'm one of them now, and I learn something every time one of the women comes in to ask for something special that she's never asked for before. They say the Chinese are like that, too, but they use different things, like bits of chicken leg and what-have-you."

Maisie nodded. "Yes, indeed. Look, when Mr. Pramal returns, would you tell him I came to see him? I want to talk to him about his sister. And tell him I have something for him—something very important that belonged to Usha." She smiled at the woman, who seemed perfectly at home in the shop that was so different from shops she might have frequented had she married an Englishman. "Thank you for your time, Mrs. Singh. I appreciate it." She moved as if to leave.

"Do you think you'll find Usha's killer?"

Maisie turned to face Mrs. Singh, looking directly into the woman's melancholy eyes. "Oh yes, I believe I will. And it might be soon."

It was predictable that the Paiges were far from happy to see Maisie.

"You! You said you'd never come here again!" said Paige. "Look, we owe nothing to Usha Pramal or her brother, her sister, her aunts, uncles, or even a dog, if she had one. We are clear, the slate is now wiped clean. Her personal effects are gone," said Paige.

"And if you must know, I rue the day I ever felt my heart go out to that first poor Indian woman I found on the street, cast out by her lords and masters and wanting for a meal and a roof over her head," added his wife.

"Yes, I am sure you must be very upset about it all. And I am glad that so much is settled now, but I have just a couple more questions for you," said Maisie. "With these final pieces of the puzzle, I think I can go on to clear your names," she added.

"Clear our names?" said Paige.

"Mr. Paige, it stands to reason that, until a murderer is found, then suspicion will fall on this house—after all, the two women lived under your roof," said Maisie. She knew she was pushing the husband and wife, who had, in truth, done what amounted to their best in terms of the welfare of women who needed help, though they had also helped themselves. But at that moment, she felt the need to press harder. She felt so close to the truth, however it might emerge.

"Oh, for goodness' sake, come in off the street before the neighbors talk even more. It's a wonder we haven't had our pictures on the front page of the *South London Press*," said Paige. He stood back from the threshold, holding out his hand as if to shield his wife from evil. As he led Maisie into the parlor, she looked back to see Mrs. Paige casting her gaze back and forth along the street before closing the door behind them.

Neither one of the couple invited Maisie to sit down, so they stood in the parlor. Mrs. Paige ran her left hand up and down her right arm, as if one side of her body were cold. Paige folded his arms.

"I understand that, for a while, Miss Pramal was working for a man called Jesmond Martin, essentially to help with cleaning and so on."

"That's right, general domestic help. They needed an extra hand in consideration of his wife's illness. But she left their employ months ago," said Paige.

"Why did she leave?"

"She wasn't needed anymore," said Mrs. Paige.

"And how did you find her the position?" asked Maisie.

"We didn't. Usually the employers or their house-keepers are attracted by small advertisements we place in certain newspapers, and we also put cards in windows of newsagents in the more well-to-do areas, within a reasonable distance of travel either by bus or on the Underground—we don't want to be racking up too many costs," said Paige.

"So, how did you connect Usha Pramal with Jesmond Martin?"

"He found us," said Mrs. Paige.

"He found you? How did that happen—through the advertisements?"

The couple shook their heads in unison. "No," said Paige. "He found us via the Reverend Griffith. At first Miss Pramal was not at all keen, but it was pointed out to her that she could fit in another job here and there."

"Was she that in awe of the Reverend Griffith, that she would do a job she didn't want to do, just because he asked her?"

"He is a man of God, Miss Dobbs. She knew he could not be refused. That would not be on," said Paige, his brows knitted. "And it would have put us, her providers, in a troubling position, and of course she would not have wanted to do anything of the sort."

"So, over a period of time—by the way, remind me; how long did she work for the Martin family?"

The couple looked at each other. "On and off for over two years, as I said before," said Mrs. Paige.

Maisie raised her eyebrows. "Really? Then throughout this period of time she was intermittently working at a job she did not wish to hold," said Maisie.

"No one wants to do cleaning work, Miss Dobbs. But it is little to ask of them when we were looking out for their future, and their well-being," said Paige.

Maisie wanted to point out that the couple were also looking out for their own well-being, but refrained from saying as much. Instead she asked another question.

"Are you aware of the connection between Jesmond Martin and the Reverend Griffith?"

"They were known to each other years ago, while Mr. Martin was involved in business overseas. I understand that they met again—" Paige looked at his wife. "Might have been not long before our reverend put Mr. Martin in touch with us, and then Miss Pramal—wasn't that it?"

The woman nodded, this time rubbing her hands together, as if she were still fighting an inner chill.

"And the minister specifically asked for Usha?" said Maisie.

"Yes. He thought that, given the problem of the wife's health, and Miss Pramal's education and obvious command of English—much more accomplished than the other women in the hostel—she would be the better choice."

"And you don't know why she left?"

"You've already asked us that question, Miss Dobbs." Paige glared as he spoke.

"I know. Sometimes the memory is jogged when it's asked again at a different time," she responded. "Do you know of a man named Arthur Payton?"

Man and wife looked at each other. Paige frowned while Mrs. Paige seemed to ask a silent question, her mouth formed in a perfect O.

Maisie asked again. "Does Captain Arthur Payton mean anything to you?"

Paige scratched his head while his wife looked at Maisie, her face blank.

"I think it rings a bell, but I couldn't say why," said Paige, at once seeming more mellow than he had just a few minutes earlier, as if something was dawning upon him, an elusive memory that he was not able to pin down, no matter how hard he tried.

"Not to worry," said Maisie. "But it might come to you later, when you are going about your business and doing something completely different. Perhaps, if that is so, you would send word to my office," said Maisie. "I believe I gave you my card, but just in case you've mislaid it, here's another. Keep it here on the sideboard, then you'll be able to find it."

Paige watched as Maisie set the plain card with her name, office address, and telephone number on the mahogany sideboard. Though kept polished to a shine, the furniture had not seen a duster of late; Maisie suspected Mrs. Paige was missing the presence of Indian women to tend to the cleaning and upkeep of her house.

"I think that's all now. Thank you for seeing me again, Mr. Paige, Mrs. Paige." She smiled, moving towards the door, which Paige stepped back to open.

"Will there be more visits to intrigue our neighbors, Miss Dobbs?" said Paige.

"I hope not. But you never can tell when a murder is being investigated," answered Maisie.

She turned to the couple as she reached the front door, to bid them good-bye.

"Will you be going to see the Reverend Griffith?" asked Paige.

"Oh, yes," said Maisie. "I'm going to see him right now."

The couple stood back as she took her leave. She walked along the street towards the junction where she would turn in the direction of Griffith's house, and as she glanced back, she saw Mrs. Paige looking up and down the road and across the square, making sure that no one had seen Maisie leaving the house. Maisie smiled, for even at a distance, she could see lace curtains twitching back and forth as neighbors took note of what was going on at the house where two murdered women had lived.

Maisie moved her motor car to another street, though when she parked it was still the only vehicle in sight. She decided to go over to the common ground where she had discovered the belongings of whoever was camped out under the low trees.

There were no children bounding around in the long grass now, no big golden dog, and no sounds of squeals and laughter. Only the muffled sounds of traffic on the canal and, more distant, the Thames—"the water," as it was known to those who lived south of the navigation—challenged an otherwise quiet day. Maisie stopped at the edge of the land, alongside the gate. Though this was the working edge of one of the busiest cities in the world, she could smell the country, as if she were in Kent at harvesttime. She stepped out along one of the many paths beaten across the common, towards the cluster of trees.

It seemed as if someone was still sleeping rough under the low boughs. The grass was pressed down, and behind a tree trunk Maisie saw a couple of empty tins of rice pudding—as acceptable cold as it was heated, thus an easy choice of quick, though not hearty, sustenance. A dappled afternoon light filtered through the trees, and after walking around the area, Maisie took off her jacket, laid it on the smooth grass, and sat down. She thought that if she lay back she might fall asleep, comforted by a lazy Indian summer breeze brushing against her skin. But she remained sitting, arms around her knees. She closed her eyes and stilled her mind—a mind that she knew was racing ahead. Was she making the same mistake as the police? Was she rushing from person to person, trying to tie up loose ends so she could move on to the next thing sooner? She sat in silence and allowed her thoughts to skim across her mind, as if they were splashes against stones in the waters of her conscience. She considered every step she had taken—including sending Billy home. It was the right thing to do, though she had underestimated the fact that she felt as if something important was missing every day as she worked. Maurice had once questioned her choice of Billy as an assistant, suggesting that his intellect wasn't up to the job. But Maisie stuck to her guns, knowing that it was Billy's heart that would stand him in good stead, and his great loyalty towards her. That loyalty had almost cost him his life, and he had suffered while trying to continue his work for her. She sighed, opening her eyes and picking at a blade of grass. But now he was moving on—and for that, this new job, she was relieved and grateful. And Sandra had proved to be more than able—more than she had ever imagined the young woman would be. The anger of widowhood had inspired her, giving her energy to propel her from her station in life to greater levels of accomplishment. What could stop her now, except the limits of her imagination?

Usha Pramal seemed to have an imagination without limits, and the determination to achieve her dreams.

But the vision of establishing a school for poor girls at home in India had been brought to an abrupt end by a single bullet from a gun fired by someone with a perfect eye for their target. Had Usha known her killer? Maisie closed her eyes again and brought to mind the woman she had never met: colorful in her fine silk sari, confident in her manner and walk. She imagined her walking along the street, cutting down towards the canal, a humid summer's day reminding her of home. But why was she walking towards the canal? Why would she leave the street where she was seen earlier in the day—according to Caldwell's notes—and make her way to a canal where barges lumbered back and forth from the river, and through the canal's dark waters? Was there something about the path that eased her heart, perhaps? Or was she meeting someone?

Maisie sighed, though her eyes remained closed. She thought of those she had met during the investigation, and others she knew only by association, dependent as she was on a picture built by question after question. She imagined Robert Martin, Jesmond Martin's missing son, to be typical of his age—perhaps somewhat lanky, possibly in the transition from a childhood during which he hung on his father's every word to now questioning each comment, question, or instruction. In the short years between boyhood and growing the beard of maturity, had he argued with his father to the extent that he would leave his beloved mother? Had he struck out on his own to prove his worth? She imagined his hair longer now, and if he was living rough—and she strongly suspected that Martin Robertson was indeed Robert Martin—he would be ill-kempt and tired. He might even be afraid. For his part, Jesmond Martin had wanted to find his son and paid good money to see him brought home. Yet he appeared to be a man adrift from any emotion—had his love for a wife who was sick taken a toll on his relationship with his son? Had they argued about the boy's mother— perhaps when Usha Pramal had helped the woman and was thrown from the house for her trouble? Was Jesmond Martin so prejudiced that he could not accept Usha's healing ministrations, when the nurse herself said that Mrs. Martin was feeling so much better? She wondered if Mrs. Martin's crippling headaches and the necessity of being confined to her room had, for some reason, brought a measure of peace to the household? In which case, perhaps Usha Pramal had stumbled upon evidence that Mrs. Martin's headaches were caused deliberately— which might in turn have placed her at risk.

Now Maisie tried to clear her mind of the thoughts that began to cascade before her—random connec- tions, more questions about Maya Patel, about Pramal, the loving brother, at home in India when his sister was murdered. She considered the Singhs—an unusual couple, yet so ordinary in their everyday life. They could have been the proprietors of any corner shop across Britain, but instead of weighing biscuits or sweets, flour or currants, Mrs. Singh was spooning turmeric and cardamom into small indigo paper bags for women who wore silks and who knew how to heal with spices and herbs blended by stone pressed to stone.

But her thoughts always came back to Usha Pramal, and the fact that, to a person, she had been described as unusual in some way, whether by her own or those outside her culture. And she had been loved, that much was clear. With this consideration, Maisie leaned her head on her knees. Would it be a leap to believe that Usha Pramal was killed by someone who loved her too much? And who would want to kill an extraordinary person who touched the lives of others with such gentleness? Who would find such beauty of spirit a threat—and take the life of a daughter of heaven?

Maisie remained in the shade offered by the branches for a while longer. She meditated for some minutes, becoming more aware of the residue of emotion left by whoever had chosen this place for refuge— for it felt like a refuge. And wasn't a place of refuge usually sought by someone who had lost something of value—perhaps a way of life, a house, a home, a lover, or simply part of themselves? Refuge. The word spun webs in her mind. She knew she would come back to that sense of a safe place in which to curl and, perhaps, escape from the world. There was sadness here, too. A suggestion of pain that went beyond the body into the heart and soul of a person, and again she pressed her hand to her chest, lest the lingering despair impress itself into her being. It was time to leave. Time to go across the common and back to the street. It was time to see the Reverend Griffith.

As she looked back at the trees, the breeze seemed to catch upon itself and the air became sharper and quicker and blew across the hay-like grass, shimmering gold in the afternoon light. She thought that, in time, those trees would become a place where children would fear to tread, that in their youthful imaginings, it would be the forbidden center of the common. Didn't children always sense evil before their elders? How many pulled back while a mother or father said, "Don't be frightened, there's nothing to scare you here." Perhaps Usha Pramal held a fear of the canal, but she pressed on anyway. And had she felt as Maisie felt in that moment, when she stepped out from under the trees and began her walk towards the gate and the road? It was the overwhelming sense that she was not alone and was being watched.

Chapter Eighteen

There was no answer to her knock when Maisie called at the home of the Reverend Griffith. She waited on the doorstep, knocked again, and listened. No sound issued from the house, though she remembered that the main rooms in Griffith's garden flat were at the back of the building. Nevertheless, it appeared that no one was home. She could not try a back door, as the front entrance was the only means of access to the house and garden. Why, then, did she have a pressing feeling that she was still being watched and that someone was at home. She knocked one more time, and when there was again no answer, she began to walk away towards her motor car. As she walked, she remembered the children and their dog, and the girl saying her mother could always see what they were up

to from the top of the house. Perhaps it was this recollection that caused her to turn and look once again
at Griffith's somewhat shabby terrace home in time to
catch a glimpse of movement on the roof. Could it have
been a pigeon flapping its wings in upward flight? She
shielded her eyes with her hand against the low light of
late afternoon. At once she was tempted to wave, just to
see if acknowledgment came in return. She waved, but
did not wait for the gesture to be reciprocated. It was
enough to know that if she were indeed being watched,
the person keeping tabs on her knew she was aware of
their presence. They would meet soon enough.

The office was quiet when she returned, though a tidy
pile of papers had been left by Sandra. On top was a
note with messages and information regarding each
item of correspondence. She'd ended the communica-
tion by adding that she would be in the office early in
the morning, as she wanted to discuss something with
Maisie. "If that would be convenient," she'd added.

There was a brief report on her visit to the other
houses where Usha Pramal had been employed, with
the conclusion that there was nothing out of the ordinary observed by the women, who she thought had
hardly ever seen Usha anyway. The Indian woman
had come to the houses, gone about her work, and left.

Next came a note to the effect that Mr. Pramal had telephoned from a kiosk, and had had just enough time to inform her that he would pay a visit to the office of Miss Maisie Dobbs the following morning. Sandra had taken the liberty of suggesting ten o'clock. Maisie nodded her head in silent approval of the appointment. And another man had walked to his nearest telephone kiosk that afternoon, possibly at some point before Maisie left Camberwell to return to the West End. Mr. Paige had left a message that he had some information for Maisie, and would place another call to her office the following morning.

Not long before Maisie decided to leave for home, but prior to departing the office, she looked up the location of the Peninsular and Oriental Steam Navigation Company. In truth, it was easier to think and talk about leaving England than it was to take the first step. But with the address in Leadenhall Street scribbled on a piece of paper, it seemed as if her imaginings could become the reality she craved. After all, plans and dreams were just words and images in the mind until she did something concrete.

She arrived back at 15 Ebury Place before James, and following a hot bath took the opportunity to sit in her rooms in silence. An uncomfortable feeling of anticipation was rising up within her. She knew that this was due in part to the case and an overriding sense—increasing as the hours passed—that she was close to identifying the killer of the two Indian women. But there was something else, too. Over the course of the days spent at Chelstone, following the news that Frankie Dobbs and Mrs. Bromley were to be married, James—who had at first been enthusiastic about the match—seemed more distant. Maisie knew the news had unsettled him, and that the status quo they had achieved in a union outside the bounds of marriage was proving, to a greater degree, to be inadequate for him. James, as she knew only too well, was a man who wanted more from her. And they both accepted that, despite their ages—she was now thirty-six years of age, James almost thirty-nine—Maisie was far from ready to take that particular leap. But was it a case of readiness? Or simply that the idea of marriage did not suit her? She rested her head in her hands, running her fingers through her hair.

James was a good man, of that she was in no doubt. She loved him as much as she could—she believed—love anyone. She knew that the past year had rocked her foundation: as time went on, the good fortune bestowed upon her by Maurice's will had not made the ground beneath her feet seem any more firm; on the contrary, she discovered that the responsibility had made her question who she was. In her plans to travel, was she hoping to find her essential self hidden in the unknown as if it were buried treasure? And when she came home, would she be ready, at last, to embrace the life she had come to know with James?

These thoughts led her once again to John Otterburn, and the case that had caused her to question the integrity of her moral compass, to lose her true north, which was a belief that all would be well and good if she acted with compassion and a sense of the right thing to do. She felt as if she had been David against Otterburn's Goliath, but holding no sling and stone with which to slay the giant—yet at the same time, this particular behemoth was intent upon protecting Britain and her people; he saw himself as the answer to a prayer not yet spoken by the common man. Therefore, she had come to the conclusion that she could no longer continue to put herself forward as a woman of good conduct in her business, when she had been complicit—in her estimation—in keeping secret the role played by John Otterburn in what amounted to murder, even though her voice had been a small one.

Could she blame James for agreeing to ally himself with Otterburn and become part of his plans? James loved his country, had fought for his country, and would lay down his life to protect the land he cherished. He was a man of good intentions, of integrity, and for that she had utmost respect, and yes, love.

It was in the midst of these considerations that James returned home. Soon there was a knock on the door adjoining their rooms. Maisie had pulled her armchair close to the window and was looking out.

"Maisie. We're both home at a reasonable hour—that makes a change." He came to her side, kneeling down before her. "What's wrong, my love? You seem so very sad."

Maisie wiped a tear from the corner of her eye. "Oh, nothing, James. Just thinking about nothing in particular. Probably my father, really."

"You're not losing him, Maisie—he's getting married, though I think that's enough to inspire thoughts of the past and of your mother, perhaps. You and your father have only had each other for so long." He smiled, holding her hand. "Well, and you've got me, I suppose."

She nodded. "Yes, you're right—it's probably down to too much excitement these past few days."

"And you're looking very tired, my love. Perhaps we should go away for a Friday to Monday, somewhere different—what about Paris?" said James.

"I have an important case on, you know. I can't just swan off, not yet."

They were quiet for some moments, when James spoke again. "Look, there's something I want to say to you, but there never seems to be the right time. I find I dither back and forth."

Maisie nodded. "Yes. I know."

"It's this, Maisie. We agreed to just go along as if all was well, as if we both found our life here suitable, acceptable. But I have realized, time and again, that I don't find things at all agreeable." James continued without further pause; Maisie looked at him, though she did not speak to counter his words. "So, here's what I've been thinking," he said, looking down at her hand nestled in his. "I have made no secret of the fact that I want to marry you, to have and to hold you for the rest of both our lives. I want to make a life with you, and even hope for children. That is the measure of my intentions. Now, I know you want to go abroad, to follow in Maurice's footsteps—and even to find part of him again. I understand all that, Maisie—in fact, I think I understand more than you might give me credit for. And you have every right to do as you wish. I know very well that you are searching for answers to questions I cannot help you with. So be it. But I want you to know that I need an answer to my proposal of marriage: yes or no." James held up a hand as Maisie's eyes widened. "Not yet though. You have a plan, as yet not fully formed—that much is clear—and I will be on my way to Canada soon after your father's marriage. I suppose we will be going our separate ways at the same time." He sighed, and took another deep breath before going on—it was clear he had a planned monologue and wanted to say every word. "Six months, Maisie. I want your answer in six months. By the end of March. We'll write to each other, of that I am sure, and you will know where I am as I will know where to find you—let us agree that much. Send me a telegram, or a message by carrier pigeon if that's the only viable option—I will be waiting for your answer on March 31, give or take a day or two. Yes Stop or No Stop. That's all I ask of you. Together until death us do part; or apart, forever. No going back." He looked directly into her eyes, still holding her hand. "That is all I have to say."

Maisie nodded. "All right, James. That is more than fair. On March 31 I will let you know. Yes. Or no."

James smiled and stood up, pulling Maisie to him. "Now, let's go and have a glass of champagne and toast to the future, whatever it may hold."

She placed her free hand on his cheek and held his gaze, though there was nothing she could say at that moment.

For some reason, Maisie felt calmer the following day, perhaps more settled than she had for some time. Now she knew, now there was a landing point for what she might become. She would go abroad. She would have several months in which to immerse herself in places new and far away, and then she would make her decision. *Yes Stop. No Stop.* In one telegram perhaps the most important part of her future would be decided. She would either marry James Compton or not. From the close of the Pramal case until the end of March, she would be accountable only to herself. The weight lifted from her shoulders, though she knew it would return in good time. But she hoped, too, that the decision, when it came, would be an easy one.

Sandra arrived at the office at the same time as Maisie. Over a cup of tea, Maisie went through files on several open cases, so that plans for the day ahead would be clear. Some assignments required only research and organization—a telephone call to a newspaper or a records office, a visit to a bank with a client—and of late Maisie had asked Sandra to take on various tasks that would have been Billy's responsibility, though on this occasion, Sandra would work only half a day with Maisie before going on to her second job with Douglas Partridge, followed by evening classes at Morley College.

As Maisie closed the final case file, which required only the preparation of an invoice, she turned to her secretary. "You wanted to speak to me about something, Sandra. Is everything all right?"

Sandra leaned forward, her hands flat on the wood of Maisie's desk. She was sitting on the opposite side, facing her.

"Well, Miss Dobbs, I thought I would let you in on what's been happening, just so you know."

Maisie pulled her chair closer to the desk, as if she were about to hear a secret told for the first time.

"A couple of things, actually," said Sandra. "The first is that, well, I might be moving, but I haven't found somewhere to live yet."

"You've hardly been in the flat a few months yet. Don't you get along with the others?"

Sandra shrugged. "It's not that I don't get along with them—it's good fun, having others around, and we all muck in to keep it nice."

"But?" asked Maisie.

"But it gets very noisy of an evening, when I'm trying to study. I stay late at the library, after my lectures, but there's the other evenings, when I'm supposed to be reading and then writing essays, so I'm trying to work out how I can afford a room of my own—a bedsit perhaps—and then still keep up my college work."

"I see," said Maisie. She had discovered that often the best helping hand was in fact an ear to listen to another.

"I didn't think I could do it, what with working part-time at two jobs, but something's happened that could help me, but I would feel just awful about it."

"I think you should tell me what the awful thing is, Sandra. Sometimes the awful things aren't half as bad as we think they are—everything sorts itself out in the end." As Maisie spoke, her own words echoed in her mind. *Everything sorts itself out in the end.* "Come on, tell me what's so bad."

"The bad thing is, Miss Dobbs, that I've been offered another job." She held up her hand. "No, not with Mr. Partridge, but through someone he knows. It, well, it pays better, and if I took it, I would have to give up working for you, that's what's bad about it. I could carry on helping Mr. Partridge on Saturdays, but this job here is different, there's something every day. I mean, it was all very well, but what with Mr. Beale leaving, and what with one thing and another and you being so busy, I couldn't just—"

Maisie held up her hand. "Hold on, hold on, Sandra. Let's just talk about the job, and what it means to you—the most important thing you should be thinking about is yourself, though I appreciate the consideration. This all might have come at an opportune time. Now then, tell me all about this job."

"It's through a friend of Mr. Partridge, like I said. He's a publisher and he's setting up by himself, a new company. He has money, apparently, and wants to publish books for students—like me, actually. Which is why he liked what I could do when he met me at Mr. Partridge's office. I've come to know a lot about the business, through Mr. Partridge, and I'm also a student and know about books—now I do, anyway. And I will be his secretary—with possibilities."

"Possibilities?"

"This man, Lawrence Pickering, says as the Pickering Publishing Company grows, so will the possibilities for me to be promoted. And he'll be flexible, he says, where my hours are concerned, so I don't have to rush so hard to get from my lectures to the office."

"Well, this all sounds wonderful, Sandra. A good job in an exciting new company, and an employer considerate of your studies. You're a clever young woman, and hardworking. The Pickering Publishing Company will be lucky to have you."

Maisie picked up a pen and turned it around in her hands, then looked up at Sandra—who was a maid at Ebury Place when they had first met; a young woman whom she had seen engaged, married, and widowed, and whom she admired anew each day with her determination to create a new life for herself. Weren't they trying to do exactly the same thing, really? To discover what the world might hold if they stepped off the well-worn path, for just a little while. *Possibilities*—wasn't that what Maisie had always wanted, even in girlhood, during those dark early-morning hours when she had stolen into the Comptons' library to teach herself Latin and philosophy, to read from books she touched with a deep excitement knowing that each one would take her on a journey of discovery? Wasn't that what James wanted, what Frankie and Mrs. Bromley wanted—the sweet sense of being touched by possibility? And now Serendipity had danced in concert with Fate at exactly the right time, and all would be well. It was as if the path were being made clear for her journey to India.

"I think you should take the job, Sandra. I think it sounds very good indeed." Maisie smiled, her eyes catching the morning light as it came in broad shafts through the window. "But make sure Mr. Partridge approves—he will know how serious this man is about his company. And I will ask just this of you—stay with me for another few weeks. Just to get some things organized here." She looked at her hands, wondering how much to reveal. "You see, Sandra, I have some plans of my own, so this is a time of change for Billy, you, and me. Sometimes things just work out the way they need to. Oh, and don't rush out and look for a new flat. I may have the answer on that one, too."

"I will stay for as long as you need me to, Miss Dobbs—I would always have given you plenty of notice, come what may."

"I know, Sandra. You're a good worker." She looked at the woman before her. "All sorted out with Billy?"

Sandra nodded. "We weren't being sensible."

"We're not always as sensible as we would like to be, Sandra—our hearts take care of that for us."

At that moment, both women started as the bell sounded. The day had begun. Pramal had arrived to discuss the case of his murdered sister with Maisie.

As Sandra came back into the room with Usha Pramal's brother, the telephone began to ring.

"I'll answer it, Miss Dobbs—then I'll make tea." Sandra pulled out a chair for Pramal, and then picked up the black telephone receiver. She shook her head; the caller had begun speaking before she had time to give the exchange and number.

"It's that Caldwell man, Miss Dobbs. Not a man-nered bone in his body." She rested her hand across the mouthpiece. "Do you want to talk to him now?"

Maisie could hear Caldwell's voice despite the muffling effect of Sandra's fingers, and smiled, thinking he sounded like a mouse in a box.

"Let me speak to him—we'll never hear the last of it." She turned to Pramal as she took the receiver. "Do excuse me, Mr. Pramal, it's our good friend, the Detective Inspector."

Maisie half-turned away to greet Caldwell.

"Good morning, Det—"

"No need for all that, Miss Dobbs," said Caldwell.

"Well then, let's get on with it—to what do I owe the pleasure?" said Maisie.

"Got an interesting bit of news for you, Miss Dobbs."

"I'm all ears." Maisie smiled.

"Man came into the Yard this morning, asking for me."

"Yes—go on." Maisie could hear the measured telling of the tale by Caldwell, teasing her with his news, as if he were dangling a length of string in front of a kitten.

"Man came into the Yard to confess to the murder of one Miss Usha Pramal," said Caldwell.

Maisie felt her smile vanish as she looked at Pramal, who met her gaze.

"What was his name, Inspector?"

"Mr. Jesmond Martin. Said he murdered her because he doesn't like them, these people coming over here.

Said she insulted his sick wife, and he was so filled with anger, he just took matters into his own hands."

"And Maya Patel?"

"Said he took her life, too—she had seen him kill Miss Pramal, so he followed her one night and shot her, just like Miss Pramal."

"And do you believe him?"

"Come on, Miss Dobbs—why wouldn't I? Man comes in, bold as you like, and admits to a crime of murder because he can't live with himself anymore. Of course I bloody believe him. Read him his rights and locked him up. The Commissioner's happy, the Foreign Office is happy—that could have been a bit tricky, what with the brother kicking up sand—and so, Miss Dobbs, I am happy. So should you be, I would have thought—though I bet you wish you'd have got him yourself, don't you?"

"No, I'm happy when a murderer is brought to justice." She ran the telephone cord through her fingers. "But tell me, does he have the skill with a gun? Could he hit a target—a very small target—with the precision that took the life of both women?"

"You thought we hadn't got that one, didn't you? Took him out and tested him with a target. Course, it was tricky, giving the man a gun—could have turned it on himself or even us, but we thought he would have done that before now, if he'd have wanted to. He was as good as gold, like a sheep, in fact. Just took the gun, leveled it up, squinted a bit at the target, and boom-boom-boom. Bull's-eye. Three shots right in the center, and after the first one the others went through the same hole. Must've been a sniper in the war—if he wasn't, he should've been, that's all I can say."

"Right, I suppose we're finished then," said Maisie.

"I've just got to find that Pramal bloke now."

"Not to worry, Inspector. He's right here in front of me. I'll tell him, if that's all right with you—or you can come to my office, if you want to speak to him."

"Nah, better give you something to do, Miss Dobbs. Can't have you going off thinking you've not been useful, eh?"

"You're smiling too much, Inspector. Remember, we've been working on a murder inquiry—people have died."

"There's always one to bring down the curtain on an otherwise excellent start to the day, eh, and I would have put money on it being you. Here I am, happy as sunshine on a rainy morning, and you have to put the damper on it. Never mind."

"Please let me know if you need any information from me," offered Maisie.

"I'll see you in a day or two—after all, you interviewed him, so we'll need to know all about that little tête-à-tête."

"Right you are, Inspector. I'll give Mr. Pramal the good news."

"That's more like it, Miss Dobbs," said Caldwell. "I'll be in touch."

"Until then," said Maisie, but she was too late—as usual, Caldwell had put down the receiver as soon as he had said everything he wanted to say.

"Do you have something important to report, Miss Dobbs?"

Maisie looked up—she had continued to twist the telephone cord between her fingers. "Yes, I have, Mr. Pramal. Apparently, a man has come forward to accept responsibility for the murder of both your sister and Miss Maya Patel. He gave himself up to detectives at Scotland Yard early this morning. It appears he has the skill with a gun that was required to take the life of your sister in an instant."

Pramal's olive skin became drawn and gray, his eyes filled with tears. It was several seconds before he could speak. "And why on earth did he do such a thing?" He thumped the desk with his closed fist. "I want to see this man, as soon as I can. And I want to see him hang."

Maisie raised a hand. "I don't think you'll be at liberty to see him, Mr. Pramal. He has been cautioned and charged, so will be moved to a prison—probably Wandsworth, I would imagine, or Brixton. He will be able to see counsel, but no one else until further notice."

"Why, Miss Dobbs? Why did he kill my beloved sister? If she had offended him, what act or words on her part could have made him take her life?" Pramal leaned forward, grief and hatred writ large in his eyes.

Maisie sighed. "He claims she was disrespectful of his wife while in his employ. Mr. Pramal, I have to tell you that I went to the man's house, I met his wife's nurse, and I learned that Usha had taken the liberty of administering medicines of her own making to ease the woman's dreadful headaches. It's no excuse, but according to his statement, he was angered beyond measure and took matters into his own hands—and much too far. Frankly, I am at a loss to understand it all."

"Did you see the man?"

"Yes, I did, and though I had outstanding questions and wanted to see both the man and his wife again, I had yet to conclude he was the killer."

"But you thought he could be, is that it?"

"Yes, I thought he could be. But a thought is only a gate to the path—it is not evidence. I must have evidence in my hands—or at least a stronger feeling of guilt from a person—to press forward with a suspicion that someone has committed murder."

"You could have been wrong, though, Miss Dobbs— and it seems you were," said Pramal, his chin jutting forward as he spoke.

Maisie took a breath to counter, but exhaled instead. Yes, of course Jesmond Martin could have murdered Usha Pramal. But if so, and if Martin Robertson was his son, as she suspected, then why did the boy alert the police to the body of Maya Patel? Unless he wanted his father caught. Unless he knew more about his father than he would have told the police.

"Mr. Pramal, in confidence, please—may I ask if you have ever heard the name Jesmond Martin?"

Pramal, so quick to answer when he had a definite response, looked at Maisie. He rubbed his chin and pressed his hands together close to his lips, as if he were about to say a prayer. Then he spoke again. "Miss Dobbs, I cannot say that I have heard this name, but you know, it seems to ring a bell."

Maisie smiled; not a smile of joy or happiness, but of irony. "Mr. Pramal, I have come to the conclusion that, in my work, the three words that are the most frustrating to hear are that something seems to *ring a bell*." She sat down, holding out her hand for Pramal to take his seat once again. Looking up towards Sandra, she saw her secretary hold up a teacup, her eyebrows raised in inquiry. "Yes, Sandra, tea would be lovely, I am sure we could all do with a cup." She turned to Pramal. "Let's see if we can get that bell clanging, because I want to know why there is even a hint of recognition when I mentioned his name."

Pramal put his hand up, as if he were a schoolboy in class. "Miss Dobbs, please forgive me for asking, but Mrs. Singh said you had something for me, something belonging to Usha."

Maisie drew her hand across her forehead. "Of course—it is you who should forgive me. What I have for you is currently under lock and key, in a safe. It is a sum of money—a rather large sum of money—from Usha's earnings while she lodged at the ayah's hostel, together with the several velvet bags full of coins I've already told you about: money she had earned outside her cleaning jobs."

"How much could be there? And how did she earn this extra money?"

"You will find Usha had saved enough money to return to India some time ago, and have some in hand, too. I believe Usha's lack of fear around those

with sickness was something for which people were
willing to pay. Yes, she was familiar with the healing
properties of herbs and spices, but she had something
else—she saw that the sick are often ignored, even in
their own homes, and as such seldom feel the touch or
attention of another human being. From what I have
learned, she never drew back from resting a hand upon
one who could not walk or see, or who was confined to
bed—and families would pay her to come in and tend
to one struck by illness, if only for half an hour here
and there. Usha could teach, too, and though I have no
firm evidence, I cannot believe she did not also earn
pin money by giving lessons on occasion. I have a feeling that your sister did any paid work that was within
her capability because she had a dream. And she was
well on the way to making it come true, I would say."

"Her dream? Her educational castle in the air? I am
sick of her so-called dream, that it brought her to live
in a way that would have made my poor father turn in
his grave. It brought her to this city that has corners no
better than the worse slums of Bombay." Pramal could
barely contain the grief that had turned to anger.

"Perhaps Usha saw something precious in those
corners, just as she saw a diamond in even the darkest person. She had that burning ambition to return to
India and to found her school for poor girls who have

no chance in life. So perhaps coming to London was a necessary part of her aspiration—or it grew within her after she arrived here." Maisie paused, her words coming more deliberately now. "I have no idea how far her savings will stretch to bring this dream to fruition, but you must know that when I give the money to you, I am placing everything your sister worked for in your hands."

Sandra returned to the room bearing a tray set for tea just as the telephone began to ring.

"I'll answer, Miss Dobbs," she said, placing the tray on her desk. She picked up the telephone, gave the exchange and number, then turned to Maisie. "It's Mr. Paige, from the ayah's hostel. He said he remembered why that name you gave him yesterday rang a bell."

Maisie reached for the telephone. "At last. A bell has rung and woken up a memory. I was beginning to lose faith."

"Miss Dobbs." Pramal came to his feet. "You should speak to your caller in private, and I am in need of a brisk walk and some fresh air." He turned to Sandra. "Mrs. Tapley, thank you for making tea, but I should take my leave. And Miss Dobbs, I will telephone to make arrangements to collect Usha's money before I depart for India. I thank you very much for your assistance in the matter of investigating my sister's death—I am most grateful for your help." Pramal bowed again, then stepped towards the door, where Sandra stood ready to accompany him downstairs.

Maisie frowned, her eyes on the doorway, before bringing her attention back to Paige and the bell that had rung in his mind.

Chapter Nineteen

"Miss Dobbs?"

"Yes, Mr. Paige. Good of you to telephone. Do you have some news for me?"

"Yes, I do— I knew the name Payton was familiar, though it's not as someone I knew, and I've never come across a Captain Arthur Payton. But I think he might be related to one of the lads who belongs to Reverend Griffith's boys club." He coughed, apologized for the interruption, then went on. "Reverend Griffith is very good with the youngsters, and could see that it's easy for them to get into trouble, especially the ones who're not working, but even those who are in the factory all day—well, they're mixing with men, and some of them learn cheating ways, don't they?"

Maisie did not want to tar every boy with the same brush, but she was anxious to hear what Paige had to say, so she agreed, then tried to chivvy the conversation along.

"Yes, I'm sure—but what of the club? And this lad?"

"He takes the boys along to that bit of meadow over the back and they have treasure hunts, and do running—all to use up the energy that might get them into trouble. He gives them elephant hair bracelets when they've completed ten tasks—climbing a tall tree, map reading, that sort of thing."

"Like Scouts, then."

"But none of these lads would join the Scouts, so it takes the place of that, really."

"Of course, I understand. But what do you know of Arthur Payton—you said you thought he might be related to one of the boys?"

"I went around to see the Reverend one day, as the boys were leaving, and I saw one of the boys carrying a knapsack with Captain Arthur Payton marked on it— the flap was open. I said, 'Bit young to be a captain, eh, lad?' He was a sullen sort and just said it was his father, and shoved his way past me."

"Did Reverend Griffith witness this incident?"

"Yes, he did, and said to me that it was best to ignore it, that the boy was experiencing difficulties at home, that his mother was very ill."

"I see." Maisie felt at once downcast. A new thread seemed to be slipping through her fingers—the only morsel of useful information that mirrored her investigation was the mention of the sick mother. But a lot of boys had sick parents, especially when a woman had gone through multiple childbirths—the streets were full of poorly women; female mortality was high in the working-class areas of London.

"But it was funny, because after the boy walked past me, to join his friends outside the house, I heard one of the boys say, 'Robertson, you coming with us, then?' I knew I heard right, but I didn't think any more of it—after all, he was just another boy being fished out of trouble by the good Reverend, may the Lord bless him for his generosity towards these young villains, because that's what some of them are on the road to being."

"Robertson? Nothing more? Did you hear another name, perhaps?"

"No, Miss Dobbs. I found it incongruous that it was not Payton, that's all. And I'm telling you this hoping you won't be back. In any case, my wife and I are considering taking up missionary work again—you get more thanks for it, and that's the truth."

"One more question, Mr. Paige—did you think this boy might be older than the others?"

"Well, he was a fair bit taller. His hair needed a good cut as well, but you can't expect the Reverend Griffith to do everything, can you?"

"No, not at all. He does enough as it is. Thank you for your telephone call, Mr. Paige. I appreciate that you had a bit of a walk to the telephone kiosk."

"Like I said, we just want to be left alone now."

"I'll do my best, Mr. Paige. My regards to Mrs. Paige."

A sound amounting to a "hmmmph" was Paige's parting comment.

"Miss? Miss, is everything all right?"

Maisie looked towards Sandra, the secretary's furrowed brow testament to her concern.

"Yes, sorry, Sandra. I was just thinking." She realized she was still holding the receiver. "Look, I want to go back to Addington Square, to see the Reverend Griffith. Also—" Maisie clicked the bar on the top of the telephone to clear the line. "I'd better place a call to Caldwell." She dialed Scotland Yard but put down the receiver before it was answered.

"Sandra, here's what I would like you to do, as I need to have some evidence to support my train of thought—and I'm hoping the Reverend Griffith can throw light on my suspicions. I want you to go along to Somerset House."

"What shall I search for?"

"A birth, approximately fourteen years ago—and I pray it wasn't in India, or it might not be registered here. Try the name Robert Payton. And a marriage—Jesmond Martin."

"Robert Payton?"

"Yes." Maisie scribbled a note on a piece of paper. "If you find any connection between these names, please telephone Caldwell at Scotland Yard, tell him what I asked of you, and then tell him where I've gone. I don't want to call in the troops, so to speak, unless there is good cause. So help me, if I'm wrong anyway, I will never hear the last of it, but it's a chance I'm willing to take."

Sandra left her desk and reached for her coat. "Very well, Miss Dobbs. I'll go straightaway. I shan't take long. You can depend on me."

"I know I can."

Maisie left the distinctive MG motor car parked on a road several streets away from the home of the Reverend Griffith. At the front door of the terraced house, she looked both ways, then knocked. There was no answer, so she knocked again, but this time, in the distance, she could hear the Reverend Griffith shouting, "All right, all right, I'm on my way."

The door opened, and the vicar—of a church that seemed to be of his own creation—stood in front of Maisie. His eyes seemed to register both shock and dismay at seeing Maisie.

"Oh, it's you."

"That's more or less what your devoted parishioner, Mr. Paige, said when he last saw me darken his doorstep. Reverend Griffith, I believe we must speak as a matter of some urgency."

Griffith sighed. "Come in. You know where my rooms are."

He allowed Maisie to lead the way to the room that doubled as a sitting room and study, where she took a seat without invitation.

Griffith sat in the chair in front of her, swiveled it back and forth, and sighed. "What do you want to know?"

"I think you know very well what I want to know. I'd like you to start at the beginning, so I might get a measure of exactly how volatile a certain Robert Payton is. I have a feeling that I could already make an educated guess regarding the young man's state of mind, and how it might have become so unbalanced—but I want to hear it from you. Because you know, don't you?"

Griffith held his hands to his face, as if to shut out the truth, then drew them down across his cheeks and rested them on his knees. "Oh, God, I have been blind and stupid."

"You thought you could control the outcome, didn't you? And you thought you could protect a boy you believe to be blameless—and he is an innocent in so many ways, isn't he? If I have guessed correctly, he might be what is termed an innocent victim."

"Of war, Miss Dobbs. An innocent victim of war."

"You'd better explain. Now. Before I go in search of him."

"You?"

"Yes. Tell me when this all began."

Griffith began to speak slowly, stuttering at first. "I knew Arthur Payton and family—his wife and baby son—just before they went to India; this must have been in 1921, I believe. I met them at a function for staff and their families going out to India. Arthur had been wounded in the war and was desperately shell-shocked—I recognized it straightaway, because of my work at the hospital in Richmond. He tried his best, but it was as if he had sustained a violence that lingered within him, and it had to come out—it was a demon that sucked on his soul."

Maisie saw Griffith falter, and urged him on in his recounting of the life of Arthur Payton. It was as if the bare outline of a person was beginning to take shape and form before her, and she felt a terrible dread as she anticipated the outcome of the vicar's story.

"Go on, please."

"In India we saw each other occasionally, and I was invited to supper, that sort of thing. I realized soon enough that he was miserably cruel to his wife. On the face of it, he put on a good show, and his wife hid her distress. But the boy was only a toddler when they arrived in the country, yet as he grew his behavior demonstrated a deep disturbance. If his father had to go up to one of the hill towns, he calmed down, became lighter and cheery. But when his father was at home, he was morose, fearful—and both mother and son had unaccountable bruising. The boy took off his shirt once—all the young boys were playing on the lawns of the club and rolling around, and they'd decided to remove their shirts and run into an ornamental pond, much to their mothers' consternation. But Mrs. Payton was horrified, because at once everyone saw the bruising to the boy's arms and back. I am sure they both suffered physically. Mrs. Payton, especially, experienced dreadful headaches, and would languish in the house for hours and hours, and the boy would have no one. I understand he would be found by his ayah weeping outside his mother's door, afraid she might leave him."

"But she didn't, did she? It was the father who left."

Griffith nodded. "Those dark demons ate his soul, and it all became too much for him. He took his own life."

"And then Jesmond Martin came along."

"He was a man thwarted in love, and—"

"Usha Pramal. He had fallen in love with Usha Pramal," said Maisie. "He was the newcomer to India who had made a foolish error in making known his love for her before she could ever explain to her family."

"Ah, so you know," said Griffith.

"I guessed it might be him," said Maisie. "But go on."

"After a brief courtship, he married Payton's widow and took her son as his own. He immersed himself into being a good father to his stepson, and in an endeavor to extinguish the past—the loss of his great love—he gave the boy his name, so they were a family complete. The boy became more settled, and it seemed as if the darkness had lifted."

"Then they came home, to England," offered Maisie.

"Yes. I understand Jesmond's adoption of Robert was registered soon after their arrival on British soil. In any case, we lost touch. I believe the return was in an effort to find doctors who might treat the dreadful headaches that tormented his wife. There were those who thought her former husband's brutality might have contributed to an injury in the brain."

"It's entirely possible, if there were repeated concussions," said Maisie. "In any case, it seems that by chance Usha Pramal—who had already traveled to

England in a bid to forget Jesmond Martin—crossed paths with the family while she was living in St. John's Wood."

"Yes. That's right."

"She and Jesmond both felt the spark that had ignited their love, and Usha left her employers, to avoid further chance meetings. But I believe it was you who unwittingly helped Martin find Usha again—rather like the prince finding his Cinderella," said Maisie.

Griffith nodded. "We met again, at a sort of gathering for men who had worked in India during the years I happened to be there, and he came to my house here—obviously, my circumstances were very different from his at that point. He was having some difficulty with his son and called upon me for advice. He passed Usha as she was leaving after Bible study. He visited me again and said he needed someone to help with his wife, so I put forward Usha's name."

"Yet you knew how they had once loved each other?"

"He was a broken man, and Usha was such a light soul, and a helpful woman, I thought that their time of love had passed and that she would be a support to his ill wife." He put his hands together in front of his lips and drew them away again. "Of course, I knew he wanted to see Usha, he wanted to have her close to him, if only in his house doing menial work."

402 · JACQUELINE WINSPEAR

"But they fell in love all over again—was that it?"

Griffith sighed. "How could they not fall in love?"

"And how could Usha not fail to help his wife, and how could the son not fail to be at once in thrall to Usha and yet at the same time feel hatred of her, for what his father saw in her," added Maisie.

"The son—Robert—came home for school holidays and occasional exeats, and it seemed that he fell under Usha's spell—and she helped his mother, whom he loved." Griffith pressed his hands to his eyes. "Oh dear Lord, forgive me. I was so unthinking."

"No, you were not unthinking, but you were thinking only of the man, of Jesmond Martin."

He nodded. "I suppose I was. I don't know how I could not have seen the outcome."

"And what was the outcome?" asked Maisie.

Griffith looked at her. "Oh, please, Miss Dobbs—you know very well what it was."

"Yes, I suppose I do. Jesmond Martin had already indulged his son—his stepson—and tried to channel his energies into various outdoor sports and activities. Was it surprising that he ran away from school and came here? Though Jesmond Martin went through the motions of wanting us to find his son, he knew in his heart where he was because at some point you'd met Robert and he'd liked you. Robert Payton—Robert

Martin, or 'Martin Robertson' was an accomplished archer, an excellent shot, and a boy who knew how to look after himself. As he crossed the boundary between youthful insolence and the beginning of an aggressive manhood, the realization that the father he had come to trust and love might also abandon him led him to lose all sense of reality. He could not take the life of Jesmond Martin, but he could take the life of Usha Pramal. And then, having seen her with her dear friend, Maya Patel—for I am sure he stalked her as if he were on the hunt for a stag—he had to ensure that Miss Patel never uttered the secret shared by Usha Pramal, that she was again in contact with the man she had loved so long ago."

"Yes, I am afraid events unfolded in much the way you've described."

"With just the odd detail out of place, perhaps? That sending Usha on her way in such an angry manner was part of the smoke and mirrors—it was to appease Robert and allow him to think his father was true to his mother, but instead, Robert had followed his father on at least one occasion—he seems to have absconded from school with ease—and knew that Jesmond Martin had no intention of giving up Usha Pramal, no matter what he had to say about her. And it seemed that Jesmond had little regard this time for the fact that Usha was drawing back again, perhaps ashamed and dismayed that her love for him had led her to such a point. Her happy mood had changed because she wanted to be free of him, of her shame. Am I right?"

Griffith nodded.

"This is surely a tragedy—a story of love thwarted, a son estranged, and ill-wrought decisions affecting a daisy chain of people. But there's something that still seems amiss to me—your willingness to put Usha Pramal in such a difficult position. You knew of her goodness and you also knew she had loved Jesmond Martin. You knew he was married—not happily, granted—and yet despite being a man of God you almost deliberately tempted two people to flaunt the Commandments. I have to ask myself what else moved you to treat Usha Pramal as if she were a commodity— almost as if she were something to be sold." Maisie paused, watching Griffith. "Were you offered money by Jesmond Martin?"

The vicar began to speak, but could barely form words through his sobs. "It wasn't quite like that. He helped me out—there were arrears on my rent and on the church rooms—he settled my debts to help me and asked nothing in return. He showed such goodness in his gesture."

"So you persuaded yourself that nothing untoward would happen between Jesmond Martin and Usha." Maisie stopped speaking until Griffith could meet her eyes. "You know, I remember reading an old legend—it may indeed have been a Hindu myth, now that I think of it. The story went that before God sent the souls to earth, he divided each one in two, so forever those divided souls would be in search of their mate. Some were never fortunate and wandered this earth alone. Some did not find their soul mate, but were happy with the love they found. Others were joined but lived unhappily. But there were those touched by destiny, who found their soul mates and experienced earthly lives of bliss and contentment." She paused as Griffith nodded his understanding. "I have wondered, as we've been talking here, whether indeed Jesmond and Usha were divided souls. Perhaps you saw this, but weren't to know theirs would be such a sad and damaging destiny."

"I was a fool, Miss Dobbs."

"Yes, I think you were, and you've woven yourself a very tangled web. Beyond a naive, misguided trust that all would be well in the end, I know why you offered the boy a place of safety; why you failed to go to the police. Not only did Jesmond Martin help you with your debts." She looked around the room. "But I think he kept quiet about something he'd guessed—you have no credentials, do you? You are a man of the cloth in name only. There was no study of theology, no ordination. You invented your church and concluded that protection of your transgression was more important than justice itself, which is why you did not go to the police when you should have. You have committed fraud on at least two counts, and have withheld information of interest to the police."

"You make it sound so very easy," said Griffith.

"Truth should always prevail, Mr.—and I do mean *Mr.*—Griffith. The way events have unfolded should tell you that what I say is right—Truth should always prevail. Eventually."

"I . . . I don't know what to do," said Griffith.

Maisie sighed. "Where is Robert?"

"Hiding, over on the common," he replied.

Maisie nodded and stood up, then turned to leave.

"Where are you going?" said Griffith.

"To speak to Robert Martin."

"But he might—"

"He might," said Maisie. "I know he's armed, and I know what he might do. But he is a boy who has had his heart broken by a man who was torn apart by war. Someone has to be a true advocate, don't they?"

Maisie walked away, leaving Griffith slumped in chair, weeping.

A bright afternoon sunshine cast shadows across the golden grasses of the common behind Addington Square. Maisie shielded her eyes with her hand as she walked towards the trees where Robert Payton, now Martin, had made a camp. Though her step was resolute, she felt fear rising as she approached the lair of a boy on the cusp of manhood; a young soul deeply damaged by a father who had sustained psychological wounds that took away all sense of right and wrong. How would she speak to him? How could she calm his temper? She pressed her hand to the center of her body and uttered simple words that came easily. *May we know peace. May we all know peace.*

Her quiet entreaty was shattered by the weeping of a child and the plea of an older girl.

"Please don't hurt her. Please don't hurt her. She's my little sister," said the girl.

"And my dad will come and get your dad, just you see," said a boy.

Maisie crept closer, bending to the ground. As quietly as she could, she rounded the trees to better view the scene. She held her hand to her mouth.

Robert Martin, stepson of the man Usha Pramal had loved, was holding a gun to the head of the smallest girl in the family she'd met on the common days earlier.

The eldest boy held their golden-haired dog by the old leather collar that seemed too large for his neck. The dog growled, and the children wailed as fear overtook them—the younger boy's darned and patched trousers bore the damp stain of terror.

"You're all sissies, that's what you are. This is my camp, my territory, and I live here—it's not yours," said Martin, his finger on the already cocked trigger.

Maisie put her hand to her mouth as thoughts swept through her mind. At once memories seemed to collide with the present and it seemed she had been in this place so many times—in a clearing in a quarry facing down a madman who threatened the lives of men who had been disfigured in the war; challenging a young politician with a secret he wanted to protect; disarming a broken soldier bent upon killing half of London; bringing an army officer to justice who had killed one of his men. Images from the past seemed to taunt her, but now she faced the insanity of war writ large upon childhood, and she knew that here, in this field, under a cluster of trees, the young were at risk of paying the ultimate price.

Maisie knew she must act now or the children—children whose mother would soon be calling them from the attic window of a house overlooking the common land—would be dead. For she had no doubt that the boy who now held his father's gun could kill every one of them. Far better she gave them the chance of freedom. She stood up, brushed down her skirt, and walked forward towards the center of the group.

"Oh, it's that lovely dog again," said Maisie, holding out her hand, palm up. "Hello, Nelson."

Robert Martin swung around, the gun now facing Maisie, who caught the eye of the eldest boy. Martin moved back again, then towards Maisie once more, the gun fanning between the children. He held on to the smallest girl, his arm around her chest.

"Who are you?" he asked.

"Me? My name is Maisie Dobbs, and these children are my friends," said Maisie.

"Is she your friend?" Martin pointed the gun at the eldest boy.

"Y-yes. Yes, she is our friend."

"Then you'd better move over there, Maisie Dobbs. Where I can see you."

"What if I don't want to move, Robert?" said Maisie, standing, facing him. He was almost her equal in height, his hair was long, to his earlobes, and his complexion ruddy from lack of sleep. His clothing seemed ill-fitting and unclean, and he wore no shoes. Maisie looked under the tree and guessed the children had disturbed him, for his shoes had been placed neatly together, almost as if he were in a dormitory at boarding school.

"Then I will shoot her," said Martin.

Maisie shook her head. "But she's only a very little girl, Robert. Can you remember how scared you were when you were that small? Can you remember, Robert?"

Robert Martin sniffed, moving his head as if he wanted to wipe his nose on his shoulder, but not quite able to.

"Why don't you let these children go back to their mother, and you hold me here instead?" offered Maisie.

"No. No. I could kill all of you before you even know what's hit you," replied the boy, his faced flushed, his eyes now glazed, almost as if he were blind.

Maisie tried another tack, and hoped she would not have to gamble.

"Don't you want to rest, Robert? You must be so very tired. You've looked out for your mother all these years, and you've done your best to be a good son to Mr. Martin, haven't you? But he's let you down, hasn't he?"

Maisie saw Robert Martin's chin begin to crease, as if he were but a two-year-old boy.

"I tell you, don't you come any closer."

"No, I won't," said Maisie. "But why don't you let that little girl go back to her mother—you would love to go back to your mother, wouldn't you? You know how she feels, don't you?"

"These are only poor kids, they don't know," the boy replied.

"Oh, yes they do, Robert. Money doesn't dictate how much people love each other, neither does color, or language or height, or whether you have blue eyes or brown," said Maisie. "Now let the children go home."

Maisie saw the boy swallow; his Adam's apple, sharp with the passage of boyhood, moved up and down as he tried to ease the dryness in his throat. His attention went to his gun, which he moved away from the little girl's head, and in that moment, Maisie caught the eye of the eldest boy of the family and nodded. He understood.

"Robert. Robert, look at me, I want to tell you something important," said Maisie.

Robert Martin turned to Maisie, and in that very second, the boy let go of his dog. "Go, Nelson!"

The golden-haired dog leaped through the air at the same time as the older boy grabbed his sister. In a split second when Maisie thought the bullet would rip through her skull, Maisie felt herself pulled to the ground, and the sound of the gun being discharged ricocheted through the trees.

Stunned, Maisie pulled herself up to see Billy move towards the prone Robert Martin, pinned to the ground by the dog, whose golden coat was spattered with his own red blood.

Four of the children were running away towards a phalanx of blue as Caldwell's men moved across the field. The older boy remained, tears streaking his cheeks.

"He's killed Nelson. He's killed him with his gun."

"Billy, what . . . how . . ." said Maisie.

"Never mind that, Miss. Later. Help this dog, would you—it'll break the lad's heart if he dies."

Caldwell and a uniformed policeman were already holding Martin as Maisie and Billy lifted the dog to one side.

Soon the trees were shadowing more policemen, with Caldwell at the center, giving orders. In the distance a gathering of mothers were holding the children to them and taking them away from the meadow. When Robert Martin was led to one side, the older boy remained, holding his dog's head in his arms as Maisie pushed apart hair and flesh to better see the wound.

"Is he dead, Miss?"

"No, he's not, but he's been hit by a bullet. He's a brave dog, you know. He saved all our lives," said Maisie.

"Oh, please make him live, Miss. Please make him live."

"Where's the nearest vet?"

"I dunno, I never took him to a vet," said the boy.

"All right, we'll find one. In the meantime, let me find something to dress this wound and stop the bleeding."

Soon handkerchiefs were gathered from the policemen and Maisie had packed a hole in the dog's shoulder. As Caldwell checked the handcuffs on Robert Martin's bony wrists, Billy leaned down and picked up the dog and began walking towards the MG, the boy running alongside them.

"Go up to Coldharbour Lane, Miss, and if there's not one there, you'll have to go directly to Battersea—I reckon there'll be one on duty. And if you can't find a vet there, it'll have to be Camden—to the new Beaumont Animals Hospital."

"Billy, how did you know I was here?"

"You'd just left and I'd popped in to see Sandra—by way of saying good-bye, I suppose. She told me what was happening, more or less." He wheezed as he bore the weight of the whimpering dog towards Maisie's motor car, the boy running next to him, stroking his dog and talking to him.

"I've been with you long enough, Miss, to know when things are coming down to the thin part of the funnel, and I knew you were walking into something dodgy. So I came over here as soon as I could. And just as well, otherwise that bullet might have hit you."

Maisie nodded. "I'll miss you, Billy. You don't know how much I'll miss you."

"And I'll miss you, too, Miss Dobbs. But we'll both be better out of this lark. I mean, I reckon I was safer in the war, even with all them bombs and that shelling."

Having accompanied Robert Martin to Carter Street police station, where he was taken into custody, Caldwell was waiting as Maisie emerged from Battersea Dogs and Cats home with the boy, Joey, and his dog, the limping, bandaged, but very much alive Nelson.

"Nelson, you say his name is, son?" said Caldwell.

"Yes, sir," said the boy.

"I know a good joke about Nelson," added the Detective Inspector.

"No," said Maisie. "No, not that one, please. He's a boy."

"Right then, I've got to talk to this lady here, so you can go home in style in one of our nice motor cars and your own driver, along with your dog—who might get a medal, if he carries on like that. He deserves a good meal in any case," said Caldwell. He reached into a pocket and brought out a few coins, which he pressed into Joey's hand. "Now, go on with you—and don't let me see that dog wanting for a meal again, all right?"

"Yes, sir," said the boy as he was led away towards the Invicta police vehicle.

Caldwell turned towards Maisie. "I reckon we've got some talking to do, eh, Miss Dobbs."

"I can drive you back to the Yard, Inspector," said Maisie. "Did Billy get home all right?"

Caldwell nodded. "Right as rain—not that we're running a chauffeur service for your assistants and their dogs here. One of my drivers took him."

"Thank you," said Maisie. "There's some blood on the passenger seat by the way, but it's only from Nelson."

"The Yard, then, Miss Dobbs?"

Maisie shook her head. "I want to speak to Jesmond Martin, if I may. And his son."

"No to both, I'm afraid," said Caldwell.

Maisie placed a hand on Caldwell's arm. "Inspector, I know we haven't enjoyed the best when it comes to working together, but I think we've reached an understanding." She paused, removing her hand. "I know Robert Martin—Robert Payton—has committed two terrible murders, but please try to be . . . to be *kind* . . . when you question the boy."

"Kind? He's a killer, Miss Dobbs, a coldhearted killer."

"Yes, and there's no getting away from the fact that he took the lives of two innocent women, and—"

"And almost took those children, too—don't forget them."

"No, I can't. I will forever see the look of fear in their eyes—and fear in a child is a terrible thing. Which is why I ask you to be as compassionate as you can with Martin." Maisie paused, bringing her hand to her mouth. "Just imagine, Inspector—imagine him as a four-year-old, an innocent, brutalized by a man himself damaged by war. Imagine that, Inspector. I do not ask for him to be absolved of his crime, but I ask for kindness. He has suffered, and his heart has been broken."

"You'll have me in tears in a minute," said Caldwell.

Maisie smiled. "A good start, Detective Inspector. A good start."

Later, Maisie parked the MG in the mews behind 15 Ebury Place, and was in two minds as to whether she should enter via the kitchen, voicing apologies to the staff for the transgression of trespass into their domain, or make her way to the front door. She decided upon the latter, only to discover that James was waiting for her to return and opened the door himself.

"At last! I thought you would never get home," said James.

"I'm only a little later than usual," said Maisie. In truth, she had almost gone straight to her flat, with the intention of calling James to make excuses for not returning to Ebury Place. However, she decided that honesty was, in this case, the best policy.

"Where have you been—and why is there blood on your sleeve? In fact, why do you have blood on your stockings and shoes? Oh, Maisie, this cannot go on!"

"James, don't worry—it was a dog."

"Did it run out into the road? Tell me that it was a dog you decided to aid in its moment of need."

"Well . . . yes, James. I saw the dog hit by another motor car, in full sight of his young owner, and I decided to help. Luckily, both boy and dog were returned to their home in good spirits, though the dog may walk with a bit of a limp in the future, and the boy might be reprimanded by his mother."

"Thank God for that. For a moment I thought you might tell me a gun was involved, and then I would have had to say something, I'm afraid." James smiled and took Maisie in his arms.

"No, don't worry—no need to say anything. All's well that ends well."

"I think you should bathe away the strains of the day, my love," said James.

"Probably a good idea—it's been a while since breakfast." Maisie drew back, ready to go upstairs to her rooms and the hot bath that she knew was being drawn for her.

"A long day, then?"

"Yes, James. It was a really long day."

"I'll have a drink ready for when you come down, darling."

Maisie nodded. Truth, she knew, was watching her as she ascended the grand staircase to the first floor, though on this occasion, she knew she had told a lie that was worth the telling.

Chapter Twenty

C aldwell had joined Maisie and Mr. Pramal at her office the day after Robert Martin—born Robert Payton—was arrested and charged with the murder of both Usha Pramal and Maya Patel, and the attempted murder of five children of the Fielding family.

"I've a mind to throw in the attempted murder of one Nelson Fielding, for good measure!" said Caldwell.

Maisie said nothing in direct response, knowing that it was Caldwell's way to be flip at tension-filled moments. She had decided, though, that she could not help but like the man; this manner was his way of coping with murder, the most troubling outcome of uncontrollable passion—whether that passion was the need to feed a family, fear, a love thwarted, jealousy, or rage.

"It's a web, Miss Dobbs," said Pramal. "This Jesmond Martin was the man my sister loved and he loved her in return—and then he married in haste when she refused him. And this deep lingering malice and her death—from a boy—is the result?"

"Mr. Pramal, as Detective Inspector Caldwell will tell you, the roots of murder often run very deep, and sadly, in many cases, are cast in childhood, in the abyss of terror and fear. Young Robert was not of sound mind, of that there is little doubt. His stepfather had tried hard to lift him beyond memories of beatings and humiliation suffered at the hands of his father, who had himself been harmed. Part of that care was in giving Robert his name, and thereafter referring to him as 'my son.' "

Pramal nodded. "I often wondered, in the war, Miss Dobbs, how men could go forward and see such death and destruction without it staining their souls forever. Yet so many have."

"And so many haven't—though I would like to think the powerful demons that subsequently tortured Arthur Payton are rare. The brutal treatment of a child is a terrible thing and is so often hidden."

"And my Usha, my dear beloved sister, was having an affair with this man, Jesmond Martin? I cannot believe it. She was pure," said Pramal.

"Yes, she was pure—and that was what drew people to her, even if they were at first prejudiced against the color of her skin. She was pure of heart and of spirit and saw only the very best in people. If called to a house to help someone—perhaps to assist in lifting an old gentleman from a chair, or washing a sick woman—she did not draw back, but tended to people with the same deep respect. In my investigation, I have discovered that children, too, were captivated by her. She need not be on a pedestal; she was a good person, a very dear person, not a goddess."

"A spirited girl, Miss Dobbs."

Maisie nodded. *A daughter of heaven*, she thought.

Pramal continued, speaking of his plans to leave Britain for India as soon as he could secure passage. He would take Usha's money with him, now safely transferred to circular notes for security during travel. The notes would be deposited in a Bombay bank as soon as Pramal arrived in his home country.

"What of Usha's dream, Mr. Pramal?"

Pramal shrugged. "I don't really know how to begin. I am an engineer, not a teacher, but I will learn how to set up a school in her name."

Maisie pushed a piece of paper towards Pramal. "May I trouble you for your address, Mr. Pramal? I am planning a visit to your country . . . perhaps . . . and I might be able to assist. Indeed, it would be an honor."

Pramal bowed his head in acknowledgment and began to write.

"You never told me about all this India business, Miss Dobbs," said Caldwell.

Maisie shook her head. "There wasn't much to tell, but you would have found out soon enough. I am closing my office and traveling abroad for . . . for a while."

"Got to be too much for you, did it, Miss Dobbs? This investigating lark?"

Maisie shook her head. "No, Detective Inspector. Quite the opposite. I realized it had become not enough."

With that she pushed back her chair and handed an envelope to Caldwell.

"My final account. You will find everything in order, and in the circumstances, I would appreciate immediate payment upon receipt of the invoice—so pass it on to one of your lady bean counters without delay, if you don't mind. I know she'll be most efficient."

"Never one to miss a trick, Miss Dobbs." Caldwell tucked the envelope into the inside pocket of his jacket. "I'll make sure they jump to the job straightaway. Right, then, Mr. Pramal—can I drop you somewhere?"

"Camberwell, if you don't mind," said Pramal. "The Surrey Canal. Now I know my sister went there to meet the man she loved—but she met her death instead. I want to be alone with her precious memory."

Caldwell raised his eyebrows and looked at Maisie.

"I think that's a good idea, Mr. Pramal," said Maisie. "Walk along the path where the children play and say farewell to Usha. You have no need to see anyone else. Then leave. As quickly as you can, leave and put this country behind you."

Tears filled Pramal's eyes. "It's leaving her that's hard, Miss Dobbs. I will take her ashes, but leave my beloved sister."

Maisie nodded. "Then hold her with you as she held her family—in the heart."

As soon as the men left her office, Maisie packed up the case map and filed away all papers—even the scrappiest notes—belonging to the Usha Pramal case. Billy's first scribbles, the almost unintelligible sentences scrawled when he first began looking for Jesmond Martin's son, formed part of that file. Every case file held not only information on the path of discovery, but something of the journey traveled by Maisie and Billy, and more recently, by Sandra. Maisie knew that in filing away those notes, she was encapsulating part of herself, part of who they were in a working partnership. And she wondered how she might look back upon those notes in years to come. She only hoped she would see some essence of wisdom reflected in the journey.

A real pilgrimage awaited her attention, and when the filing was complete, before the more arduous task of packing away over four years of work under the business name, *Maisie Dobbs, Psychologist & Investigator*, she traveled to Leadenhall Street, to the offices of the Peninsular and Oriental Steamship Navigation Company, to book her passage. In the middle of October, she would board the SS *Carthage* to India. She would travel as one of the one hundred and seventy-seven first-class passengers on the ship, which also carried the Royal Mail service to India and the Far East. From Southampton, she would sail via Gibraltar, to Naples, Port Said, through the Suez Canal, to Aden, and then Bombay. The SS *Carthage* would leave with Maisie on board in just four weeks— time enough to close her business, to have the many files transported from Fitzroy Square to be stored in the cellars of The Dower House, company for the boxes of Maurice's archived notes. It would be time enough to see her father married and with a loving wife at his side. She would be leaving after James, for his departure was already booked for the day following her father's wedding—from Southampton, he would sail for Canada. The oceans would part them, perhaps for now. Perhaps forever. Leaving Leadenhall Street, her ticket safely tucked in her document case, Maisie walked towards James Compton's office. Yes, he would be busy. Yes, there was work to be done. But for now, perhaps he might be persuaded to leave work early to return to Ebury Place together. In fact, she knew he would.

Maisie's list of loose ends to tie up seemed to grow each day. Amid the packing, the cancellation of the lease on the Fitzroy Square office, the necessary hours spent with her solicitor, Bernard Klein, and the process Maurice had called their Final Accounting—the essential visits to places and people encountered during work on the Usha Pramal case, a task that brought work on a particular investigation to a more settled close—she realized that this would not be the final accounting of a single case. She knew that, if he were with her, Maurice would counsel her to look critically upon the years since she first began work on her own, from the time she moved into the dusty office in Warren Street, when a man named Billy Beale, who recognized her as the nurse who had saved his life in the war, had come to her aid on her first big case, and had, ever since, been at her side—to the point where he had saved her life when Robert Martin discharged the gun, spattering her with the blood of a dog who tried to protect the children he loved.

"*Oh, Billy*," said Maisie to the silent room as she lay down her pen and pressed her hands to her eyes. "Oh,

Billy, bless you, dear man. Bless you for risking everything for me."

From the Surrey Canal in Camberwell, to the house
where she saw the "For Sale" sign—the Paiges really were leaving—she retraced her steps in the Usha
Pramal case. The Reverend Griffith was gone now—
there was a sign indicating that rooms were available for rent in the house where he'd lived—and the
building that served as his church was boarded up.
On a fine day in early October, Maisie stood for a
while looking across the common land close to Addington Square, before setting off towards the clump
of trees where children had played, where a boy she
hardly knew, but knew so much about all the same,
threatened a young family and was saved by their
loyal dog. It was here that she sat down, that she lingered under the dappled light of a willow tree and
rested her head against its trunk, to finally face the
past and what it might mean to step out into another
future.

"The trouble with you, love, is that you think too
much." The oft-spoken warning from her father—a
light admonishment that she would accept and he would
offer with a smile that hid his true concern—echoed in
her mind and almost led her to leave this place where

a tragedy had been averted, where the blood of an animal still stained the ground. But she remained, sitting, thinking, allowing her thoughts to roam across time and the lives she had touched and been touched by in return.

How different now was her life from that of the girl who left a small house in Lambeth to work at a grand mansion in Belgravia. Ebury Place. She was, to all intents and purposes, mistress of that same house now, yet at once she remembered the feelings that caused her to weep as she made her way towards the kitchen entrance on a blustery day so long ago. She had just turned thirteen, still grieving the loss of her mother, when she left her father's house that morning. He was then a man suffering the death of his wife so deeply, he had considered the best future for his daughter was one away from a house with the curtains closed against the light of day, and a widower father clad in black whose heart was broken.

It was at Ebury Place that she had been summoned to meet Dr. Maurice Blanche, and from that moment, her life would never be the same again. How she had worked for that future—Frankie Dobbs could never have imagined such possibilities for his beloved daughter, who then pushed all opportunity aside when war touched her.

"You think what you can do for these boys," her friend Enid had said as they watched the wounded being brought through Charing Cross Station in early 1915, after the crossing from the battlefields of France. Within hours Enid was dead, killed in an explosion at the Woolwich Arsenal where she was a munitions worker—a tragedy that inspired Maisie to make a decision that would define the person she became, the person she still was. Perhaps more than anything else, going to war had changed her life.

"Doesn't death always change a life?" she heard herself say aloud. And with that sentence, she knew the die had been cast from that time. In her work as a nurse, as Maurice's apprentice, and as a woman with her own inquiry agency, she worked in a realm where death always changed lives.

And now, under the trees, as a chill seeped across the land from the river, along the thoroughfare of the canal, she looked at life after life, at the people she had met: those she could help and those who would never be saved. She remembered Tom, the man who tended the Nether Green Cemetery because his son, wounded in the war, now lay there beneath the soil. She thought of those men who had lost their facial features in battle, and whose masks—designed to allow them to live lives alongside their fellow men—now ceased to keep pace with age, so that on one side their features were young, untouched, as if they had never been to war, and on the other the years had creased and folded their skin. She had saved a group of such men from the power of another damaged man. And what did it mean for a woman to lose her sons, her husband to war—she remembered bringing to justice a woman who had murdered those she deemed responsible for the lost loves of her life. Billy had wept as the woman was led away into police custody, for he understood how it felt to be drawn under by death. What was it like for him to lose his brother and descend into dependence upon narcotics to dampen the pain of his own wounds? One case after another came to mind, as if her future demanded one last look at the past, a reckoning on her conduct in each investigation. Images of the women who'd given out white feathers to young men they'd considered shirkers merged with the face of a man who had clutched at the enemy on the field of battle and had been held in return, their terror mingling with tears and blood. There was an artist maligned, and a man cast out of his family for his love of another man. A speck of light had begun to shine in her life once more, when the Gypsy woman who'd foretold her future—and whose earthly belongings had burned in a fiery ritual of death and renewal—encouraged Maisie to dance again.

It was as if a moving picture of her cases were playing in her mind. Soon there came the young cartographer who had gone far afield in search of adventure; it was a case in which she had learned that love, most assuredly, could again be hers. These were all recollections which, in this quiet place, brought her to the death of Maurice Blanche. Maurice, who had given her the tools to measure the path ahead, who had provided her with all she needed to map her own future—a future that might, or might not, include marriage. Finally, John Otterburn seemed to stride into her mind's eye and take his place—how she detested his part in the death of two men, one of them an innocent in the ways of those who would wage war and end war. She might be closer to accepting her powerlessness against him, but his actions had, ultimately, led her to question who she was and who she might be. And now this. Usha Pramal, whose love reached out to others with the same smooth touch of her silk sari against the skin. Maisie felt the immediacy of her spirit. She felt as if the hand of this woman, who came from a country so very different from her own, had in some ways beckoned to her, had drawn attention in death, as much as she drew so many to her in life.

Maurice had always cautioned her to look for patterns in her cases. He'd taught that certain elements of an investigation came in threes, as if Fate itself were a teacher. She had seen such phenomena during her apprenticeship, but now she identified something quite different—the way in which all those cases had come together to press her onward towards this moment in time, this place and her decision to leave. Who might she be when she returned? That was in itself a mystery, but Maisie knew this, as certainly as she knew that Pramal would found a girls' school in his sister's name, that Billy would do well at his new job and Sandra would go on to surprise them all. And she knew that whatever presented itself to her, and whatever lessons she had learned along the way, she would be well equipped. Like Maurice, she would be prepared for whatever turns the future might take.

Priscilla was vehement in her opinion of Maisie's plans.

"Oh for goodness' sake, Maisie! Are you completely mad? I know you said you planned to do it, but really, I never thought it would come to this. You have a dear man who loves you, a good business—which is getting better. You have a father about to be married—which gives you a delightful stepmother. Even your paramour's parents think you're the best he could land—and you are going off to India! How could you possibly deprive my dear boys of their beloved godmother?"

"Don't lay it on too thick, Priscilla. I don't know how long I will be away, and anyone with an iota of observational power would see that your boys are growing fast and rather prefer the company of boys their own age—soon it will be girls."

"Heaven forbid! I don't know how I will cope with an endless trooping through of the young party set," said Priscilla, pressing a cigarette into the long ebony holder she favored.

"You'll love it. They'll give you nothing but sublime joy," said Maisie.

"But I will miss you!" said Priscilla. "Now I will be well and truly stuck with these silly women who do nothing but, well . . . talk."

"You love talking."

"About things that count, Maisie. You know that as well as anyone." Priscilla took only one draw on the cigarette holder before pressing it into the ashtray.

"Yes, I know. But we can write, and you never know, I might be home, here, before next summer."

"It's a long bloody way, India."

"I know. But if I have had enough after a fortnight, I will return—or go somewhere else. I haven't even set foot aboard ship, and I confess, I feel bitten by the bug of travel."

"Heaven help us. I can see myself trailing around the seven seas in your wake."

"Whether you're here or in France, I will find you when the time comes. And I will write to the boys."

"Don't expect anything in return. I have yet to see any semblance of the writing cells being passed from Douglas to his sons."

Maisie shrugged. "But at least they'll know I care."

"And they would care a bit more if you married James."

"If I go anywhere on board an aeroplane, they will be the first to know—and I'll take photographs."

"Do you really have to leave?" asked Priscilla.

"Yes. I do," said Maisie.

Further visits followed, blending the past with the most recent case. Maisie visited the lecturer, Dr. Harry Ashley, at the Camberwell School of Art, and went from there to see the boys who had found the body of Usha Pramal, where she pressed a coin into the hand of each lad, telling them all to buy something nice for their families. The Fieldings were now treating Nelson as if he were canine royalty; he was not left in the concrete yard at night, but enjoyed evenings in front of the fire, his belly full with dog biscuits and leftovers.

The Allisons were surprised to hear the outcome of the Usha Pramal case, and seemed saddened to know the reasons for her death. They talked across each other, and to each other, but despite the chatter that was a hallmark of their union, Maisie could see they were genuinely affected.

She did not make any attempt to see Jesmond Martin, who had been released from custody on bail following a full admission of guilt by his stepson. Martin could still be charged with perverting the course of justice. In questioning, it was revealed by the boy that Robert had indeed committed both crimes alone, having followed his quarry and killed in such a way that he could move the bodies alone before covering all evidence of his footprint and presence in the locations where Usha Pramal and Maya Patel were found. Jesmond Martin had secured the services of a respected legal firm, and the boy could expect expert counsel working on his behalf. Robert Martin's age, and the circumstances of his mental state, would serve to keep him from the gallows, but Maisie knew he would likely never see the bright light of freedom ever again.

As cooler evenings drew in, she and James turned down invitations to parties or "Friday to Monday" excursions, and instead spent their time together, sometimes close in conversation, and sometimes in silence, but feeling the comfort of each other close by.

"So, are you nearly finished?" asked James one evening.

Maisie nodded. "The van is coming to collect the filing cabinets next week, and a carter will be taking the office furniture to sell. There's nothing there worth much, to tell you the truth; I never invested in the best desks and chairs. We're having our post forwarded to my flat, and Sandra will ensure that all inquiries receive a response."

"Hard to believe, isn't it? I mean, have you forgotten that over four years ago your first big case really caught your imagination when you heard from my mother that I was planning to go to a place called The Retreat?" He paused. "It seems unbelievable that I had reached such a state of terrible desperation—enough to want to leave my world behind. It's a different time, isn't it? I mean, despite the fact that we're both stepping out into the unknown. Neither of us really knows what is there, do we?"

Maisie reached for his hand. "Perhaps we must allow ourselves to be brought gently into the future by the good times, taking those dear memories with us and not allowing the worst of times to hold us in its grip—to hold us back, really."

Dame Constance, in a move that was not customary, reached through the grille that divided the visitors' room from the plain cell where she came to meet Maisie, and touched her hand.

"Maisie, I believe you have come to hear words of encouragement as you set out on your path. There is no encouragement, save for me to say 'Godspeed.' May you find the person you are most seeking, Maisie. May you discover who you might be in the wider world, now that so much has come to pass."

Maisie was silent. Her respect for Dame Constance had grown in recent years, and she knew that, especially since Maurice's death, she had come to the Benedictine nun in search of the mentorship she so missed.

"We are all apprentices, Maisie. Even when we think we've graduated to another rung on the ladder of experience, there is always much to learn. Every soul who comes to me for counsel gives me another lesson in return, and I am humbled and made new by each fresh opportunity to serve."

"I understand, Dame Constance." Maisie felt the elderly nun's fingers press her own.

"Godspeed then, Maisie. I look forward to hearing about your adventures."

"I'll write."

"And I would expect you to."

With that Dame Constance smiled, and instead of the usual snapping of the small door across the grille, she pulled it closed slowly. Maisie sat in the room with the red carpet, the fire in the grate, and a view across the Romney Marsh. She heard only the sound of the nun's skirts brushing the floor as she made her way back into the silence of her realm.

Khan was resting when Maisie called at the white mansion in Hampstead, and instead of an audience with the man she believed to have been Maurice's closest mentor, she received a brief note. The English was perfect, and though Maisie thought he had not written it himself, he had without doubt dictated the brief message.

"Go forward with a light step, my child. Your heart will open with every mile traveled. Fill it wisely."

She folded the piece of paper and held on to it as she walked away.

The final name on her list was Lakshmi Chaudhary Jones, who had invited her to tea. Maisie arrived at the apartment in midafternoon, as the autumn sunshine was reflecting a golden light across trees filled with yellow, red, and rich brown leaves. The mild summer and still-warm days had given London a resplendent and lingering Indian summer.

Tea was served by a maid dressed formally in a black dress with white collar, cuffs, and apron and a small white cap to keep her curls at bay. Mrs. Chaudhary

Jones was again wearing a colorful sari, this time of lavender with a deep purple border. Her hair was secured with an amethyst pin, and her beaded shoes, too, reflected the colors of her clothing.

"It's lovely to see you, Maisie—may I call you Maisie? I ask this to do you a favor really, because Lakshmi Chaudhary Jones is such a mouthful, isn't it?"

Maisie smiled, and agreed. "Thank you—Lakshmi."

"So, I understand you are leaving for my home country, and soon."

"Yes," said Maisie. "Just a couple more weeks, actually."

"And you have a wedding on the cards, too—I hear all the gossip, you know." Lakshmi offered Maisie a sweet dessert to enjoy with her cup of tea.

"My father, who is getting on now, is to be wed. To my housekeeper. I'm rather thrilled, to tell you the truth. I think they will be very happy, and my home will be looked after very well while I'm away."

Lakshmi nodded, sipping her tea. "And no marriage for you? Yet?"

Maisie shook her head. "I—I . . . Well, no, not yet."

"You're afraid of losing your place, aren't you—I think 'independence' might be the word."

"I'm not sure anymore," said Maisie. "I think that's too simple for me now. I have come to believe that I must garner a greater understanding—of the world, of myself—before I could make a good wife."

"Oh, that old chestnut," said Lakshmi. "What, I wonder, is this person, the 'good wife,' when she's at home?"

"Someone who knows herself, so she won't get lost." Maisie was aware that her words had been spoken before she could take the measure of what she wanted to say. She reddened.

Lakshmi Chaudhary Jones set down her cup and saucer, and touched the corners of her mouth with the edge of a table napkin. "It comes down to knowing what you stand for, I think—if I were to discern the nub of the matter. If you both stand for the same things, then you can go forward together and apart, whatever the day may bring. That doesn't mean you agree on everything. I don't agree with my husband's work for that man, John Otterburn, but—"

"You don't?" Maisie could not hide her surprise.

The woman shook her head. "No. I don't care for such ostentation and the impressing of power upon others, but knowing my husband shares my essential way of thinking, I know he believes he is reflecting something important in his work—which is quite apart from his lecturing at the Imperial College, you understand." She paused, looking at Maisie, who was stirring her tea. "That is something to think about, Maisie. If you are looking at marriage, or something akin to it."

"Lakshmi, I want to ask you something, if I may. You know I was involved in the murder case of a young woman who had come to this country to work as a governess, and also of her friend?"

"Go on," said Lakshmi.

"Well, here I am, preparing to leave this country, to leave my father, my new stepmother; to leave James, my dearest friends, my business—to leave everything behind. Yet though I feel brave enough, I feel quite astonished at myself, as if I have made a decision to go away from all that I love. I wondered—when I learned more about those women, and when I met you—I wondered, how that felt, and how you mustered your resources to, well, I suppose, to get through the distance, the leaving—even if it was your choice."

The woman looked at Maisie with her deep brown eyes.

"I'll tell you this. Leaving that which you love breaks your heart open. But you will find a jewel inside, and this precious jewel is the opening of your heart to all that is new and all that is different, and it will be the making of you—if you allow it to be."

Maisie could feel her eyes fill with tears.

The woman before her, serene in her confidence, continued. "It is like the fracture of a delicate blue egg, when the bird-chick is ready to face the world. Such a struggle, such a rent in the casing that has most protected the small creature; but look what awaits—the learning to fly, and the grand adventure of migration. Yes, there is the risk of death, the sorry promise of starvation, of exhaustion, but that struggle is unavoidable. For you, the mystery of departure awaits."

"Yes, I understand—I think," said Maisie.

Lakshmi Chaudhary Jones smiled. "Perhaps. But you might not begin to understand until you are on that ship. I came here as a young bride, and I thought I would never, ever be part of this country—but it is now as much part of me as my home, India." She reached to pour more tea. "Perhaps you must leave to come home to yourself—and you must experience this exile before you can return, forever, to your James."

"Yes. You may be right," said Maisie.

The women talked on, and when it came time for Maisie to leave, it came as no surprise that Lakshmi Chaudhary Jones ignored her proffered hand and instead reached to kiss her on either cheek.

"I will welcome you to my home again, Maisie. Of that I am sure."

Epilogue

I t was with little ceremony that Maisie handed over the keys to the Fitzroy Square office to the landlord and met Billy at the front of the building, where he waited with Sandra.

"All done, Miss?"

Maisie nodded.

"Right, better get this finished, eh?"

Billy stepped towards the brass plaque to the side of the door, and took a screwdriver from his pocket. Maisie and her two employees looked at the plaque with its polished engraving: *Maisie Dobbs, Psychologist & Investigator.*

"Better than your first business name, eh, Miss?" said Billy.

"Trade and Personal Investigations? Yes, it's a bit more professional," said Maisie.

"I think I like that better, actually," said Sandra.

Maisie laughed. "It's done now, anyway."

Billy unscrewed the brass fitting and held the plate out towards Maisie. "Want to keep this?"

"Yes, I think I'll take it." She reached for the plaque and placed it in her document case.

"Might need that again, isn't that so, Miss Dobbs?" said Sandra.

"You know, I might. Anyway, now that's done, we're going to have a bite to eat; something a bit different," said Maisie.

"Celebration?" asked Billy

"Yes, a celebration. I thought we would go to Veeraswamy. The food is reputed to be very good," said Maisie.

Billy crinkled his nose, and Sandra almost followed suit, but instead smiled at Maisie.

"He has no imagination, Miss. Well, I'm up for it, anyway. I'll brace myself," said Sandra.

Billy laughed. "Oh, all right then. As long as I don't get Delhi belly, I'll be all right—bet Doreen'll have something to say about it, though."

"She doesn't have to know," said Sandra.

"Oh, she'll know all right," countered Billy.

"Come on, you two—this is our last day, and we're going to see it off in style," said Maisie. "Each of us is moving on to fresh pastures, so let's sample something new while we're at it."

Having discharged all final responsibilities in connection with her business, Maisie turned her flat over to Sandra, had her personal belongings removed to The Dower House at Chelstone, and spent the remainder of her time with James in London, and at Chelstone, though there was little for her to do in preparation for her father's forthcoming marriage. The cook at Chelstone Manor was planning the wedding feast for what seemed to be a much larger gathering than at first anticipated. Not only would staff at Chelstone be in attendance, but a goodly number of Frankie Dobbs' old friends from London, and a few of Mrs. Bromley's family members, plus villagers who had come to know them both. Priscilla and her family would be traveling down from London for the event, and the Compton family would of course be present. Frankie and Mrs. Bromley had spoken to the vicar about a slight change in the ceremony, to account for the fact that—as Maisie's future stepmother pointed out—"There would be no giving away, and no best man fumbling for a ring! We'll walk up the aisle as we will walk for the rest of our lives—together." For Maisie, the only pall on the day was the fact that James was due to leave the following morning, and had decided that he would travel to Southampton alone—there would be no tearful dockside good-byes in anticipation of his departure. Maisie would embark upon her journey four days later, although her father, together with the new Mrs. Dobbs, plus Billy and his family, Sandra, and Priscilla and Douglas and their sons, had decided that they would be there to bid her farewell. She was dreading it, and thought James' determination to board ship without accompanying relatives and friends was a very good decision after all.

On the day of the wedding, Mrs. Bromley, who had bought a new dress of peach silk for the day, together with a matching coat and hat, was at The Dower House preparing for the wedding, while Frankie was at his cottage. At precisely half past ten, he would walk to The Dower House, where the couple would be taken to the church by the Comptons' chauffeur. Already staff were at The Dower House, preparing the dining room for the reception. Maisie had bought a dress of pale violet silk with beading to the hem, neckline, and waist, and wore a new hat to match, with a brocade band and rosette at the side. Her shoes were of deep violet, and she wore a light cashmere wrap in case it became too cold. It was soon clear that she was not needed in The Dower House, so she made her way down the path towards her father's cottage home.

"Dad, how are you getting on?"

"Bloody tie. Never wear the things, and all of a sudden, here I am, having to wrestle with this bit of cloth."

Maisie regarded her father, standing before her, fidgeting in the new bespoke suit she had persuaded him to wear for his wedding. Jook stood to one side, her ears envelope-flapped in anticipation of something unusual in the air.

"Did you think your old jacket, your corduroy trousers, and a red neckerchief would make Mrs. Bromley swoon?" said Maisie.

"Now then, before you start, my Maisie, come and help me with this tie."

Maisie stood before her father, took the two ends of the tie, then pulled one longer than the other. Her father spoke again as she lifted his chin and began to work to achieve the perfect knot.

"I won't forget your mother, you know," said Frankie.

"No, Dad. I know you won't. But you've been lonely for long enough," replied Maisie.

"Broke my heart, you know, losing her. And losing you."

"You never lost me, Dad," said Maisie, stepping back to check the tie. "Don't ever regret anything you did, because you had my best interests at heart when you found me a job in service. And it all worked out the right way in the end, didn't it? Even better than we could ever have imagined."

"Maisie," said Frankie. "I know you loved Dr. Blanche, and I know I could never have given you all that he gave you—the education, the books, and the learning. But did I do right by you?"

Maisie placed her hands on her father's shoulders. "You did everything right for me, Dad. Everything. And you did everything right for Mum. She loved you more than anything else, and you loved her to the end of her days."

"And beyond," said Frankie. "And beyond."

"But it's time to walk up that hill now. Your future awaits, and I think Mum would have been so very happy for you. I know I am." She leaned forward and kissed her father on the cheek. "May I escort you to meet your bride?"

"Jook's coming, too, you know."

Father and daughter walked the path to The Dower House, followed by the cross-bred dog with a large white bow around her neck. James joined them to wait for Mrs. Bromley to walk down the staircase into the hall.

Frankie Dobbs smiled as his bride stepped onto the landing above.

"Would you care to come to the church with me and be my wife, Brenda?" said Frankie.

"Yes," said Mrs. Bromley. "I would be honored, Frank."

James took Maisie by the hand. "We'd better get going, Maisie. We don't want to get there after the bride and groom, do we?"

As James drove away from The Dower House and towards the church, Maisie opened her mouth to say something, but stopped, for she realized she didn't know what to say. James filled in the silence.

"March 31st, Maisie. You need say nothing until March 31st."

The chauffeur came to collect James before dawn the following morning. The house was silent, and before the crunch of tires was heard on the gravel driveway, Maisie and James had been sitting in the kitchen, where Maisie prepared a breakfast of tea and toast.

"Write, James. Tell me how things are faring. And—I know this sounds trite—please, do please be careful. I don't trust aeroplanes at the best of times, and—"

"Don't, Maisie." James placed his hand on hers. "I am involved with John Otterburn's plans to test new fighter aircraft, and I must see this through because I believe in what he is trying to do. I won't take unnecessary chances, and believe me, much of my work will be on the ground—I've not the reflexes of the younger aviators. I'm too much of an old graybeard, I'm afraid."

"I know all that, but—"

"But nothing." Approaching headlamps cast a light across the ceiling. "That's my transport, Maisie. Now, you must take care, too. You're the one going off into the unknown, and you're the one who must write with news."

"I promise."

"Good. Now, let's get this over with, shall we?" He stood up and pulled Maisie to him, holding her tight. "I love you, Maisie. I love you and I will miss you."

"You too. Yes, you too, James."

They drew apart. "Right then, better be off now, before we both get maudlin," said James.

Maisie waited by the door while luggage was loaded onto the motor car—a trunk had already been dispatched to Southampton.

James looked back one more time before taking his seat in the motor car.

"It's been a good time, James. Really. To be loved so much . . . it's been a very good time," said Maisie.

"That's what it was meant to be, Maisie. I wanted us always to have a good time."

He waved, and as the vehicle turned and drove away, then through the gates of the Chelstone Manor estate, Maisie felt herself overcome, and at once fearful of the future.

"Godspeed, James. Take care, and Godspeed," she whispered into the chill morning air.

Southampton was a teeming mass of people. Relatives kissing loved ones, passengers lining up to go through the disembarkation area, and others looking up at the ship to give a final wave. Maisie said goodbye to everyone who had gathered to see her off, and was even kissed and held by her eldest godson, who had reached an age when such affection did not come easily.

"You're honored, I must say," said Priscilla. "Those kisses stopped finding a way to my cheek about two months ago—it happened far too quickly for my liking."

"You have men in the making, Pris, not boys anymore," said Maisie.

"I'm trying to keep my youngest innocent. I might bind his feet and feed him only broth."

Maisie saw that her friend was fighting back tears.

"Pris?"

"Oh, for goodness' sake, Maisie. I'm all right. Now then, let's all say what we have to say and do what comes next. This ship will leave without you if you don't get a move on."

Maisie looked at those gathered, and decided it might be a good idea to go now—eyes were red and watering wherever she looked. She hoped Frankie would not crumble as he and Brenda accompanied her to her cabin.

"This is a very nice cabin, Maisie," said Frankie, setting her small leather case inside the door. "First class and supper at the Captain's table, I would imagine—very posh."

"I remember, when we crossed the Channel over to France, in the war, I was dreadfully sick—so I thought I'd splash out for some comfort."

"Hardly a troop ship, is it?"

"No, but I'm going a lot further than France."

"The bed seems comfortable enough, Maisie," said her stepmother, pressing down on the mattress. "When will your luggage be brought up? Do you know?"

"Soon, after we're under way, I would imagine," said Maisie.

"You've packed enough books with you, in any case," said Frankie.

"A few of Maurice's diaries are in there, too—I can travel with him, retrace his footsteps." Maisie had not told her father that in the trunk of books and belongings that would be brought to her cabin, she had also packed a wooden box containing the ashes of Maya Patel, which she would return to the land of her birth.

Frankie nodded, and was about to say something else when a horn sounded to alert guests that they must leave the ship before she began her voyage toward the first port of call—Gibraltar.

"That'll be us, Bren," said Frankie.

"Oh dear. Just when I've got a daughter, I'm losing her." Brenda Dobbs grasped a handkerchief from her sleeve and dabbed her eyes.

Maisie first held her father, then kissed the new member of the family on the cheek. "I love you both. I will write. I will be safe, and I will be back before you know it."

"Promise?" asked Frankie.

"I promise," replied Maisie.

"Better go."

"Yes, better go, Dad."

Maisie came back to the rail to watch her father and his wife leave the ship, joining the others on the dockside. Priscilla's boys were whooping and calling out to her, while Billy's sons seemed more subdued, almost overwhelmed by the number of people waving and shouting. Billy held up his baby daughter, taking her hand to effect a wave. Another deafening sound came from the ship's horn, and a rumble seemed to escalate from the depths of the vessel.

People cheered and waved even more furiously. At once, Priscilla began singing, and soon it seemed the crowd on the dock had picked up the verse from the wartime song and gave voice in unison, all the while trying to keep their loved ones in sight as the ship began to move.

Goodbye-ee, goodbye-ee,
Wipe the tear, baby dear, from your eye-ee,
Tho' it's hard to part I know,
I'll be tickled to death to go.
Don't cry-ee, don't sigh-ee,
There's a silver lining in the sky-ee,
Bonsoir, old thing, cheer-i-o, chin, chin,
Nah-poo, toodle-oo, Goodbye-ee.

And Maisie did wipe her tears, and though they could not possibly hear her, she shouted out that she would write and so must they. The children cheered, and she saw Priscilla wave to the point of jumping. Her father put his hand to his forehead in mock salute, and she knew he would think of her constantly, stopping the postman every single day looking for her letter. And at once she remembered her new friend, Lakshmi Chaudhary Jones, and her words on a sunny afternoon over tea, as the autumn light came in shafts to reflect against the colors of her silk sari. She had told her that in leaving everything most loved, Maisie would break her own heart. In fact, she could feel it now, this much-wounded heart that she had worked so hard to protect from the dragon of her memories— that she had cradled gently so it might not be broken, again, by love—was, as she waved and called out, being fractured by her own desire for something more, something different. But she trusted Lakshmi's counsel, her assurance that, in leaving, she would shatter this precious part of her to open it again—and in so doing, she would cast aside all fears and instead claim the colors and scents, the sounds and minds of other places that would fashion who she might now become, and fill her anew.

How long might she be away? Might she decide to linger at her first port of call, then return home? At what point would she have seen enough of the world, for now? And what would she do, come next March 31st? There was a frisson of excitement in the fact that she had no ready answers to her own questions.

Again the ship's horn sounded, and a whooping came from the throng on the dock, who, she realized, were becoming smaller and smaller with distance, faces indistinguishable until they became one. She felt the waves catch the ship, the engines roar again, and the propeller taking her forward. Gulls swooped overhead as she turned, pulling up her collar and clinging to the guardrail while trying to find her sea legs. She began to make her way along the deck, her hair catching in the wind, her face already tingling against salt air. She had no idea what might lie ahead. But she was sure of one thing: She would be back. Yes, she would be back.

About the Author

JACQUELINE WINSPEAR is the author of the *New York Times* bestsellers *Elegy for Eddie*, *A Lesson in Secrets*, *The Mapping of Love and Death*, *Among the Mad*, and *An Incomplete Revenge*, as well as four other nationally bestselling Maisie Dobbs novels. She has won numerous awards for her work, including the Agatha, Alex, and Macavity awards for the first book in the series, *Maisie Dobbs*, which was also nominated for the Edgar Award for Best Novel and was a *New York Times* Notable Book. Originally from the United Kingdom, she now lives in California.